REFLECTIONS OF YOU

She looked at him. The abundance of firm muscle rippling across his chest and forearms immediately took her breath. He was right. His body moved her to places she'd long forgotten and to a place she longed to visit again, only with him.

His body was flawless perfection. There was no other way to say it. Every muscle, every bone, every tendon was precisely placed beneath his sun-kissed skin. Skin streaked crimson red by her nail imprints when she'd hastily opened his shirt.

"I don't jump through hoops for anybody," she stated soundly.

"I never asked you to."

Reflections of You

Celeste O. Norfleet

BET Publications, LLC
http://www.bet.com
http://www.arabesquebooks.com

ARABESQUE BOOKS are published by

BET Publications, LLC
c/o BET BOOKS
One BET Plaza
1900 W Place NE
Washington, DC 20018-1211

All Kensington Titles, Imprints, and Distributed Lines are available at special quantity discounts for bulk purchases for sales promotions, premiums, fund-raising, and educational or institutional use. Special book excerpts or customized printings can also be created to fit specific needs. For details, write or phone the office of the Kensington special sales manager: Kensington Publishing Corp., 850 Third Avenue, New York, NY 10022, attn: Special Sales Department, Phone: 1-800-221-2647.

First Printing: March 2004
10 9 8 7 6 5 4 3 2 1

Printed in the United States of America

Fate & Fortune

Acknowledgments

To my sisters, Amanda Mitchell and Karen Linton, for always showing me the best times, getting me over the rough ones and forever being in my corner.

To my sister authors, Michelle Monkou, Candice Poarch and Angela Winters, your friendship is unending and I am forever grateful.

To my sisters of the heart, Angie Jenkins, Renee Salnave, Betty Moore, Francis DeLoach, Charlene Murray and Andrea Jenkins, I look to your strength for encouragement and joy. Thank you for always being there for me.

Lastly, thanks to my BET family, Linda Gill, Glenda Howard, Kicheko Driggins, Selena Spencer, Evette Porter, Demetria Lucas, Guy Chapman and Ericka Caine.

Chapter 1

Angela Lord was far too practical for old wives' tales. The boogeyman, things that go bump in the night, invisible monsters under the bed and other such nonsense had never plagued her as a child. The only monsters she feared were those she already knew.

Still, the icy shiver of nothingness made her shudder nonetheless. The pit of her stomach quivered and the short hairs on the back of her neck stood on end. The old ones swore that when the feeling came, it meant someone had just tread across your grave. But Angela was far too sensible for such absurdity. Yet, the uneasy feeling remained and she'd had just about enough of it.

Even without looking up she could feel the chill of eyes continuously glaring at her. For the last four hours the old woman gawked, and stared. It was unnerving. *This is ridiculous,* Angela told herself. *What is this woman's problem?*

Angela lowered her book, looked up and glared back at the woman seated across the narrow aisle. Annoyance darkened her usually pleasant features as their eyes met and held. The old woman stared back, fixed and unwavering. Angela shivered again.

Eyes as cold and vacant as an arctic abyss returned her

stare. With crystal clarity, the old woman's cold, unfeeling eyes were hauntingly eerie. Deep burrows of torment knitted her brow giving her pale, ashen complexion a mask-like appearance.

The woman's lips quivered slightly; yet, her expression remained unchanged as she stared back. It was as if she looked right through her. Angela shook her head in astonishment. The old woman didn't even have the decency to turn away with embarrassment. She was a troubled woman and it appeared that Angela was her source of pain.

Eventually, Angela looked away in exasperation. *Why am I letting this woman creep me out like this?* she wondered silently as she leaned over and peeked out the small round window. *The sooner I get this over with, the better,* she thought, as she looked at her watch impatiently. In another half hour they would be landing.

Although she planned to stay for only two weeks, she hoped that her quest would take less time. She needed to finally get this behind her and get back and figure out how to put her professional life back together.

The corner of her coral-painted lips creased upward into a half smile as she lowered her eyes to the open book still in her lap. *By the time the plane lands, the old woman will be a distant memory,* she assured herself halfheartedly as she drummed her fingernails repeatedly on the armrest.

Maybe her friend, Elliot, was right. She did need to loosen up a bit and try to relax. Even she had to admit that she was wound too tightly lately. This thing had had her in a tangle of nerves ever since she first received the report. She smiled when she thought about Elliot's other suggestion. *An island fling with a Latin lover would be an interesting diversion at the very least,* she considered with pleasure. But that was definitely not on her schedule of things to do.

"Ladies and Gentleman, this is your captain speaking. In a few moments we will be landing at the Luis Munoz Marin Airport in the beautiful city of San Juan. The temperature is a

balmy ninety-six degrees, with a light southeastern breeze. The skies are crystal clear and the time is approximately eleven-twelve A.M. on this beautiful March morning. At this time, I'd like to take the opportunity to thank you for flying Eastway Island Air and wish you a pleasant stay. Please observe the attendants as they prepare for our landing procedure. Enjoy your stay in Puerto Rico and thank you again for flying Eastway Island Air."

Angela reached over to the tiny shade covering and glanced out of the small circular window. Pulling the bottom edge gently, she released, letting it glide effortlessly upwards, exposing the beautiful Caribbean skyline. A small rectangular land mass surrounded by still, blue water slowly came into view. A shudder of excitement surged through her. Finally, she'd have her happy ending.

As the pilot began to make the final approach, the plane dipped to one side, allowing the passengers to get an eyeful of the island's splendor. Angela smiled in awe. The radiant scenery was breathtaking. She soaked in every inch of the visual treat. The water, crystal turquoise blue, flaunted tiny foam crests as the waves lapped lovingly toward the glimmering sun-stroked shore. A hint of iridescence glittered and sparkled on the stark white sandy beach. A myriad of colorful buildings arose from the spectacular landscape as natural as the lush green vegetation surrounding them. Rich royal blues, deep purples, warm greens, scarlet reds and vibrant golds combined together creating a sensational feast for her eyes.

Ding. Ding.

Angela looked up. A soft bell chimed as an attendant proceeded down the aisle checking seat belts and securing food trays. Angela nervously pulled at the safety harness across her lap. "Well, here goes nothing," she muttered quietly, assuring herself that this trip would finally bring an ending to her long search. She closed her eyes and relaxed back into the soft leather, allowing wayward thoughts to trespass.

She smiled inwardly. She'd waited a long time for this opportunity, a whole lifetime to be exact. In the past five years she'd spent a small fortune on detectives, each one in turn giving her the same hopeless answer. But she refused to give up. This was too important to her and to her future. Slowly she opened her eyes and stared out of the small window at the island below. Somewhere down there was her answer.

The sound of massive engines grew louder as the plane descended. Angela instinctively gripped her seat's armrest tighter. At the first solid thump of rubber onto asphalt, she nervously drew a sharp breath. The wheels touched a second then third time. It wasn't until she felt and heard the sound of rubber rolling on the tarmac did she realize she'd nervously been holding her breath the entire time.

The plane landed smoothly then taxied to the receiving area and came to a complete stop. Angela gathered up her purse and book and waited for her turn to collect her belongings from the overhead storage compartment.

Excited chatter arose all around her as passenger after passenger disembarked. Angela returned the smiles of the eager, carefree tourists whose only thoughts were sun-soaked beaches and long walks through ancient ruins. Slowly her strained smile vanished, realizing what the next two weeks could mean to her life. Moments later she impatiently stood to take her turn to disembark.

Angela eased closer to the plane's open door. She exhaled in joyous relief. She had finally arrived! The flight was over and she was here in Puerto Rico, the island of love, fantasy, and romance. Where dreams meet reality, and romance was just a stranger away. At least that's what the travel brochures professed. But the last thing she wanted or needed was an island romance, she didn't care what Elliot said.

Out of sheer curiosity, Angela looked across the aisle to where the staring woman had sat. To her relief, the seat was now empty. Angela quickly scanned the immediate area. The woman had scrambled hastily to be the first in line to exit the plane. *Adios*, she thought as she bid the woman a final good riddance.

* * *

Rosa Delores Martinez raced to the passenger receiving area looking feverishly for her husband. She spotted him across the aisle casually waving a local newspaper to get her attention. Quickly, she ran to his side. Her short squatty legs couldn't seem to carry her fast enough. "Juan, my dear Juan, you would not believe it," she panted anxiously, "who I have seen, Mother of God." She crossed herself and kissed the tiny crucifix hanging from around her thick neck. The frightened woman continued rasping breathlessly. "She is back, Juan. She's come back for him."

Juan, stunned by Rosa's outburst, grabbed hold of his wife as she charged into him. He'd never seen her so distressed. She was usually a very calm and patient woman. "Rosa, que pasa? What is it? Why are you so upset? Is it your sister? Has her illness worsened?"

"No, Juan, it is Angelina, she has returned," Rosa said slowly, still fighting to breathe evenly.

"My sweet Rosa, calm yourself. You have imagined this. Angelina is gone two years now. You have simply dreamed her," Juan patiently reassured his wife as he held her tightly and stroked her back to calm her.

"No, no. She was on the plane with me; I saw her. She is here," Rosa insisted.

"No, Rosa, she is not," he said, firmly placing both hands on her shoulders and bending slightly to look into his wife's worried eyes.

"Then you look," Rosa insisted, pulling back from him and turning in the direction of the other passengers entering the waiting area. "See with your eyes that I speak the truth."

Juan looked up just as Angela passed through the door's narrow opening. He watched as the woman paused, looked around, then looked directly at him. "Mother of God, Angelina," Juan said as he slowly crossed himself and shook his head in sheer disbelief. He was just as amazed by the vision standing there before him.

"You see, husband, Angelina has returned," Rosa murmured

quietly under her breath. She kissed the small silver-beaded rosary again. "You've come back for him," she added in her native tongue. "It seems even the devil himself could not keep you away."

After a snail's pace of unexplained delays, the line through to the passenger walkway began to move again. Then, after another few minutes, Angela had finally arrived at the passenger's waiting lounge. As soon as she entered the small area she spotted the strange staring woman. She was standing with a man by the check-in counter. The man looked up straight into Angela's face, dropped his newspaper to his side and crossed himself slowly.

Not you too, buddy, Angela thought to herself absently. *Is everybody on this island nuts?* To her annoyance she could only shrug off the tiny nagging voice that kept saying, *they're not staring at anyone else; they're only staring at you.*

Determined not to let the couple annoy her further, Angela ignored them and went directly to the luggage claim. Within a few moments of her arrival, the cranking sound of machinery began churning and sporadic pieces of luggage began circling a turnstile. Spotting her luggage, she retrieved the two pieces then proceeded through the crowded airport.

Busy with eager passengers hurrying to begin vacations and weary tourists ready to return home, Luis Muñoz Marin Airport was a bustling hub of activity. Joyous reunions and fond farewells surrounded Angela as the sounds of island salsa accompanied her as she strolled through the terminals.

On the way out, Angela spotted a little souvenir shop near the main entrance. She stopped and browsed the magazine and book racks. She found a number of romance novels both translated and untranslated. The familiar cover art was universal. Hulky, bronzed, godlike warriors embracing to the point of dominating freely submitting docile yet wanton maidens. The stories were ubiquitous, of hope, love, and possibilities.

Always the same happily-ever-after ending. If only life were that simple.

Angela eventually decided on two books, one, a spy-thriller mystery, and the other an untranslated romance novel. She decided that along with her pocket Spanish/English dictionary and her high school and college courses, she'd enjoy the challenge of reading the Spanish version. She understood, read, and spoke a passable degree of Spanish.

After browsing for a few more minutes, she gathered her purchases and moved to the checkout counter. As she stood in line flipping through several island tour brochures, she failed to notice the man and woman watching her from a safe distance just outside of the store's entrance. They stared for a few moments then continued on their way. Angela looked up just as they turned and walked away. She frowned, slightly disturbed by seeing them again. She watched as they disappeared through the main entrance.

She decided that seeing the couple again was just a coincidence and not to let her imagination get the best of her. She paid for her books and picked up several travel brochures and left.

After a not-so-quick ride to her destination, Angela paid the taxi driver then followed a stiff-backed doorman into the plush hotel lobby.

Once inside, Angela stopped and looked around in awe-struck wonder. Her first quick glance was a startling surprise. The Paradise Island Hotel was just that, paradise. It was a spectacular oasis surrounded by nature's perfection and everything the brochures proudly boasted. It was as if she'd walked through a time portal that brought her to a utopian Shangri-la.

A blast of vibrant color and deep, dark lush foliage grew within its walls and encompassed the entire inner sanctum. In the center of the lobby was an elaborate fountain filled with numerous coins tossed in by hopeful tourists. Brilliant sunlight streamed down through fan-shaped palm trees that soared to the towering glass-vaulted ceiling above. The sweet aromatic scent of island flowers and salt water tantalized her nostrils as a tranquil feeling of serenity engulfed her. *Maybe this wasn't a bad idea after all,* she mused to herself as she hurried to catch up with the bellman already waiting for her at the front desk.

Angela quickly registered as the receptionist instructed the bellman to take her luggage to her room. She turned to follow.

"Pardon, señorita," a small gentle voice echoed behind her just as she turned away from the front desk. Presuming the man called to someone else, Angela continued walking. "Señorita Lord."

Surprised at hearing her name called, Angela stopped. She turned around. There, standing two feet from her was the same couple from the airport. Neither spoke for a second's heartbeat as they both just stood and stared at her.

The man repeated her name, "Señorita Lord?"

"Si," Angela finally responded cautiously, realizing that the couple had obviously followed her from the airport.

"Señorita." He smiled broadly at her response.

"How did you know my name?" Angela questioned.

"I overheard the receptionist at the front desk." Angela nodded slowly as he continued. "Señorita, me llamo Juan Martinez." He held out his hand. Angela looked at it suspiciously, then tentatively grasped his hand to shake. He continued excitedly. His rapid Spanish caught her off guard, yet she quickly discerned his greeting.

"How may I help you, señor?"

"You speak English quite well," he assessed with noted interest. "Is it your first language?"

"Yes."

"I gather then that you are from the United States?" he asked through a heavy black mustache and sparse Latin accent.

She nodded slightly. "Yes I am," she stated coolly. Having grown up and lived in the Bronx, Brooklyn, and D.C., she had become an expert at spotting scams, con artists, and cheats. So she waited impatiently for the inevitable pitch.

Juan smiled warmly, gently pinching together a host of crow's feet at the corners of his muted green eyes. "That is good, very good," he said, then nervously looked at the woman standing behind him. He nodded, she returned his gesture curtly. "Señorita, please forgive this intrusion. May I introduce my wife Rosa, Rosa Martinez." He beckoned the timid woman closer. Reluctantly, she came forward and nodded her head awkwardly, oddly refusing to look at Angela.

"My wife and I would like just a few moments of your time," he said.

"Is there a problem?" Angela asked with typical jaded interest.

"No, no, señorita. There is nothing to be concerned about."

Still cautious, Angela adjusted her purse and looked toward the bellman as he stood patiently at the elevator with her luggage. "Look, señor, if you're trying to buy or sell me something, I'm not interested." She took a retreating step back.

It took Juan a few seconds to understand her meaning. Then without warning he burst with joyous laughter. "Señorita, please, I assure you I am not trying to sell or buy anything. But I do wish to offer you something."

Every fiber of her being shouted to turn on her heels and walk away but for some reason she didn't budge. There was something about the way this man looked at her that piqued her curiosity. "And what might that something be, Señor Martinez?" she asked suspiciously.

Juan bowed his head courteously. "Santos," he stated simply. Angela looked puzzled, more by the shocked reaction of his companion than the cryptic single-answer revelation.

"Santos," she repeated.

"Si, Rosa and I would like to invite you to be our guest at Club Santos this evening."

Angela took a moment and eyed the two fully. Her gut instinct immediately screamed, *no way*. So, as usual, she went with it. "That's very kind of you, señor, but, no thank you." She turned to continue walking.

"Señorita," Juan called out again. "Un momento, por favor." Angela reluctantly stopped and turned again. "I realize this is a very unusual request. Please believe me when I say that I am not accustomed to inviting complete strangers out to dinner," he began. He reached into his pocket, pulled out a card and handed it to her. "But I assure you, this is a legitimate invitation to have dinner at Club Santos."

Angela took the offered card and read its elegant script. It simply read *Club Santos* and a phone number. She looked up to meet the eyes of the woman standing behind him. Although she'd relaxed significantly, she was still guarded. "I'm sorry, señor, but I've made other arrangements for this evening."

"I see," Juan replied, not intent on accepting her rebuff. "That is unfortunate." He paused a moment then continued. "Señorita, I feel I must be completely honest with you. I realize you do not know us, but my wife saw you on the flight this morning and I too must admit, I was amazed when I first saw you."

"And why is that, señor?" Angela questioned skeptically, glancing again at the still-staring woman and the bevy of tourist activity surrounding them.

"When I saw you enter the terminal, I could not believe my eyes. I am still unable to trust what I see standing right here before me. You see, señorita, you resemble someone we once knew." He turned briefly to his wife for conformation. "This woman passed away suddenly several years ago." Rosa Martinez crossed herself automatically. "The resemblance is truly astounding," he continued. "Imagine our shock seeing you. My wife feared she was seeing a ghost." He smiled briefly.

Angela nodded slowly. "I see."

"We mean you no harm and we surely did not mean to alarm you." He continued to stare while shaking his head in disbelief.

"No harm done," Angela said, smiling graciously.

"Señorita, are you visiting family here on the island?"

Rosa asked. Speaking for the first time, her voice was a mere whisper.

Angela briefly considered her reasons for choosing Puerto Rico then decided to answer. *No*.

"No?" Rosa said, surprised by the answer. "So you are here on vacation then?" she added, still uneasy with the uncanny likeness.

"Something like that," Angela said, frowning at the woman's sudden interest.

"Puerto Rico has many wondrous sights. You will surely enjoy yourself," Juan added. "I can assist you in arranging for an exclusive tour of the island if you wish."

"That's very kind of you, señor, but that's not necessary. Thank you for the offer." Angela secured her purse on her shoulder in a feeble attempt to end the conversation again. She took a casual step back as she glanced at the bellman, who was now talking to another bellman at the elevators.

Juan nodded his understanding, then followed her. "Señorita, is this your first time on the island?"

Angela stopped again. "Yes it is," she answered, obviously getting annoyed by the questions.

"Then please, you must be our guest for dinner this evening at Club Santos. It is your first night here and there is no better way to spend your first night on the island than at Club Santos," Juan declared proudly.

"That's very generous of you, but, as I said, I do have plans," she insisted.

"Señorita, it is your first night in Puerto Rico. Come, experience the hospitality and flavor of paradise. Please, we have thoughtlessly taken so much of your time. Let us offer dinner this evening to atone."

"That really isn't necessary."

"Nonsense, we insist. It would be our most sincere pleasure," Juan continued. "Should you perhaps be able to attend after all, I will have a car waiting for your convenience at eight o'clock. I promise you an evening you will not soon forget."

Chapter 2

At twenty minutes before eight, Angela took one last look at her reflection in the bathroom's full-length mirror. Remembering Juan's words, she stepped closer and wondered just how much she really looked like this other woman. The thought faded as she turned around, curious to see the back of her outfit. The fiery scarlet of the flared halter dress was much brighter and shorter than she usually wore, but she couldn't resist purchasing it after seeing it the small boutique's window.

The look was elegant, sleek and sexy, and it caressed every curve of her feminine physique. She smiled admiringly as she spun around and watched the multitude of tiny lined pleats dance against her bare legs. She adjusted the straps of the laced bra-like top and modestly pulled at the front's low dip that exposed the swell of her generous cleavage.

She fluffed the crop of thick curling ringlets dancing about her soft brown shoulders. Absently, she considered a thousand and one reasons why she shouldn't go this evening—all of which made sense. But the nagging pull of the bright red dress and her reflection in the mirror persuaded her to go anyway.

Stepping closer to the mirror's reflection, Angela eyed the

scant makeup she adorned for the evening. The barest touch of deep rose blush enhanced her chestnut cheeks and a hint of glimmering color was lightly brushed above her almond shaped eyes. Her long thick lashes were curled perfectly and the barest suggestion of perfume kissed the sensitive pulses of her body. Satisfied with her appearance, she picked up her small beaded evening bag and shawl then headed out the door.

Several appreciative heads turned as she smoothly sauntered through the plush hotel lobby. Once outside, she stopped and glanced around. The hotel's entryway was crowded with numerous evening guests. Their attire ranged from bathing suit casual to black tie formal. Her eyes fell on a young man casually leaning against a sleek black sedan smoking a thin brown cigarette. His amorous eyes scanned the shape of every woman who passed through the lobby's glass doors. As soon as his eyes drifted to her, he immediately dropped and stamped out the cigarette and strolled over. He greeted her with an overly exuberant grin.

"Buenas noches, señorita," he purred seductively.

"Buenas noches," Angela returned as she continued to look around the open area. The young driver eased closer, seemingly unable to move his eyes away from the swell of her breasts. As he made his second pass down her long bare legs and stiletto heels, she cleared her throat to get his attention. "You wouldn't happen to be the driver sent by Señor and Señora Martinez?"

The young man looked stunned, then extremely bewildered. He sighed heavily. "Si, señorita, me llamo Carlos. Es usted Señorita Lord?" She nodded. He instantly readjusted his black chauffeur's cap to a more conservative angle, and then he hurried around to the rear passenger side of the waiting car. He held the door open, gallantly bowed, and helped her inside.

Angela settled comfortably against the plush interior. She ran her hands against the cool leather as she watched Carlos slide into the driver's seat. As soon as he started the engine, he began speaking rapid Spanish. Angela realized that it was impossible for her to understand. "Carlos, habla usted ingles?" She interrupted.

He looked in the rearview mirror. "Si, señorita."

"Good," she said, relieved. "Would you please repeat that in English," she requested with a smile that would melt ice. She wanted to make sure she understood everything he said.

Carlos sighed his admiration as he looked in the rearview mirror again. "Sure, of course, no problem," he said. His English was perfect and his accent was nonexistent. "Mr. and Mrs. Martinez will meet you at Club Santos. So sit back and enjoy the ride. We'll be at the club shortly. I'll be happy to point out local landmarks of interest, if you'd like."

"That would be great, Carlos, thank you."

Angela sat back against the dark leather of the car, letting the distinct smell of newness surround her and the cool air conditioning refresh her. This was so unlike her. She would never consider doing this in Washington. Going to a club simply because she received an invitation was ludicrous, not to mention dangerous.

The car glided smoothly through the center of San Juan. Tourists still cluttered the streets as the beginning of dusk settled low on the quaint island paradise, washing the early evening sky with hues of purple, red and gold. Angela marveled at the spectacle.

Carlos entertained her by pointing out several interesting landmarks as they passed. Angela shifted her head from side to side, trying not to miss a single thing. She made mental notes to return to some of the sights Carlos had suggested. They passed richly adorned churches, lovely little shops and the most whimsical and enchanting town homes she'd ever seen. The splash of color ignited an array of excited images. She had to admit, Puerto Rico was everything it promised and more.

They drove through the center of Old San Juan, then cruised along the coastline of Puerto Rico's northern shore. The rich blue-green water sparkled in reds and oranges as the sun set just beyond the horizon. In the distance she spotted two large cruise ships as they left the dock. They looked like glittering Christmas tree ornaments decorated with hundreds of tiny twinkling lights all bouncing and reflecting off of the water. Angela watched as they slowly, peacefully sailed from sight.

Just then the car turned a corner and traveled down a narrow street. Within a few minutes, a line of people standing in front of a newly remodeled building came into view. "Is there an evening celebration here or something? Why are all these people standing out here in line?" she asked, as they slowly drove past the extended line.

Carlos smiled and nodded his understanding with pride. "You mean the crowds," he chortled. "These people are all waiting to enter Club Santos. It's like this nearly every night; sometimes it's even worst."

Angela was amazed. "All these people are here to get into a club? That's amazing."

Carlos nodded and smiled broadly. He motioned toward the waiting crowd. "Sometimes they wait outside for hours to get inside the Club. When it's really crowded, Señor Santos opens the lower decks and sends waiters out to take drink orders."

Carlos pulled the limo up behind the last waiting car. There were several cabs in front of the building so Carlos slowed and waited his turn in line behind those waiting for valet parking. He put the car in park and pulled out a small phone and pushed several numbers. He spoke softly then slipped it back into his pocket. He turned and smiled at Angela. "Señor Martinez will be right out." She nodded absently, still amazed by the throng of people.

After a few minutes the cars drove off and Carlos pulled the car directly in front of the building. An attendant hurried over to open the rear door. "Buenas noches, señorita, enjoy Santos," Carlos called out as Angela took the offered hand and slid from the back seat.

"Gracias. Buenas noches, Carlos," she said as she stepped out of the car and into the swell of excitement. She looked up at the front of the building. The grand marquee was beautifully adorned with a backlit stained-glass window that prominently proclaimed CLUB SANTOS.

The building, several stories high, with huge windows on each of four floors, nearly took up the entire block. The front of an exaggerated entrance was lined with three sets of double doors, each anchored by neatly dressed attendants. To the far side, beneath a deep burgundy awning, was the separate VIP entrance, separated with a velvet-chained partition. The line of eagerly waiting revelers extended to the near side. And on the opposite side were numerous outside umbrella tables occupied to capacity with exuberant, celebrating restaurant customers.

Escorted by one of the doormen, Angela felt like a celebrity as all eyes turned to her as soon as the car door was closed. Being driven in a sleek black Mercedes with tinted windows felt special. Being delivered to the front door and welcomed as soon as she stepped out was spectacular. The attendant, a huge man dressed in all black, immediately ushered her toward the VIP entrance.

"Señorita Lord." Angela looked up as the door opened for her. A familiar voice greeted her with a warm smile and firm handshake. "¡Bien venida! Welcome to Santos. I am glad you could make it."

"Señor Martinez, good evening. Thank you for inviting me and please call me Angela."

"Very well, if you would do me the honor of calling me Juan." She nodded. "Please come this way," Juan said with a generous smile, obviously enthused to see her. Juan held out his arm, nodded to the attendant and escorted Angela inside.

The heavy bass music reverberated through her as soon as she set foot inside. They walked through the VIP doors amid whispers and stares by several VIPs already inside. Juan continued through the main lobby, moving quickly toward the elevators.

Angela walked briskly, keeping up with Juan's rushed steps. She quickly soaked in the club's atmosphere. A blur of sights whizzed past her in flashes of color and excitement.

"So Angela, how do you like our Santos so far?" he asked proudly.

Angela smiled as she continued to look around. "It's incredible," she said, raising her voice over the joyous music.

Juan laughed with joy. "Yes it is, isn't it." He looked around with pride then began telling her about the club's many specialized private rooms.

An older man on the far side of the room began waving his hands to get Juan's attention. "Un momento, Angela." They stopped walking as the silver haired man approached and whispered something into Juan's ear.

In mid-sentence he stopped suddenly, and looked at Angela's face. The stunned expression of shock registered in his eyes. Angela smiled and nodded politely. She hoped this wasn't going to be the norm for the remainder of her time on the island.

Juan looked up when the man stopped speaking. A knowing expression crossed his face as the man's face turned ash white. "Chevis, this is my guest, Señorita Angela Lord. She is a visitor to our island and a very special guest of Club Santos this evening. Angela, this is my assistant, Chevis de Long."

"My God, you look just like . . ." Chevis began but was cut off by Angela.

Angela looked to Juan. "Yes, so I've been told. Nice to meet you, Señor de Long." She held out her hand to shake. He seemed hesitant, almost afraid to touch her. Finally, he grasped her hand reluctantly, still staring at her face, unsure of his own eyes. Eventually he continued talking to Juan as Angela stepped away and continued to look around the Club.

Divided equally into two separate sections, the club entrance and the restaurant entrance, Club Santos was enormous. The expansive entryway was lavishly decorated with mirrors, glass doors, and stained glass. Its plush, overstuffed club couches with generous throw pillows were clustered together on highly polished wooden floors. Angela was more than slightly impressed by the grandeur of the Club.

She watched the wide range of patrons mingling around the area. Most were heading in the direction of the intense Caribbean rhythms. Others passed through the thick glass doors leading to the restaurant section. Still others simply mingled in the immediate area, lounging on the plush sofas talking, laughing and enjoying themselves.

Club Santos was phenomenal. She'd never seen anything as grand and exciting. The air was charged with excitement and the ambience was electrifying.

She noticed that several waiters and waitresses openly stared and more than a few drinks were spilled as dinner guests pointed or even bumped into each other at seeing Angela standing in the lobby.

"Señorita Lord." Chevis took her hand. "Welcome again to Club Santos.

"Thank you." She smiled graciously.

"It was a great pleasure meeting you, señorita. I hope you enjoy your stay on our island." Chevis smiled timidly and hurried off in the same direction he'd arrived.

Juan offered his arm. "Shall we continue?" Angela nodded and took his lead. She was relieved when Juan guided her to the elevators. As they stepped inside, Juan exuberantly chatted about the history of the building, noting particularly its current tenants. He explained in great detail the Club's basic setup and his duties as manager.

As the elevator ascended he commented on each floor's unique specialty as he held the door open so that she could briefly glance around. "The first floor is the restaurant and club entrance. The second floor is the private club entrance; the third floor are the executive offices."

Angela noted the fourth floor button on the panel. "What's on the fourth floor?"

Juan smiled. "The fourth floor has secured keyed entry. It's off limits. Only the owners have access."

"Sounds mysterious. Is that where all the bodies are kept?"

"I'm afraid it's not at all that dramatic or intriguing." He chuckled aloud. "It's merely their private apartment."

"Their?"

"Si, Club Santos is owned by two brothers. They have several other enterprises on the island."

As the elevator glided to the third floor, Juan spoke of several must-see sites while on the island. He offered to personally arrange a tour but again Angela declined, wanting to experience Puerto Rico on her own.

When the elevator door finally opened on the third floor, Angela noticed that it was nearly deserted. They passed several open doors, most leading to empty offices and storage space.

At the end of the hall, Juan stopped in front of a pair of double doors. He opened the doors and escorted Angela into a large office that belonged to the owner of the club. "Angela, if you would please wait here. I shall check on your dinner arrangements," he said before leaving.

Angela looked around the room duly impressed. It was magnificently decorated with stylish modern furnishings mixed with exquisitely selected antiques. Each piece in the room was perfectly placed right down to the fanlike stack of popular magazines on the large marble coffee table. This was definitely a professional decorating job, she decided as she continued to move about the room.

She walked over to the oversized mahogany desk at the far end of the room and placed her purse down. She ran her fingers along the wood's beveled edge. The piece, antique, perhaps circa 1920, was beautifully hand-carved with a high-polished reflective surface, ornate detail and the original brass hardware. And, like the rest of the office's furnishings, it was expensive, very expensive.

Directly behind the desk was a large alcove inset with an enormous bay window that overlooked the club's dance floor with a perfect view of one of the club's two huge bars.

Angela moved to the dark tinted glass windows. Through the darkness, shafts of multicolored light beams pierced the space around her. Lasered and lavish, the lights jumped and pulsated to the rhythms emanating from the invisible speakers that surrounded the two lower levels.

A thin layer of smoke hovered just above her eye level making the colored beams of light resemble an alien invasion. She squinted, looking down at the dance floor but couldn't see much—the floor was filled to capacity. A mass of humanity would have been considered an understatement. It seemed like every available spare inch was taken up by waving, twirling, gyrating bodies and everyone was having a wonderful time.

Further back, beyond the dance floor, was a semi-circle bar packed three deep with eagerly awaiting patrons. A mirrored wall loomed behind the bar shelved with rows and rows of bottled libations of every imaginable kind.

Above the two bars were huge 3-D video screens that showed images of the dancers and the band. The camera, viewing from points unknown, showed flash images as it panned the entire club. As soon as someone realized that they were on the enormous screens, the crowd around that person went wild. Angela laughed at the comical antics some of the revelers performed when their faces appeared.

Everywhere she looked there were smiling, laughing, partying people. Some were huddled together laughing and talking while others sat on tall stools at small cocktail tables attended by sparsely costumed waitresses.

A lively salsa band performed on the platform to her immediate left. Dressed in bright trendy costumes and accompanied by scantily dressed dancers, the sweat-drenched musicians performed Latin rhythms with dazzling intensity. Angela could feel the heavy beat of the bass guitar and the drum reverberate through her body.

The rich Latin music penetrated the window and flowed into the office. Angela began to move her head and hips to the pulsating beat. She watched smiling, enjoying the show below as shoulders shimmied and hips gyrated. Helplessly, like the masses all around her, she soon lost herself in the hypnotic rhythms of Club Santos.

Chapter 3

Juan hurried down the steps to the lower level. He met Chevis rushing up. "My God, Juan, have you gone mad?" Chevis exclaimed, out of breath and still stunned by seeing Angela.

Juan rushed past him. "Not now, Chevis. I have to find him."

Chevis grabbed Juan's arm to halt him. "Juan, listen to me. Get her out of here, now, before he sees her. Put her back on a plane to wherever hell she came from. My God, Juan, what were you thinking?"

Juan frowned at his friend. "Would you prefer that he see her on the street, or that she wander in here by chance, or perhaps that Roberto find her first and bring her in here to torment him? Tell me, Chevis, which would you prefer?" He began walking down the stairs.

Chevis lowered his head, defeated, as his mind swam with questions. He followed Juan. "Who is she? Where did you find her? Where did she come from? Why is she here?" The questions rapidly burst from his lips.

"She is as she appears," Juan answered, looking beyond Chevis, catching a brief glimpse of a man across the lobby completely surrounded by women. "She seems to have no idea of any of this."

"But, Juan, surely you cannot be serious. This is madness. Bringing this woman here is insane. Marco will . . ." He shuddered, shaking his head woefully at the thought of his employer's temper.

Juan laid his hand on his friend's shoulder. "I know your concerns and I share them. But not now, we will speak later." Chevis nodded his understanding then continued up the stairs. As he reached the top step he turned and watched in dread as his old friend continued down the stairs toward Marco.

Juan scanned the crowded open area of the front lobby until he spotted his quarry again. Standing a generous ten inches above the hovering mass of spiked heel femininity, he wore an easy smile. Surrounded by the ceaseless chattering, he never let his stately patrician expression or his cool, detached facade waver. Dressed in his usual black-on-black, he seemed more like a hunted desperado than the owner of the most popular nightspot in Puerto Rico.

His eyes, blacker than a raven's wing, and always watchful, continued their constant scan of the area. Within seconds he spotted Juan and Chevis talking on the stairs.

Then his attention was successfully gained by an admirer who ran her bright red fingernails through his main of thick, shinny black locks. He turned and halted her wandering hands as they reached his broad shoulders. She puckered and pouted her scarlet lips until he brought her hand to his lips and kissed the nail tip. The other women instantly swooned and sighed.

Juan shook his head. The last thing needed in this club was a dozen or so more drooling woman. Marco's playful encouragement was all it took to set eyelashes fluttering and hearts pounding.

His deep, rich, masculine laugh held the women captive, as did his generous smile. They yielded willingly to the passion his dark beguiling eyes promised. Enraptured, they were hopelessly imprisoned by his charm or maybe it was the aura of power that continually swirled around him. To please him body, mind and soul would be their greatest desire. They would freely surrender to his bidding.

The women varied in appearance to suit his diverse tastes; rich, dark chocolate with long, wavy blond hair, creamy porcelain with full, thick lips, café au lait with sea-blue eyes and tightly curled locks. Standing in a swirl of fragrant perfume, the perfect faces worshiped in skimpy swatches of flimsy fabric held up by the barest threads. All yearning one objective: to entice, incite, enthrall and capture the sovereign, Marco Santos.

This was his domain. He was czar and king, ruling Club Santos with a velvet fist. Under his skillfulness the club had reached unimaginable success. It was packed to capacity every night with standing-room-only crowds inside and as always an anxiously awaiting crowd outside.

Marco smiled and eyed his old friend hurrying toward him. Juan's worried expression didn't concern Marco in the least. He knew that just about everything grieved him. Juan's brows knotted when a mainland shipment was overdue or when a waiter accidentally dropped a glass or when a band member sneezed. Getting him to relax was an impossible quest that Marco had given up long ago.

Marco lowered his ear to Juan as soon as he reached his side. "We need to speak," Juan whispered quietly in their native tongue. "Privately," he added firmly. Marco nodded and excused himself from his many adoring admirers. A pouty moan echoed behind him as he laid his arm across Juan's shoulders and drew him aside.

"I have a woman in your office," Juan began.

"Juan Pedro Martinez," Marco chuckled, flashing his dimpled cheek, then exclaimed with amusement, "I'm surprised at you." He smiled the crooked smile that drove women to distraction. "Granted, it's your affair, but you realize, of course, that Rosa will strangle you with her bare hands when she finds out. And be assured, women always find out." Marco laughed as he began walking up the stairs to the third level. Juan hurried along behind him.

"Actually, Marco, this is a very special woman. She is not for me, she is for you."

Marco threw his head back in joyous laughter again as the two approached the third floor level. "Matchmaking is for little old women and nosey busybodies without grandchildren. You, Juan, have seven grandchildren and are awaiting your eighth. Since when do you need to take up the annoying sport of marriage broker?" Still chuckling, Marco's long stride reached and crossed the third floor hallway within minutes. An out-of-breath Juan hurried, half running, half walking behind him. Marco reached the door of his office a few seconds before Juan.

He entered. Angela, still entranced by the club's music, had her back to the men so Marco had the opportunity to observe her at his leisure. He watched as she seductively moved to the rhythmic melody emanating from the club below. He had to admit, he liked what he saw so far.

The crimson dress dripped fluidly over her luscious hips. A night's pleasure could definitely be had wrapped in those long lovely legs. He smiled, savoring the fantasy.

"So this was the woman who has caught your eye? Very impressive," he whispered to Juan as he entered, while nodding his approval. As his eyes leisurely caressed the silhouette of her body, Marco indulged his fantasy as he smiled at the delightful possibilities. His mind's eye conjured up a number of uses for her long legs and full hips.

Her skin was the color of dark island rum, *Ron del Barrilito*, Puerto Rican rum, a luscious treat he often savored late in the evening. He could almost taste the bittersweet full-bodied richness in his mouth. He feasted on the image of sampling every delectable drop. He decided at that moment that he would know this woman intimately.

Hypnotically his eyes followed the sensual movements of the backless dress as it swayed to the music. Surrendering to his primal need, he smirked with pleasure. Then, he saw the reflection of her face in the darkened glass at the exact moment she saw his. The image of a woman he'd known a lifetime ago stared back at him. The vision spun around abruptly. His amorous smile quickly faded as their eyes met head on. "Angel," Marco breathed in a whisper loud enough to make Angela gasp.

With the jubilant celebration behind her, long forgotten, Angela stared at this tall, dark stranger. His black silk shirt and matching tie gave him a dangerous air of the forbidden. His look was of cautious anger. But there was something just under the seething stare that sparked something inside of her. She found herself drawn to him instantly.

His eyes, like coal from Satan's den, pierced right through her. Masked by his neatly trimmed beard, he had the face of a god and the eyes of pure sin, hot and wild. The fiery look he bestowed upon her bespoke of passion and peril. She couldn't tear her eyes from him. She scanned every inch of his magnificent body as if to brand him in her memory forever.

Well-toned muscles lie just beneath the surface of his arms, legs and the flat of his stomach. The slim narrow of his waist and the generous expanse of his chest made her fingers itch to touch what seemed an irresistibly impossible vision. He stood tall, regal and confident as attested by his proud stance and bold actions. The sense of danger flowed through her as he approached.

Marco walked over to Angela slowly and purposefully. Each step was carefully placed and perfectly measured. Eye to eye, they stood staring at each other for several moments, both lost in their own thoughts. He reached up to touch her face then paused. Without releasing the connection of their piercing eyes, Marco uttered to himself, "Quien es ella?" Then, louder, he spoke. "What is this deception, Juan?"

Juan walked over, turned to Marco and said, "Marco Santos, I'd like to present Ms. Angela Lord. She is the woman I spoke of earlier." Juan looked to Angela and smiled meekly. "The resemblance to Angelina is uncanny is it not?" Juan said nervously, trying to gauge Marco's reaction to Angela.

Absently, Marco rubbed at his neatly trimmed beard. He

meticulously examined Angela, then slowly leaned in closer. She felt his warm breath as he intruded into her invisible shield of personal space. He stepped around behind her. Closing his eyes briefly, he inhaled deeply until the scent of her penetrated his blood. She smelled of sweet innocent wonder and wanton erotic fantasies. The mix set his blood on fire.

He reached out and boldly fingered a loose lock of Angela's hair before she jerked her head away. He smiled at her reaction and stepped in, edging even closer. He looked over to Juan. "Yes, it is unbelievable, too unbelievable." His mock amusement turned darker and the deep crevice of a scowl slashed across his brow.

The face belonged to his Angelina, yet the body and eyes belonged to a stranger. His Angelina's eyes sparkled with coy mischief. But these eyes, which bore into his soul, held secrets of pain or pleasure, he couldn't be sure of which. Her body was fuller, more womanly than Angelina's thin willowy frame. Every curve flowed fluidly into the next. In perfect rhythm, her body could wrap firmly around a man's vision of paradise. The dark rich rum tones of her skin begged to be touched. He imagined the taste of her was just as intoxicating. Being drunk in her arms would be any man's fantasy or nightmare.

Angela had had enough of this scrutiny. She inhaled deeply, thrusting her chest out proudly, defiantly. She lifted her chin upwards in challenge after sensing the anger burning inside of the man behind her. His golden honey-toned skin singed red with heated passion as he all but glowed with rage.

He moved around to face her. She could feel her own anger rising, escalating to match his. Angela held on to his eyes as fiercely as he held on to hers. She watched until the tiny golden flecks disappeared into the blackness of his temperament.

Years in New York City's foster care system had taught her that at times listening was far more advantageous than speaking. So, she held her tongue. The ability to immediately assess her surroundings had served her well for twenty-nine years. This time was no different. The setting may have changed but the hostility was the same. So, she held her tongue, but far more importantly, she held her temper.

Marco circled again to stand directly behind her. His already squinting eyes pinched and darkened even more. He spoke. This time the tone in his voice was anything but placid. Instantly, he and Juan engaged in a heated argument in their native tongue. With Angela's substantial language skills, she found it easy to understand the rapid discussion.

Angelina. The woman's name came up several times. Angela assumed Angelina was the woman she resembled. She also fathomed that Marco didn't appreciate Juan bringing him a dead ringer for this Angelina. Angela reached over and picked her purse up from the desk and began walking to the door. Juan turned to follow.

He stepped between her and the door. "Angela, Angela, please, por favor, stay." He pleaded, then looked to Marco. "Marco, this is not how we treat a guest to our island and in Club Santos."

Exasperated, Marco yielded to his friend and walked over to Angela. He looked down the length of her bare back, "Señorita Lord, perdón por favor," he said after composing himself. "Me llamo Marco Santos." He held his hand out in greeting. His voice was as smooth and satiny as warm molasses on a hot summer day. The base of his deep, rich baritone voice reverberated inside of her like the lasting tone of an ancient Tibetan chime.

Slowly she turned. Her clear soulful eyes blazed into him as his hand enveloped hers without being offered. An electric spark surprised both of them as witnessed by their expressions. She nodded curtly. "Angela Lord." The cautious tone in her voice was devoid of warmth.

Her voice was deep and exotic and instantly filled his thoughts with possibilities. Intrigued, he immediately wanted to hear more. Marco smiled openly for the first time since seeing her face.

The stubbornly assured way she leveled her stare at him

threw a coal onto the continuously heating blaze in the pit of his stomach. Marco smiled, enjoying the ember of desire that stoked the slow growing flame within him. "Señorita Lord," he began, then spoke in rapid Spanish. He continued until he saw Angela look over to Juan. Grimacing, Marco also looked to Juan. "Que?" he asked.

"English is Angela's first language," Juan said to the still bewildered Marco.

"I see. I assumed you were fluent in our native tongue," he said. Marco spoke to Juan as he rudely turned his back to her. His anger and annoyance were still very obvious, yet his tone was calm. After a brief debate between the two men, Marco again directed his attention to Angela.

Her temper spiked as she easily translated the discussion.

"Juan tells me that you are here on vacation," he commented in perfect English. She nodded and he continued. "I also understand that you profess to have no family on the island." She glared at him. "How could you possibly resemble someone so closely and not be related? You must have distant relatives here," he offered.

"Anything's possible," she scoffed, "but I doubt it. My family isn't Latino."

He looked at her as if she'd doused him in Arctic ice. "You're not Latino?" he exclaimed, sounding completely astonished.

"No," Angela replied, "I'm not."

Marco moved to just inches from her face. "Then what are you?" he questioned as if amazed by her absurd admission.

"What do you mean what am I? You realize, of course, that there are other nationalities in this world." He remained silent and her eyes narrowed. "For the benefit of your obvious ignorance, I'm African-American," she said pointedly.

"Ah, sarcasm. You're definitely African-American," he smirked with a condescending tone.

That was the last straw. She'd had enough of his snobbish, patronizing attitude. The one thing that she didn't tolerate was bigotry. As far as she was concerned, war had been declared and she had gleefully accepted. He was in for the battle of his life. "And what's that supposed to mean?" she asked, allowing her temper to gain the upper hand over her good sense.

"No offense intended," Marco offered with another smirk, then continued with the inquisition. "I would also like to know why . . ."

She threw her hand up to stop him. Without a word she maneuvered past him and headed for the door. "Juan, thank you again for the invitation, but I had a long day and I think I'll go back to my hotel now."

"Arrogant jerk," she mumbled as she burst through the office door and quickly walked to the elevator. She impatiently mashed the glowing button several times then noticed the stairs and quickly hurried down the three flights.

On the last step of the first floor level, she bumped into a solid wall of muscle. An attractive man clad in white silk and white leather and wearing dark sunglasses stood blocking her way. "Sorry," she apologized and tried to continue past him but found that the stranger had clamped on to her wrist.

He uttered a few words in Spanish then removed his glasses.

"I suggest you let go of my wrist. Now." Angela said, getting more and more agitated by the outcome of the evening.

"My God, it's true, Angelina," the stranger added.

"No! I am not Angelina," she snapped. "Is everybody on the island nuts?"

"Roberto! What are you doing here?" Marco demanded as he quickly sauntered down the stairs, catching up with Angela.

Juan hurried to Angela's side, positioning himself between the two men. "Señorita Lord, Angela, please stay. I apologize for the misunderstanding."

"There was no misunderstanding, Señor Martinez." She glared at the stoic Marco. "I understood him perfectly."

"Buenas noches, Marco, Juan y muy bonita señorita," the suave stranger cooed, lowering his lips to kiss the hand of the wrist he continued to hold. "Me llamo Roberto Santos, encantado. Command me, I am your obedient servant."

"Silencio, Roberto!" Marco demanded. Roberto chuckled then responded in Spanish beneath his breath. Whatever he said shocked Juan and further angered Marco. Marco hissed a warning between tightened lips and lowered a glare at Roberto that could freeze the sun. "Don't start with me tonight, Roberto, not tonight," he said, snarling between gritted teeth.

Marco's challenge was met with a mischievous glint in Roberto's eye. "Por que? Why? What are you gonna do, Marco?" Jaws clinched and fists balled. The two seemed ready to go to blows when Angela had had enough. She turned, snapped her wrist free and hurried to the nearest exit.

"Way to go, bro, I see you've managed to run another one away," Roberto said as Marco glared and brushed past him to follow Angela.

Once outside, Angela spotted Carlos casually chatting with several women standing at the front of the line. He quickly tossed a lit cigarette butt into the street then dashed around to the side and opened the car door for Angela.

"No thank you, Carlos, I've had enough Santos hospitality for one evening." Her last remark, directed at the approaching Marco, had Roberto snickering as he came up to her opposite side. Angela looked down the crowded street. She spotted a row of waiting cabs. She threw up her hand to hail one. The cab driver started the engine and shifted into gear. Marco held up his hand to wave him back. The cab immediately stopped.

"Perhaps you will join *me* for the evening, señorita," Roberto urged smoothly. His casual charm radiated all around him. "My car is right over there." Marco stepped between Roberto and Angela.

"I'm warning you, Roberto," Marco hissed.

"I suggest you get my cab up here," Angela demanded of Marco.

Marco turned to face Angela as Juan chimed in, "Ms. Lord, Angela, please let us go back into the office. It seems we have become the center of attention."

Juan was right. They all turned to look around. Several

people standing in the front of the line had turned their interest to the two men vying for Angela's attention. Juan turned to distract the waiting crowd as Marco took Angela's hand. The same twinge went through her when his hand enveloped hers.

"Shall we?" His touch matched the soft gentleness in his voice. Instinctively she pulled away, then yielded. It occurred to her that there might be a better way to teach him a lesson in manners and respect for others.

"Please," Marco offered. "I will see that you return safely to your hotel," he promised as he smoothly placed his hand at the base of her back and guided her back toward the club's open doors.

Angela nodded absently, finding herself melting to this desperado's newly acquired charm. Her feet found their own ruling and followed him obediently. They moved in silence to the elevator and returned to the office.

As soon as they entered, Marco stalked to his desk and Roberto plopped down on the sofa and began absently flipping through a magazine on the coffee table. Angela stood in the rear of the room by the bar. The room was tomblike silent for a few minutes, then, without warning, hostilities erupted. The battle lines had been drawn, and the two caballeros were at war.

The argument was in Spanish and much too fast for Angela to completely understand. But she picked up enough to know what the gist of the altercation was about. It seemed to center on Angelina again.

Angela sat down on one of the bar stools and watched in amazement. *Unbelievable,* she mused. *Two extraordinary men arguing over a dead woman while she sits here.* Her self-esteem had definitely taking a major blow this evening. *How can an interesting, reasonably attractive, highly intelligent woman be overshadowed by a corpse?* She chuckled to herself at the absurdity. Her friend Elliot would love this.

She tilted her head in fascination as she became captivated by the two Latin hombres. They were clearly related.

The similarities between them were obvious. Both men had deep, dark, golden skin kissed by years of island sun. Their faces were classic, chiseled firm with dark eyes, nearly black, framed by long curly lashes. Together they represented the universal icon of male virility. One youthful and quick, the other mature and seasoned.

Marco turned. He faced the alcove window then looked down at the packed dance floor below. Angela watched every move he made; every minute gesture drew her keen awareness and undivided attention. She couldn't take her eyes off of him. He was truly magnificent. His broad muscles flexed across his back when he removed his jacket and placed his hands against the glass. His narrow waist, strong legs and firm buttocks reeked havoc on her senses. Lacking the underlying playful demeanor of the second man, he was defiantly the seducer of women.

He had a sexy mouth with full, tempting lips, shaped and styled for long leisurely kisses and soft tender nibbles. And although Spanish poured out, understanding didn't really matter. She just liked the way his mouth moved, his jaw tightened and his lips formed.

This man was trouble, she concluded. His brooding arrogance and charismatic charm made a dangerously intoxicating mix. Angela found herself being helplessly drawn to his strength. Marco turned back to the room and stood before his desk with his arms crossing his chest. His dark eyes blazed passionately as his powerful body leaned against the front edge of the desk. *Umm . . .* Angela mused. *Imagine unleashing all that power in the bedroom.* She shivered at the tantalizing wayward fantasy.

Whoever Angelina was, she must have been an incredible woman, Angela resolved. Then, with surprise, she caught to herself. *What am I doing? My libido must be on serious overdrive.* It had definitely been too long if just watching this man move made her body burn.

She took one last look at the two men. One dressed in dangerous black, the other donning pure white, both in heated dispute over one woman. She slid down from the bar stool and left the club virtually unnoticed.

Twenty minutes later her cab arrived at her hotel.

She breezed through the lobby on her way to the elevators, but realized that she was still too wound up and perturbed to retire for the night. So she decided to stop in the hotel lounge. As she neared the entrance, the boisterous crowd grew louder and louder. She stopped. The last thing she wanted to be around right now was more people, so she turned and headed toward the outside terrace she'd noticed earlier when she arrived.

To her relief the small outside veranda was secluded and nearly empty. She looked around. Several couples sat talking beneath cabanas while others strolled down the path leading to the beach. Angela hesitated for a moment. Two by two, like Noah's Ark, they walked, talked, and sat, paired up for life or for however long it would last. The sudden familiar solitude gripped her without warning as she stared into the darkness.

She hated the loneliness when it came. But more than that, she hated feeling sorry for herself. Emptiness and isolation had always been burdens she'd carried. She had friends enough, and a wonderful family she'd created over the years, but the oneness and the yearning for companionship sometimes saddened her.

Melancholy, Angela walked toward the center fountain and sat down on the marble and granite ledge. The sweet, colorful floral scents and calming gentle breezes soothed her as she dipped her hand into the cool water then watched the water trickle down from the adorned spouts into the darkened pool.

Angela looked deep down into the fountain's darkness. Her image in the troubled water bespoke her life. Awhirl with turmoil, she had always sought peace and solace. The sparkling reflections of soft candlelight and muted stars glistened on top of the water's surface. She sighed heavily, willing the subtle splashing of water to soothe her troubled heart.

Eventually, her mind whirled with images of the last few hours. The pleasant ride with Carlos. The beauty of Puerto Rico at sunset. The expression of delight from Juan as they met. The splendor and glamour of the Club, and then there was Marco Santos. The most vivid image of them all.

She stilled her nervous hands as her heart lurched at the mere thought of his name. He was the epitome of power and control and definitely the most impressive man she'd met in a long time. He didn't just enter a room he took command of it, along with everyone and everything there.

The compelling effect he had upon her at first sight nearly toppled her forwards onto the glass. She remembered looking up from the dance floor and seeing his reflection. He was a vision beyond belief. Then, when he spoke her name, *Angel,* the room spun as she turned to witness his true image.

Breathtaking beyond imagination, he was attractive in a way that caused a woman to yield everything. Succumbing to the lustful feel of his body, the sensual sound of his whispered promises and the dark danger in his eyes, any woman would be instantly enticed by the alluring aura surrounding him. Begging to be invited into the temptation of his arms, she'd find herself lost and adrift forever in his dark beguiling eyes. Loving him would surely be as easy and natural as breathing.

In shameless disregard and abandoned pleasure Angela could almost feel herself, even now, being captivated by his magnetism and enraptured by his power. In spite of everything, his unrestrained temperament, his judgmental comments and deplorable behavior, her body's immediate reaction to him was unmistakable. Her blood ran hot, and she wanted Marco Santos to quench her lustful thirst.

Angela shuddered and shook her head to dismiss her wayward thoughts. The draw to Marco was more intense than she realized. His powerful presence had apparently lingered long after she had departed from him. Chilled by the assertion, she wrapped her hands around her arms and looked away. She could still feel his presence surrounding her.

"You left without saying good-bye to Juan."

Angela looked up across the fountain. Marco's dark, piercing eyes greeted her. A second of hesitation gripped her as she fathomed for a moment that he was merely a vision from her wayward imagination. Her heart instantly lurched as every nerve in her body tingled, when she realized that he was actually standing there in front of her. She swallowed hard. "He was busy at the time," she said.

Marco walked around the side of the fountain. "May I join you?" he said, sitting, not waiting for an answer.

"Actually, no. I think I've had quite enough of your interrogations for one evening," she said, as she looked away into the dimness around them.

Marco smiled at her quick remark and settled comfortably next to her. He stared at Angela. His expression was unreadable, as his eyes traveled every inch of her face. "I apologize if my inquisitiveness was offensive. Your appearance at Santos this evening took me by surprise. I didn't expect to see this face again." His voice trailed to a whisper as he reached out and stroked the side of her cheek.

She let him before realizing what was happening, then she leaned away. "Look, I'm sure it must have been strange to suddenly see a doppelgänger of this Angelina. I understand. Apology's accepted. Now, if you'll excuse me, I'd like to be alone."

As if hypnotized by her likeness, Marco shook his head to clear his stayed thoughts. "Of course," he said but remained seated. "But, you should know that this is a very small island. No one is ever alone in Puerto Rico."

"I'm beginning to see that," she said, as she looked up and watched as another couple walked hand in hand down the path toward the beach.

"Where are you from, Señorita Lord?"

"Washington."

"D.C.?"

"Yes."

"What do you do there?"

"I work."

"As?"

She took a deep breath then sighed heavily. "I'm an architect, I design home and office environments."

"I see. And you have come to Puerto Rico to see our buildings?"

"You're interrogating me again."

Marco smiled at her quick wit. "I apologize."

"Look," Angela gathered her purse and stood. "I'm not sure why you're here or what you think this will accomplish. I am sure that I need to leave now. So," she turned to leave, "buenas noches."

Marco instantly stood. "I'll walk you to your room."

"That won't be necessary," she added as he followed her back to the lobby area. She stopped at the bank of elevators and pushed the button. They stood silently for the extended moments that it took the elevator to arrive. When it finally did she stepped on and turned. Marco was there. "Look," she raised her hand for emphasis, "you don't need to walk me to my room."

Marco stepped closer to Angela, allowing her hand to rest on his chest and letting the elevator doors close behind him. A spark of intimacy singed them both as Angela quickly removed her hand from the broadness of his chest. She watched intently as Marco reached down, took her hand, and pressed each finger to his lips. Then, in the most erotic, mesmerizing action, she watched as he slipped her finger into his mouth and tasted her.

Angela tilted her head in sheer amazement. The feel of his tongue suckling her finger took her breath away and left her awestruck. The simple action, something she'd done often after a tasty sticky treat, had turned into a heart thumping, toe curling, mouth watering, erotic performance.

If his intention was to arouse her sexual desire, then *damn,* he definitely had a head start. Spellbound, she watched as her finger slipped from his mouth, and his tongue lay to rest on the very tip. Next, the muscle of his mouth gently moved quickly and purposefully, taunting the sensitive tip of her finger, and her body moistened instantly. This man was good.

Then, in an instant, he captured her mouth, and the elevator soared skyward. Backed against the corner, Angela relished the intensity of his passion as his tongue searched for an opening and she gleefully accepted him into her warmth. She felt his hands encircle her, pulling her even closer, pressing his unmistakable desire into her.

Breathless with passion, they kissed and touched, conveying a lifetime's desire in a few fleeting moments. His hand fell to her breast and gently caressed the delicate fabric, kneading her nipple to beg for freedom. Angela gasped at his boldness.

Her thoughts hazed with desire as each touch and each kiss drove her closer and closer to begging him to take her right there, right now. She knew this was wrong. She didn't know anything about him. All she knew was that he made her feel alive and wanted. He made her body yearn with an undeniable need that she knew only he could satisfy.

Scorched remnants of kisses trailed down her neck as the intensity of her need propelled her to grasp him, drawing a moan of pleasure so powerful and intense that he gripped her upwards and she immediately wrapped her leg around his waist. She could not get close enough, and he could not have her closer, lest he penetrate her body at that very instant.

Transfixed by the moment, Angela drowned in the pleasure of feeling, letting her senses swim in the pool of her desire. The hunger she felt in his touch excited her. Attuned completely as one, she knew everything he craved without a word ever being spoken. She had the power to control him and wield it freely.

Marco paused suddenly and looked into the eyes of this new woman. A woman whose face he'd already seen, whose touch he'd already felt and whose body he was now driven to know. Familiar, but not. She was inside of him and had gone far beyond his recall to push her away. In this instant, she had captured and held his heart to do with it what she willed. She had become an aphrodisiac, his drug, his poison, his pleasure.

The anticipation of her whim excited him.

The chime at the arrival of the elevator to her floor sounded, sending Angela scrambling through the opening doors. She paused, and without turning, knew instinctively that Marco would follow. "Don't," she rasped, still breathless from the passion they'd shared.

Marco stayed in the elevator and watched as Angela hurried down the hall and disappeared through the doors at the far end. The elevator doors slowly closed.

Numbly, Marco watched the numbers descend slowly as his body still ached for the feel of Angela. He looked at his reflection in the brass doors. A stranger looked back at him. He had no idea what made him follow her when he saw that the red dress had left the Club.

All he knew now was that he needed more of her. This woman, whose face bewitched him and whose body enticed him, was definitely more than she appeared. She was a dream-fantasy come to life. She was the image of a memory and the feel of reality. She and Angelina could be one, yet the differences were many.

The doors opened and he remained stoic. A part of him wanted to go back up to her room and finish what they'd started. But he knew that it wasn't the right time. He left the elevator then exited the hotel. He needed to find out more about this woman, particularly why she'd suddenly appeared in his life.

Chapter 4

Angela leaned back against the door and sighed heavily. What was she doing? What had she done? What happened to the teach-him-a-lesson idea? The second she looked into those devil dark eyes, she'd melted into mush. God, that man was gorgeous. He had a body for sin and his face could weaken and crumble the strongest heart.

And when he kissed her she nearly fainted. She held her hand to her chest to stop her heart from beating so fast. That was too much. She nearly attacked the man in the elevator of a hotel, for heaven's sake. Maybe this was getting out of hand.

She kicked off her heels, tossed her purse, and walked across to the bed. In one timbered plop, she fell down onto the bed and looked up at the ceiling fan as it slowly spun. The dizzying feel of Marco Santos took her breath away. And if she wasn't careful, he'd take her heart away too.

Then, on mindless automatic, she prepared for bed.

She shook her head in total disbelief as she pulled the oversized T-shirt over her head and dragged the cotton sheet back and crawled into the bed. It was amazing how her life had spun so completely out of control in the span of just a few days. Less than a week ago she had been sitting at her drafting table recalculating the dimensions of a newly modified foyer when Lewis Carter, her boss, stormed into her office.

"I need you to redo this by Monday morning." He tossed an already approved job on her desk then turned to leave.

"I won't have time, I'm leaving for my two week vacation in two days." She pushed it aside and continued working.

"You'll have to postpone it. I need this for a client meeting first thing Monday morning. You'll have to work over the weekend to get it done."

Angela quickly looked at the blueprints tossed across her desk. They were laden with yellow sticky notes and bright red marker changes. "These have already been approved by the client and the city planning commission. We can't make changes now."

"I can do anything I want including make changes. Remember, I own this company."

"Actually, Lewis, your father owns the company. And you don't understand. Once blueprints have been finalized and approved, you can't make changes, not without going through the entire process all over again."

"I know how the process works, Angela," he huffed, growing more and more indignant. "Just make the changes. I'll handle the client and the city. I have connections," he gloated. "I've made a few notes with ideas I had. I'm sure the client will find them more interesting than these specs. The changes shouldn't take any longer than a few hours."

"But my vacation . . ." she began.

". . . will have to be postponed," he finished.

"I've already postponed my vacation for three years straight. I'm taking this one."

"You do and you're fired," he warned.

"You can't fire me just for taking a vacation that I earned."

"I can and I will." He turned and left the office.

Angela threw her pencil at the closed door. Every fiber of her body screamed QUIT! She stood and walked over to the window and looked out at the gray day. She didn't need this. She was already as nervous as a cat in a dog pound.

That's how Elliot Richards found her five minutes later when he exuberantly burst into her office. "They're here," he sang in his usual lilting tone. Angela turned around and stared at the package in his hand.

Elliot saw her face. "What the hell happened to you?" He dropped the package on her desk then walked around behind her chair as she sat down. "What's wrong, girlie?"

"I'm not going to Puerto Rico."

"What? What do you mean you're not going?"

"I can't go. I have all this work to do." She pulled at the blueprints in front of her. "Lewis just gave me this rush assignment. He needs it in a few days."

Elliot walked back to the front of Angela's desk and plopped down in the chair. "You're kidding, right? You've been talking about going to Puerto Rico for the last three years. We both know that you need to do this. And personally, I think it's about time to just finish it. It's the only way to get the answers to your questions."

"I just can't, not now."

"Since when do you let people push you around?"

"It's not that. I have a responsibility. This is my job."

"Your job, yes, your life, no. And the only responsibility you have is to yourself and your happiness."

"You don't understand."

"Like hell I don't. Since when do you let people take advantage of you? Angel girl, the only reason you're even considering Lewis's request is that you're too damn scared to finally finish this thing."

Angela glared at Elliot. She remained speechless until she finally looked away. "I don't have time for this right now, Elliot. I have a million things to do," she complained as she turned back to her computer screen to pull up the specs on Lewis's rush job.

"Oh please. You're just too afraid to go," he affirmed, ignoring her refusals.

She shook her head no. "I'm not afraid. I just can't go right now because I'm swamped with work. I have two jobs on the board, one in construction, four quotes to work out and this new rush job. I can't believe I even considered going in the first place. What was I thinking?"

"What you were thinking, girlie, was that you need to handle your business. Now get your butt up out of that chair, take these tickets and go to Puerto Rico." Elliot stood and walked behind her desk and looked at the design on her drawing table then at the revised computer rendition. "First of all," he began, as he massaged her stiff shoulders, "the two jobs on the board are both six weeks earlier than the expected timetable. The job in construction is ready for my brilliant interior design expertise, and the quotes aren't due until the end of next month."

"The showcase . . ." she began.

". . . is done," he finished.

Angela closed her eyes and reveled in the sensation of feeling Elliot's talented hands. She rolled her head and he gently stretched his fingers down her slim neck. "What about the showcase?" she muttered, trancelike.

"We've already submitted. There's nothing to do but sit back and wait for the committee's decision." He continued to knead her shoulders and back. Angela moaned her pleasure. "So you see, Angel, there is nothing so pressing that you can't take a few weeks off," he said while his fingers made tiny circles at her temples. "Right?" he prompted.

"Right," she said hypnotically.

"Good, now march yourself into Lewis's office and tell him you're taking your two weeks' vacation."

"Right," she repeated hypnotically.

"Then it's agreed, you'll go to Puerto Rico."

Angela moaned a hypnotic, "Um . . . hum."

"Good, then my work here is done." Elliot instantly stopped the massage.

"Hey wait, don't stop." He laughed as he walked to the door. "Elliot," she called out just above a whisper. He turned back to her. "Do you think I'm doing the right thing by going?"

"No one can answer that question except you, Angel. You have to do what feels right for you. But if that's where you think you'll find the answers that will make you happy, then you can't be doing the wrong thing, can you?" Angela shook her head, agreeing to his reasoning. "Just promise me that you won't go down there and forget to have a little fun. Lay on the beach, sip a couple piña coladas, make a few sketches, have an island romance. Then, handle your business and do what you have to do."

With that, Angela marched into Lewis's office, refused to work the weekend and was promptly fired. That was just two days ago.

Angela snuggled deeper beneath the covers and reached over and grabbed her cell phone. She dialed her best friend. He picked up on the second ring.

"I do hope you won't be phoning me every few minutes," Elliot quipped indignantly after an overly extended yawn. "Some of us still have to work for a living." Angela smiled at hearing his welcoming voice, wisecrack and all.

She and Elliot were as close as two people could be. Both survivors of New York's foster care system, they were beyond friends—they were family, the only family each had ever really known.

"No, Elliot, I won't be phoning you every few minutes," she sassed back with just as much spark. "I just called to see how everything's going."

"Girl, you would not believe what's been going on around the office since you left," Elliot continued with his usual exuberant tone, as he quickly removed his sleep mask and sat up in bed.

"You mean since Lewis fired me, don't you?" She paused, still angry about the events leading up to her untimely dismissal. "But wait, don't tell, let me guess. Lewis ripped apart my office then threw a bon voyage party in my honor," she jeered sarcastically.

"Better than that. Apparently stupidity doesn't always run

in the family. Caroline found out what her idiot brother did and had a fit. She screamed at Lewis for an hour. Bottom line, they want you back."

Elliot was and had always been her only supporter when it came to her dream. He understood her reasoning having also been in foster care at an early age. She laughed at his typical sarcastic remark. "So, Lewis wants me back, that's a laugh. I have no intention of going back there. He has some nerve."

"Lewis may be a lot of things, simpleton, idiot, imbecile and jerk, but he's no fool."

"I can't believe it."

"Believe it, girlie. But enough of that dreary stuff. How's it going down there so far?" Elliot asked while stretching and looking out of his bedroom window to gauge the weather and temperature outside.

"It's interesting. I'm going to try to locate the records office tomorrow."

"Records office? Angel, girl, you're on an island paradise, 'interesting' is definitely not the word to describe Puerto Rico," he reprimanded sternly.

"You're right. The island is unbelievably beautiful."

"Well dish: have you met any interesting natives yet?"

"Elliot, give me a break, I just got here this afternoon. You're the only one that works that fast."

"True that," he admitted freely.

"But actually, I did meet a strange couple who seemed to think I looked like a dear friend of theirs. Apparently seeing me scared the devil out of them. They invited me to have dinner with them tonight."

"I don't even have to ask, I know you didn't go," Elliot said, dripping with sarcasm.

"Well, believe it or not, I went."

"Well?" he said, pulling out the word as if it were salt-water taffy. "Do tell, what happened?"

"I met a couple of more nuts. I had an argument with the

owner of a club. Then, I made out with the same gorgeous hunk of a man in the hotel elevator."

"Angel, girl, only you could go a hundred miles away and wind up starring in your own soap opera. What's the name of the club?" He chuckled.

"Club Santos," she said absently as she leaned up and fluffed the pillows behind her head.

"Club Santos! You've got to be kidding. You got into Santos on your first night? Girlie, that's almost impossible. Santos is one of the hottest clubs in the Caribbean. You go, girl! I am too impressed!" Elliot said as the second line buzzed through. He glanced at the caller I.D. It was Lewis's home number. "Listen, Angel, Lewis just buzzed through, no doubt he's still looking for you. Let me shoo him off and get back to you."

"No, wait. I'm exhausted, I'm gonna crash. Let me call you later."

"Okay, Angel, you take care; have a wonderful time and good luck with your search."

"Okay, talk to later," Angela said.

"Ta, doll," Elliot replied as he hung up.

Angela hung on to the phone a few more seconds before hanging up. She was still surprised to hear about Lewis wanting her back. Then, as if a bolt from the blue, the image of Marco Santos in black pierced her thoughts. She smiled then caught herself, looked around as if she were a school child cheating on a test. She lay back, closed her eyes and dreamt of warm breezes, soft music, Caribbean sunsets and Marco Santos.

Chapter 5

At seven o'clock in the morning, Club Santos's stilled silence was tomblike and eerie. The only sign of life came from the occasional swing of the kitchen door as preparations continued for the evening's opening. The clang of pots and the rattle of dishes were the only music played as the first-shift kitchen staff danced their familiar steps of preparation.

Juan looked up at the bearded man strolling into the dark, deserted club. He picked up his cup and tipped the steaming hot liquid to his lips. After a long sip he lowered the cup and continued typing on the laptop computer that sat on the table in front of him. The rumpled man paused at the circular table. Juan looked up into haunting ebony eyes. The man's face was still darkly shrouded in annoyance. The expression on his face was evident. He was definitely not in a good mood. "You look like hell," Juan ventured where few men dared to tread.

"Who asked you?" Marco grumped as he slid into the booth across from his friend. He glared at Juan for a few seconds then threw his head back onto the high leather backed cushion. His glassy eyes stared up at the darkened ceiling. Slowly, he rolled his head and let his eyes drift toward the stilled mirrored ball above the enormous dance floor.

Marco thrived on the living pulse of Club Santos. The loud music, flashing lights and twirling dancers were all part of his heartbeat. He fed on the high energy that the club provided. Every night he reenergized himself. This was his addiction, his vice, and his obsession. She was his world and every part of her was his life. Club Santos was the lover that would never disappoint him. She would continuously give of herself without taking anything in return.

"Do you want to talk about it?" Juan questioned as he took another sip of the steaming hot liquid.

"Do I look like I want to talk about it?"

"Yes," Juan admitted truthfully. "As a matter of fact you do."

Marco fixed his stare at Juan. "Exactly what were you thinking when you brought that woman in here last night?"

"Would you prefer to accidentally walk into her on the street, or maybe have her wander in here inadvertently?" Marco said nothing. "Or perhaps Roberto could have met Angela first and brought her in here." Juan closed and exited a computer file, then pushed the laptop aside and focused his attention on the man seated across from him. "Marco, the presence of Angela Lord isn't the problem here. You are."

"Really? Then by all means, Juan, tell me, how am I the problem? Everything was going just fine until you brought that woman in here last night."

"Everything was not going just fine. There has always been and will always be something that will remind you of Angelina. The curve of a woman's smile, the tilt of her head, a passing scent—these things are natural. These are the fond memories we cherish of our departed loved ones." Marco looked over, anticipating the next words as Juan gauged his mood, then proceeded, "Up to a point."

"Meaning?" he stated, more of a warning than a question.

"You are a widower, Marco. Angela does not resemble your wife. She resembles your dead wife." The heat in Marco's eye flared.

"I'm well aware of my marital status, Juan."

"Apparently not," Juan continued. "You have been in mourning for the past two years, and it's time to move on."

"So, the best way for me to move on in your opinion is to be reminded of my late wife, and have a woman that could be her identical twin walk into my office?"

"No," Juan continued. "The way to get on with your life is to put Angelina behind you."

"Up until last night, I thought I had." Without uttering another word Marco stood and walked into the darkness.

Angela stood at the mammoth medieval fortress in awe. She gazed reverently at the aged foundation dating back to the mid 1500s then reached out and lightly touched the great wall. The sun-drenched, muted tan color of the varying stone reminded her of the solid body of a lion laying in wait, ever perched and ready to protect its own.

A formidable barrier to approaching invasion and pirate attacks, Castillo de San Felipe del Morro was all but impregnable in its day. Solid rock fifty feet high, twenty feet wide and six miles long stood between it and the betrayer from the open sea.

San Juan's ultimate fortification took over 240 years to complete. The immense construction was an architect's dream and an enemy's nightmare. The imposing structure boasted an intricate system of dungeons and tunnels intertwined through six levels of island history. Angela reveled in its magnificence.

She looked up at the ring of rectangular sentry boxes dotted along the upper wall. Cannons still perched in defense of the island's protection. Smiling, Angela could almost hear the thundering cannons hurling huge ebony pellets through thick air clouded with black gun powder and soot.

She sat down on a stone bench a few meters from the wall and prepared to go to work. A few simple drawings later, she paused and glanced down at her guidebook and scanned the page dedicated to Old San Juan's turbulent history. She frowned, reading of the constant threat from distant civilizations that led to many violent years for the simple inhabitants of this beautiful land.

Drawn back from centuries past, Angela looked around her, then quietly continued sketching. Numerous boisterous tourists stood around chattering nonstop and taking turns snapping posed photos. Wide-brimmed straw hats, brightly colored shirts and Bermuda shorts surrounded her momentarily then excitedly moved on. Their stark contrast to the majesty of the ruin was apparent. Angela scoffed in ridiculed annoyance. Lost were the historical significance of the structure, the architectural importance of the few remaining remnants and the bequeathed promise of its grand future.

These were the true treasures of time. Though ravished by wind and rain, they remained untouched by man's destructive powers. Built on a solid foundation, this structure could last well into the next century and beyond. A strong foundation was the key. Everything needed a solid foundation, be it a building, a country or a child.

Sorrow shaded her thoughts as she turned the page and began another drawing. Minus the guidance of parents, she was left to build her own foundation. But she was a lucky one. Eventually she had help by a loving, caring foster family. With their support she succeeded where so many others had failed.

"My God, I can't believe all these people actually get up this early to look at rocks." The deep masculine voice startled her. Cautiously she closed her sketchbook and looked around the now-deserted area. Directly behind her she spotted a tall muscular man casually leaning against the base of the century-old wall. He tossed the remnants of his icy snow cone treat into the trash, squinted, blew dust from his dark sunglasses then put them on. He hooked his thumb into the waistband of his white shorts then innocently cocked his head and gazed at her.

"Are you talking to me?" she asked. He grinned and nodded curtly, treating her with the same debonair smile as the night before. The stunned Angela opened her mouth then clamped it shut. She recognized him. The bleached blond hair, dancing dimples, smiling eyes and handsome features were impossible to forget.

He casually pushed away from the wall and strolled closer then stopped again in front of the aged gray stone. He reached up and felt the roughness against his perfectly manicured fingers. "We learned about this place in grade school," he chuckled to himself then clicked his tongue. "I haven't been here in years." He turned to Angela and tilted his head, questioning. "Is this why you came to the island, to look at some old rocks?" Angela gathered her books, stood and walked away.

Following the route outlined on the map, she headed back toward the center of Old San Juan. Multistoried buildings with pastel rainbow facades greeted her at every turn. Refurbished and renovated Spanish colonial and Moorish architecture, exaggerated by stark white details, outlined the vibrantly colored storefronts, restaurants and fancy boutiques. Wrought iron gates and floral-draped balconies gave the mixture of traditional, modern, and old, an eclectic brew that was totally, solely, uniquely Puerto Rico.

She coolly strolled down the promenade then paused before a most extraordinary building. She looked at her guidebook then back up at the building. *Casa Blanca,* she surmised, then stepped back to get a better look at the foundation, structure and composition of the elaborate design.

She walked through the gateway into the enormous garden surrounded by numerous ornamental fountains. She smiled, looking around at the obvious pun. The home of Juan Ponce de Leon, who searched in vain for the fountain of youth, having his home surrounded by so many fountains. She smiled again.

"It's the ancestral home of the first governor, Juan Ponce de Leon." The now familiar voice interrupted her thoughts again. Smelling of subtle spiced cologne and lemon ice, he eased closer. "I believe that was before his search for the fountain of youth." Roberto Santos smiled mischievously as he admired her form before he gazed back up at the white building.

Angela turned her head to the side. "Is there a reason why you're following me?" she threw over her shoulder without actually looking back at him.

He ignored her statement and moved to stand right beside her. "The building's a museum now," he said then looked over at her. "Historical legend has it that Ponce discovered Florida but died in Cuba still searching for the fountain. His bones were supposed to have been brought back and laid to rest in the San Juan Cathedral." He paused. "Some believe he actually found the Fountain of Youth but was killed for the knowledge and its location was subsequently lost. They also say that his single-minded obsession with living forever drove him insane just before he died. But, I don't think so."

She turned directly to him with annoyance. "Oh really, and why is that?" she huffed.

"Because I saw him out partying a few nights ago. He still looks great for a guy over five hundred years old." He'd caught her off guard. The barest twinge of a smile tugged at the side of her mouth. She wanted to laugh but refused to give him the satisfaction. "Come on, Angela, you know you want to laugh," he teased mischievously.

She broke down and graced him with a friendly smile then rolled her eyes and looked away. "Don't make me like you." He smiled warmly and boyishly pushed his hands deeper into his pockets. He turned to completely face her, shaking his head in amazement. The brilliance of his white T-shirt peeking out from the open silk shirt that blew restlessly in the early morning breeze caught her attention.

"Believe it or not, most people don't have a choice," he said. Angela smiled, shook her head, and chuckled. "I still can't get over how much you resemble her. It's like the two of you were identical twins separated at birth." He stepped in closer, lowered the tiny oval sunglasses down his sculpted nose, then squinted at her. "It's uncanny."

Sighing heavily to show her disinterest, Angela turned slightly and looked back up at the white building. "So I've heard," she said sarcastically.

He peeked at the sketch she'd just completed then up at the building. "That's pretty good. Are you some kind of artist or something?"

"Or something." Angela closed her book and continued walking into town.

After several minutes, Angela finally strolled down the narrow stone streets of Old San Juan. Shops and cafés lined both sides of the narrow path. She wandered along easily, leisurely, soaking in the natural wonder of her new surroundings. She stopped before a roadside display and noted the wares before entering the store.

Hand-crafted masks of coconut husks and papier-mâché hung horned and frightening above small-carved figurines representing the deities of the Catholic, Santeria, and Yoruba beliefs. Rows of candles and incense perfumed the small store with an aura of heavily laden musk.

A royal blue fringed shawl instantly caught her attention. Beautifully designed with playful paisley and slashes of gold thread, it was the most beautiful thing she'd seen in a long time. Playfully she fingered the long delicate threads before walking out to look through another store window.

She paused before a street band of small children. Some played tambourines, maracas, kalmias and conga drums while others danced in response to the music. *Bomba y plena,* in rhythmic synchronism, the cadence of their lyrical movement enthralled the assembled crowd. Angela clapped her hands and laughed as several tourists began dancing their weak rendition of the dancer's movements. When the entertainment had finished a small child came up to her and offered a large hat to collect gratuities. Angela dropped in several dollars and continued her walk.

Roberto followed a half step behind her and watched every move she made. "I'm sure you realize by now that ignoring me is a waste of time." His dimple playfully winked at her in the store window. "I have a very compelling personality."

Angela looked up at the store window's reflection. Apparently this man couldn't grasp the subtlety of her hint. "Annoying would be a better word," she said.

"Semantics."

Angela looked at Roberto closely. In the brilliance of morning light, he looked even younger than he did last night. "What exactly is it that you want from me?"

As she spoke she noticed several women walk by and openly stare at him. Roberto was younger and definitely less intense than Marco. His body was just as firm and his white linen walking shorts and white silk T-shirt curved around every muscle. But as attractive as he was, he was no Marco.

"You know, you remind me of my mother," he confessed haplessly.

"If you're flirting with me and that's your best pickup line, I'd seriously consider shaving my head and joining a monastery if I were you."

The boisterous laughter caught her off guard. She didn't expect his overly exuberant reaction. Roberto reached up, removed his dark glasses and wiped his moist eyes. He nodded his head in complete agreement. "Yep, that's definitely something my Moms would say."

Angela strolled on. He easily fell into step beside her. "Me llamo Roberto Santos. I am your obedient servant," he announced in a grand gesture.

"Yes, I remember. You were my obedient servant from last night."

"And you are Angela Lord from Washington, D.C." She stopped. He could have easily gotten her name last night from Juan but there was no way he could have known where she was from.

"What makes you think I'm from Washington?" she asked as she continued walking again.

He smiled. "I know a lot about you, Angela. You grew up in New York foster care, supported yourself through college, majored in architecture, and now you work at Carter Architectural and Design Firm. I hear it's one of the most prestigious design firms in the D.C. area, thanks to you. Is it?"

"You seem to have all the answers, Roberto, why don't you tell me?"

He smiled boyishly. "I love it. And you are so good. Quick and pointed, intelligent and beautiful, you're perfect."

Angela stopped again. Having her life recited for her wasn't the easiest thing to hear, particularly from a complete stranger. With her fist now planted firmly on her hip, her stance anything but obliging, she tilted her chin up in preparation for battle. "What do you want?" she asked blatantly.

Slowly, the corner of his slanted lips turned upwards. "I didn't mean to alarm you, Angela. Honestly. I just wanted to get your attention."

She glowered, and one thin neatly trimmed brow rose defiantly. "You have it."

"I asked you a question earlier," he said. The last thing on Roberto's mind at this point was the question he'd asked. Surprisingly, his mouth began salivating at seeing her rose-colored lips pucker and pout in anger. He knew she was angry. Yet the composed passion in her deep exotic voice was erotic and he relished every time she spoke.

"Refresh my memory."

"Looking the way you do, I find it hard to believe you came here to Puerto Rico just to look at some old rocks. Why did you come?"

Angela took a deep breath and sized up the man in front of her. He was a lightweight compared to her. She'd devoured his kind every day. On work sites, in the streets, in clubs, his kind was always angling for the advantage in a situation, using words to enhance their position. Well, if words were his game, play on. "If I told you I came here on personal business, would that satisfy your curiosity?"

"Maybe. Did you?"

She shrugged her shoulders, smiled and moved closer. The plot from the book she purchased at the airport popped into her mind. "Maybe I'm an international spy who's been surgically altered to resemble your Angelina." His smirk faded as she began reciting several more plots from her many romance and mystery novels. She removed her sunglasses to give him a better look at the seriousness of her expression.

"Maybe you were right earlier. Angelina and I were twins and I've come to avenge my sister's death. Or, perhaps I am actually Angelina and suffered amnesia for the past two years. Or, maybe I'm just a figment of your imagination." She moved even closer, whispering up to his ear. "Or, possibly, I'm Angelina's ghost, and I'm a wandering spirit unable to cross to the other side."

Her voice was now the barest whisper. "Or maybe I'm just a tourist here for some sun and sand." She stepped back and replaced her glasses. "You make the call." She began walking away.

Suddenly, a wide grin replaced the hard, stern expression. "Not bad." He nodded his head approvingly. "Not bad at all. He caught up to her, "But, if it's all the same to you, I think I'll go with the spy scenario. It sounded more intriguing."

"Whatever." She shrugged her shoulders and walked on. He watched her walk off then hurried to follow.

"So, what's your code name?" he asked as he caught up with her.

"It's classified."

"What's the mission?"

"Top secret."

"Is there anything you can tell me?"

"I could, but then I'd have to eliminate you."

"We've all got to go sometime," he said, enjoying himself immensely. "But before you eliminate me," he paused and looked around casually, "how about some lunch? I'm starved."

Angela stopped again and looked at the man at her side. He was charming, funny and about as tenacious and stubborn as a puppy. "Sure, why not." She looked him up and down. "You look harmless enough."

A few moments later the two walked the bustling side

streets of Old San Juan. Laughing wildly at Roberto's many
humorous stories, Angela loosened up and began enjoying
herself. Roberto guided her toward a small outside eatery in
the center of the Old San Juan village. The charming café was
idyllic for an early afternoon meal. With its picture-perfect
view of the century-old plaza, Angela gazed awestruck at the
ancient Spanish style architecture encompassing the area. In
amazement, she watched as busy tourists hurried by, completely oblivious to the surrounding historical treasures.

Roberto motioned towards two empty seats beneath an
open umbrella. He pulled out a white-painted wrought iron
chair with a brightly colored padded cushion. "You're not
Latino, are you?" He seated her.

She raised her brow with warning. "No."

Roberto beamed. "I didn't think so."

"And why is that?"

"You have a different way about you."

"Is that good or bad?"

"Neither, it's just different, a refreshing change from the
norm," he said, as he waved to a couple walking by.

"Is that a problem for you too?"

Roberto smiled. "No, not that I know of. Why?"

"It seemed to be a problem with your brother."

"Marco, nah, he's just overly tense."

She let the statement pass and looked around the café. There
were several other customers sitting in the outside area. A
table of women constantly glanced over to their table. Their
interest in Roberto was evident. Angela smiled as one woman
leaned over to the other and fanned her face with her fingers.
"You said that I reminded you of your mother. Is she Latino?"

The smile returned. "Nah, like yourself, she's African-
American. Also from New York. Also sarcastic, stubborn and
beautiful. Must be a character trait." His dimple winked boldly.

"Yeah, must be," she said. He stared again as she absently
fiddled with the silverware. "Sounds like you have a good
relationship with your mother." Roberto nodded.

"We do, although I don't see her that often. She still lives in Manhattan.

"Really? She's not here on the island?" she asked, tilting her head questioningly as she waited for him to continue. He waved his hand nonchalantly to dismiss the subject. "It's a long story." The waiter appeared with two glasses of iced water and menus. As he set them down he recognized Roberto. The two spoke for a few moments then the waiter disappeared into the restaurant still carrying their yet unseen menus.

"Did you just order for me?"

"How did you know? I'd heard you didn't speak or understand Spanish," he asked suspiciously.

"Who told you that?"

"You do speak Spanish, don't you?" he affirmed.

She smiled her vague non-answer. "The waiter took the menus back. It was obvious."

"Oh. Right. Yes, I did order for us," he said without a second moment's thought.

"Why?"

He opened his mouth but realized he had no answer. "Because . . ." He curiously scratched his head, then after few seconds of thought leaned closer. "Trust me, I promise you will enjoy the meal."

"Trust is not an option. Trust is a luxury most people can't often afford."

Roberto's face turned to stone in its sudden seriousness. The expression seemed foreign to him. "How sad," he uttered softly.

"Not really. Life is cruel. You learn to trust very few, and then you get over it."

"Sounds like experience talking."

She smiled politely but didn't answer yet her piercing eyes spoke volumes. A moment of silence drifted between them as she gazed out over the plaza. "So what did you order?"

"You're going to love it," he began, as she looked skeptical and he elaborated on the food selection. "First, the island mystical nectar, *cielito lindo,* also called small beautiful sky. It's a spectacular splash of rum, fruit juices and blue curaçao with plenty of fruit on the side. Then, arroz con pollo, which is spiced chicken with rice, asopado with mounds of seafood and fresh vegetables served on an bed of fluffy rice and beans. It's like a paella. Also, mofongo, spiced and battered plantains and for dessert," he glanced down her long crossed legs, "who knows. Maybe we'll improvise." His cocky self-assured expression was impossible to resist.

"What if I told you I don't like chicken, rice or red beans. I'm allergic to seafood and I never ever eat anything spicy." To that statement she got the desired result.

"Really?" Roberto's eyes widened. He was mortified as he began searching the area for a waiter. Then, realizing her temperament and hearing her chuckle, he turned to her, squinted his eyes and a broad smile emerged as he wiggled his finger in her direction. "You," he began. "I'm going to have to be very careful with you, and I see that now."

"I suggest you allow me to order for myself in the future."

"In the future?" he asked while waving at several locals walking by. "Yes, there will indeed be a next time."

She gave him a *we'll see* expression, noting that he waved at practically every other passing motorist. "Are you an island celebrity or something?"

He laughed openly. "Why do you ask?

"You seem to be very popular, like you know just about everybody on the island."

"Santos is a very important name on Puerto Rico. The lineage goes back several hundred years. My family has influence in certain places."

"So, I guess I should be impressed."

"Are you?" he asked hopefully.

"Not really," she admitted truthfully.

"I didn't think so," he said, laughing.

The waiter arrived with two icy, tall glasses of blue liquid. Angela removed the tiny colorful umbrella and sipped the delicious nectar. The cool, sweet iced drink chilled her mouth while the heat from the dark rum warmed her throat. The mix of sensations was delightful. Moments later the abundant meal arrived along with the second round of small beautiful sky.

The conversation during the meal was light and flowed easily between their travels, businesses and interests. The food was as Roberto promised—exceptional. Angela ate heartily, leaving only a small pile of gathered red beans on the side of her plate.

Over a lazy dessert platter of freshly sliced pineapple, passion fruit, mango and guava, Angela's curiosity got the best of her. "Tell me about her."

"Who?"

"Angelina."

He smiled. "Angelina Carita Rivera Santos; she was my brother's wife."

"I assume that was your brother last night?"

"Yes, Marco. He and Angel had been married for about five months before the accident. The marriage was annulled after the third month. It's a very long story." He waved his hand to dismiss the conversation as he had done earlier.

"I see." She watched as he tilted his head and grimaced. "What? What is it?" She questioned.

"It's funny, the more I look at you now, the less you actually look like her. I can barely see the resemblance now. It's amazing. There's nothing remotely similar about you and Angelina."

She smirked. "Good, I'm glad to finally hear that." The conversation lapsed into an uneasy silence.

"Sometimes you look so distracted, and sad at the same time. Why is that?"

She looked him squarely in the eye. "Why so curious?"

Holding her stare, he responded without missing a beat, "Why so sad?"

She smiled. The conversation was about to turn in an uncomfortable direction. So, she changed it. "I get the feeling you'd like to use me as a pawn in this drama between you and your brother."

"Wow, where did that come from?" he questioned.

"I learn quickly. You like to play head games, don't you?"

Laughter answered the truth of her remark. She felt assured that she'd more than figured Roberto out. "Don't take this the wrong way, Angela, and I'm not talking romantically or anything, but I think you and I are going to get along famously."

"You think so?" she acknowledged comfortably.

He felt the need to clarify his position. "No, seriously. I really like you. You've got gumption."

"Comes with the territory."

He nodded his sincere approval. "Apparently." Roberto couldn't stop grinning at his kindred spirit. Angela was exactly as she appeared and he loved it. He was right when he first assessed her. She was just like his mother; she too was the love of his life.

Chapter 6

When the meal ended, Angela said her good-byes to Roberto then went back to her hotel suite. She showered, wrapped herself up in the hotel's fluffy robe then relaxed outside on the small terrace. Beneath the crystal blue sky she reviewed and examined the sketches she'd done earlier that morning. She studied the details of the fortress's brick facade and jotted down a few ideas for future design uses.

Admiring her work, she mused, *maybe this trip wasn't such a bad idea after all.* Then she remembered her first night and she changed her mind. Last night's fiasco at the Club seemed more like a bad dream that had been washed down the drain with the warm water of her shower. Then there was the ride in the elevator with Marco. A flush of heat blushed her cheeks. Suddenly she wasn't in the mood to draw, so she donned a pair of shorts and a T-shirt, found the hotel's exercise room and worked out the last of her frustrations.

She returned an hour later, completely exhausted. She'd barely had enough strength to slide the key card through the slot and open the door.

Just as she collapsed onto the bed there was an annoying knock at the door. She looked at the clock. It was nearly five P.M. already. Instead of getting up, she lay there, wishing the person would go away. They didn't. The knock came again, this time much harder, louder and more persistent. "Yes, okay I'm coming," she shouted then grumbled. She was prepared to murder the unfortunate being on the other side of the door. As she swung the door open the overwhelming scent of fresh flowers greeted her along with two grinning bellmen.

"Buenas dias, Señorita Lord, para usted," one of the young men said as he handed over a large basket of assorted fresh flowers. Then he turned to the second bellman and handed her the second one, a glass vase filled with dozens of pure white blooms. Angela was speechless. "Oh, ahh, gracias, un momento." She took both bouquets, placed them down on the side credenza, then reached for her purse to tip them. The bellmen declined, stating that they had already been very well compensated. The two smiled, bowed slightly then bid her good evening.

A broad smile crept across her face as she looked at the beautiful display of cut flowers. "Elliot," she said aloud, knowing exactly who must have sent the wonderful gifts. She went back to the credenza and inhaled the aromatic assortment of fresh flowers then gently caressed the tall magnificent calla lily blooms. Sculpted to nature's perfection, the slightly furled blossoms gracefully yielded to her gentle touch. She marveled at their simple and distant elegance. Then, gingerly, she searched both bouquets for cards.

She opened the first small white envelope. *Looking forward to your next history lesson, Roberto.* She shook her head. "You don't give up easily do you?" she said aloud then chuckled to herself while opening the second card. *Dinner at Santos, nine o'clock, Marco.* She chortled then read the card a second time. "I don't think so," she stated firmly as she sat both cards on the dresser, concluding that Marco's audacity was unbelievable. After another whiff of the fragrant flowers she kicked off her sneakers, peeled down her damp socks and padded barefoot into the bathroom.

The third shower of the day with much cooler water was

even more refreshing than the first and second. After a generous amount of aromatic moisturizing lotion and a quick swipe of the moist mirror with the damp towel, she stopped and gazed longingly at her reflection.

A flawless rich complexion of softened African tones muted by decades of diluted ancestors stared back at her. "Who are you?" she asked the question always nagging in the back of her mind. "Where do you come from?" Satisfied by the ever-present silence in answer to her wayward questions, she looked away from her reflection in failed misery.

Her conversation at the Club with Marco Santos brought back a myriad of painful memories from her childhood. The loneliness of solitude. Never feeling comfortable enough to connect with any one person or family. She'd readily accepted her sentence of oneness, yet questions were always perched in a dark corner of her heart. They'd threaten to emerge at the least provocation. No, she wasn't Puerto Rican as Marco had assumed. She wasn't anything. No past, no history. She just was.

Then, with the sheer will of might, she reached deep down within herself to replenish her spirit's strength. She refused to accept pity, even from herself.

She stepped out onto the terrace again to soak in the heavenly view. It was spectacular. The steeple of a nearby church pierced the skyline like a sharpened needle through a colorful quilt. The crest of flamboyant floral-topped trees, the endless blue sea horizon and distant mountains seemed to almost be within arm's reach. Angela watched as colorful exotic birds and sea gulls scattered across the open expanse of blue sky. Each soared and glided, fell and climbed as the gentle breeze prevailed.

The picturesque scene was a kaleidoscopic of God's perfect handiwork. Within moments she was back to feeling the power of one. She wondered how she could bottle this relaxing feeling and open it the next time a contractor uttered, *Angela, you might want to look at this, are you sure this will work,* or the most popular from her clients, *Angela, I changed*

my mind again, can we go back to the first design you had.
She felt her shoulders begin to tense again so she got up and
strolled back into the floral-scented room.

She quickly dressed in a scant one piece bathing suit with
matching cover wrap, then slipped on her sandals, grabbed
her straw bag and headed for the door. On her way out to the
hotel's poolside she paused at the two bouquets and took another deep inhale. She picked up the card from the lilies and
read it again. *Dinner at Club Santos, nine o'clock, Marco.*
"No phone number."

Angela started for the door then stopped. She grumbled
loudly, then opened and searched her purse for the card Juan
had given her. The only number listed was to Club Santos.
She picked up the phone and dialed the number. A voicemail
message recited several options. She chose to leave a message
declining Marco's dinner invitation then hung up. She tossed
the business card and floral card invitation, on the dresser
along with the four tiny colorful drink umbrellas from lunch.

At poolside, Angela found an empty lounge chair beneath
a large blue striped cabana. She spread out the beach towel,
sat down, lay back and put on her dark sunglasses. When the
waiter arrived she ordered a drink then sipped it slowly as she
watched the children playing in the water. Then after less
than a brief conversation with the man in the seat beside her,
she pulled out her new romance novel and read the first line.

Surprisingly, after just a few paragraphs, she read and
translated the story easily and became completely enthralled.
Lost again in the familiar throngs of passion, Angela let go
of her insignificant existence and delved into the familiar
world of romance. A comforting world she knew all too well.
Welcoming the passionate words as a benevolent lover, she
found her solace then gave herself permission to hope, to
dream and to desire.

*. . . Clayton smiled lecherously and crooked his
finger. "Come here, wench," he commanded gently . . .*

* * *

"Excuse me, miss, miss, may I get you another drink from bar?"

"Humm?" Angela looked up, still wrapped in the comfort of her novel. "Oh . . . yes, thank you," she said, ordering a second virgin banana daiquiri. Slightly embarrassed, she smiled to herself as she shook the last remnants of romance from her mind. She snapped back to reality with a heavy sigh. Relaxing her shoulders, she eased deeper into her canvas-cushioned seat and dreamingly placed the opened book across her chest.

Feeling a little ridiculous about her silly adolescent obsession, Angela sat up straighter and glanced around the pool area, pleased with herself. After a morning well spent, drawing sketches of architectural ideas, she decided to relax at the hotel's pool then grab a light dinner before stopping by the casino. She finished her first drink then tilted the book up, and continued to read.

> . . . *Clayton's masterful hands slowly, gently and skillfully unbraided the laces on the front of Bridget's drenched garment. His watchful eyes never left her lowered face. Her heated breath escaped nervously as millions of tiny fluttering butterflies tickled the inside of her belly. His fingers brushed across the swell of her ample breasts as they protruded against her taunt bodice. He smiled at the once lowly tavern wench. Barely able to move, she shyly looked up into Clayton's raven eyes and saw her troubled past disappear and her future open up to a hundred new and exciting possibilities. She was ready . . .*

"Umm, what a man," Angela moaned as she unknowingly licked at her rose-colored lips and smiled the contented smile of a woman in anticipation. Her excited hands scarcely held on as she continued.

* * *

   *. . . She was ready for this. Clayton's head dipped
and captured her mouth in a kiss meant to curl her
toes and weaken every fiber of her being. He succeeded. Her mind was a complete haze of wanton desire. Her thoughts swirled and blended until nothing
seemed real. His hot powerful hands branded her
body with loving strokes. She whimpered as his mouth
left her swollen lips and began their assault on her
slim neck. Then, he pulled back from the kiss and his
dark stormy eyes brazed her heart. He made quick
work of her remaining garments as they puddled hap-
hazardly atop her bare feet. With her heaving breasts
completely exposed, he smiled a knowing smile, then
he . . .*

Angela began to wonder. Why wasn't there a Clayton out
there for her? Or Charles or Cliff. Hell, at this point she'd take
a Wilbur. Clayton was the personification of the quintessential
man. He was sheer masculine perfection. He was every
woman's ideal fantasy lover. He was a tall, dark, dangerous
stranger turned hero and savior. A man with a stormy past
who rises above it to become a champion of the downtrodden.

He was ready at the blink of an eye to sweep his heroine
off her feet and whisk her away from the drudgery of her existence, then destined to worship and adore her for eternity.
The men in Angela's romance novels were all like that, strong,
powerful yet gentle, gallant and very, very sexy.

Glass clinked against glass as the waiter, placing her second drink on the small side table, interrupted her thoughts.
She smiled at the colorful fruit filled concoction. After signing the tab she pulled out the paper umbrella then took a sip
from the long red-and-white plastic straw. *Umm, perfect,* she
thought, then went back to reading her book.

   *. . . With her heaving breasts completely exposed,
he smiled a knowing smile, then he . . .*

* * *

She began to read again, then, as if on cue, a loud, obnoxious snort interrupted her thoughts. She looked over to the man seated in the next chair with annoyance.

Comically, his mouth gaped open like a hippo in water while his fluttering lips resembled flapping leaves in a windstorm. His contorted facial features, the plump redness of his cheeks, along with the big bushy crop of hair and his stout body, gave him a humorous appearance that reminded her more of a squatty cartoon character than the world-traveling businessman he professed to be.

Yet, his apparent friendliness was a welcome distraction. As soon as she sat down he talked nonstop about himself then pulled out an overstuffed wallet filled with photos of his wife, eight children, pet dogs, cats and iguana. By that time, he'd had his third drink and she'd heard his entire life story including career triumphs and future goals.

Actually, she thought he was kind of sweet with his sun burned freckled skin and cherry red nose. That was, until he began to hit on her somewhere during the fourth drink. He confessed every cliché in the book: *My wife doesn't understand me; we have an open marriage; I'm only staying for the children.*

By his fifth drink, he dutifully fell asleep. Angela shook her head in disgust. Lord, she'd love to just once meet an honest man with minimal baggage and maximum character. In the past few years, she'd had her fill of the half-stepping, jive-talking, lame-excuse-for-a-man types. But, as her foster parent Mother Mitchell always said, "You have to squeeze a lot of lemons to make lemonade, but anything worth having is worth putting the time in."

Well, at twenty-nine she'd taken all the time she intended to take. Soon to become one of the unmarried statistics she'd always read about, she accepted her new status in life begrudgingly. It wasn't fair. But then, few things in life were. She of all people attested to that truth.

Ideally, she had everything a woman could ask for. She

had a loving family of sorts, attentive friends and a fabulous
career that she adored. So, finding a companion at this stage
in the game wasn't exactly top priority. Even if it were, when
would she possibly have time to look? Working in the office
for twelve hours a day then trudging around on construction
sites dressed in dusty jeans and a hard hat wasn't exactly
conducive to finding "Mr. Right."

But that was the nature of the job. A job she loved. She
poured her heart and soul into her designs and was amply re-
warded with an impressive client list. Yes, her life was satisfying. She was truly blessed. But, there was that part of her
that still wanted more, needed more, and deserved more.
Like the heroines in her books, she wanted it all plus someone to share it with.

In the years it took to firmly establish herself in the com-
petitive Washington, D.C., market, she'd lost interest in the
traditional dating game. The men who approached her now
were either married, broke or emotionally needy. So, with
the serious lack of possibilities, Angela unsuccessfully convinced herself that her life was pretty much complete.

But deep down inside she wished and hoped, like a young
schoolgirl reading fairy tales, that her Prince Charming would
someday come along. Going home to an empty home just
wasn't satisfying any longer. With that notation firmly in
place, she relaxed back, adjusted her sunglasses, took a long
sip of her drink and continued reading. She repeated the last
line again, then went on.

> *. . . With her heaving breasts completely exposed,
> Clayton smiled a knowing smile, then he . . .*

She was impossible to miss. The bright yellow swimsuit
spoke volumes as it caressed every envied inch of her curva-
ceous body. Lush flesh tones of chestnut, cherry and mahogany danced across her body's palette as she moved with a
rhythm he heard so clearly. Marco stood completely unseen

at the smoked glass pane of the atrium wall of windows and observed her from the blessed coolness of air conditioning.

He watched her hips sway seductively across the poolside and frowned as several men followed her path with their lustful eyes. She sat down and pulled out a book from her straw bag then carelessly laid it across her ample chest when the waiter took her drink order. His dry mouth salivated with desire as memories of the elevator danced in his head.

He rubbed at his beard absently, seething when a man next to her garnered her full attention. What was wrong with him? He had lost all control. He'd become tormented by his wayward thoughts. All he could think about since first setting eyes on her was this mysterious woman. He was fixated on her. Somehow, she had slipped into his system. She had become a drug, and he was hopelessly addicted. The cravings were too strong and he weakened each time he thought of her which was more often then he cared to admit, even to himself.

He had to end this slow torture, one way or another. He didn't care where, when or how. All he knew for sure was that he needed to either be done with her, or to be with her. Then, without further thought he stormed through the glass doors and within seconds stood before his addiction.

Angela looked up. This time she was interrupted by a shadow falling across the pages of her book. At eye level, perfectly tailored black linen pants stood rigid in front of her. Her gaze continued upwards, resting on the slim narrow waist, then the black fitted T-shirt smoothed over a chest of rippled muscle. Her gaze followed the natural progression upwards until she looked into the reflective sunglasses of Marco Santos.

He stared down at her. His lips slowly crept into a dubious curve reminiscent of a smirk. "I'm sorry, I don't mean to stare."

"Yes you did," she challenged with certainty.

Sudden surprise crossed his hard facial features then just as suddenly melted into a vibrant smile. "You're right." He relaxed, lowered his head, embarrassed, and pulled at his diamond studded ear lobe. "I did. I just didn't mean to get caught."

"Obviously." They stared a few moments, sunglasses to sunglasses. Angela, suddenly self-conscious of her attire, placed the slightly trembling book across her thighs. Her body warmed and her mind whirled. The mere sight of this man could melt the polar caps.

Shaded, Marco's eyes followed the book at rest then continued down. "You look so much like her," he confessed.

"Yeah, so I've heard," Angela said coolly, trying to distance her traitorous emotions. She realized that keeping her wits was going to be challenging around this man. He was too dangerous and way too sexy. Everything about him screamed: touch me.

"Your resentment is misplaced."

She looked up lazily at the magnificent man. "If I thought about it, and I don't, I'd have every right to be annoyed."

At that moment a short squatty man rushed up to Marco, anxious to get his attention. Angela assumed it was the valet or some waiter wanting drink orders until she saw that his name badge read HOTEL MANAGER. He pulled a huge white handkerchief from his inside jacket pocket and began nervously wiping his damp face.

"Buenas tardes, Señor Santos, a pleasure to see you again, sir. I'm, I'm sorry, I didn't greet you when you first arrived. No one told me you were coming in today. What, what can I get for you?" he asked ardently.

"Excuse me," Marco said, obviously bothered by the interruption. He turned his attention to the nervous little man. "Buenas tardes, Enrique. This is simply a social call," he assured the profusely sweating man.

Enrique looked at Angela, puzzled. "Ah, si, I understand. Will you and your guest be joining us for dinner on the terrace this evening perhaps, or maybe a private dining room?" the manager offered.

"No, gracias," Marco said pointedly and turned away, dismissing him. "Good evening, Enrique."

"Si, si, good evening, sir." The man nodded and rushed off just as quickly as he had arrived. During the exchange between Marco and the manager, Angela noticed several other employees had their attention drawn to the two men.

"Excuse the interruption," Marco apologized, getting back to their previous conversation. "Look, we got off on the wrong foot last night. I didn't mean for my remark to come out as it did. The shock of seeing you took me off guard. It's not an excuse. I'd like to start over tonight. Please have dinner with me."

"To tell you the truth, the last thing I need is a repeat of last night. Thanks, but no thanks," Angela said as she picked up her book to return to her reading.

"I received your message."

"Uh-huh," she said with her face still in the book.

"Very few women turn me down, Ms. Lord."

"I bet," she said, sending the throaty pitch of her voice lower for emphasis.

By the barest thread of composure, Marco's mounting desire wavered on the brink of arousal. The flame she'd coerced earlier had returned in full force. Marco's solitary desire at that moment was to hear her throaty-pleasured moan at his intimate touch.

He removed his glasses and crouched down to her chair. His jet black eyes sparkled as bright as the large diamond in his ear. "I'll send a car at eight-thirty. I suggest you join me." He looked at her with complete assurance.

Angela smiled. There was something about this man that intrigued her. "I won't be there," she assured him.

He smiled. "I think you will."

"Do you always get your way?" she asked, half joking.

He stroked his beard with the back of his hand. "Yes, as a matter of fact, I do," he replied. As he stood up, he wished her a pleasant day, then walked off, obviously used to the effect he had on the women around him.

"Marco," she called after him. He turned to face her several yards away. "Thank you for the lilies. They're beautiful."

"You're very welcome," he said with Roberto's sweet boyish grin that gripped her heart. He put on his dark sunglasses, turned and walked away. As he crossed the pool area he was followed by the eyes of every woman over the age of seventeen, each drooling in her own romantic fantasy.

Angela shook her head and made a mental note to stay as far from him as possible. He was just too tempting.

Leaning against the glass window, just a few yards away, Chevis de Long huddled in a corner behind a tree trunk his cell phone to his ear. Diligently, he watched the interaction between Marco and Angela. His eyes widened with concern as a tense voice chimed in his ear.

"Calm down, estúpido," she demanded sternly, as her exceptional breeding would not permit her to yell at the simpleton. She picked up then twirled the ever-present silver hand mirror at her side.

"Si, of course, you are right, as usual. It's just that seeing this woman is like seeing a ghost. She is Angelina's exact duplicate. I would not have believed it had I not seen and spoken to her personally," Chevis continued anxiously.

The woman on the other end of the line graciously walked out onto the balcony of her lavish Miami condominium. The weather was perfect as always. The sky and ocean spread out below her as if to proclaim her arrival. She casually glanced down at the myriad of people mingling beneath her penthouse abode. Ocean Drive in South Beach was packed as usual. A swell of haughtiness washed over her as she assumed her seated position above the common masses.

She listened intently as the man on the other end rambled on. He paused hesitantly. "Are you there?" He panicked as silence returned his comments about the mysterious woman with Marco.

"Yes," she said calmly while continuing to eye herself in the mirror. She smiled admiringly. The swelling had gone down considerably and the remaining bandages would be off in days.

"Well, what do you want me to do?"

"Do nothing," she said, running a slim finger down the side of her swollen face.

"Nothing?" he shouted aloud then looked around as several passing tourists looked in his direction. He turned his back towards the tree trunk. "Nothing? Didn't you just hear what I said?" The small gasp of displeasure that came from her caused him to lower his voice again and drastically change his tone. "I'm sorry, forgive me, my sweet."

She ignored his current apologies and ramblings. "Do nothing; I shall be down shortly," she assured him, then hung up.

Chevis closed the tiny cellular phone and watched as Marco rounded the pool and headed for the hotel's lobby. He quickly moved to avoid being seen. As Marco continued walking, Chevis pulled a white tissue from his pocket and wiped the beaded sweat from his upper lip and brow.

He wasn't sure that this affair was worth the trouble it had began to cause in his life. Lately she had become too demanding of his time and his attention. But just as quickly a smirk of pleasure crossed Chevis's face and he had his answer. She was definitely worth it.

Chapter 7

The loud, high-pitched squeal, then the clamorous clanging sound of falling coins drew Angela's attention a third time. The woman sitting on the stool a few feet from her had just won another jackpot in less than ten minutes. Angela frowned her annoyance then glared back at the traitorous machine in front of her.

The multicolored device promised great wealth for a scant price. It temptingly displayed numerous images in various possible combinations. Each assured to be a winner. Angela tapped the silver tray with her fingernail then slipped three coins into the narrow slot and pulled the long handle. Immediately the tiny fruit wheel began to whirl.

The first row jerked to a stop on a grouping of three brightly colored cherries. Using all her mental abilities to will the cherries to appear a second and third time, Angela stared at the spinning second wheel. It stopped. She smiled as a second grouping of cherries appeared. Angela watched as the third row continued to spin. "Come on, cherries, come on," she muttered subconsciously. It stopped on a lemon. Angela smirked. "Figures," she mumbled.

She looked into the small, depleted bucket of coins. Grabbing the last five silver dollars, she quickly plopped them into the machine. With one last all-or-nothing grimace, she placed her hand on the large round knob and prepared to pull.

"I'm not accustomed to being stood up." She knew without turning it was Marco. He laid his hand on top of hers, preventing her spin. Quickly he dipped his mouth to her ear to add to their private conversation. "I didn't like it."

Angela stared straight ahead. "Then I suggest you seek professional help. It sounds like you have a personal problem." The dry bite of her sarcastic comment did little to quail his appetite. Instead, he relished her throaty quips. He enjoying the husky rasp of her voice each time they bantered.

Marco smiled. Her voice was low and raw. The kind of voice that nudged you awake at dawn to make love. "I ate alone."

"I'm sure you enjoyed the company."

His plastered smirk was replaced with a genuine smile.

She yanked the handle down with his hand still covering hers. The dials spun quickly as the handle snapped back into position.

"Was that an assessment of my character?" he asked. The first dial stopped on three solid bars.

"It's a statement of fact, much like my decline of your dinner invitation earlier this evening."

"Very few people refuse me, Señorita Lord," he warned. The second dial stopped on three bars.

"Get used to it, Señor Santos," she challenged.

Marcos smiled openly. The cool detached contrast of her icy veneer steamed his blood to a boil. "Looks like I brought you luck."

The third dial stopped. A loud bell rang as dozens of silver dollars tumbled into the large tray. She whooped loudly, thrilled by her recent turn of luck. She gathered the coins into the bucket, leaving one in her hand.

She dropped the single coin in the slot then pulled down on the handle. Three different fruits appeared. "I don't think so."

He smiled and leaned in closer after deciding that a change

in approach was necessary. "You would have thoroughly enjoyed our evening together, Angela." She tensed as his warm breath made the gathered curls below her hairclip scatter across at her neck. The insinuation was apparent. He'd planned to have more than just a simple dinner with her.

"You overestimate your appeal, Marco," she countered evenly. "You're not that enticing."

His brow rose in challenge. "Ah, but you have yet to try me, Angela," he dared.

"Another invitation so soon? Careful, Señor Santos. You're beginning to sound desperate." She turned around. Her breath caught in her chest at the sight of him. He was so devastatingly handsome dressed again in all black.

"You enjoy provoking me, don't you?"

"Of course not," she promised innocently.

"I believe I'm correct. You do enjoy it."

"I've noticed that you seem to think that you're always right."

"I usually am."

Angela chuckled. "You're not that good."

Marco raised his brow. "Try me," he challenged again. She knew exactly what he implied. "Interested?" he asked, seeing the curious glint in her sparkling eyes. She raked her lower lip between her pearl-white teeth. He watched in anticipation. She had a way of seducing him with the slightest, most innocent action.

Her obvious curiosity was unmistakable. "You're enjoying this little game, aren't you?" she asked, stepping back to get a grip on her runaway senses.

He smiled menacingly, watching her move back to lean against the machine. "Yes, I am," he replied honestly. Then he moved closer. The small space between the two seemed to evaporate as his arms straddled her when he leaned both hands against the rimmed edge of the slot machine. "Just as you are enjoying it, Angela."

She opened her mouth to object, but began speechlessly shaking her head no. Then she felt him lean in even closer.

His eyes narrowed on her open mouth while he nodded his head yes. "Foreplay," he mouthed for her ears only. Surprise registered on Angela's face. Her heart slammed against her chest with the force of a fallen anvil through silk.

His mouth came to within a hair's whisper of hers. Their breath mingled erotically. Then his lips barely touched hers in the briefest of joining. He tasted the sweetness of her lips. She was exactly as he'd remembered and fantasized. Neither exerted pressure toward the mock kiss; yet both felt its scorching effect.

Reprimanding herself for her overpowering physical reaction and lack of restrain, Angela came back to her senses. "Was that your feeble attempt at seduction?"

Marco smiled arrogantly. "I do not seduce women; I must confess, I've never had the need." His cocky smile tipped the scale decidedly in his favor.

"I suppose every woman you meet endeavors to seduce you?" she asked mockingly, but was less than surprised when he confirmed her query with a subtle tilt and nod of his head. Angela sighed, relieved when he leaned back. "Don't assume you know me because I resemble someone else, Marco. That would be a mistake."

"I don't profess to know you, Angela. I do however profess to wanting you."

"What games are you playing?" She tried to appear as unconcerned as possible. But one brief glance into the raven-black of his eyes was all it took for her to lose all senses. Her heart thundered loudly and her stomach twirled in circles.

"I could ask you the same question."

Then, she nodded her head slowly. "An island affair, a brief distraction with a tourist, is that what you're looking for?"

"If you prefer," he said, calling her bluff. "When I see something I want I go after it."

"As do I."

"Shall we." he said firmly.

They stared into each other's eyes. The stalemate had been achieved and he had left it up to her to make the next move.

"Fine, let's go," she found herself saying, before she'd weighed all of the consequences. She took his offered arm. Several patrons smiled and spoke as he escorted her through the crowded casino to his waiting car.

They drove in silence. Yet Angela's mind was a whirlwind of conversation. *What am I doing here? This is crazy.* This wasn't like her. She was extremely cautious when it came to men. But it seemed that nothing about her and Marco made sense. He unnerved her and that scared her. His eyes seduced her; his lips enticed her and his body aroused her. His blatant confession of wanting her threw her over the top.

They arrived at Club Santos amid the same outlandish party atmosphere as the night before. He laid his hand gently on the base of her back and led her through the VIP entrance, to the elevator then to his office. He opened the door and followed her inside.

Angela walked over to the large glass window and looked down at the jubilant crowd on the dance floor. Marco watched her as he stopped at the small bar in the corner and poured two glasses of champagne. He removed his jacket and carried the filled glasses to the window. He opened a small panel and touched a button. Angela looked around for a change in the lighting but noticed nothing different.

Her questioning expression prompted him to answer. "I darkened the privacy glass. We can see out but no one can see in." She nodded her understanding. Their fingers brushed lightly as she took the offered champagne flute. The fiery spark sent a heated chill through her stomach. Angela looked up into Marco's shadowed face.

His eyes, soulful and proud, were deep dark pools of liquid fire. Black, smoldering eyes that had paralyzed her senses on more than one occasion. She could very easily lose herself in his eyes. The notion alarmed her; suddenly she stepped away and moved toward the desk. Needing a distraction, she took a sip from her glass and looked around the room. "This is an interesting building. How long have you been here?"

"A while," he said as he sat on the desktop.

"Did you renovate it?" He nodded yes. "What was it before?"

"Ruins."

"From what little I've seen, you've done an exceptional job."

"I like it," he stated.

She motioned to the packed dance floor below. "Is it always this crowded?"

"Are you going to ask questions all night?"

"One last question. You said you wanted me; I want to know why."

"You want the usual list of compliments? Fine." Exasperated, he sat his glass down on the desk and moved in front of her. "You're beautiful; you're intelligent; you're witty; you're sexy." He tossed out the words rapidly as if scripted and he was mentally checking them off a list one by one. Then when he looked at her, really looked at her, into her eyes, he paused as sincerity gripped him. Breathing deeply, he added, "You fascinate me. Not your resemblance, *you*."

He took her glass, disposed of it next to his own and continued. "I like watching you move when you don't know I'm watching," he confessed, smiling slyly. He reached out to her hair clip, freeing the heavy mass of waves. "I like the way your hair rests on your shoulders." He lowered his hand to grasp a handful of soft curls. "I like the way your body smells of sweet coconut, bubble gum and cotton candy." He smiled and licked at his lips. "I like the taste of coconut, bubble gum and cotton candy." Each word was punctuated with arousing passion. His eyes drifted to her lips as his fingers gently touched them. "I like the way your lips pout when you get angry." He stopped.

Breathe, she ordered herself mentally. But the simplest of actions would not come easily. She had been swallowed whole by the intensity of his eyes. His words barely registered when his eyes spoke to her as they did at that moment.

"Are you a dream," he whispered, then paused, "or a nightmare?"

"I'd say that would depend on you."

The kiss was sudden and consuming. Without hesitation Angela reciprocated, matching force for force. Their lips pulsated, releasing the hunger that raged inside and demanded to be fed. Her hands pulled at anything and everything, as he nudged her away from the window.

Guiding her backwards toward the sofa, he continued his worship as he dipped his mouth to the sensitive throbbing pulse at her neck. She freely exposed her throat to his ravenous assault. Greedily, he feasted, then he lowered his body to her temple. Shamelessly, she grabbed fistfuls of soft black curls when he buried his head against her stomach. They were starved, famished, and gluttonous with insatiable need and desire.

Her blouse opened as by its own doing. Marco covered the scant satin lace of her bra with his hands. She moaned, savoring the feel of his touch. As he eased her downward, she collapsed, absorbed by the softness of the thick cushions and the ardor of his savored mouth.

She pulled at the buttons that selfishly prevented her hands from touching him. With ease she tugged his shirt over his shoulders, freeing herself to touch him, and she did. The warmth of his skin sent a blade of hot passion cutting through her. This is what she wanted. He was what she needed.

Breathlessly, the kiss ended with her laying on the sofa and him poised motionlessly above. He lowered his mouth to her again. This time, gentle brief kisses followed in slow-motion secession, each more inviting than the last. The taste of his champagne mouth mingled deliberately with hers. She closed her eyes, listening to the playfully wet sounds of their mouths dancing in unison. His tender lips left her mouth and traveled down her neck. Angela arched back, reeling with the wave cresting above her as his hands found her breasts.

She stopped cold.

"What did you call me?" she sputtered in shock.

"What?" he muttered in the haze of desire too thick for him to penetrate.

Angela sat up, gathering her open blouse. "You called me Angel."

"So?"

"So? That's what you said the first time you saw me. That's what you called your wife, wasn't it?" She pushed away from the sofa. "Marco, I'm not Angelina and if you're looking for this to be some sick, twisted reunion between you and your dead wife, you can do it without me." She stood and stalked to the door.

"Wait." He stood and shouted out. Ignoring him, she continued moving to the door. "Don't walk away from me," he demanded when she continued to go. "I said stop!" He ordered louder.

She whirled around. "Excuse me? You may think your Santos name runs this island, but your name doesn't mean squat to me."

The fire of lust and anger clouded his eyes. "My name may not move you, Angela, but my body does," he stated definitively as he moved to her. "Doesn't it?" He let his open shirt slowly drop to the floor. Her breath caught in her throat as she stared at his beautiful body. The waistband of his pants, still unbuttoned by her needful hands, lay waiting. She turned to look away. "Look at me, Angela," he demanded. "Look at me."

She looked at him. The abundance of firm muscle rippling across his chest and forearms immediately took her breath. He was right. His body had moved her. It moved her to places she'd long forgotten and to a place she longed to visit again, only with him.

His body was flawless perfection. There was no other way to say it. Every muscle, every bone, every tendon was precisely placed beneath his sun-kissed skin. Skin streaked crimson red by her nail imprints when she'd hastily opened his shirt. "I don't jump through hoops for anybody," she stated soundly.

"I never asked you to."

"What do you want from me, Marco?"

He slowly ran his hand over the braid of his muscles and his rock hard chest then paused, letting his fingers rest on the waistband in front of his pants. Her eyes followed hypnotically as his hand seductively glided over the hard firmness of his body. Her fingers tingled, begging to be the caresser. "I thought that was obvious," he said with his eyes still blazing with anger turned back to desire. "You, Angela Lord, excite my blood, I want you. I want to make love to you. Take this moment, Angela. Come, be with me now." He reached out to her.

She took her fill of his body, broad shoulders tapered to a narrow waist and hard well-formed abs above a perfectly flat stomach. With just a sparse whisper of black hairs leading to her downfall at his open pants, she took a slow deep breath and raised her eyes to meet his.

Impulsively she stepped closer, reached out, and grabbed the back of his head and pulled him to her demanding mouth. Devouring him seemed to be the natural thing to do. She pulled back and gently caressed the tiny silky hairs on the sides of his face. "You don't know what you want, Marco. You look at me, but you don't see me. You see a second chance to have things differently with Angelina. You see a way to have her back in your arms. You may someday get over her. Or maybe you never will, I don't know. I do know that when you look at me you don't see me, you see her. You weren't touching me just now; it was her you wanted to make love to tonight, not me."

He opened his mouth to speak but she placed her fingers across his lips and shook her head. Slowly, she let her hand drift down, feeling the solidity of his chest. He closed his eyes, letting her touch seep through his body. "And you know what?" His eyes opened when she continued. "It's a shame, because I think we could have really been good together."

With one last longing smile she turned. "You're gonna have a hell of a time getting over me." She opened the door and left. "Good-bye, Marco," she whispered from the other side.

He stood there, staring at the door. She was right. Until he could separate the two women, physical intimacy with Angela would be meaningless. And for once in a long time of faceless bodies, he wanted making love with her to be special for both of them.

Her last words still echoed in this thoughts. *You're gonna have a hell of a time getting over me.* "Tell me something I don't know," he uttered, as he picked up his discarded shirt and walked back to his desk.

Chapter 8

Angela briefly scanned the information she'd just received from the lobby's tour desk. Ponce and the El Yunque Rainforest were two places she definitely wanted to see. But today, she had something else to do. Not looking, she began walking toward the lobby's main doors.

"Good morning," he said brightly. "Where to this morning?"

Angela looked up at the devilish dimple and smiling face. "Good morning, Roberto. Don't you have a job to go to or something?"

"As a matter of fact I do."

"Then go."

"I just got off."

"Really?" He nodded. "What do you do besides seducing young virtuous women?" He looked at her questioningly until she nodded across the lobby toward the young woman still eyeing him and giggling with her two girlfriends.

He turned, following her gaze. "If seeing me with them makes you jealous," he said smiling impishly, "then I assure you they were merely an innocent tryst."

"I bet," she said, mocking his innocent expression.

"Why do I have the feeling you do not believe me?"

"Of course I believe you, why wouldn't I?" she added sarcastically. Angela noticed the small tour bus arriving outside. "But as for today, I've already made plans."

"Good, I hate making plans, too confining." He leveled his arm out for her to accept. "Shall we go?"

"Not this time, Roberto," she said, seeing her shuttle beginning to fill with passengers. "I've got to get going. I'll see you later." She hurried off, leaving Roberto standing alone in the lobby of the hotel. Within minutes Enrique, the hotel manager, raced up to him. After a few words and several bows, the two men walked into the bar followed closely by three giggling young women.

Angela looked at the numbers prominently displayed on the small white building and then to the slip of paper given her by the detective a year earlier. They matched. She smiled, suppressing the sudden elation bubbling inside of her. This would be a turning point in her life. Here, she could possibly find the answers to all of the questions that had plagued her all her life. She looked up at the building again, breathing in a shallow nervousness.

Without hesitation, she eagerly hurried up the steps. As one foot after another landed upon the brilliant white marble, she felt a sense to fulfillment wash over her. This was a long-recognized dream of hers. One way or another she would complete her search.

As she reached the top landing she walked to the massive iron gate. The intricate design, latticed with a delicate floral pattern, was extraordinary. She gripped the cool metal handle and pulled. The rusted, squeaking sound crept out as the door easily opened to reveal an old wooden door already ajar.

Angela paused a moment for her eyes to adjust from the brilliant glare of the sun to the shadowed darkness of the inside hall. She stood blinking as a young woman walked up to her. "Buenas dias," the woman said cheerfully.

"Good morning," Angela replied. Her eyes, nearly fully adjusted, focused on a lovely young woman standing in front of her, dressed in what could only be stated as librarian drab—sleeveless gray dress at midknee, black soft-sole shoes double-laced, white-laced handkerchief collar and enlarged tortoise shell glasses. Angela smiled and inquired. "Do you speak English?"

With a perfect Bostonian accent she answered, "Yes, I do. My name is Rita Mendez. How may I assist you this morning?"

"Hello, Señorita Mendez. My name is Angela Lord." They shook hands in greeting. Angela winced in surprise. Rita's hands, although thin and strong, were as cold as ice.

Rita smiled her understanding as she purposely hid her hands behind her back. "How may I assist you?"

"I need some information," Angela stated simply.

Rita nodded. "If you'll follow me to my desk, you can tell me exactly what you are looking for." Rita motioned for Angela to follow her into the larger room. She turned to lead the way back to her office. Angela smiled in spite of herself. There, prominently displayed, was the typical librarian hair bun skewed with several chewed pencils.

"A relative perhaps?" Rita offered, as she moved behind a paper-cluttered desk and sat down in a decrepit, old chair barely stable enough for a toddler.

"Yes, a child."

Rita looked up, a frown creasing her seemingly placid face. "A child? Yours?"

"No, this particular child was born in New York in 1974." Angela slowly sat down in the chair opposite Rita's desk and retold the exact story told to her by the last detective she'd hired. Although she purposefully omitted the fact that she was the child. Rita listened without interruption, smiling pleasantly and nodding appropriately.

When Angela had completed her tale, Rita placed her elbows on the desk and arched her fingers to her pale lips. Silently she thought for a moment. "Ms. Lord, I'm not sure I can help you with your search for this child."

"Oh, no, I not looking for the child; I'm looking for information on the child's parents or grandparents, whichever the case may be."

"I see. And the detective informed you that his search led him to the shores of Puerto Rico." Angela nodded. "And you say he was positive that one parent, possibly the father, lived here on the island." She nodded again. "You are searching for your parents, correct?" Angela smiled and blushed, embarrassed by her attempt at deception.

"Yes, I am searching for my parents."

Rita reached into her side drawer, pulled out a yellow legal pad then scribbled a few notes. She looked up at Angela and smiled. "What is the name of the father?"

"I don't know."

"Okay, we will begin with the maternal side. What is the name of the mother?"

"I'm not sure." Angela hurriedly pulled documents given to her from the first two detectives she'd hired. She pulled a single paper from the bulging folder and handed it across the table. "This is the child's, my birth certificate." Rita took the paper, adjusted her glasses on her nose then scanned every word. "The mother's and father's names are listed but I was told that the names were more likely than not aliases."

Rita nodded as she continued to scan the paper in her hands. After a few moments she looked up at hopeful Angela and smiled politely. "Ms. Lord, if these names are indeed aliases as you suggest, I'm not sure what I can do to assist you in your search. Your parents used these false names for a reason. It seems that they did not wish to be found out." She placed the birth certificate on the yellow legal pad then sat back in her creaky chair.

The realities of Rita's words were sledgehammer-targeted. They reverberated in Angela's mind like the inside of a church bell. How could this not have occurred to her? It was so obvious. "They didn't want to be found?" Angela unconsciously questioned out loud, as she stared at the oversized calendar just over Rita's left shoulder. "They didn't want to be found?" she repeated again.

"Yes. That may or may not be the case, Ms. Lord. It is nevertheless a possibility you might want to consider, however distant or remote."

Angela smiled at her folly. "A possibility that seemed to have eluded me all this time," she said as she focused back on Rita.

Rita thought a moment then spoke as she leaned in and began to write on the pad. "I'm afraid, unlike the States in the midseventies, an unwanted pregnancy—please excuse my frankness—was an instant shame to any family here on the island. Thus, given that mentality on the island, there was still a very real stigma on an unwed mother, presuming, of course, that she was unwed. That would be reason enough for a woman to leave early in her pregnancy to deliver her child elsewhere."

"I always assumed that my parents were married."

"That may be the case, but then one would ask: why give up your child?" Angela nodded her agreement. "Poverty perhaps, unable to care for yet another child, or just not willing to parent. These are all valid possibilities when one considers adoption."

An icy chill crept through Angela at the word "adoption." Angela closed her eyes in shame, wishing that, indeed, that were the case. Without hesitation she spoke. "Rita, I was not put up for adoption. I was abandoned in a New York state hospital."

A small gasp escaped Rita. Her mouth hung open as her eyes blinked wildly. She swallowed hard. "I'm so sorry." The sympathy in her eyes and voice were real. "I assumed you were an adopted child looking for your birth parents."

Silence hung in the room until Angela slowly reached across the desk and took the birth certificate back. She placed it in her folder and gathered her purse. "Thank you for your time, Ms. Mendez. You've given me something to think about." She stood to leave.

"Ms. Lord." Angela turned. "If you have time, might I suggest you scan some of our newspaper files from the early and midseventies? There might be a clue of sorts. This is a small island, and the most remote gossip would be considered newsworthy. Since we do know the date of your birth we can go back eight or nine months. We can also look at the travel reports a few months before you were born. This may be a huge waste of time, but then again, some suggested that so were the pyramids." Rita smiled at her attempted humor.

"That would be more than I can hope for at this time, Ms. Mendez," Angela said.

"Rita," she corrected.

Angela smiled. "Thank you, Rita."

"It's my pleasure, Señorita Lord."

"Angela." Rita nodded and smiled as she stood and came from behind the desk.

"I'll show you to our file room. I'm afraid it isn't as tidy as it should be, but I assure you, the records are all intact."

Together they walked deeper and deeper into the bowels of the empty building where the distant smell of must and mildew increased with each step. The soft clicking of Angela's sandals bounced and echoed off the book- and cabinet-lined walls. Angela looked down at the dulled surface of the aged wooden floor. They looked as if they were the original planks when the building was initially erected.

They passed a series of doors titled in Spanish, yet simply enough stated that Angela easily could read and understood. At the end of a hall they entered a stairway, descended, then walked along a narrow path that lead to a single door.

Rita pulled out keys and unlocked the glass door with the words NEWSPAPER ARCHIVES written in Spanish. "This is it," Rita said as she ushered Angela inside and turned on the fluorescent lights that blinked and twitched, seemingly sluggish for having been awakened. The room eventually brightened to a bevy of computer and microfilm monitors.

"I'm afraid a good number of our earlier archives were lost or damaged during Hurricane Hugo in nineteen eighty-nine. We managed to save most items, but sadly some were lost. I believe we have complete records for the dates you mentioned." Rita moved to the nearest monitor and turned on several switches. It immediately came to life. "Please sit down and make yourself comfortable. I will gather the film you'll need from the archives in the next room."

Angela sat down and placed the folder she'd been carrying on the desk next to the monitor. The monitor came to life with a Spanish prompt. Confused, Angela stared, momentarily forgetting she was, in essence, in a Spanish-speaking country. Dumbfounded, she just stared at the terminal.

Angela jumped when Rita silently appeared over her shoulder and punched in several keystrokes. "Since I presume you would prefer English, I have pulled only the English-speaking newspaper files. I will search and translate the Spanish newspapers later this evening." She punched a few more keys and the terminal's language changed to English. "This should be more helpful to you. There is an intercom on the wall by the door. Please call if you have questions." She turned to leave.

"Thank you, Rita, for everything."

"It is my pleasure to assist you." Rita smiled brightly, turned to leave again then paused. "Angela, my terminal upstairs has an excellent search program. I've used it on occasion to assist in locating missing relatives for some of our local residences. I would be happy to begin a search for you, if you'd like."

"I don't know what to say. That would be wonderful. Thank you. I would appreciate anything you can do. Do you need more information from me?"

"Yes. Initially you suggested that it was more likely that your father had lived on the island. What led you to that assumption?"

"The last detective I hired came to that conclusion during his investigation. He followed a lead to a doctor with prenatal care records listed with my birth certificate number. One of the documents listed a Brooklyn address but it had been abandoned shortly after I was born. Another document listed the patient as a resident of New York and by all accounts she was a U.S. citizen. Unfortunately, it was a dead end, so the detective dropped that lead and moved onto my paternal lineage. After a lot of searching he found documents related to the hospital admittance paperwork that listed a phone number. The phone number had a Puerto Rican area code and exchange. Unfortunately the remaining digits of the phone number had been torn away."

"I see. Is there anything else you can tell me about your birth mother or father?" Angela looked down at the folder lying next to the monitor. It was something she'd guarded fiercely for years. Inside was every slip of paper, shred of evidence and piece of the puzzle that was her life story. There were only two copies. One in her safety deposit box and the other here. Reluctantly she handed over the folder to Rita.

"Yes, the information in here might be helpful."

Sensing Angela's hesitation, Rita offered, "Angela you have entered this life as no child ever should. I assure you I shall do my best to seek the answers for which you search, and in my opinion to which you are entitled. I will care for this folder as due its importance to you and your goal."

"Thank you, Rita, thank you for everything."

Chapter 9

Dressed in basic black, she opened the door of the office and brazenly walked inside. This was all so familiar to her. She went to the bar and poured herself a glass of cool sparkling water then sat down comfortably behind the large desk.

She glanced around the beautifully decorated office. It was just as she remembered. Her eyes fell upon the door leading to the fourth floor. Marco's private apartment. She smiled knowing that one day she would climb those stairs and be welcomed.

She spun the chair around to the large window above the dance floor. The dimness of the room cast her reflection onto the glass. She shifted her face from side to side then lifted her chin to check her surgeon's work. He had done an excellent job. She was just as she had been twenty years ago. She smiled at the reflection. She could very easily pass for her mid-thirties.

Satisfied, she spun the chair back to the desk and lifted her long slim legs and rested them on the desktop. She smiled at their impressive appearance in the three-inch spiked heels. Although well into her fifties, she was still a very attractive woman. Young, virile men constantly approached her, attracted by her slim body, tight skin and newly implanted perky breasts.

She was an expert at illusion. For years she had perfected the ultimate deception, a happy family. Since her father, of name and money, had left the family and—most particularly—her mother practically paupers, she had learned to live by her wits and rely on her feminine wiles to attract men with money.

Eventually she had married for money a man she didn't love, and rarely tolerated. He was beneath her socially and had no family lineages to speak of. But he was rich. He adored her and gave her everything she desired. His untimely death was merely an inconvenience until she found out that he had left her far less than she'd anticipated.

Who would have known that all the furs, clothes, jewelry, cars, houses, boats and exotic vacations she'd purchased over the years would add up to economic failure. If her husband hadn't died of a heart attack, she would have strangled him herself.

It wasn't until Angelina mentioned the name Santos did her luck change. Then, insisting her daughter marry Marco Santos, she would be back were she belonged. As soon as the alliance was made, she had insisted her daughter secure her a sizable allowance that would ensure for permanent comfort. Now, all that could change if Marco continued to see that other woman.

That she couldn't risk. Not after all she'd done to secure her financial security. There was only one thing to do to permanently secure her future: an alliance of her own.

Having been forewarned of her presence, Marco opened the door of his office and found the woman comfortably seated behind his desk. He smiled, well aware of her manipulative prowess. She was a troublemaker, but still, for a while, she had been the only woman he had called mother. "Buenas dias, Señora Rivera," he greeted in their native tongue.

She looked up as a well-timed tear ran down her surgically modified face. "Marco, my son. It's so good to see you after so long a time."

Marco dropped a clipboard on his desk and walked around to the woman. He helped her to her feet and embraced her slim frame hesitantly. "It has been a long time, señora."

"Señora?" she questioned. "Since when do you call your long-lost mother Señora Rivera?" She lovingly stroked the side of his bearded face then laid her hand firmly on his broad chest. "What happened to Isabella? That's what you always called me before . . ." She suddenly weakened, letting her delicate body sag against his broad chest.

Instinctively, Marco grabbed her to his body to prevent her imminent fall. He helped ease her back down into the chair and placed the glass of water in her hand. She sipped the cool refreshment then nodded her recovery. "Isabella, that's what you called me before"—she gasped and paused for effect—"before the accident."

"That was a long time ago, señora. . . ." She looked up at him woefully. He relented predictably, to her delight. "Isabella," he continued, "a lot has changed." He sat half on the desk in front of her and stretched out his long legs.

"What has changed? You are still my family." She caressed then laid her hand on his upper thigh. He took her hand, held it a second then rested it on the arm of the chair.

"No, Isabella. I was your son-in-law, but no longer."

"But, Marco, at one time I was the only family you knew. I will always be the only mother you have."

"Isabella." He stood and walked to the window behind the desk. Brightness greeted him instead of the usual darkened club atmosphere. Absently he watched as several employees walked around in last minute preparation for the evening's opening. "You do realize of course that my mother is still alive."

Isabella slowly spun the chair around to face him. "Yes, of course. But you don't have contact with her, do you?"

"No," he admitted, turning away. "When I have need of a mother, I will contact her."

Isabella stood and moved to Marco. She held his waist and nuzzled close in his limp embrace. Then she took his hand to her lips, kissed it lovingly then slowly let his hand rest against her ample new breasts. "My poor dear Marco. I know it's been hard without Angelina. That's why I'm here. I've come to help you with all of this. You need me with you, now more than ever. I see this now. You need me to help you get your life back in order. Together we shall ease our pain."

"Isabella, what are you talking about?" he said quickly, moving his hand away. "Angelina has been dead for over two years. There is nothing to get over."

"How sad—you have forgotten Angelina already. Have you also forgotten your unborn child she carried to her grave?"

Marco glared at her in heated rage. "Child, Isabella?" he questioned. "What about the child?"

"Our child, Marco, my grandson and your son." Isabella crossed herself at the mention of the unborn infant. "Surely you haven't forgotten that Angelina was pregnant when she died?"

Marco tensed as a muscle tightened in his jaw. "Was she? No, Isabella, I have not forgotten Angelina's claim of the child she said she carried. I've merely gone on with my life. I suggest you do the same as best you can. I don't need your help. I don't need anyone's help."

She eased closer to Marco's side again and intertwined her arms around his waist. She closed her eyes and reveled in his strength as she silently cursed her daughter for her stupidity. "But that is where you are wrong; you need me now more than ever, Marco." Her leathery, taut face softened.

"Why would I need you now, Isabella?"

She walked away slyly. "I have ears. I hear things. Yes, even in Miami, I hear things. Things that are improper. Your wife, barely dead two years and you turn to other women for comfort. You don't need other woman, Marco. You have me. Come to me, Marco."

"What?"

"And the new one. You had that woman up here last night." Marco frowned and moved away. "She is the devil come to erase my dear child's memory. See? Look around this room. Where are all the pictures I sent you? Where are the things to remind you of Angelina?"

"I don't need anything to remind me of your daughter, Isabella."

She gasped in horror. "See?" She pointed her finger accusingly. "See? This devil woman has already corrupted your mind." Quickly she crossed herself and rushed over to him. "Marco, my dear, let me take care of you; let me take care of all of this for you. I will ease your pain if you allow me." She caressed his face in her hands as she softened her voice to a gentle whisper. "Santos and Rivera. Our families belong together, Marco, don't you see. Together we are a dynasty. It will be Santos and Rivera again."

He jerked away angrily. "What are you talking about? There will never be another Santos and Rivera union."

Isabella moved to the door that led to Marco's private apartment on the fourth floor. She was sure that if she could get him upstairs in a more conducive setting, she could twist him to her way of thinking. "Maybe we should take this conversation upstairs for more privacy," she suggested innocently.

"Not necessary," Marco stated sharply.

"We would have more privacy."

"The discussion is finished, Isabella. Angelina is gone, you have to move on."

"Marco, how could you?" Isabella's face darkened in pain as her eyes filled with tears. "It's that woman, isn't it? You cannot deny that the devil woman has been here." She looked around and crinkled her nose in disgust. "Beware of her charms; she is only after your money, my son. She wants to be a Santos as my Angelina once was. She will seduce you into wanting her with her face of memories and her mouth of lies. I warn you, Marco, don't take this devil woman to your bed. She will capture your soul."

"I think it's time for you to leave, Isabella. I have a lot of work to do."

"But, Marco, my love . . ." Isabella implored.

"Isabella," he stated firmly. She stopped in her tracks. "Who comes in this office and who sleeps in my bed is no concern

of yours. Now, if you'll excuse me, I have a club to open."
He crossed the room, sat behind the desk and picked up the
clipboard.

Isabella angrily grabbed her purse from the desktop and
marched to the door and yanked it open. "Mark my word,
Marco, she will bewitch you and steal your heart."

When the door closed Marco looked up at the empty room
than over to the sofa. The memory of Angela's body still
burned in his mind. "She already has, old woman; she already
has." He spun the chair around to the window and stared out.

The Club would open in a few hours. He needed a distraction. Angela Lord had been on his mind and in his dreams
all day and all night. The puzzle of her resemblance to Angelina
was troubling; yet, it was her eyes that transfixed him. She'd
pulled him into her web of desire and left him there.

Involuntarily, his body became aroused at the thought of
their evening together and the possibility of more evenings
to come. Now that he'd tasted her, he realized that no one
else could satisfy his burn. He needed Angela.

Chapter 10

Pirate's Cove had been ideally named. Over numerous centuries it had well earned its impressive yet timeless lineage. Hordes of 15th, 16th and 17th century merchant and warships had seen to it. It was a mausoleum, a graveyard, the final resting place on a long voyage never completed.

Fleets of Spanish galleons destined for the new colonies lay to rest just beneath the crystal clear blue waters of the Caribbean. Each carried a wealth of gold and silver unimaginable in their time and unparalleled in ours. Some vessels completed the journey; others endured the hardships of man and nature. Some floundered and sunk on the jagged reefs and others were downed by mighty hurricanes. Still, some were set upon and sunk by bloodthirsty pirates, privateers and buccaneers.

Ruthless and cruel, they preyed and plundered the Spanish vessels with all the tenacity of a flock of gluttonous vultures. Attacking with a vengeance, the pirates left no witnesses. With canons blazing and swords slashing, they'd swoop down on their objective and gut it of its booty then sink the skeletal remains to the silence of the bottom of the Caribbean sea. Driven by the greed of gold and treasure, they were the perfect thieves committing the perfect crime.

The promise of lost treasure, pirate's gold, and sunken ships might have also lured some of Angela's excited companions. Ecstatically, they pursued their fortune. Bullion, bars, coins or ingots, gold or silver, it didn't matter to them. They swam in search of riches, she swam in search of solitude.

The tranquility just below the surface of the water was her serenity. The cumbersome goggles and snorkel afforded her a perfect view of the most spectacularly colored coral reef she'd ever seen. She drifted below the gentle waters. Her flippers padded gracefully while her arms waved almost motionless at her sides.

She luxuriated in the weightless feeling of buoyancy as her thoughts wandered to the interlude at the Club the night before. Marco had been on her mind, then in her dreams all night. She questioned herself constantly. If all she wanted was an island fling, then what was the big deal about his saying Angel? Most of her closer friends called her Angel. Why did she make such a big deal when Marco said it? She knew they had nothing in common beyond the intense physical attraction. Nothing serious would have come of one night of passion. So what was the big deal?

She watched a school of small colorful fish swim by. Their tiny bodies effortlessly glided to the movement of the water's ripples. The warmth of the water caressed her body as Marco did just the other night.

She could still feel his mouth on her, licking and tasting her scalded flesh. Everywhere he touched she singed with desire. The intense burning he dispensed incinerated all rational reasoning, leaving her with a desire so intense she craved him even now. Where was her plan to teach him a lesson? Where was her resolve to put him in his place? The only thing she'd accomplished was to burn for him.

Angela surfaced and perched the snorkel apparatus atop her head. She spotted the beach and decided to float in its direction. She rolled her tense shoulders then stretched her neck as far back as she could. After a short time she completely relaxed, amazed how therapeutic the simple act of floating on water could be. She lay on the surface of the warmed lagoon with her face upward. She opened her eyes. The sky was a pale blue streaked with long finger cloud formations interrupted by an occasional gliding seagull.

With slow, steady kicks she raised and lowered her arms at her sides, smoothly skimming the water's surface and propelling her body towards the shoreline. Regretfully, she left the water and walked to the secluded paradise-like cove. Away from the awaking tourist crowds, it was the perfect refuge to rejuvenate her labored spirit. She lay in the recessed tranquility afforded by the secluded, sheltered bay of palm trees.

The open sky was now replaced by tropical foliage overhung by decades of untouched natural splendor. Beneath her, white pristine sand coated her sun-kissed body on the soft padded beach towel. The gentle breeze carried the sound of steel drums hammered to an upbeat calypso rhythm.

After a long restless night, the recuperative healing powers of nature were just what she needed. That and the sane voice of reason. She adjusted the oversized brim of the floppy straw hat then placed the tiny cellular phone to her ear. She punched in Elliot's office number. While the call connected, her thoughts traveled the decades.

She had met Elliot at her last foster family placement. Elliot, a nerdy brainy kid who was constantly beaten up at school because of his overly flamboyant personality, had already been comfortably assimilated into the Mitchell family. When Angela was placed with the family, she felt like an outsider.

Having long suffered the abuse of money-motivated foster families, Angela assumed her new placement would be no different. She was wrong. The Mitchells, a childless older couple, weren't the usual New York foster family to which she had grown accustomed. They were caring and nurturing both to body and spirit.

Arriving at age 14, angry and hostile because of her many

temporary displacements, she instantly disliked everything and everyone. Spewing harsh, angry words at everyone within listening distance, she refused to adapt. It was the loving, gentle patience of Mr. and Mrs. Mitchell and her increasingly growing friendship with Elliot that finally turned her life around.

Their continuous words of encouragement became the catalyst she needed to make her dreams come true. By the time she graduated from high school she was a completely different person. She'd gone on to college and studied a profession she'd always dreamed of, architecture. Yet the inner scars of her pain still remained and continued to grow and fester just below the surface. Those, she could never remove. They were too painful, a constant reminder of her status as an abandoned child.

The brash voice of reason interrupted her fond memories. "Girlie, the only reason you'd better be calling me this time is to say: 'There's this guy and he's got a brother.'" Angela laughed at the ironic truth in his flippant remark. "Well, que pasa, sistah, what's happening?" Elliot, the perpetual night owl, was never at his desk before nine o'clock in the morning. And when he was, he was hardly upbeat and cheerful. Hence, the influx of lively banter in his voice was a pleasant surprise.

"Well you see, there's this guy and he's got a brother . . ." Angela began, knowing it would add an upbeat lilt to his cheerful tone.

"Very funny," he responded, after a timid sip of his hot black coffee and a quick adjustment of his dark sunglasses.

"Who's joking? I'm serious," Angela assured him as she glanced at her watch. "What are you doing at your desk this early in the morning? It's barely seven."

"With Caroline on a rampage, Lewis still dragging his knuckles on the ground, and you gallivanting around the Caribbean, someone has to pick up the slack. So, give me a break; I'm trying to behave responsibly. As a matter of fact, I'll have you know, I got into the office this morning at six-thirty."

Surprised by the absurd statement while sipping her drink, Angela unexpectedly sputtered, sending fruit punch spritzing across her chest.

"Serves you right for laughing at me," Elliot added with his usual pout, then, unable to refrain from the horrendous lie, he burst with laughter at hearing Angela guffaw and choke again. "Are you all right, Angel girl?"

"Yeah, I'm fine." She coughed several more times and wiped the wayward tears from her eyes. "But I know you too well, Elliot. You were out partying all night long and have yet to go to bed. Right?"

He smiled at her insight. "Guilty."

"Did you have a good time?"

"The best."

"What did you do?"

"No way. You first: how's Puerto Rico so far? And don't tell me interesting; I've heard that one already."

Angela happily looked around and smiled at her lush seaside surroundings. "It's beautiful. It's everything you said it would be and more. I love it here, I could stay forever."

"Did you get to the hall of records yet?"

"Yes, yesterday. I was there most of the day and evening."

"Find anything?"

"Not really. I know the detective said that there was a strong possibility that the search might continue here, but so far I haven't found anything, no birth records, no certificates, no nothing."

"Maybe some of the locals could help you. Have you asked around or talked to anybody?"

"There's a Rita Mendez who works at the hall of records. She's been very helpful. As a matter of fact she said she'd dig out a few more things for me to go through. I'm going back there again tomorrow."

"You'll find something. You've waited this long. Be patient. Something will break. I have a good feeling about this trip."

"I hope so."

The conversation went silent for a few seconds. "So, girlie," he drawled out. "Tell me, have you gone to Club Santos again?"

Marco Santos immediately came to mind. "Yes, as a matter of fact I did. And believe it or not you hit it right on the money earlier—there really is a guy and he really does have a brother." She picked up a handful of silky white sand and let it slowly sift through her closed fist.

"Ohh, sounds intriguing," he sang encouragingly.

"Unfortunately there's also a wife."

"A wife," Elliot declared with surprise. "Girlie, don't you tell me you're kicking around with a married man. Have you gone down there and completely lost you ever-loving mind? You know better than that. Mother Mitchell would tan your hide if she found out."

"Actually, he's not married now; he was married. He's widowed."

"Are you sure? 'Cause, girlie, you know how these men like to play their games on us girls."

Angela smiled as always when Elliot adapted his card-carrying female role. "I'm positive," she answered, remembering the numerous conversations regarding Angelina's untimely demise.

"So what's the problem then? You can have yourself a good old fashioned island fling with a handsome hunky cutie then come back home wearing a perpetual grin for the next few days."

"It's not that simple."

"Rocket science it ain't, Angel. Just sit back and enjoy the ride, no pun intended."

"I wish I could," Angela sighed wistfully. "I just have a feeling that if we started something, it would get out of hand real fast, and I'd rather not have my heart broken."

"Broken hearts! Girl, who's talking about broken hearts; I'm merely suggesting a quick island fling. You know, body-to-body, sweatin', bumpin', horizontal dancing. That's all. Everybody has them and, of course, what happens on the island stays on the island."

Angela thought hopefully for a moment, considering Elliot's suggestion. It was one of those ideas that only looked good on paper. She knew that if she and Marco ever submitted to their attraction, there would be no turning back. "Not this time, Elliot, not with this guy. He's just too . . ." Angela sighed, remembering the last time she and Marco were together, ". . . magnificent. There's just something about him that screams heartbreaker."

"Please," Elliot said dryly. "Girlie, ain't no one that fabulous, except maybe me." Elliot pulled his dark glasses off and squinted against the bright office lights. "Who is this Island Romeo?"

"His name is Marco Santos . . ."

Elliot stopped clicking the computer keys and leaned back in his chair. "Are you referring to one of *the* Santos brothers? The owners of the Santos Club plus? If so, then damn, girlie, you're definitely living large."

"One and the same. I gather you've heard of him?" she asked, hardly surprised by his recognition. Elliot knew just about every notable name and celebrity in the western hemisphere.

"Of course I've heard of the Santos family. Even if you've only spent an hour in Puerto Rico, you've heard about the Santos family. The brothers in particular. And you're right, they are incredible. The locals treat them like demigods."

"Have you ever seen Marco's wife?"

"No. But she's out of the picture, right?"

"Yes."

"So, I still say go for it. If I remember Marco Santos like I think I remember him, then it would be worth it."

"There's more to it than that, I think he also has a problem with African-American women."

"You can get around that," Elliot assured her positively.

"What about the fact that I'm a dead ringer for his dead wife?"

"You're making this too difficult, Angel," Elliot said, placing his coffee mug back on the tile. "Forget about the minor details and just do it."

"Is that the best you can offer?" Angela lamented while digging her brightly colored red-polished toes into the silky white sand.

"What can I say? I've been to the club, I remember Marco Santos; he's a prized catch. Women break their necks just to stand next to him. Tell me, is he interested?"

"That's problem number three. It seems we have this mutual physical attraction. He can't seem to get past the dead wife thing and I can't get past the fact that he's an arrogant, pompous snob."

"Sounds like true love to me." Elliot roared with laughter. "Angel, only you could go on vacation and wind up starring in your own mini drama."

"Tell me about it." She laughed along. "Believe me, it wasn't easy." She sighed heavily and watched three young children carrying buckets of water. After digging a huge circle into the sand, they poured the water in around the center mound. "What's going on there?"

"Same ole, same ole. Lewis is losing it and Caroline's biting her nails. They know they're going to have to step up as far as you're concerned."

"It's too late for that. I still can't believe how bent out of shape Lewis got when I told him I was going to take a few days off. He had a fit. I haven't had a vacation in years."

"Like I don't know that."

"Anything else?"

"Your friend Elmer, the city inspector, asked about you yesterday when he stopped by. Funny, he had no idea you were going away. I guess you forgot to tell him."

"Yeah, I guess I did," she said with a chuckle as she shook her head and rolled her eyes. Elmer was a married man with delusions of player. Every time he walked into the office, he made a beeline to visit her and run his pathetic game. "How are your projects?" Using small plastic shovels, the children heaped mounds of sand on top of the center pile.

"Smooth as silk," he declared easily. "I've already reviewed the specs on the Seventh Street Boutique. The initial blueprints arrived two days ago. It looks like I won't be able to save as much of the original structure as I hoped. The present foundation is unstable. Everything's going to have to come down."

"That's unfortunate. I know you were looking forward to keeping the stone wall in front and two of the surrounding walls," she said, slightly distracted by the children at work. "Are you going to alter your designs to fit the new specs?"

"I have to, I've got no choice."

"Sorry to hear that. Your first designs were fabulous."

"Yes they were," he said proudly.

Angela laughed. "Elliot, you are much too much."

"True that." They laughed together. "Angela, on a serious tip, everything will work its way out. You'll find exactly what you're looking for. And if it happens between you and Mr. Gorgeous, fine. Otherwise, it just wasn't meant to be. You can't force feelings, Angel, you know that."

"I know, and you're right," she added, "as usual. I gotta go; I'll talk to you later."

"Wait, Angel, you can't force feelings, but you can nudge them along, if you get my drift."

Angela smiled at Elliot's last remark. "Loud and clear. I'll talk to you later."

Angela ended the conversation by flipping the small cell phone closed. She picked up her punch drink and looked out on the water's horizon line. She smiled then held her glass up to toast. "To a gentle nudge," she vowed.

She laid back, relaxed and eventually drifted off to a warm, serene nap. For the most part, she slept peacefully and soundly, interrupted only by the occasional seagull wail or distant child's giggle.

By noon they had come in droves, sun worshipers, day-trippers and sightseers. From fish-belly white to leather-skin tanned, they baked, broiled and basked in the searing, sweltering heat of the Caribbean sun. At five minutes past high noon, the once comfortably crowded Luquillo Beach was packed beyond capacity and threatening to spill out into the Caribbean sea.

Angela sighed miserably, her once-secluded spot under the shade of two crossing palm trees had been invaded by land-loving intruders and their obnoxious offspring. Surrendering to the inevitable, she left.

"Well it's about time you got back."

Angela swung around to see the person with enough nerve to chastise her. Bright, sparkling eyes bathed in humor greeted her. Roberto grinned with his usual boyish charm. Angela sucked her teeth. "I thought I got rid of you yesterday." She continued walking to the waiting elevator doors.

"I'm sure by now you know how impossible that is." He stepped into the elevator behind her and pushed the button to her floor. She noticed, but was barely phased by his presumption. They chatted meaninglessly as the doors opened and he continued following her to her room. Without a second thought she opened the door and he breezed in behind her.

She tossed the straw hat and bag on the bed and kicked off her sandals. Going straight to the bathroom, she reached into the shower stall and turned the knobs, feeling the cool, refreshing water stream between her fingers.

Roberto took a quick tour around the welcoming suite. He paused to delight in the two distantly different bouquets of flowers sitting on the side credenza. Then, admiring himself in the large dressing table mirror, he moved to the balcony's glass doors and looked out. Hearing the shower in the next room, he unlatched the balcony doors and stepped outside.

That's where Angela found him fifteen minutes later, sitting asleep in one of the two lounge chairs with his feet perched up on the iron rail. Angela cleared her throat, then again, much louder this time. Roberto finally lazily looked up from his nap and lowered his legs.

"What are you still doing here?" she asked, not entirely surprised to see him still in her room.

Roberto looked her up and down, assessing her new attire. She'd changed into white denim overalls and a white midi T-shirt and bright white ankle-high socks. He beamed with joy. "You look delightful."

"Thanks," she said as she turned and slipped into her white sneakers. She plopped down on the bed and rustled through her large straw bag. Grabbing the romance novel she'd been reading at the pool the other day, she stuffed it into a smaller bag and stood. "So, what are you still doing here?"

Roberto walked to the door, smiling eagerly. "I'm hungry. Let's go eat."

How could anyone resist this man? He was as lovable and friendly as a six-week-old puppy. "Something tells me you're always hungry." He nodded his agreement as he handed her the card key and closed the door behind them.

After a harrowing forty-minute ride in Roberto's speeding red convertible Mercedes they surprisingly arrived safely in front of a large, newly constructed building with a small patio garden in front. The sign out front announced CAFÉ SANTOS. Angela smiled, remembering Juan and Elliot's assessment of the Santos brothers. Then she began to wonder just how many Santos enterprises there were on this island.

They walked through the open patio surrounded by crowded tables of smiling, satisfied customers. Roberto greeted several of the clientele as they passed through the busy eatery. Several heads turned as eyes stared, noticing the newly arriving couple.

Isabella couldn't believe her eyes. It was as if Angelina arose from the dead just to spite her. Her narrowing eyes followed the pair as they casually strode through the open patio area. They stopped to chat at a few of the tables then continued on their way without interruption.

Feeling a slight tug on the sleeve of her designer jacket, Isabella leaned over to her dear old friend. "Sweet mother of

Jesus, Isabella, who is that woman with Roberto Santos? She looks just like your Angelina." All ears at the table perked up to hear the reply.

Isabella's troubled smile was as cold as ice and just as sharp. "My Angelina?" she said, stunned by the implication. "Heavens no. There's barely the slightest glint of semblance to my sweet child." Slyly she leaned nearer to the center of the small circular table, immediately bringing all four of her lunching companions with her.

She smiled, lowering her voice to the barest whisper, and looked into each woman's eyes. "I heard that Roberto Santos was so distraught over Marco's relationship with Angelina that he went searching for a duplicate. Apparently this is the best he could find." She edged her nose skyward, showing her contempt at his actions.

Her snobbish companions all leaned back slowly, nodding and understanding completely. They stared at the couple as they entered the main dining area inside. Pity, contempt and disdain registered on their condescending faces. Isabella smiled triumphantly as the women began uttering commonly known gossip about Roberto and his infamous love affairs. The victorious smile faded just as quickly when Isabella realized that this strange woman's resemblance to Angelina was no mere coincidence.

Over an enormous plate of traditional paella, without red beans, Angela and Roberto talked endlessly. Their seats, slightly distanced from the other seating in the trendy restaurant, afforded them the perfect view of the precision performance around them. Angela marveled at the exceptional skill of the proficient staff. She also noted that Roberto, although seemingly engulfed in their conversation, kept an ever-watchful eye on the surroundings.

Café Santos was slightly right of elegant and left of family casual with a healthy chunk of style and panache thrown in. It was classy, contemporary and earthy, and apparently just as popular as Club Santos. The atmosphere could only be summed up as tropical chic. The abundance of ceiling fans, natural island greenery and the centerpiece waterfall made the ambience complete. Low-hanging Tiffany lamps with an impressive view of the ocean from nearly every seat added the right touches to the already impressive master-piece.

After their plates were cleared, Roberto escorted Angela outside and along the path leading down to the sandy beach. She was impressed. Few restaurants boasted a private beach on its grounds.

Their walk along the gently lapping water's edge was easy and comfortable, just like Roberto. Yet Angela sensed that he wanted to talk, so she asked questions and he answered them. The two talked about the history of the island and its people. Then they laughed at his humorous ideas and thoughts on every subject imaginable, from rap to Pavarotti and from ro-mance to Rapunzel.

Then, in one stilled moment of silence, he looked out to the Atlantic Ocean. "My older brother can be difficult, but not impossible. You're the first woman to get to him like this. You made a real impression."

Angela looked skeptical of his assessment. "What about Angelina? I have a feeling that to be Marco's wife, she had to have made some kind of impression on him."

Roberto shook his head negatively. "Angelina is a totally different case altogether."

"How so?"

"Their relationship wasn't as everyone assumed. Few knew differently." Angela nodded, presuming the obvious by what little she'd learned of the couple.

"How did they meet?"

"I introduced them." That she didn't expect.

"Then why didn't you two hook up? You were obviously fond of her."

"Two words: Isabella Rivera." Roberto saw Angela nod, noting the concept of another woman. "It's not what you think."

He looked back out to the ocean for a few moments, staring pensively into his past. When he spoke again his voice was hoarse with emotion. "I met Angelina in Miami. We did the club scene; you know, partying until dawn and whatnot. She was perfect, tall, slim and busty. She was a free spirit but sort of delicate inside like a wounded butterfly." The pain in his voice was growing more obvious.

Angela stepped in front of him and took his hands. "Roberto, you don't need to tell me all this."

He smiled and gently laid the palm of his hand on her cheek. "Yes, I do. If things are ever going to play out as they should, you need to know what you're up against." Angela frowned, not completely understanding his concerns. "A few weeks after Angelina and I met, Marco and I opened the Café Santos. I invited her down as my guest. She came along with Isabella, her mother.

"Apparently Angelina had told her mother of our recent acquaintance. Isabella is originally from Puerto Rico but moved to the States some years back. She was very familiar with the Santos name. Once she got down here, she impressed upon her daughter to involve herself with Marco since he was the oldest and more responsible. And of course, more likely to inherit the bulk of the Santos estate. Angelina refused and insisted that she wasn't ready for a long term relationship with anyone, least of all Marco."

Angela interrupted. "But she went with Marco anyway to please her mother." He nodded sadly. "So why didn't Marco back off her when he knew that you were with her?"

"That's just it. Angelina and I were many things, but we were never intimate, although many people assumed we were because of my somewhat colorful reputation. Marco came to me questioning my intentions toward Angelina. I told him the truth; we were just friends, and that there was nothing romantic between us."

"So, getting the green light from you, he went for it," Angela surmised.

"With Isabella's consent and encouragement, the two quickly wed. A month or two later Angelina began hanging out here at the café. She was deeply troubled and regretful. She never told me why. I assumed that she and Marco were having marital problems, but she hinted that whatever it was, it was much more. Isabella stepped in again and forbid Angelina to see me. Then she told Marco that I was the cause of their marital trouble because I still wanted Angelina."

"Wait, I don't get it. Didn't you already tell Marco that you weren't interested in Angelina?"

"In Marco's eyes Isabella was the perfect mother. She could never lie or manipulate for personal gain. So when she insinuated an affair between the two us, it seemed reasonable, given Angelina's recent behavior and her constant presence here.

"As the weeks went by, Angelina grew more and more edgy. She and Marco argued constantly; afterwards, she would come running to me. By this time Marco and I were barely civil. The night she died, they'd argued and she came to me as usual. I sent her back to Marco; there was a sudden storm, and her car ran off the road. The report stated that her body was never found."

"That's so sad."

"I don't think Marco will ever forgive me. I don't think I can ever forgive myself."

"For what?"

"I should have stopped her. Instead I sent her back to him."

"Did you know it was going to storm that night?" He shook his head no. "Did you know her car was going to crash?" Again, he shook his head no. "Then how can you possibly blame yourself for an accident?"

"That's just it. I don't believe it was an accident. I think she did it on purpose."

"Suicide? Why? If she truly wasn't happy all she had to do was divorce Marco, no big deal. Even with a prenuptial, I'm sure Marco would have been more than generous financially."

He admittedly shook his head no. "Impossible, she would never have done it."

"Contrary to popular belief, Catholics have divorced on occasion. What about an annulment?"

"That's another ironic part, Marco and Angelina had already signed off on an annulment, although only a few knew about it. The marriage was already technically void months earlier. So, it wasn't the church Angelina feared, it was Isabella."

Angela remained silent at this point. She was stymied. It was a sad ending to a sad story. How could anyone fear their mother so much that suicide was the only way out of a troubled marriage? Having only experienced foster mothers, Angela was perplexed by the hold Isabella had on Angelina. She also felt extremely lucky. She couldn't conceive of growing up under the rules of a woman like Isabella Rivera.

"Come on," Roberto said, suddenly cheerful as if a great weight had been lifted from his chest. "I'll take you back to your hotel." Their afternoon walk ended shortly before four and Roberto drove Angela back to her hotel. She thanked him for the lunch, the tour and the talk. Roberto explained that he'd made plans to go to the States and would be back in a few days, then asked to see her when he returned.

Angela gladly accepted as Roberto kissed her softly on both cheeks and said good-bye. "Remember," he added before driving away, "difficult, but not impossible. Sometimes my big brother just needs a little nudge in the right direction." He winked and sped off faster than legally allowed.

Angela smiled at his interesting choice of wording. Elliot had essentially said the exact same thing to her just hours earlier. Maybe there was something in their reasoning. Marco was definitely worth a second look.

Chapter 11

"Hola, big brother," Roberto said with a spark of mischief in his eye. "You miss me?" he asked playfully.

Marco looked up briefly then continued writing. "The café opens for dinner in an hour. Shouldn't you be working?"

Roberto bent down and opened the small refrigerator beneath the office bar. "Unlike you, big brother, I know how to delegate. I hire capable people and delegate to them. It gives me the freedom to explore other options." He pulled out a can of soda then stood up. "You should try it."

"I prefer the more hands-on approach."

Roberto shrugged his shoulders. "To each his own." He opened a bag of peanuts sitting on the bar and dropped a few into his mouth and chewed enthusiastically. "I'll be in the States for a few days. I want to look around before we finalize on the Miami property."

"I thought we decided to offer a bid."

"We did. But I want to make sure we aren't missing anything. I have a lead on something else."

"Another solo venture like your Texas Phoenix?"

Roberto stopped chewing and looked at Marco, stunned by his mention of his club in Texas. "How did you know about Phoenix?"

"The Club Phoenix may be your solo venture, Roberto, but it's not entirely without distinction. It still holds the Santos name. I hear it's quite nice."

"Care for a visit? I could get you in cheap."

Marco looked at him sternly. "You know that I've vowed never to set foot in the States again."

Roberto smiled. "Just checking."

"So, if this new property isn't in Texas, where is it?"

"More to the north."

Marco eyed Roberto suspiciously then looked back down at his papers. "If you're referring to New York, I strongly disapprove," he said coolly, knowing Roberto's affection for their mother and her hometown.

Roberto shook his head. "Not this time, bro. I have someplace else in mind." Roberto smirked openly.

Marco looked up from his desk, nodded his head then looked back down at the papers he'd been reviewing. Roberto smiled happily while pulling the tab off of the canned soda. He leaned across the bar's counter and stared at Marco. After a few minutes Marco looked up at him. "What?"

Roberto beamed innocently. "Nothing." He dropped more peanuts into his mouth.

Marco tossed his pen on the desk and glared at Roberto. "So, you finally have what you've always wanted."

Roberto came from behind the bar and strolled over to a chair opposite the desk. "And what might that be?"

"Angelina."

Roberto burst out laughing. He continued with renewed spasms each time he looked up into his brother's angry eyes. "Does the phrase 'obsessive-compulsive behavior' mean anything to you?" he finally managed to get out.

Marco picked up his discarded pen and absently fingered it, sending it weaving through each finger then back again. He leaned back in the chair, smiled menacingly and tapped the pen on the desk. "Does the phrase 'Am I my brother's keeper' mean anything to you?"

"Oh please, don't start quoting the Bible to me."

"Cain slew Abel out of jealousy. You, little brother, don't have the guts."

Roberto coolly slouched in the chair and extended his head lazily back. "Same old song. Don't you ever get tired of listening to yourself talk?"

"Get out. I've got work to do." Marco lowered his head and began scribbling something in the margin of the top sheet of paper.

"She is beautiful, isn't she?" Roberto sat up straighter and eyed his brother closely. "She wants you, you know." The serious tone in his voice was different.

"I'm busy, Roberto, get out," Marco said.

"I bet if you were just a little nicer, you could get her to come out and play with you. She might even let you play with her toys." The glint of mischief returned to Roberto's eye.

Marco laid his pen down again and stared at his brother. "What games are you playing now, Roberto?" Innocently, Roberto shook his head and shrugged his broad shoulders, confused by the question. "It's a small island, and, as you expected, word got back to me that you and Angela were together earlier."

Roberto smiled broadly, "You're right, this is a small island . . ." he began. Then he stood up and tossed the empty soda can across the room into the trashbin. The can tapped the rim then tumbled in. Roberto raised his arms in mock celebration. "And it seems that you were also seen with the very lovely Angela." An angry muscle in Marco's jaw twitched. "But the difference is, big brother, she doesn't want me."

"Just like Angelina didn't want you?" Marco said coldly.

"Whatever you say, Marco." Dejected, Roberto turned and headed for the door. In a few minutes the same old argument would erupt. But today, Roberto was in too good of a mood to listen to Marco's accusations. He stood staring at the door for a moment then grasped the knob. "For the record, your wife didn't know what she wanted. Sort of like you now. But if you asked my opinion, what she really wanted, what she finally has, is her freedom. Hasta luego, big brother."

Marco slowly stood and leaned both fists on the desk as

he watched the door close silently. He stood there staring across the room as memories of the final slammed door crept into his thoughts. He waited a few seconds, then he heard it. Always the same: the slamming door, the screech of tires then the stillness of silence as the rain began to fall. He ran outside and stood, drenched by the sudden cloudburst. That was the last time he saw Angelina alive.

Their fights were just as fierce as their lovemaking. With Angelina it was all or nothing. Her passion for life was equal only to her love of family. Marco had no doubt that she loved him in her way. He also had no doubt that Isabella was in-strumental in both forging their marital bond, and breaking it.

Marco looked down at the papers on his desk. On the top sheet he noticed a name scribbled repeatedly in the margin. "Angela," he read aloud. He picked up the phone and dialed. The front desk picked up after the second ring. After speak-ing a few words in Spanish, he was connected to the room. The phone rang unanswered several times before he hung up. He grabbed his jacket and left the office seconds later.

Enrique slammed the phone down angrily. His day had gone from bad to worse. Helena, his niece, was driving him crazy. She had altered another requisition order, sending dozens of brand new toys to the hotel's new day-care center she'd set up four months ago, also without his prior approval.

Ever since he'd hired her to be his administrative assis-tant, things had been totally out of control. It was more like he was working for her instead of the other way around. He'd have fired her months ago if he wasn't certain that his sister would ring his neck. He made a mental note to himself to find another position for her as soon as possible. The buzzing intercom broke through his strained thoughts. "What is it now, Helena? I'm busy."

"Oh, I just thought you might want to know that doorman just called," she chirped brightly.

"And?" he prompted with annoyance.

"He told me that Marco Santos is on his way in." Enrique gasped loudly. "Oh, hi, Marco," Helena said as Marco entered the outer office. Enrique gasped again at hearing Helena's conversation with Marco.

Sweat poured from Enrique's forehead as his jaw dropped open. This was the third time in as many days that Marco Santos had come to the hotel. Something was terribly wrong. He'd been general manager for eight years and could only remember seeing Marco in the building twice before. Now, suddenly, here he was again. Enrique pulled the oversized handkerchief from his jacket pocket and wiped his moist face.

Never once did he remember Roberto dropping by for a visit as he had the day before and earlier. Something was going on; he was sure of it. Maybe the Santos family was assessing his management skills for a promotion. Enrique smiled happily then gasped, his eyes widening to saucers. Maybe they were selling the hotel, or worse, maybe they were dissatisfied with his performance.

Fearfully, he rushed to the door and flung it open just as Marco raised his hand to knock. "Señor Santos." He beamed nervously. "Please come, come in. A pleasure to see you again so soon, sir. Uhh, not that you can't come to the hotel whenever you'd like. You're always welcome here. Of course, you know that; it's your hotel." He chuckled nervously. "What I mean is you can come whenever you please, uh, not that I'm telling you what to do, of course. And I'm not saying that you have to stop coming all the time because I am very effective and we don't need you here. But I'm not saying we don't want you here. Because of course it's your hotel, and you can come here whenever you like, not that you need to, but . . ."

Marco smiled graciously as he patiently listened to Enrique continue with his elaborate explanations while all the time pumping his arm in a lengthy, exuberant handshake. "Thank you," Marco finally said to Enrique, ending his extended dissertation.

"Please come in," Enrique said, stepping aside quickly.

"Have a seat. Is there anything I can get you?" Before Marco answered, he hurried back to the open door. "Helena," he called out to the young woman playing solitaire on the computer. He gasped loudly as his eyes grew wide with shock. He ducked his head back into the office. "Un momento, Señor Santos." He bowed low several times, pulled the door closed, then ran out to his niece.

"Are you mad, child? Are you trying to ruin me? How could you sit there playing that, that, that"—he motioned to the card game displayed—"game? Have you any idea who that is in there?"

"Yeah, Roberto's brother, Marco Santos," she answered nonchalantly.

Enrique all but lay down on the floor and kissed the carpet in praise at the mention of his name. "That's Marco Santos."

"I know, that's what I said," she said, as he beckoned for her to lower her voice.

"Shhhh," he hissed after peeking back to his office door. "His family owns this hotel. That's his signature on your paycheck every week. And you're just sitting here playing that, that, that . . ."

Helena stared at her uncle oddly, watching sweat pour from his brow. The usual smoked-pink of his friar-balding head was bright red and getting redder by the second. "Are you okay, Uncle?"

He whipped out the familiar huge white cloth and covered his face quickly. "No, I'm not okay," he raged through gritted teeth. "Because of you we could be out of a job by tomorrow."

She shrugged her shoulders as he cringed in fright. "Go, go, go." He quickly pulled her chair from behind the desk. "Get Señor Santos a drink from the bar." He peeked back to his office door. "Hurry."

Helena shook her head in pity then stood and headed for the door. "Wait, wait, wait, where are you going?" Enrique shrieked out in a hushed voice.

Helena gave him a *duh* expression. "To get the drinks from the bar like you just told me."

"No, no, no, come back here," Enrique stammered in exasperation. "Get this, this, this"—he pointed accusingly to the computer game—"this thing off the screen before Señor Santos sees it."

Helena blew at her curled bangs that dipped into her eyes and strolled back to her desk. After clicking a few buttons, the game disappeared and a screen saver of a very muscular man in the briefest of swimming trunks appeared.

Enrirque's mouth dropped to the floor and his eyes comically blew up to the size of dinner plates. "What, what, what, what . . ." He pointed fiercely and stuttered like a sputtering motorboat. It was all Enrique could do, given the circumstances. He was speechless.

"Marco," Helena said as Marco stepped out of Enrique's office, "I'm on my way to the bar to get refreshments. What kind of drink would you like?"

Seeing that her uncle was still pointing and sputtering, she addressed the question to the man standing behind him.

Marco lowered his head and snickered shamefully at Enrique's dilemma. "How about a cold soda; any kind will be fine." Helena nodded happily and left the room.

Enrique held his breath with his eyes still glued to the screen saver when Marco spoke. "Enrique . . ." he began.

"Señor Santos," Enrique interrupted, "I can explain." He paused a moment to wipe the pouring sweat from his brow again. "Please forgive the appearance. We're not usually this lax in our professional decorum. I apologize for my niece's ideas of professionalism; I will very sternly speak to her when she returns."

"Enrique," Marco moved to the man and put his arm around his shoulders, "you fret for no reason, my friend. I have no problem with Helena's choice of computer images. It's her computer and whatever makes her comfortable is fine with me. Also, I too have been known to play an occasional game of computer solitaire." Enrique breathed for the first time since seeing Marco at his door. "Come, I'd like you to pull some information on one of your guests."

Chapter 12

After waiting in line for half an hour, Angela stepped up to the door and paid the club's admission price. The sound of a live salsa band hit her as soon as she crossed the threshold. They were loud and the crowd loved them. The noise level was deafening and very close to being off the Richter scale. It was easy to see why this was the most popular nightspot on the island. The place was pandemonium and she loved it immediately.

She eased her way through the throngs of pulsating bodies and found an opening at the bar. The bartender, a tall, wiry man with sun-bleached white blond hair against a deep tanned complexion, glanced at her, looked away, did a double take and stared. Trancelike, he moved to her. His sea-blue eyes never left her face. She smiled knowingly. "Yes, I know who I look like. May I have a piña colada, please?"

The man stared a few seconds longer, then walked away to prepare the coconut and pineapple drink. When he returned, he motioned for her to come down to the other end of the long oblong-shaped bar. She nodded her understanding and followed him to the empty seat close to the dance floor. He placed the frothy fruit-and-rum concoction on the counter in front of her and leaned in closer. "The resemblance is amazing," he yelled out over the loud music.

"You think so?" she responded at the top of her lungs as she continued surveying the frantic party ambience around her.

He nodded, still entranced by her face. "Have you met the boss yet?" She nodded yes. "Are you a relative or close friend of the family?" She shook her head no. "If you'd like, I can call up to the office and let him know you're here."

"Thanks"—she looked down at his name tag—"Emilio, bar manager, but that won't be necessary, I'm not staying that long. I just wanted to actually see the inside of this place. It's wonderful."

Emilio looked around. "Yeah, it's not too shabby. I've been in worse. You're not from here are you?"

"Nope." Slowly she began to loosen up and release her inhibitions. "I grew up in New York, Brooklyn, the Bronx, Spanish Harlem."

"Get out, really? I was raised in Brooklyn, just over the bridge. That makes us neighbors."

Angela reached her hand across the bar. "Angela."

"Nice to meet you, Angela," Emilio said. shaking her hand.

Angela took a sip of the drink. "Um, this is delicious," she said, then slipped a twenty-dollar bill on the bar.

"Sorry, your money's no good on this end of the bar."

She smiled. "Oh really, and why is that?"

He leaned closer. "You're sitting in tonight's lucky seat. Anyone who sits there gets all their drinks on the house." He smiled and shrugged his shoulders. "Besides, you're a homegirl." He turned, seeing a customer beckon for another round of beers.

Angela smiled and shook her head. "Thanks Emilio, but that's really not necessary."

"Sorry, those are the bar rules." He tossed the clean white towel over his shoulder and walked away.

Suddenly, a speaker close to the bar blared out music. The crowd thickened around the semicircle as the three bartenders began their nightly performance. Juggling, spinning, twirling, and tossing bottles into the air, glass bottles flew from all directions. They wowed the crowd with double-dip pours from one end of the bar to the other and spinning bottles into single shots, ten glasses at a time.

At one end of the bar, fire flared in an open glass as hot ice steamed from another glass. Six bottles were simultaneously tossed high into the air. They came down in perfect procession as the three bartenders, in precise synchronization, made the exact same drink at the exact same time.

When the performance ended, applause rang out in a tremendous uproar of whistles, screams and chants. The DJ introduced the three bartenders as the winners of the Extreme Bartending & Mixologist Competition. The crowd went wild again. The three bowed and waved, loving the complimentary applause.

Emilio came back over to Angela's end of the bar.

"You were incredible."

"Thank you," he said as he finished preparing several drinks at one time. "Can I freshen that up for you?"

"I'm fine."

He nodded as someone called to him from the other end of the bar. "I'll be right back."

She nodded and spun the bar stool around to get a better view of the crowded dance floor. Her mouth instinctively opened in awe. She'd never seen so many outlandish costumes in one place. Fringed skirts, bra-like tops, sequins, beads, and skin-tight, strategically torn T-shirts were everywhere. She sipped her drink and got into the flow of the music.

The Afrocentric, ethnic blend of rhythms led the tempo straight to her body. It felt so natural, as if she were born to this music.

Emilio served several customers then coolly stepped to the opposite side of the bar. He pressed a small button under the counter then looked up at the darkened window. He assumed Marco heard the page in his office and was standing at the window. As casually as possible he looked up at the window, nodded, then looked down to the other end of the bar.

A few seconds later the office's darkened glass brightened. Marco stood staring at the end of the bar just short of the dance floor. Moments later the window faded back to black.

Marco stood hypnotized by the laughing woman at the end of the bar. Juan moved to stand next to him. He looked down at the bar, the small dining area and finally at the dance floor. Nothing seemed unusual. "What's the problem with Emilio?" Juan asked. Marco didn't speak.

Juan continued to scan the area to no avail. "What is it?"

"Did you invite her here tonight?" he asked as he rubbed his beard.

"Who?" Juan asked, then watched as Emilio elaborately poured a drink then walked with a big smile to the end of the bar. He leaned over and presented the drink while taking away the half empty glass. The woman took a sip then said something that made Emilio laugh. He tossed the towel over his shoulder, glanced up to the darkened window then moved to help another customer. Angela turned back to the dance floor. "Ah, I see Angela found her way back."

"You didn't invite her?"

"No, not this time," Juan assured Marco. "I wonder what brought her back here?" Juan continued speaking as an interested frown burrowed across Marco's brow.

At that moment, a man stepped up to Angela and held out his hand. She smiled, grasped his hand then slid down from the barstool. The man led her to the center of the dance floor. They talked for a moment, then he wrapped his arm around her slim waist and began easing her around the dance floor.

Following his lead closely, Angela did exactly what she saw the other women on the floor doing. Her arms went up and she took a slow, swaying, grinding turn with a cha-cha two-step. She felt good. She felt sexy. And apparently her dance partner agreed because his mouth dropped open to the floor and his eyes comically bulged out twelve inches from the socket.

The tight-fitting dress afforded her little room, but she swiveled her hips and gyrated her pelvis each time the music's rhythm pulsated. The heavy conga beat quickly seeped into her heated blood, prompting her body to take over. Within a few minutes she felt and looked like a native on the dance floor.

She raised her arms again and slowly twisted her hips and spun around. Her dance partner's eyes immediately went to the round tightness of her buttocks then down to the shortness of the tight dress then down her bare legs. When she completed another slow seductive turn, she grinned excitedly. He nodded his approval. Then with a loud yelp he spun around. He grabbed her hand and spun her around several times then tucked her back into his arms. She slammed hard against his chest and laughed hysterically. The song ended on that beat. She giggled and laughed like a schoolgirl.

The band played three successive songs and Angela danced each one with the same partner. He proudly glided her through the meringue, the samba and the lambada. When the beat slowed down she excused herself and went back to the bar.

Exhausted and out of breath, she picked up her drink and downed the last few sips just as Emilio brought over another one and a glass of iced water. "Thanks, Emilio," she barely rasped out. She took a long sip of the water and fanned her damp face and neck with her fingers.

She could feel the perspiration dot her upper lip. Emilio handed her several napkins then wiped the bar with his white towel and smiled. "Having a good time?" he asked.

She nodded enthusiastically and, still breathless, added, "Definitely." A young man came up to her and grasped her hand. She politely declined his offer to dance, choosing instead to sit out a few to catch her breath. She fanned her face with her fingers again then took another sip of the water. "I forgot how hot it gets on those dance floors," she said. Emilio nodded his agreement before attending to another patron.

Angela sat listening to the slow, alluring rhythms of the salsa band. She tapped her toe on the rim of the bar stool and sipped her coconut drink when another young man eased up. He was smooth. He slid his arm around the back of her chair then slyly began stroking her back. Angela politely eased away.

"One dance," he promised. "Just one dance. And you will beg me to take you home with me."

Angela smiled then shook her head and looked back to the dance floor. "I'm going to have to pass. It's just too hot and too crowded out there for me."

"Believe me, baby, once we get started the heat will be the last thing on your mind." He laid his sweaty hand on her knee and squeezed. She eased his hand away and declined his offer a second time. "Come on, baby," the young man said as he began grinding his hips seductively against her leg.

"Hey, Angela," Emilio called out across the bar. "Can I get you another drink?"

"No thanks, Emilio, it's getting late." She shifted her dangling purse on her shoulder then slid down from the stool and leaned across the bar. She took Emilio's hand. "Thank you. You're the best. I had a great time." She slid two twenty-dollar bills across the bar and dropped them into the overflowing tip glass. Emilio nodded and winked his thanks. "Come back and visit us again."

"I will, I promise," she threw over her shoulder as she turned to leave.

"Yo, baby, what about my dance?"

"Sorry, the lady has a new dance partner," Marco said, appearing out of nowhere. He took Angela's arm and escorted her through the crowded area. Together they walked up the stairs to his office. She angrily marched inside. He followed. Then, as soon as he closed the office door, she spun around.

But before she could get a single word out, Angela found herself backed up against the flat of the door with Marco blocking her only escape. They looked at each other murderously. She opened her mouth to speak but without warning Marco's mouth was on her. Angela wrapped her arms around his neck and pulled him closer. Hard and punishing, the kiss continued until the human need for air overtook them.

More angry with herself at that moment for still craving

the taste of him, Angela pushed him back hard. "What the hell is wrong with you?" She fumed as he barely budged an inch.

"What?" Marco rasped out, still breathless by the kiss and his mounting desire.

She pushed him back again, feeling the solidity of his chest. A quick quiver of delight jetted through her body. "You heard me. What was that idiotic display of testosterone?"

He chortled. "Testosterone?" He turned his back on her and walked away. She followed as he knew she would.

"Yes, testosterone. How dare you pull that lame Rambo crap on me?" she added as they moved past the large office window to a side door.

He continued walking. "You obviously needed my assistance." He opened a side door and began climbing the stairs. She followed.

"Did I ask for your assistance? Did it look like I needed rescuing down there? Did it ever occur to you that I might have wanted to dance with that man, that I might have been attracted to him?" That got the expected response she wanted to see. Marco stopped walking, turned and slammed the door behind them. "You can't go around bullying people and charging into my life like that. Who do you think you are?"

He smiled smugly in response to her rhetorical question. A smirk of interest turned the edge of his full lips upwards.

She shook her head in amazement. She'd seen that look before. "You are truly unbelievable and you have an ego the size of a . . ." Suddenly she became aware that she was no longer in the club's office but in the fourth-floor private apartment. She looked around quickly, taking in her surroundings. The large room was dark, lit dimly by several low lights along the headboard of the huge bed. "Oh, you've got to be kidding. If you think that for one minute . . ."

"Do you ever shut up?"

Appalled, Angela gaped her mouth open. "I beg your pardon?" she uttered slowly, placing her fist on her hip indignantly.

"You heard me. Do you ever just shut up and listen?" She

opened her mouth, then clamped it shut without saying another word. "I didn't bring you here to seduce you. I brought you here to talk." She glared at him suspiciously when he turned to the large bed. "Nothing will happen here unless you want it to."

"Fine, then talk," she commanded.

"I want some answers. Why did you come here? What are you really after?"

She smiled. "Why don't you tell me?" she answered, humored by his direct question.

"I suspect the same thing every woman wants."

"And what might that be?" she asked.

He smirked. "Money, power, revenge, sex, the eternal control over men."

"You've got to be kidding." She said while laughing. "Tell me, what part of your anatomy told you all that?" The rage in his eyes was exciting. She sauntered up to him and leaned closer to his ear. "I'll tell you a little secret." He glared at her. "You're not even close."

The fire in his eyes increased as did the heat in his body. The teasing way her playful eyes glared at him had turned his blood to molten lava. Watching her innocent expression and the lustful mouth, he fought hard for control. The simple way she stood sent a flash of heat to his very core.

He instantly recalled the way she moved on the dance floor. He had been so hypnotized that it had taken Juan four times to get his attention. Each slow, seductive turn twisted his insides. When she smiled at her partner, his rage was complete.

He began moving forward, forcing her to retreat back farther and farther until the backs of her bare legs rested against the foot of the bed's frame. He leaned in as she plopped down. The bed moved. She shrieked. Marco grabbed her struggling body and quickly pulled her up. Angela held on to him, then turned to see the bed as it continued rippling with water.

Marco closed his eyes, mentally fighting with his body

for control. Realizing that Angela's body was too intimately pressed against his, he backed away. "Answer the question, Angela, what are you really after?"

She glared at him then walked back to the door.

"You." She flung it open and stormed back down the steps into the office. She gasped when she spotted Roberto standing behind the bar laughing. Embarrassed by the display he had to have witnessed, she breezed over to him. "He's all yours." She slammed out.

Marco stood in the doorway with his arms braided across his chest and his eyes raging with murder. "Why didn't you announce your presence earlier?"

Roberto smiled and shrugged. "I'm easily amused." He swallowed the last of his drink and picked up the empty bottle.

"Apparently." Roberto burst out laughing under Marco's murderous glare. "Shouldn't you be somewhere managing something?"

"I've got the late shift," he quipped, settling comfortably on the barstool. Marco shot him another murderous look. He immediately sat his bottle down. "I think that's my cue to leave." He did.

It took several swigs of ice cold water and a stiff drink to ease Marco's thoughts of Angela. The remainder of the night was a meaningless blur of faceless women all vying for his attention. But only one woman was privileged to garner that bestowed accomplishment—that woman was Angela Lord.

Chapter 13

For the next two days Angela, alongside Rita Mendez, diligently worked in the hall of records while only being slightly distracted by the complete silence from Marco.

While Rita translated Spanish chronicles, Angela forced herself to focus on her search using the English periodicals. She spent hours digging through large, cumbersome books and miles of microfilm with few prominent leads. Growing more frustrated as the hours slipped by, she decided to leave and return after a few days or when and if Rita found something promising. She realized that her focus was too divided between her search for the truth of her birth, and Marco.

There was definitely something wrong. She couldn't stop thinking about him. She was supposed to remain detached and simply teach him a lesson in respect or have a simple island romance. But she began to realize that her emotions were getting too involved. Marco had gotten to her.

Angela shook her head, still unbelieving. She was sure that Marco would contact her after the night at the Club. Maybe she'd overplayed her part and he was weary of her. Maybe she wasn't seductive enough and he was no longer interested. Or maybe he grew bored with the chase and moved on.

Whatever the reason, Angela chose to accept it as another one of life's little lessons and move on. She decided to concentrate on enjoying herself; she still had over a week left on this beautiful island and intended to start taking full advantage of its many wonders.

She leaned against the rough bark of the century-old tree. She looked straight up, some one hundred feet to the ceiling of green and marveled at the royal poinciana tree's exaggerated limbs and bright red blossoms. She rubbed her hand against the tree's bark. The outer texture was hard and jagged to the touch. But there was something about its resilience of age through centuries of warfare, pestilence and natural devastation that was wondrously gentle and majestic.

Anxious to start her second, more detailed tour of the wonders of lower El Yunque Rainforest, she looked at her watch then back at her lush surroundings. It was getting late. She removed her light-weight jacket and tied it around her waist. The early morning tour took her to the higher, skyscraper altitudes of the rain forest and the guide warned of chilly surroundings and crisp, cool air. Afterwards, she'd taken a jeep ride down to the lower ranges where the air was thick with warm, tangled, gentle breezes.

She longingly gazed down the starting path taken by the members of her early morning tour group fifteen minutes earlier. Maybe she should have just continued with them through the lower rain forest instead of waiting for her private "rent-a-guide" to arrive. He was already a half hour late.

The anxious manager glanced out of the rear window and checked his watch a second time in just a matter of minutes. Suddenly, the front door of the small tourist center burst open. The man's smile was genuine.

"You, my man, have a very annoyed customer on your hands."

"Where?"

The center's manager nodded his head in the direction of the entrance to the forest hiking trial. The tardy guide quickly grabbed the waiting company vest from the counter and pulled it on. He slapped at the many flapped pockets, quickly feeling for the standard issue supplies. He grabbed the small walkie-talkie, tested its battery reserve, noted the center's emergency channel, then looped it on his khaki shorts buckle. The cumbersome load of day-long necessities was comparatively lighter than the backpack he'd slung over one shoulder. He nodded his thanks to the man behind the counter and set off on a day's work.

"I like the new look; good to have you back," the manager called out to the guide retreating to the back door. He laughed as the tour guide turned and nodded. "You'll get used to it again." The door closed and he quickly walked across the parking lot toward the trails.

Angela quickly looked upwards in the direction of the squawking sound. Three brightly colored parrots flew overhead. Their loud cackling brought a smile to her face. *The music of nature,* she surmised with pleasure. She watched as the three birds were joined by a fourth then began a dance of swooping pirouettes and swirling turns as they circumnavigated the mountainous trees. Her eyes held to the delightful sight when the masculine voice interrupted.

"Vamos," he ordered as he began marching down the well-tread hiking path. Within seconds the tall stranger was several yards ahead of her, moving in a very determined pace.

Angela grabbed her backpack and hurried to catch up with him, but was never quite able to match his long strides. Five minutes of complete silence passed as they hiked deeper and deeper into the throngs of Mother Nature's verdant metropolis.

The skyscraper trees grouped tightly together gave the forest a claustrophobic sense. Its mile-high canopy of fat leafy greens hung high, draped like Christmas tinsel by cords of thick twining vines. The surrounding vegetation, dwarfed by its little regard for sunlight, was unusually thick. Delicate fernlike trees and miniature orchids dotted the landscape along the uneven path.

Just as she was about to ask a question, the guide turned a

corner, leading to an observation point. He stepped aside and allowed her to pass before him. She stepped up and stood in wonder. Her bright eyes took in all the splendor of the enchanting view before her. She gasped silently then sighed at the vast mixture of God's handiwork.

The panoramic spectacle of nature was almost surreal in its absolute perfection. Never had she witnessed such splendor and such magnificence in one place. She felt humbled by the overwhelming enormity of her surroundings. The pigments of color were those she'd never experienced before. The greens, reds and yellows weren't simply shades of color; they went beyond verbal description. She pulled out her camera and began taking numerous photos in every direction.

She stood silently for a few moments then turned to the guide who had dipped his cap lower on his face and was poking at the ground with two long, shaved tree limbs he'd picked up. He jabbed one stick into the ground roughly, then pointed with the other toward another trail leading downward.

"Vamos," he stated.

"Señor, what is your name? Señor, pardon, por favor, como te llamo?" she asked.

The man remained silent and beckoned with the waiting stick.

"Do you speak English? Usted habla ingles?"

He answered again with silence. "Oh great," she muttered, then pulled out her Spanish-English dictionary. She quickly ran her finger over the many translated verbiage then stopped at the phrase she sought. "Señor . . ." she began.

The guide ignored her and looked off into the distant horizon at the approaching darkened clouds. "Vamos," he insisted.

"Wait," she called out as he began hiking back to the main trail. She caught up with him within a few moments then followed wordlessly until they came to a second trail. Instead of taking the marked path the guide marched forward through a grouping of unmarked trees. Several large drops of water plopped down on the surrounding vegetation. The sky grew dark, making the area beneath the canopy of hundred year old trees seem like midnight.

Dutifully Angela followed until she realized that there was no longer a marked trail and the usual cut back groundcover had thickened. "Hey, wait a minute," she called out. "Where are you going?" Then thinking quickly, she translated the question into Spanish. "Señor, adonde va?" she began, then hurriedly pulled out her dictionary as the guide descended down the steep side of a small hill.

She continued flipping pages when she heard the first rumble. "Señor . . ." she called out again.

The man seemed to quicken his pace to an almost trot. He glanced back several times to make sure she was keeping up as the huge droplets continued to fall. "Señor . . ." she called out again as she tried to put her jacket back on. But the last call ended with a frightful shriek. The guide turned just in time to watch her slip on loose thicket and tumble down the side of the small hill. He reached out to her to no avail.

Angela tumbled, falling several yards before she came to rest on a small plateau just over a small grass covered ridge. Landing hard and surprised by the sudden jolt, she landed on her bottom. Before she could catch her breath, her guide came barreling down the hill and quickly grabbed her as he collapsed by her side.

Stunned for the second time in as many minutes, she pushed back from him. She barely moved him. "What the hell are you doing? get off of me!" she demanded angrily, then she froze. Something about the way he held her was all too familiar. She looked up into the man's face.

He was all too familiar. She squinted her eyes distrustfully and mentally altered his appearance; much shorter hair had replaced the long shoulder length locks. A neatly clipped goatee had replaced the beard and mustache. Awareness suddenly registered like ice cold water poured down her back on a hot summer day. *Marco Santos*. "You son of a . . ." she yelled to the sound of rumbling thunder.

Marco swallowed her words instantly with a kiss before they reached completion. With little refrain, she wrapped her arms around his neck and pulled him down to her body.

"Are you hurt?" he finally asked with worried concern. He looked down the length of her carefully.

After sitting back on his heels, he squeezed down her arms, legs and shoulders. She was covered with leaves and dirt, but apparently unscathed. "What are you doing here?" she demanded as she batted away his roaming hands, along with the dirt and leaves from her denim shorts and T-shirt.

"Rescuing you again, apparently," he said wearily. Thankful that she appeared physically unharmed, he quickly got to his feet and pulled her up, then bent down to pick up her nearby jacket. "We need to get to some cover," he yelled over the roar of thunder. She nodded, agreeing to the soundness of his suggestion. He scanned their location. The darkness around them did little to impede his catlike vision. He took her hand and together they ran toward a small, covered cave-like structure. The rain began to fall.

After pulling back the tangled overhang of vines and foliage, Marco gingerly entered the cave with Angela close behind. Marco yanked at a few hanging roots deeply embedded in the cave's roof. With a pocketknife, he cut a path for them to sit comfortably.

They sat at the entrance of the cave until the sudden fierce downpour finally subsided to a steady drenching rain. For the first few moments she was too furious to speak. By the time the rain eased again she had calmed down considerably. Hopefully, it would just be a brief shower.

Angela shrieked. Marco spun around, seeing several frogs leap through the threshold. He aided the eagerly departing frogs on their way as Angela cringed in the corner.

"They're called *coqui*. They're commonly found here on the island. You'll find them all over the forest floor. They're said to be the island's good luck charm."

"I don't care what they're called. They're frogs and they're disgusting," she yelled. Then her voice hushed when she looked around and spoke again. "Snakes," she whispered breath-lessly.

Marco smiled at the woman who could certainly defend herself in any big-city situation, yet here she sat afraid to even speak aloud. "Excuse me?" he prompted.

"Snakes," she repeated and looked around as if they would hear and understand her.

"What about them?"

"Are there any snakes here?" she whispered as her eyes watched carefully for any movement inside of the cave.

"Yes, a few." Her head snapped around and her eyes widened. Her mouth slowly opened and closed without words. She made a sudden move to leave the cave but Marco quickly grabbed her waist to still her. "Relax, snakes are scarce in the forest and none of them are dangerous."

Angela glared at him, not sure if she should believe him or not. Against her better judgment she nodded her head and slowly eased back down, huddled away from the jagged wall, and inched closer to him.

Marco pulled a bottle of water from his discarded back-pack and handed it to Angela. She took a deep swig then handed it back to him. He drank. "I presume we're going to be stuck in here until this lets up," she said. He stared at her then nodded absently. He hadn't realized until now that the rain had soaked her thin T-shirt and now the thin wet layer of cotton clung enticingly to her breasts.

She peeked out beyond the hanging vines. "How long is this going to take?"

"Long enough for us to talk," he said softly.

"We have talked."

"No, we've yelled, shouted, argued, battled and even attempted to make love, but talking is something we've never done. This time, we will actually talk."

"Fine. Talk about what?" she answered, still riled by his ruse.

"For starters, the other night." She looked at him in confusion. "Your unannounced appearance at the club," he reminded her.

She stiffened and raised her chin defiantly. "My apologies; I wasn't aware that I was supposed to check in with you every time I decided to leave the hotel," she whipped back sarcastically.

"I didn't say that."

"That's what you implied."

"Enough of these word games. You know exactly what I meant."

"I usually go where I want, when I want. I paid my money at the door and as far as I know it's still a free country. It's not my problem that seeing me bothers you."

"You have no idea," he muttered beneath his breath as his eyes swept over the damp T-shirt a second time.

"And I refuse to hide out for two weeks just because you can't separate me from your dead wife."

"That," he emphasized, "I am finding easier and easier to do."

"Isabella, as I told already you, I have no idea where my brother is. If he's not at home or at the club, try Vieques. He mentioned something about visiting father."

"Roberto." She eased closer, sensing he was deliberately misleading her. "I just want to help him. You boys are like my own sons. I am the only mother you know."

Roberto looked at her as if she'd lost her mind. "Apparently you've forgotten with whom you're speaking? Don't confuse me with my brother, Isabella. Your cheap bubble gum tricks don't work on me. Marco and I have a mother who's very much alive and well."

"But she abandoned you so long ago. What kind of woman would abandon her children and husband to live in some far away land? She is not a mother. She is a disgrace to all of us who truly treasure the sacred care of our young."

Roberto felt the sting of her hurtful words but smiled. "If I were you, old woman, I'd mind my tongue before you find that it has been ripped out."

Her eyes grew wide with alarm. "Roberto, forgive me." She lowered her head shamefully. "It was the ramblings of a devoted mother who misses her dear departed child."

"Get off of it, Isabella. You miss Angelina about as much as you miss being poor. What you miss is the money and power she married. Without her and the Santos name you're just a shriveled-up old prune with a hard-on for her ex-son-in-law." Roberto smirked and ventured further. "Rumor has it you're actually trying to get Marco to take you upstairs."

It was a direct hit, to his surprise. He'd actually just made it up.

Isabella gasped as her head snapped up. She looked at the door guiltily, then back at him. He laughed, adding fuel to the fire. "How dare you insinuate such sacrilege," she hissed slowly. She reached up to slap him across his face but was halted in midair by his iron clamped grip.

"I dare because I am Santos, something you will never be." He pulled her wrist forward, throwing her off balance, allowing her to ram into his arm. "So I suggest you go crawl back under whatever rock you crawled out from and leave my brother and my family alone. Do you understand me?" She nodded pitifully.

Tears began to roll uncontrollably over her cheeks as desperate heaves of pain gripped her. Her once placid face pinched into one of pain and suffering. "Roberto, I know you do not mean what you say." To that he smirked wider then arched his brow. "You know in your heart that I only want the best for you and Marco. I have always tried to be a good mother to you boys, for my Angelina's sake. Oh, how I sacrificed for my child," she lamented sorrowfully.

Roberto laughed. "Lady, you have no idea of what a good mother is. The only sacrifice you've ever made was pushing Angelina onto Marco because he was too young for you and our father didn't want you. But either way you thought you'd won, that was until Angelina couldn't stand your constant demands any longer. She never wanted to marry Marco—you made her, with a lie."

Isabella gasped again as hatred darkened her face. Still held by Roberto's iron grip, he pulled her closer. "You see, Angelina and I weren't lovers as everyone assumed. I was her confidant. Her walking, talking diary, if you will. She told me everything. Everything," he reiterated with intense pleasure. He released her wrist and she pulled away.

"You don't know anything," she shrieked while rubbing her wrist. "You think you can blackmail me?" She strutted around proudly. "I don't think so."

Roberto laughed. "I don't need to blackmail you, Isabella. You don't have anything I want. But I warn you, don't push me or you'll regret it."

"Don't you dare threaten me," she huffed nervously.

Roberto smiled innocently. "I don't need to threaten you, Isabella. We both know I have the power, the money and enough malice to enjoy putting you through hell repeatedly. Now, I suggest you leave before I get angry."

Fully weeping, Isabella hurried from the office of the Café Santos. This had obviously not gone as she'd expected. Apparently that evil woman had already gotten to Roberto as she'd feared. He was completely lost. But, she thought hopefully, she could still save Marco. Determined for success, she piled into her car with her cell phone to her ear and sped in the direction of her next destination.

Twenty minutes later Isabella rang the doorbell and waited patiently. There was no answer so she rang the bell again. She curiously looked up at the large stone structure surrounding the main house. It was an old design. One she no longer cared for. These days she preferred the splendor of her Miami high-rise condo with all of its extravagant amenities. She glanced back at her car, annoyed to see several children at play around the expensive vehicle. She was about to blast their ears when she heard the sound of the door latch open.

Rosa Martinez cautiously peered through the cast-iron gate at the richly dressed woman. She recognized the woman instantly; it was Isabella Rivera. Tentatively, she walked through the small courtyard, unlatched the gate, and swung open the large doors to greet her unexpected guest. "Si, may I help you, señora?" she said, recognizing her instantly as the one person who had never accepted her and who never would.

Isabella, dressed in an elegant white pantsuit with expensive shoes and handbag, turned quickly to face her. Courteously, she removed her dark sunglasses to reveal severe eyes on a harsh face with a satirical expression. Her cruel mouth, covered with blood-red gloss, cracked into something resembling a smile.

Isabella glanced openly into the modest open courtyard. "Buenas dias, Señora Martinez," she began in the native Spanish. "My name is Isabella Rivera. I'm not sure if you remember me, I am—"

Rosa interrupted the woman. "I know who you are. You are Angelina's mother. I am sorry, madam, but Juan is not here at the moment."

Isabella smiled happily at the instant recognition of her notoriety by the peasant woman. "Señora, I did not come to speak with Juan. It is you I have come to speak with. I assure you, it will only take a few moments of your time. It's very important." Rosa eyed her skeptically. "It concerns my son-in-law, Marco Santos."

At hearing the mention of Marco's name Rosa cautiously stepped aside and allowed the woman into her home. "Please follow me," Rosa said sternly. She led the woman along the narrow-tiled path around a center fishpond through an open courtyard to the door of the main house.

Rosa glanced back several times at the well-dressed woman. Juan had spoken many times of Isabella's devious actions. She was known to be famous for her quick temper and biting tongue. Rosa knew that Isabella lived by the old standards of class and considered anyone below her station as worthless.

The perpetual grimace she displayed on her leathery face left little to interpretation.

When they arrived at the door, two young children hurriedly ran out into the fresh air. Each child hugged Rosa's waist then continued running outside. Isabella grimaced at their filthy hands and leaned away so as to not get dirty. When Rosa turned to her she quickly replaced her abhorrent expression with one more suitable. "Your grandchildren are precious," she lied expertly.

"Thank you," Rosa stated proudly. She held the door open for Isabella to enter the large living area. "Please come in. I was just about to fix myself a cup of tea. Would you like one?"

"Si, thank you. That would be lovely." Rosa smiled pleasantly as she escorted Isabella to a seat, then went into the kitchen for refreshments. Isabella looked around with her new nose haughtily perched to the ceiling. She frowned and crinkled her nose distastefully. She expected more of Juan's home.

Juan Martinez was a man of distant name and noble blood. His family had been titled when they first arrived in Puerto Rico. How he came to such lowly ruin was appalling to her. And how he even considered marring a peasant such as Rosa Delores, who was obviously well below his station, baffled her completely.

Nostalgically, Isabella fantasized back to the age-old years of chivalry and honor when a name meant something and those without title and name knew their place, accepted it and remained there.

People of her ilk did not marry commoners. Yes, granted, they were useful for meaningless affairs, but it was always understood that those of noble bloodlines only married others of noble blood. That was the unwritten law. That was the way. The only way.

Isabella raised her nose another notch. She was a descendant of noble blood as were the Santos family. Thus, it would stand to reason that their names and bloodlines be joined together. It was unfathomable that Marco couldn't see that.

It was true that her grandfather had disgraced them and squandered the mass of the family's fortune, but things like that happened. Marrying into money was the only alternative.

With an astute eye, Isabella scanned the room more thoroughly. The large open space, bright with filtered sunlight through the many surrounding windows, was elegantly designed with terra cotta tiles and Spanish marble. The disappointing decor was an unbalanced jumble of French antique and contemporary furnishings. Large fernlike greenery and pricey antique knickknacks did little to accent the muted tones of the drab interior.

"You have a lovely home, Señora Martinez," she lied when Rosa returned carrying a large tray.

"Gracias, Señora Rivera," Rosa replied as she placed the tray on the coffee table between them. She picked up the ornate teapot and poured two cups.

Isabella accepted her cup gratefully. "Please call me Isabella."

Rosa smiled happily and nodded her head appreciatively. She knew the old ways. A person of Isabella Rivera's stature would never consider sitting down to tea with someone of her background. She was a descended of farmers and workers. Isabella was descended from royalty. Having her here in her home was a great honor. Isabella was the epitome of high social standing and gentry. Her face had graced magazine covers showing her exquisite style and taste.

Although rumored to have been impoverished financially until Angelina's recent marriage to Marco, her name was once synonymous with Spanish royalty dating back hundreds of years. She was said to be a direct descendant of the Queen Isabella of Spain. Whether or not the rumored lineage was true didn't really matter since Rosa considered it true and conducted herself accordingly.

"And I insist you call me Rosa."

Isabella sipped her tea and declined Rosa's offer for a short-bread cookie. "Rosa, I'll get right to the point," she began. "I have not seen this with my own eyes, but I have heard from a very reliable source that there is a woman on the island who very closely resembles my dear departed Angelina."

Rosa's eyes widened. Isabella smiled to herself at the woman's reaction. Apparently she'd chosen the right person for an ally. "I saw this woman," Rosa said excitedly. "We arrived on the same flight from the States almost a full week ago."

Isabella opened her mouth in an exaggerated gasp. "Then it is true," she said sadly.

"Si, yes, I have seen this woman, Angela Lord. She is the exact duplicate of your Angelina. How is this possible? Is she a distant relative?"

Isabella did not hear Rosa's questions. Her mind raced with fear. There was only one way that this Angela Lord could so closely resemble Angelina. She stared off as her mind wandered.

"Isabella? Are you all right?" Rosa asked with concern.

"Yes," Isabella snapped at hearing her given name on the lips of this lowly peasant. "Of course." At Rosa's stalled reaction Isabella eased her tone. "I am just so fearful for my son Marco."

Rosa frowned her confusion. "What do you mean?"

Dramatically, she sighed heavily and lowered her head. "May I confide in you, Rosa?" She nodded encouragingly and Isabella continued. "As a mother, I knew my daughter's faults. She was spoiled, pampered and selfish. In a lot of ways she was still very much a child. Marco knew this and accepted her completely." Isabella placed her teacup down and stood to walk to the window. She noted her car and saw that the dirty children were nowhere near it. A smile of satisfied relief graced her face.

After a few moments she continued. "But with all of her faults, of one thing I was always certain, she loved Marco and he loved her." She turned and walked back to sit by

Rosa. She reached down and took Rosa's hands tightly. "As you know, Marco is like a son to me. I am the only mother he knows. I'm afraid for my son. If Marco associates with this woman because of the resemblance to his cherished wife he will only get hurt when he realizes she can never be his devoted Angelina."

A slow, skilled tear crept down her perfectly powdered face. "Oh, Rosa, what can we do to help him?" she begged.

Saddened by a mother's pain, Rosa gripped Isabella's hand in solidarity. "She will not hurt him, Isabella," Rosa promised. "We will think of a way to prevent this from happening."

"I'm afraid it may already be too late. The foreigner has already bewitched my son."

"No, Marco must not be hurt by this intruder. Together we will see to it."

Isabella sighed sadly. "Si, maybe together we can come up with a way to save poor Marco." Rosa's eyes widened with hopeful anticipation. Isabella smiled behind her delicate teacup. Rosa was now her ally. Isabella realized that she would do almost anything to stay in her good graces. As well she should.

Chapter 14

Having just averted being caught in the sudden rain shower, Roberto lowered the convertible top of his red Mercedes and tooled eastward along the coastal highway. The twisted road's numerous curves were second nature to him, so he was driving far beyond the posted speed limit, as usual.

Slightly detracted by his earlier conversation with Isabella, he watched as the small rain pellets speedily crawled upwards across his windshield leaving tiny streaks of perforated water along the way.

Isabella Rivera was a vicious and devious woman whose only desire was money and power. For years she'd presumed it her responsibility to insinuate herself into their lives because of Angelina's relationship with Marco. The fact that Angelina was no longer in her life didn't alter her presumption in the least. She still craved and expected the privilege of her previous Santos connection.

Mindlessly, Roberto maneuvered to pass an upcoming car with rental tags. He eased into the passing lane then began to accelerate. The car suddenly zoomed into the passing lane to block his passing maneuver. Roberto eased back into the side lane. He smiled menacingly at the childish stint. He loved a good dare.

The Mercedes' heavy motor roared with power as he shifted the late model sports car into a lower gear for the upcoming curve. The rental car, driven by what appeared to be a tourist, sped up not knowing about the severe curve ahead. Following closely, he paced the car for several yards then just before the sharp curve he shifted gears and floored the accelerator as the other car quickly, fearfully, adjusted his speed to accommodate the treacherous road ahead. With complete ease Roberto overtook and passed the vehicle then threw his hand up to wave his appreciation of the challenge. The tourist angrily blew his horn in reply as he slowed to round the road's bend.

Roberto smiled at the trivial diversion. Most of the island tourists didn't bother him. He accepted them as a steady source of capital for his family's many endeavors. Yet, there were the occasional few that visited the island with a seemingly superior mentality. They assumed everything was for their benefit and comfort. Their apparent delusional divine right to whatever they desired was whimsically astounding. The cocky attitude, the arrogant demeanor and the disdainful conduct was truly bewildering. The era of conquest was over, yet some still felt the need to dominate.

Roberto pulled into the entrance of his destination. He parked and hopped over the top of the car door then coolly strolled to the private box seats.

El Commandante Racetrack was usually packed this time of day. Both islanders and tourists sauntered around the thoroughbred stalls in hopes of finding the next winning trifecta.

Not seeing his father in the family box, Roberto strolled into the dining room. He lowered then raised his dark shades and scanned the area quickly. He spotted a distinguished man sitting alone eating while carefully eyeing a racing form. Smiling, he went over and took the seat across from him.

The two men sat in silence for a few moments. Then the older gentleman turned a page of his racing form and sipped from his miniature cup of strong black island coffee.

Roberto absently fondled the napkin at the place setting

in front of him. There was nothing unusual about their greeting. Arturo Santos was the patriarch of the Santos familia. When summoned, as Roberto had been, he came without question. And once in Arturo's presence you waited until he was ready to acknowledge you.

Roberto gazed at the man from behind his dark sunglasses. His strong, solid build and tight, firm skin attested to his good family genes. His honey-toned face, ever kissed by the island's sun, and his still wavy salt-and-pepper streaked hair gave the appearance of a much younger man. The brilliant gleam of an unending band of gold encircled the third finger on his left hand. Roberto smiled at the statement of commitment that the gold band still made.

Without realizing it, Arturo, using his thumb, slowly spun the ring around his finger. It was a mindless action that often conjured up fond memories of the matching band of gold. Roberto smiled, thinking of his last meeting with his mother.

Her smile radiated a beam of such pure warmth that even now, months later, and miles away, he still felt her presence. Missing her was an understatement. He could never understand how Marco refused to acknowledge her existence. After over twenty-four years, he still blamed her for abandoning him and returning to the land of her birth. At two, Roberto was certain he was too young to understand much of what occurred but of one thing he was certain, he loved Ava Santos and always would.

After a second sip from the cup, Arturo cleared his throat and finally spoke. "You're late," he said, without looking up.

"I was unavoidably detained."

"I hope she was worth keeping your father waiting."—he glanced at his watch then back at the paper—"almost twenty minutes."

"As a matter of fact she wasn't. Isabella Rivera stopped by the club."

"So I heard."

Roberto shook his head in amazement. His father's intuitive knowledge about just about everything going on the island was astounding. Even though he lived on the neighboring island of Vieques he had more contacts than the average local government and more clandestine connections than most secret service agencies. His vast repertoire of friends and associates kept him well informed of everything no matter how minuscule, particularly when it came to his two sons.

"I assumed she'd go crying to you," Roberto said.

Arturo gazed at his son for the first time since he sat down. "She said that you were rude to her."

Roberto smiled his acknowledgment as a waiter arrived bringing a menu. He looked over to his father's empty plate of food then just placed a drink order. When the waiter departed he continued. "No ruder than she to me."

Arturo took a sip from his cup, dotted his lips with the white linen napkin, then fingered his salt-and-pepper mustache. "Never lower yourself to another's level. Isabella is . . ." he paused, waving his manicured hands in the air, ". . . what can I say, she is a woman in great want and need."

"I agree, she wants Marco and she needs money," Roberto mumbled after the waiter placed a circular coaster and tiny glass in front of him, then walked away.

"Isabella Rivera has always been excessively concerned about the best interest of the Santos family. She has also been kind enough to point out some of your rather indiscreet escapades from time to time." Roberto opened his mouth to rebut, but closed it after eyeing his father's brow raised in warning. "She also tells me that we have a tourist, a woman who is the exact image of Angelina."

"Yes, Angela Lord."

"I assumed you'd already knew of her." Arturo smiled as he stood. Roberto stood up also and dropped several bills on the table then followed his father as he walked out of the dining room.

"Yes," Roberto replied.

The men walked to the family's private spectator's box. Shortly after they entered, a waiter clad in a knee length white apron followed with their drinks.

Arturo picked up his waiting field glasses and casually scanned the horses assembling for the opening race. He mentally sized up his horse along with the others waiting impatiently at the gate. "And is she indeed the image of Angelina?"

"The uncanny resemblance is definitely there; the two could be twins, at the very least sisters," he said, then frowned wordlessly.

"That is troubling," Arturo announced as he lowered the binoculars and glanced at his son. "But . . . ?" Arturo prompted Roberto to continue.

"But, after talking and being with Angela for a while you realize just how different they are. Angela Lord is actually nothing like Angelina. They're like opposite sides to the same coin. It's a strange contradiction until you separate the two mentally and ignore the physical appearance. Then they're the exact opposite."

A gunshot fired from the opening gate. The first race of the day had begun. Immediately, the gates pulled away and the horses tore out. Roberto, impartial, looked to the running horses, his thoughts still on Angela.

"Interesting. And you say they look so much alike that they could be sisters?" Roberto nodded. Arturo nodded and stroked his mustache again. "Isabella is concerned for Marco's welfare. She seems to think that Señorita Lord will invoke unpleasant memories that will damage him emotionally."

"The only damage will come from Isabella and her greed." Arturo tilted his head in warning to his son for his blatant disrespect. Roberto sighed heavily then rephrased his response. "Really, Poppy, I don't know why you still insist on putting up with that woman. You know how disruptive she is."

Arturo raised the binoculars again and focused on the lead horse. "Everyone has a purpose, son, this you will learn to understand and accept in time." Roberto frowned his irritation at Isabella's constant intrusions into their lives. He reached over and toyed with the strap of binoculars draped on the narrow counter. "Isabella's personality does not concern me at this point. Her insistence that Señorita Lord will harm Marco is my only concern."

"Then you needn't concern yourself; Angela can only show Marco that not all women are like Isabella. And since she's African-American, she'll also show him a different side to his bias to mother."

Arturo lowered the binoculars and raised his brow with extreme interest. A wily smile crossed his face. "I see." He raised his binoculars again to view the horses as they rounded the last leg of the muddy course.

Roberto looked at his father suspiciously. "Meaning?" he questioned as he continued toying with the binoculars' hanging strap.

Arturo smiled wryly as his horse accelerated at the last moment and crossed the finish line a nose ahead of his nearest challenger. "Meaning, it seems that Señorita Lord has acquired a champion in my youngest son." He lowered his binoculars and looked at Roberto.

Roberto smiled and chuckled, remembering Angela's strong character. "Believe me, Poppy, the last thing Angela needs is a champion. She has enough fortitude to stand up against Marco's issues and Isabella's deceit without my help."

"A fighter?" Arturo asked with added interest.

"A survivor."

Arturo mulled over the newly acquired information with great interest. A steward tapped lightly on the wood panel opening of the private booth. Wordlessly, he held up a fresh pot of black coffee on a small silver tray. Arturo waved him away as if shooing away a pesky mosquito. "It appears my son knows more about Señorita Lord than just merely a passing acquaintance."

"We've talked."

"I hardly think, given the kind of woman you just described to me, that she openly admitted personal information that would indicate her survival instinct."

Roberto smirked and shook his head, conceding to the cunning of his mentor. The old man was sharp. "I asked around," he said as he leveled a self-satisfied grin to his father. "You're not the only one with important friends in the important places."

Arturo nodded at the aptness of his son's ability. "So what else did these important friends tell you about Señorita Lord?" Roberto exchanged most of the information he'd learned on Angela with his father. Arturo reminded silent as his son extensively relayed her schooling and professional histories. "And her personal life? Her family?" Arturo asked. "What of her life before Washington?"

"Brick wall."

Arturo nodded his understanding then turned his body, leveling his piercing raven eyes at his son. "And your interest, Roberto: what is your agenda here?" Roberto looked wounded until his father continued with a satisfied, open smile, "You, son, have much of your mother in you." Absently, he looked out across the grassy-mounded meadow beyond the dirt-packed racetrack. "She too attempted to right the wrongs of the world. But a word of caution." He looked back at his son. "Be careful not to lose sight of the smaller picture while advocating for the just. Sometimes it's the little things that matter most in life."

The slight rapping drew both men's attention immediately. The same steward appeared, then bowed from the waist to excuse his intrusion. "Señor Santos," he began, "you asked to be informed upon the arrival of your guests." Arturo nodded. "Shall I show them in?" Arturo nodded again and the man quickly vanished behind the tall wooden panels.

Roberto stood and gazed out at the still green hills in the far distance. "I'll be in the States for the next few days. I'm leaving first thing in the morning."

Arturo smiled, imagining his son's final destination. "This is rather sudden, isn't it? Is there a problem? Would you like me to accompany you?"

"No," Roberto answered as nonchalantly as possible.

"Business or pleasure?" Arturo asked with a slight smirk. He knew exactly where his son would be going and who he'd be seeing.

"Both. I'm going to stop in Texas, then check out some property in Miami, then head up to New York."

Arturo smiled slyly. "Texas again? One of these days you're going to have to tell me why the sudden interest in Texas." Roberto looked away evasively. "But not today, I gather." Roberto looked back at his father, keeping Texas as his secret. "So, New York, huh." Roberto joined his smile and nodded knowingly.

Loud talking and generous laughter erupted as a number of fashionably dressed guests arrived at the doorway of the private boxed area. Knowing them as having long been close family friends, Roberto greeted each with due respect and sociable familiarity.

He kissed the cheeks of the women, flirting with each in turn, then grasped hands with the gentlemen while speaking briefly of business, cockfights, and his alleged nightly rendezvous with the fairer sex.

Amid woos of tempting invitations to stay and enjoy the upcoming festivities, Roberto bid his fond good-byes to all. Then he turned to the now-standing Arturo; they smiled knowingly and hugged generously and lovingly. "Safe journey," Arturo said. Roberto nodded and turned to leave. Then, as a passing thought, Arturo said to his ears only, "Give her my best."

Roberto turned. "You already have." He winked then bounded up the two steps that lead out of the Santos private box.

Chapter 15

"So, at birth you were sent to your first foster home, then what?"

"Why all the questions?" Angela asked as she waved away a buzzing mosquito from her ear.

"Just making conversation," he assured her as the two trudged through the thicket of wet rainforest plant life.

Angela shrugged her shoulders matter-of-factly. "Then nothing. I stayed in the foster care system until I was eighteen."

Marco took her hand and helped her up a steep incline. "So, you just moved from home to home and family to family constantly."

"No. Sometimes I'd stay with one family for a few years. But," she paused and looked out into the distance, "there was always the knowledge that I would leave one day."

"So you never formed any attachments," he said sadly.

She turned and looked at him as if he'd read her thoughts. "Don't pity me, Marco. I considered myself lucky. I got to choose who I wanted to be and who I wanted in my life. I had no past to regret and no family to tie me down. My future was open to any possibility. A lot of people can't say that." She stiffened her chin as they stared at each other for a while.

She looked around the area nervously. "Are you sure you know where we're going?"

"Positive, I was a trail guide here when I was a teen."

"You?" She sounded surprised.

"Yes, why is that so hard to believe?"

"I would have thought a Santos would be above getting his hands dirty. Guess I was wrong."

"About a lot of things," he acknowledged with a level eye. He handed her the water bottle. She sipped then handed it back to him. He drank then replaced the bottle in his backpack.

She stared at his face for a moment then smiled. He returned her smile. "What's with the new look?" she questioned.

"Do you like it?"

She shrugged her shoulders noncommittally.

He automatically rubbed at the missing whiskers on his chin. "Actually it's an old look. I grew the beard and let my hair grow long after Angelina died." He began to walk.

"Was that some kind of penance?"

"Penance?"

"You're Catholic, aren't you?" He turned to her and nodded his head yes. "So were you trying to atone for something?"

"I assure you, there was no need for me to atone."

"So why'd you grow the beard?"

"Why so many questions?"

"Just making conversation," she said, mimicking his earlier response. He smirked with a nod and chuckle, then turned his back to continue leading the way.

Angela shrieked. Marco spun around, seeing a twelve-foot boa lying atop and rock enjoying the streaks of sun beaming through the canopy of green above. She ran to his opened arms and punched at his chest. "I thought you said that there weren't any dangerous snakes in the rainforest," she yelled, now safely distanced from the reptile.

"There was no reason to unduly alarm you. The boas in this part of the of the island are completely harmless."

"There's nothing harmless about a snake that size. I don't care if it's dangerous or not."

He took her hand. "Let's go." She snatched her hand away and with a *humph* marched past him a few yards. She looked around, then stopped. There was no visible path and every direction she turned to looked exactly the same. She realized that she had no idea where she was or where she was going. Marco eased up by her side. "Maybe I should lead."

She rolled her eyes childishly. "Whatever."

They walked in silence, each in his own thoughts. Marco took a side path through a thicket of tall bushes then rounded an enormous tree and headed for a narrow wooden bridge with knotted rope guides for handrails.

"Are we supposed to cross that thing?"

Marco kept walking. "I assure you it's safe."

Angela had her doubts. She watched as Marco, without a moment's hesitation, walked briskly and confidently across. She removed her jacket, tied it around her waist and stepped out onto the narrow path. It wasn't as rickety and flimsy as it had appeared. The wood beneath her feet was solid and stable. As a matter of fact, it was more stable then some of the ground she'd trod on recently. She continued walking carefully then stopped when she heard a distant rustling noise. She looked around, then up and down the waterway below her.

"What's that noise?" she called out. Marco turned. He spotted Angela standing midway on the bridge leaning over the knotted ropes. He walked back to the center and stood by her side. "Where's that noise coming from?" she asked again.

Marco smiled and took her hand. "Come on, we're almost there."

A short while later Angela complained, "Where exactly are we going?"

"There." He pointed upwards just beyond some trees and a grove of yellow and red floral adorned shrubs.

Angela's voice caught in her throat as she looked in the

direction of his pointing finger. "Oh," she proclaimed in a tiny whispered voice. The scene, completely serene in its perfection, gave an aura of timelessness. It was as if it had been captured on canvas centuries earlier only to be witnessed at this exact moment. "This is incredible." Angela pulled out her camera and began photographing the timeless beauty of her surroundings.

Within moments Angela was completely lost in the world around her. Her mind's eye swam with ideas and images of artistic designs and structures. Nature had always influenced her designs so she was truly in her element. Patterns, shapes, and configurations forged structural images of architectural formations. Her imagination went wild as she conjured up idea after idea.

The way the light trickled through the canopy of shadows gave her an idea for a ceiling skylight she'd been tinkering with for weeks. The textured play of rough bark against floral bursts and verdant green sent her thoughts in the direction of extreme surface characterizations. The thought of contrasting appearances was exciting.

She reached into her backpack and pulled out a small notepad. In quick, simple sketches and hastened notes, she outlined the general feel of her ideas.

Marco looked over her shoulder as she worked. "So, is this what you do?"

"Sometimes."

She continued hurriedly. The ideas were flowing and she didn't want to miss a single one. Marco stepped back and observed her at work. The excitement radiating from her was contagious. He'd never realized that nature in its abstract shapes could influence so many architectural forms. After a few more minutes she paused and lowered her sketchpad.

"We're almost there," Marco said as he raised several low-hanging branches and fan palms, affording them the gateway to an enchanting path of stunning reds, blues and violets and dazzling yellows, golds and greens. Angela stepped through the arch in wonder as she gazed hypnotically at the cascade of beauty. Spread out like a buffet of edible rainbows were succulent colors in every conceivable form.

Multicolored butterflies daintily danced along the tops of flowers that hung delicately from vines which grew up from vibrant green stems.

Angela stood for a moment taking in the beauty of her surroundings. She gazed upwards. Through the canopy of green leaves came shafts of brilliant sunlight illuminating the colors like spotlights on a muted stage. When her eyes adjusted to the brightness, she glanced beyond the tree trunks to see a sparkling cascading waterfall splashing playfully down a cluster of natural boulder steps.

Hurriedly, she scurried along the path, leaving Marco in her wake. As she grew closer, her excitement escalated into sheer joy at the sight of sparkling water falling into a natural pool formation.

She reached small opening and continued through. Suddenly, as if on cue, a mass of hundreds of butterflies raised up from the path in front of her. She gasped, stopped and stared in awe as a bubble of giggles arose from inside of her. Marco held up her camera and began clicking away. Giddy, like a child at play, she laughed and spun around with her head to the sky, watching as the butterflies fluttered and scattered in search of another undisturbed resting place.

Marco marveled at Angela's candid reaction. Surely this wasn't the alluring temptress who aroused his primal needs each time she glanced at him. The woman before him now innocently giggled and frolicked with butterflies as naturally as she gyrated seductively on a crowded dance floor. Riveted, he was unable to take his eyes from her, followed every movement of her playful butterfly dance.

Then in wonder, she looked straight up, a hundred feet into the sky. The perfect blueness cracked in the center and tears from heaven poured down. Against the backdrop of a now bluing sky, dozens of dark shiny boulders lay toppled and tumbled down the front of the waterfall. Each tonnage had been scattered and fixed, rested and arranged, in rigid positions centuries ago. White crests of foam flowed against the shiny rocks, making them glisten in the warm sunlight.

"This is too incredible," she called out.

Crystal clear water cascaded down in sprays, splatters and splashes to finally pool into a beautiful reflecting pond. Surrounded by vibrant greenery and colorful flowers, it was the most exhilarating sight she'd ever witnessed. "My God," she said in a whisper. "This is unbelievable. How? Where?" She looked to Marco.

"From the mountains." He answered her incomplete questions.

Slowly she walked toward the water's edge. "It's so beautiful." She dropped down to touch the oasis of calm water amid the dense surround of plant growth. The tranquil pond's water was warm and cool at the same time while still refreshing to the touch. She splashed at the water then watched as circular ripples dispersed repeatedly, growing wider and wider until they finally dissipated into nothingness.

Giggling like a schoolgirl, she playfully spattered the tepid water up her bare arms. "It's so cool; it feels so wonderful," she uttered in wonder, sensing Marco's recent arrival behind her.

"The stream and waterfall run down from the Sierra de Luquillo mountain range. The water is kept cool by the overhang of vegetation."

She stopped and looked around. "It's so beautiful here," she said in wondrous delight. "What's it called?"

Marco smiled, pleased by her admiration of his favorite retreat. "This place doesn't really have a name. But it's referred to as *puerta Eden's laguna*." She smiled and easily translated: the door to Eden's lagoon. He nodded and watched as she drizzled cool water down her neck then rebraided her hair, securing it into a small knot at the nape of her neck. Then with wet fingers she drizzled water down the front of her, causing the now dry T-shirt to plaster itself against her skin once again.

Marco knelt down beside her, having already removed his

backpack, vest and her camera. "This is my favorite spot. I came here a lot when I was younger."

Angela stopped playing in the water long enough to look around and nod her approval. "This must be what the Garden of Eden looked like," she said as a haze of innocent wonder overwhelmed her.

The rushed sound of water splattering against the boulders gave a tranquil aura to the underlying ambience. The subtle undercurrent of calm radiated throughout the entire setting. It was almost too perfect.

Angela inhaled deeply; the scent of sweet gardenias, luscious jasmine and succulent orchids scented the warm, moistened air. Noticing the obvious absence of others, she asked about their newfound seclusion.

"This is an old trail; it hasn't been a marked sight for visitors for some time. Years ago, there was a problem with tourists getting a little carried away by the serene ambience. In the evenings the local teens used it as a make-out spot." She looked at him, surprised. "You did mention its resemblance to the Garden of Eden," he added.

Her mouth opened into a perfect letter *O*. "I see." Then, several moments later, she turned to him and cocked her head. "Is that why you brought me here, to make out?"

"No," he said, looking deep into her brown eyes then off into nothingness. "I just thought you might enjoy the beauty."

"You know, you can be rather charming when you're not being a complete and total pain in the butt."

He laughed. It was the first time she'd heard his relaxed and genuine laughter. It was pleasing. She was pleased. "I take it that was a compliment?" he asked. She nodded righteously. "Thank you." He laughed again. "Thank you very much."

Quickly she averted her eyes. Look at him any longer and she would surely pounce on top of him right at the water's edge. "It's so incredible here." She sighed, seeing luxuriant greenery everywhere she looked. She picked up her camera and began clicking away.

"There are well over a thousand species of plant life in El Yunque and over two hundred types of trees," Marco began. "The rainforest is divided into several distinct areas and gets over two hundred inches of rain annually. Taconic is below two thousand feet and has tall straight trees, flowers and shrubs. The Palo Colorado is above two thousand feet and is distinct for its ancient Colorado trees that grow to age more than a thousand years. The highest range is known as Cloud Forest or Dwarf Forest. There the trees are twisted by the strong winds and grow a mere twelve feet tall."

"What does El Yunque actually mean?"

"Perfectly translated, it means 'the anvil'."

"The anvil? Why?"

"The north side peak is said to resemble an anvil."

She spotted a small green parrot in a nearby tree. Its beautiful brightly colored feathers, highlighted with red and blue, danced against the deep greenery of the background whenever it extended its wings. Marco came closer. "It's called *el iquaca*. They're near extinction. In all the time I've been in the rainforest, I've never actually seen one. I've heard them, seen photographs, but never seen one until now."

"*Iquaca,*" Angela repeated the name as she picked up her camera and clicked away. "It's beautiful, but so small. The parrots I saw earlier were a lot larger and much different in coloring."

"This particular species is the smallest found in the Caribbean. As I said, they're almost extinct. Right now their existence is in the center of a political dispute between the Fish and Wildlife Service, the United States Forest Service and the Puerto Rican Department of Natural Resources."

The bird flew off to points unknown and suddenly Angela became very aware of her surroundings. The vibrant plant life seemed to sparkle that much brighter; the sounds around her muted to a soft hushed pitch. The sweet-scented air around her stilled and calmed to placid tranquility.

She lowered the camera, sensing the presence of Marco closer behind her. She turned sharply. He was there staring.

She stepped closer then raised her hands to touch him. The solid power of his chest excited her while the heat of his body permeated her flesh. She looked up into the dark abyss of his black eyes. They spoke of need and of desire, with promises of fulfilled fantasies.

He touched the secured knot at her nape, releasing her hair to fall freely through his fingers. He cupped the back of her head and lowered himself to her. They kissed. But, more than just a kiss, they connected on a level so intense and so absolute it left her breathless and wanting. Marco swept her up in his arms and lowered her to the ground. Angela drifted on a wave of perfect bliss as Marco's arms completely surrounded her. Comforted by the soft blanket of cool damp grass, Angela lay back cuddled in Marco's arms.

She wasn't sure how long they had been kissing, how long they'd been lying there, or even how long they'd existed. All she knew was that she never wanted this feeling to end. She never wanted to be without Marco's arms embracing her.

A playful tongue, a loving stroke and gentle caress all added to the heated sensation seething inside her. How did she survive all these years without this man's touch on her body? Her mind soared, caught up in the bliss of Marco's embrace. Angela was sure that this was either heaven or hell. And one way or another she was going to pay for it. But until that time she intended to savor every delectable second with this wonder of masculinity.

At that instant she realized that she felt more for him than just a simple island affair would suggest. Her intense emotions were way out of control. She'd never opened her heart to anyone as she had done with Marco, and it scared her.

Breathlessly, she pulled back. This was moving too fast and she was far out of her league and absolutely over her head. Marco had her head dizzily spinning. She was completely out of control. She looked around for refuge. "Can we swim?"

Marco barely nodded when Angela pulled from his embrace and began removing clothing. Marco watched the enticing strip with unabashed attention. Baring a pink floral bikini, she stepped to the water's edge and dipped her toe in. She giggled and turned to him.

Dry mouthed, Marco could only smile. Seconds later she perched on the edge then dove in. Marco watched as she swam a few yards then stopped in the center of the pooled water and waved him in. Slowly he undressed.

She swam to the giant boulders and cautiously climbed into the small recess. Like a perfect shower, the water poured down with mists spraying all around her. Marco climbed to her side. They held each other and the waterfall lovingly caressed their bodies and curtained their kiss.

Then together they swam to the center of the pond. They splashed and played like children. Then the moment turned. Treading water, Angela slipped into Marco's embrace and looked into his dark eyes. Pools of molten fire greeted her. Who was she kidding? This was going to happen. They were going to happen.

"How long can you hold your breath?" he asked.

"What?"

"I want to show you something. How long can you hold your breath?"

"How far?"

Marco slowly turned her body and pointed to the waterfall. "Just on the other side."

The spark of adventure gripped her. "Let's go."

Chapter 16

They dove beneath the surface and swam in unison toward the turbulent force of the waterfall. Moments later they surfaced in an dark cave-like chamber. A bright streak of muted light arched down the side of one of the walls, allowing her just enough light to see her surroundings. "Hey, we're on the other side of the waterfall."

Angela looked around as Marco got out and walked toward a large boulder against the far wall. A cool, refreshing mist rose from the surface of the water, giving the inner chamber a mystical feel. She looked behind her in the direction from which they swam. There was a wall of rocks but she could hear the flow of water beyond. Small sporadic openings between the cracks allowed water to drizzle through, creating a gentle continuous stream-like fountain flowing back down into the pooled water.

Cautiously, she followed Marco toward the small sandy patch of land completely dried by the steady flow of warm air spinning between the rocks.

"What is this place?" she sputtered blissfully as Marco helped her from the underwater shelf separating the sand plateau from the deep water. It was like a dream, complete with subdued lighting, gentle sound effects, and scented air.

"This," Marco smiled and open his arms wide, "is Eden."

"I have a feeling that this place isn't on the regular tourist map either."

"No, not exactly."

She watched as he removed several extra large towels from a sealed plastic bag. He unfolded them and laid them down on the soft sand. "How obscure is this place?" she asked.

"Completely."

Angela smiled as she continued to look around at the cozy chamber. "So at the moment, that would make you and me the only two people on this planet." She moved closer, stepped into his welcoming embrace. She inched her hand into his, entwining their fingers as one, then placed his hands around her waist.

"I thought a bit of privacy was in order," he said softly, his voice deep and husky with desire.

"Oh you did, did you?" Angela's angelic smile was openly wanton and sexy as she reached up and stroked his newly shaved face. She bit at her lower lip and gazed into his dark, smoldering eyes. The stark emotion she witnessed there was so intense, it took her breath away. The pit of her stomach did a sudden jolt. This seduction scene was taking too long. She wanted him now. "Kiss me," she commanded without hesitation.

Marco smiled, reached up and took a tangle of her damp curls in the palm of his hand. He gripped her hair then lowered his face to inhale its sweetness. Then, in one swift movement, he cupped and angled her head to meet his.

Just inches away he paused and asked in the softest whisper, "Do you want me, Angela?"

"Yes, I want you, Marco. All of you. Now."

Tantalizing and teasing, his tongue gently touched her mouth. Her lips parted of their own volition as his mouth took hers. In heavenly bliss they united. Their mouths moved together in magical perfection. Their tongues danced, savoring the joy of the long awaited reunion. His kiss was firm and passionate, meant to stir the heart and heat the body. It was as if they had always been together. Reunited from another time, in another place.

Instinctively, she pressed her body into his, molding her peaks and valleys against his broad strength. As one, in form-fitting passion, they held each other while their mouths indulged the desire of their passion. Her stomach fluttered, her mind whirled, her limbs weakened and her heart thundered. The urgency of their desire would not be denied. Not until the union was joined as one.

"Touch me," he instructed.

Through his damp shorts, she felt his desire press against her stomach. She reached down and grasped the length of his need through the cloth. He was hard and throbbing and his desire excited her. His short primal gasp and heavy sigh urged her on, making the boldness of her actions that much more enticing. The newly found power she wielded excited her. She unsnapped and unzipped his shorts, letting them fall to the sandy beach.

He was set free from all restraints, long, thick and full. In all of his masculine grandeur, he stood beyond perfection, swelled and ready. Angela felt the swim of excitement seethe through her as she anticipated this masculinity deep inside her.

Now, only a thin layer of Lycra separated her from her desire. She yearned for his touch. Then, as if he'd read her mind, Marco's hands began to explore. "Now," he said softly, "I'm going to touch you." His hands began slowly. She felt the singe of his long fingers on her face. His hands roamed across her brow, down her cheeks, then behind her slim neck. The simple tie of her haltered bikini top was released.

Gently he gathered the ties in his hands while still holding the top in place. Angela inhaled sharply. At any moment, at his will, she would be freed. To her relief, the plaster of pink flowers that danced on her breasts lasted only the briefest of moments. Her burning need erupted as he lowered himself down, bringing the straps of her thin suit with him.

Bare. Uncovered. Uninhibited. Her taut nipples instantly perked to freedom. Marco gazed lovingly as he knelt down, reached behind her and completely removed her damp swim-suit top. She stood before his kneeling body topless and exposed.

Pleased with his prize, he wrapped his arms around her and held her tight, pressing his face between her breasts. Slowly he kissed and nibbled gentle trails across her breasts, setting each peak afire as his hands roamed to her buttocks and kneaded the tight muscles beneath the fabric still in place. Her breath quickened. His hands on her body felt so good. She leaned in, grasping fists of his shortened wavy hair. This slow torture had to end.

She needed the fabric gone now. She stood firm, willing her trembling hands to remove the last barrier of cloth between them, but his hands stopped her. "No, not yet," he promised. "I want more. I want all of you." With that he continued his assault, taking his fill of her body while seeking more. Touching. Taunting. Tasting. Tantalizing. He sent her writhing to the very edge of pleasure then started all over again.

Angela easily conformed to his beckoning need as her body came alive with each touch. Willing and eager, she opened her soul to him as unleashed desire seethed through her body, scorching a path to her heart. She wanted Marco here, now, forever.

She knew that this wasn't a simple island affair as she so wittingly agreed. The clarity of her feelings for Marco sparked the obvious. She was in love with him. And this moment may very well be their first, last and only.

A brief instant of nervousness needled through her. She'd never done anything like this before. Not with a man she'd only known for less than a week. But, somehow, knowing him for such a short period of time made no difference to her. In her heart she felt as if they'd known each other a lifetime. Angela tried to savor every second of the moment. She sought to be frozen in time in this place called Eden.

Marco continued as he took a pebbled nipple into his mouth and suckled his fill, then brought both breasts together and savored the joy of two. Replacing his mouth with his cupped hands, he kneaded her breasts while his fingers toyed relentlessly with the rest of her body. Slowly, he angled lower, tempting and enticing her tingling skin with tiny teasing nibbles, driving her wild with anticipation. She gasped faintly as her legs weakened beneath his astute skill. She grasped the thick black curls on his head as his mouth indulged her body, sending her to points beyond her realm of reason.

In mind-blinding response, she weakened and gave in completely to the onslaught of his assault.

He stood and lifted her to wrap her legs around his waist—an idea he'd envisioned since the first night he saw her reflection in the glass. He backed her against the smooth cave wall and kissed her with unbridled passion. Her legs gripped tightly when his mouth captured her breast. She screamed out in ecstasy.

"Do you feel me, Angela?"

"Yes," she moaned, barely audible.

"Do you want me, Angela?"

"Yes," she nearly screamed as his slow torture persisted.

"Tell me what you want, Angela."

"Everything," she rasped, "all of you, now."

"Are you sure, Angela?"

"Yes. Yes. Yes. Now."

In amorous excitement, with the twist of her body still around his, he lowered her down into the cool mist onto the towels he'd placed on the soft sand earlier. He reached for his discarded shorts and pulled a silver disk from his pocket and handed it to her. She ripped the package open and rolled the thin latex over his length. Her slow, methodical dressing and torturous hands inched him too close to the edge. A groan rumbled from deep inside of him. He was about to explode.

She lay back and smiled when she had completed her task. The mist slowly weaved around their bodies. "Mi amor ahora," she beckoned in his native tongue. "Love me now."

He obliged willingly and positioned himself above her. In

anticipation he looked down at her lush body. She raised her hips, aiding the removal of the last barrier.

Marco paused and smiled. She was beautiful, and now she was his. Slowly he eased into her tightness, filling her with his hardened need. She secured herself around his waist then arched her hips upwards, sending him deeper in a sudden rush that pulled a breathless gasp from her lips. "I see you want more," he quipped.

Angela nodded her head and moistened her dry lips. "Yes, more," she instructed. "I want more. I want all of you." Then, in paced thrust after thrust, he delved deeper, filling her completely. He rocked his hips back and forth, in and out, plunging deeper and deeper, reaching her core and tantalizing the sweet point to her fulfillment.

Angela's hands roamed over his back and down his waist, settling on the firm richness of his buttocks. She felt his movement and raised her hips higher to his tempo. The dance's pace quickened as the mists around them swirled recklessly. Again and again he thrust into her and she took all of him. In frenzied tension they built wave after wave of rapture. Surging forward, then pulling back, forward then back, in and out, until the moment they plunged together, swept up in the rapture of passion, the sated fulfillment of desire, and, in intense eruption, their love washed over them.

Sated, he lay heavily on top of her for a brief instant before rolling to the side and bringing her with him. The once hastened swirl of mist settled gently, tenderly over their bodies. Like a soothing blanket of haze, it lay across them entwined by their passion and sated by their love. In perfect rapture, they lay in each other's arms letting timeless moments drift by.

Angela had drifted off to sleep in his arms. Dizzied by the memory of their love, seconds slipped into minutes and minutes faded into wistful peace. When time passed and Angela stirred, she looked around, comforted by the man at her side.

Marco leaned down and kissed her tenderly, then stood and gathered their discarded clothing. Angela lay back in luxurious wonder. She watched Marco dip their damp sandy clothes into the water, then lay them out on the large rock. "Where'd the dry towels come from?" she asked.

"The park keeps a survival kit for emergencies." He walked over and reached behind a large rock and pulled out a knapsack. He unzipped the bag. Inside were clear plastic bags containing water bottles, dried fruits and nuts, a first aid kit, flashlights, compass and more.

"Boy scouts, trail guides, always be prepared?"

"In the rain forest, anything can happen; always be prepared." He replaced the items and secured the emergency kit behind the rock then looked around and smiled at the memory of their union. He reached out his hand to her. She grasped it and he pulled her up against his body. "Ready to get back to the real world?" He handed her the two bikini pieces.

"No." She took and secured the wet fabric as he slipped into his wet shorts.

He reached out and took her hands. She stood flat against his body as they entered the pool of water together. "Ready?" She nodded. "Let's go." A knowing smile was sealed with a slow passionate kiss as together they dipped beneath the surface of the water and swam out and away from Eden.

Moments later they popped up on the other side of the waterfall back to the reality of the real world. Marco encircled her waist and drew her closer. He kissed her again, passionately, forever sealing the memory of their time in Eden.

Quite literally, Marco Santos took her breath away.

Whooping howls broke the silence of the rainforest as a small group of island teenagers passed by and saw the lovers' watery embrace. They hollered and cheered, causing Angela to suddenly jerk away from Marco. She swam to the edge. The young teens continued on their way, leaving Marco and Angela their privacy, but with an awkward silence as he followed her out of the water.

Angela grabbed her T-shirt and pulled it over her bikini. "Do you think they saw us earlier?"

"Behind the waterfall? No way."

Relieved, Angela sighed then asked, "In the water?" Marco

looked up to the raised platform where the teens had stood. "The last kiss, definitely, but anything else, I doubt it." Angela looked up to the now emptied space.

"Regrets?" he asked hesitantly.

"No, none."

"Are you hungry?"

"Starved."

"Good," Marco said then stood up and walked to his backpack. "I had our chef whip up a small picnic lunch for us." With that he began pulling out container after container of food from his heavy backpack.

Angela knelt down by his side in awe. "This is considered a small picnic?" she asked sarcastically.

"For a Santos restaurant chef it is."

She hurried back to the pool of water, washed her hands then began opening the containers and spooned small portions onto the accompanying small plastic plates. "Wow, this really looks fabulous." She sampled some chilled penne, shrimp and lobster salad. "Oh God, this is heaven. My compliments to your chef."

Marco took his prepared plate and began to eat. He nodded proudly. "She is the best."

For the next half hour they sat together eating, talking and enjoying each other's company. Then, Marco pointed to a grouping of large boulders just beneath the waterfall. "See that spot right over there?" She nodded. "Legend has it that's where the forest nymphs live. Right there, between the split second of sunlight and darkness."

"Why am I not surprised?" she asked. "Pixies, fairies, and sprites, oh my," she mused as she mimicked Dorothy from *The Wizard of Oz*.

"And spirits," he added.

"Spirits?"

"Island spirits, guardians of the forest, protectors of all you see." Marco went on to tell Angela of local folklore whispered down from generation to generation. Tales of betrayal, unrequited love, suicide and murder.

Angela listened intently, her eyes riveted as he told the last tale of a princess nymph who could transform herself into a beautiful maiden. "She'd wander the land searching for handsome young men to lure into her kingdom. There, they would live somewhere between their world and her world, spending the remainder of their natural lives in service to her desires. If asked if they would rather return to their previous lives, they would instantly decline. Hence the word 'nymphomaniac'."

"Okay, you almost had me. But you blew it with the nymphomaniac thing. I happen to know the origin of that word is Greek, not Spanish or Puerto Rican."

He shrugged his broad shoulders and raised his brow, smiling. "Who do you think they got it from?" Angela laughed unexpectantly. The joyous sound was music to Marco's ears. He realized that he never wanted to live without having the sound of her laughter in his life.

"This is the land of the ancient *Tainos*. They were the protectors of *Yukiyu*, the spirit of the forest. It is said that the *areytos,* their ceremonial dance and songs, still travel on airstreams of El Yunque. Like conch shells found on the sandy beaches, if you listen closely you'll be able to hear their epic chants."

"Puerta Eden's laguna; this is such a magical place."

Together they gathered the makeshift picnic and returned it to his backpack. He led the way as they continued to the main trail to return to the tourist center. "Tired?" he asked.

"No, not really," she answered as she hiked up by his side. They were in sight of the visitor's center. Several tourists mingled around waiting for guides to begin their early evening enchanted tours.

"What are your plans for the rest of this evening?" he asked as he took her waist, helping her over a fallen log.

"Why?"

"Come to Vieques with me tonight." He paused to look at her.

"Vieques?"

"It's a small island off the eastern coast of Puerto Rico."

"Why?"

"I'd like to show you something."

"Again." They smiled knowingly. "The last time you wanted to show me something . . ."

He finished her statement. ". . . we had an amazing moment in Eden."

Angela blushed and looked away. "Marco," she exhaled deeply, "I really enjoyed myself today, more than you can ever imagine. But I don't think we should push our luck."

"Come tonight, please; I promise you won't regret it."

She looked at him, wanting desperately to say yes. But better judgment won out. She didn't want to ruin the wonderful afternoon they'd just had. "I don't think that's a good idea."

He could see the uncertainty reflected in her eyes as he took her hands. "Angela, once you wanted to know if I'd gotten over Angelina; I have, a long time ago. Seeing you simply brought back some painful memories; that I'll admit. But I know you're not her. She could never be you."

Angela's arms goose-bumped at his admission. *She could never be you.* The words of his confession reverberated in her mind like bells ringing in a tower. *She could never be you.*

"Please, come with me tonight."

Shyly she looked down to fondle the bright red flower she'd picked up along the trail. She smelled the sweet fragrant flower then presented it to him. "You are persistent, aren't you?"

"When I find something I want, yes."

With much cajoling, Angela finally consented to accompany Marco to Isla Vieques. After a quick stop at the tourist center to return his gear, they drove to the ferry dock. Ninety minutes and seven miles later their launch from Fajardo arrived on the magical shores of Vieques.

After the ferry arrived on Vieques they immediately boarded a second smaller vessel. The small boat set out less than a mile from shore then continued along the coastline. Their destination was Mosquito Bay, also called Fluorescent Bay because of the wondrous waters.

As the small boat reached a secluded location the engines were cut and the anchor dropped. The vessel drifted freely on the mystical glowing waters. Angela gasped in wonder. "What are they?" she asked, astounded by the sight.

"They're microscopic protozoan called pyrodiniums or 'whirling fire.' They're actually microscopic bioluminescent organisms. They live near the surface of the water." Gasps of wonder and amazement continued as their traveling companions also observed the strange phenomenon.

Angela gazed with astonishment at the tiny creatures. En masse, they quickly darted away as the small vessel drifted near, leaving eerie blue-white veins just below the water's surface. "They look like tiny lightning bugs underwater," she continued, still amazed by the sight.

Angela was so enamored by the sight of the tiny creatures that she didn't notice that several of their companions had discarded their clothing and were preparing to enter the glowing water. Angela sat back in amazement as Marco pulled his shirt over his head. "Come on, let's go in," he said, smiling.

She looked at him as if he'd lost his mind. "You have got to be kidding. No way."

"No." He kicked off his Dockers. "It's perfectly safe. It's like swimming with fireflies or dancing with butterflies."

No matter how curious she was, Angela couldn't get her legs to move. The idea of swimming with the tiny glowing creatures seemed insane.

Though he tried, Marco was only able to get Angela to dip her fingers and feet into the water. Swimming, she'd decided, was totally out of the question.

They stayed on Vieques for several more hours. Since there was no ferry that late at night, Marco and Angela boarded an island flight back to Isla Grande Airport in the heart of San Juan. He promised her an unregrettable experience but what she got was unforgettable.

Chapter 17

As a prominent realtor of high-end residences and executive relocations, Ava Santos worked primarily out of her home office. Her home was a multi-level townhouse elegantly furnished with the very best money could buy. Every piece of adornment was meticulously chosen and placed for optimal effect.

She was right in the middle of faxing several interesting prospects to a client when she heard keys jingling in the front door. Since there were only four keys to her home and Roberto and Arturo were the only people who possessed them, she walked to the foyer expecting to see one of the two men.

Their embrace was nothing less than sheer unbounded love. Roberto beamed; the advancing years did little to impede on the beauty of the woman before him. He adored her. She was, in his eyes, the perfect woman. He kissed each smooth brown cheek lovingly. "Hola, Mama."

Ava closed the door and watched her handsome son stroll comfortably through the foyer and deposit his single bag beside the stairs. She followed, interested and curious about his unannounced arrival. "This is a pleasant surprise," she said as she moved by his side.

Roberto turned and smiled lovingly. "I'm just a few weeks early. I had some business to take care of in Texas and Miami."

"Texas?"

He waved his hand evasively. "It's a long story."

"Santos North?" she questioned, knowing the complete details of Marco and Roberto's plans to open a restaurant and club in Miami. "I thought everything was on schedule and you were ready to make the bid on the Miami property."

They embraced a second time. "I think I've found a more feasible location."

"Is that why you were in Texas?"

He smiled and climbed the front stairs. "Actually, I was in D.C." Ava grimaced at the unexpected location and followed Roberto to the second floor. They passed several closed doors, one of which was Marco's bedroom. A room he'd didn't know about and had never seen it was always available to him when he was ready for it. In the room, on the mahogany nightstand by the four-poster king size bed, a fourth front door key sat in an envelope also available when he was ready.

Roberto moved silently down the thickly carpeted hall. The five-bedroom abode was always perfect no matter what time of day or night. Everything was always in its place. Ava relished order and precision. Unlike Roberto, it was obvious to see from whom Marco got his quality of perfection.

Roberto opened his bedroom door and looked around. He sighed in comfort and relief. He was back home. At times he considered this more his home than his small island villa in Puerto Rico. He loved the island and his home there but here he found contentment. Here he could relax and just be himself. He didn't have to be the youngest offspring of the legendary Arturo Santos or the equal to his perfect, straight-laced brother Marco. Here, he was simply Roberto Santos.

Roberto dropped his bag on the floor and crossed the large room to open the drapes. The room was immediately drenched in mid-afternoon sunlight. He looked down at the beautifully manicured patio. It was an oasis of perfection in the center of a bustling metropolis. The newlybudding trees hung just low enough to give shade without being bothersome. The bare flowerpots surrounding the perimeter offered the promise of fragrant floral scents and colorful petals just a few months' time as perennials casually awakened from the long winter's nap.

Closely examining every trace of his honey-toned face, Ava tilted her head curiously to the side. There was something definitely different about him. The pleasant ever-smooth skin she'd found so masculinely attractive was pinched tight with weighted concern. She sat down on the side of the bed and gently patted the space beside her. "Talk," was her only command.

Roberto melted into the open space beside his mother. She knew him too well and always would. He was troubled. Troubled and concerned by a woman he knew nothing about and the one he knew all too well. "There is a woman on the island, Angela Lord," he began. "She looks enough like Angelina Rivera to be her identical twin."

A short, deep crevice dipped between Ava's hazel eyes. The image of her older son flashed into her mind. "Marco."

"Yes, Marco."

"Is she threatening to him other than the obvious?"

"No, as a matter of fact, I think once he gets his head out of his, ah . . ." He paused to look at his disapproving mother. "Angela is good people. Marco just has to realize it."

"I see."

"She's beautiful, that goes without saying." He smiled, remembering. "And her voice is husky and throaty, in a sexy kind of way. She's got an inner strength that you just don't get in books or with schooling. She's been through a lot, you can see it in her eyes."

"She's had a hard life?"

"Hard, difficult and complicated." Roberto paused to think about his words. "Also, she has this flippant, don't-give-a-damn attitude that drives Marco wild. He loves it but he's too proud to say so or do anything about it."

"So what concerns you?"

"Isabella."

Ava looked away. That was a name she hadn't heard in many years. The last time she saw Isabella was at Marco's wedding. Isabella sat perched in front as proud as a glorified peacock. Ava sat in the rear, far away from the main festivities. Unnoticed, she graced the last pew then slipped out after the vows were exchanged. She made sure Marco hadn't seen her. That was the last thing she wanted on his special day. "How does Isabella fit into all of this? What is her relation to this Angela Lord?"

"That's just it, she doesn't. According to Angela, she doesn't have any family at all."

"Does this Angela know Isabella or Angelina?"

"Nah, she had no idea about any of this."

"Are you sure?" Ava asked protectively, suspicious of anything that might endanger either one of her sons.

"Positive."

Ava stood and walked downstairs to the kitchen, closely followed by Roberto. He immediately went to the refrigerator and scanned its contents. Pulling out a large selection of lunch meat, bread, lettuce and tomatoes, he prepared to make a sandwich. Ava stepped up and took over the task. Roberto sat and opened a bag of chips that he found in the cabinet. "Tell me more about Angela," she requested.

Roberto grabbed a soda from the refrigerator, popped the tab and sat down on the counter top. Ava looked at him as only a mother can. He soon hopped down and took a seat on a stool. "Her name's Angela Lord. She's African-American, an architect. She works in a design firm in Washington, D.C., but she's originally from New York. No parents or family, she'd been in foster care all her life." His spreading smile was contagious.

"And . . ." Ava prompted.

"She's got this energy that draws you to her. It's intense. It makes you want to be around her all the time. She's bold and cool and definitely doesn't take any crap, even from me."

Ava smiled. "Sounds like you care for her."

"I do, I admire her. She's strong. She reminds me of you; as a matter of fact I told her that."

Ava chuckled. "You told this woman that she reminds you of your mother. I bet that went over well."

Roberto grinned, knowing she correctly assumed Angela's reaction. "I consider it a lesson learned." He smiled broadly at his mother. "Not one of my best lines." Ava returned his smile. "To be honest," he continued, "I flirted innocently, but that was it. I always saw her for Marco."

Ava finished preparing the sandwich, put it on a plate and placed it in front of Roberto. "So what does Marco think of her?"

"That's the funny part," he said as he stuffed half of the sandwich into his mouth. "He's got this thing for her but he's too stubborn to give into it. They both are. It's like watching a love story where the two main characters circle each other but never get together."

"This thing he has for Angela Lord, is it because she looks so much like Angelina?" Ava slid a cloth napkin next to the plate.

"I don't think so. Maybe it started out like that at first but I doubt that's the reason now. You see, after you're with her for a while you realize just how different they are. Angela's strong willed and determined. Angelina was kind of fragile and timid. Particularly when it comes to Isabella." After devouring the rest of the sandwich, Roberto downed the last of the soda and looked at his mother. She was lost in thought. "What are you thinking about?"

"The obvious."

Roberto looked confused by Ava's cryptic words. "What do you mean? What's the obvious? What am I missing?" he asked, wiping his mouth.

Ava smiled knowingly. "Isabella has always been a difficult woman. At this point there's nothing anyone can do, Roberto." She stood and began preparing a second sandwich.

"But what happens in the meantime? Does Marco just let

Angela get away and live the rest of his life regretting his stubbornness?"

Ava smiled at her son's deep concern for his brother. "Marco is a grown man with a good head on his shoulders. I'm sure, given time, he will open up to Ms. Lord and see Isabella as she truly is," she said, purposely holding her tongue. "Be patient, Roberto, time will tell."

Roberto grabbed a handful of chips as the discussion lapsed to more upbeat conversation of his time spent with Angela Lord. Still, Ava pondered Isabella's fervent interest in her oldest son.

She was well aquatinted with Isabella's overzealous motivations. She remembered the challenges she faced when she and Arturo began their relationship. Apparently Isabella and several of her close friends decided that she was not worthy of a man as wealthy and powerful as Arturo Santos. They did everything in their power to keep them apart, including lies, deceit and every manner of deception imaginable.

Ava finished preparing a second and third sandwich and placed it in front of Roberto. He took a huge bite of his sandwich as Ava pulled two sodas from the refrigerator. She placed one in front of Roberto and sat down to drink the other. "I know my son—Marco will certainly come to his senses in time. And if Angela is half the woman you say she is, she won't want to pass up a good thing."

The telephone began to ring. Ava excused herself as Roberto picked up the remote control and found a soccer match to watch with his third sandwich.

Ava took the call in her office. It was an associate, Jasper Hall, a private investigator she used fairly often when she was unsure about the credentials of a particular client. He faxed over several documents that justified her hunch regarding a potential client.

"Jasper, I have another job for you," she began. "This one is personal. I'd like a full workup on an Angela Lord out of D.C." The laughter from the other end of the line caused her to grimace. "Something funny?" she queried with guarded annoyance.

"If I weren't a scrupled man, I'd take this job, no questions asked," Jasper began.

"Are you refusing the job?"

"Hold on now, as I was saying if I weren't scrupled man, I'd take the job and collect a fat check from both of you."

Ava instantly understood. "Arturo?"

"You know I don't discuss my other clients, Ava."

"That's not what I heard." Jasper chuckled again. "When?" she asked.

"A few days ago."

"Do you have anything yet?"

"Nothing promising. Looks like I'll have to do a double report on this one."

"Thanks, Jasper, I'd appreciate that."

Ava hung up the phone just as Roberto walked into her office. "Hey, I'm starved, let's go to that little Italian restaurant on the corner. I feel like some pasta."

Ava smiled, shook her head then grabbed her purse and jacket. Moments later they walked arm-in-arm down the chilled streets of Manhattan in March, in search of food for Roberto.

"Buenas dias, Arturo," Isabella said as she was escorted into his veranda by his attentive housekeeper.

Arturo lowered his morning newspaper and looked up to the unannounced visitor. Still dressed in his satin paisley bathrobe, satin pants and satin slippers, he stood and gentlemanly greeted her with an innocent peck on each cheek. "Buenas dias, Isabella."

Anxiously, she looked around the open green of the perfectly manicured grounds atop the hilly residence. She was nervous. This was a huge risk. Arturo wasn't the average man. If he were, she'd have long ago bended him to her will and been his wife. But today's objective was different—she wasn't after Arturo, she wanted Marco.

Her immediate survival depended on having Arturo on her side. He had the parental influence she needed. This was her agenda and she'd come equipped with every means of persuasion in her vast arsenal. She'd even plead and beg if necessary. Anything to get Marco Santos back under her control.

"What brings you out to the island this early in the day?" Arturo asked as he motioned for her to have a seat across from him. She sat and slowly, seductively crossed her long legs, smiling seeing Arturo's brief glance.

The maid immediately appeared carrying a second cup. Poised to pour, she halted her movements, waiting for her employer's approval. Arturo waved his hand to Isabella. She nodded graciously. The coffee cup was filled and the maid disappeared as quickly and quietly as she'd come.

Isabella took a polite sip of the steaming hot liquid then dotted her full lips with the supplied napkin. "Arturo, I'm very concerned for Marco."

His brow rose at the mention of his eldest son. "How so?" He neatly folded his newspaper and set it aside, giving her his undivided attention. "I spoke to him earlier, he seems perfectly fine."

She uncharacteristically fidgeted in the chair. "I, uh, I wanted to warn you about a woman on the island. Her name is Angela Lord." She watched closely, seeing Arturo's expression never falter or vary. "This woman looks exactly like my Angelina."

Arturo waved his hands nonchalantly. "And your concern is that Marco might become troubled by her appearance if he saw her."

Isabella reached over and grasped Arturo's hand. "I fear he already has," she said sadly. "This woman's undue influence will hinder his healing process." An easilymanufactured tear began building in the corner of her overly made-up eye. "Arturo, I just don't know where to turn. I consider Marco as my son." At this Arturo's brow raised again; this time there was annoyance on his face.

"No need to concern yourself, Isabella. Marco is a grown

man, and I am certain he will make the right decision for himself." He finished his coffee and stood, dismissing her. "I am sorry you came all this way with your concern. But after this talk I encourage you to lay your worries to rest."

Isabella stood and eased closer to the handsome older gentleman. "Arturo," she cooed seductively while running her manicured finger down the collar of his robe. "You and I have . . ."

He grabbed her hand to stop its progress. "Isabella, we were a long time ago; we were teenagers. The time has long since past. Ava is my—"

"Ava isn't here," she interrupted. "I am."

He smiled at her persistence throughout the years. "On the contrary, Ava is always here"—he pressed his hand against his chest—"in my heart. She always was and always will be."

Isabella frowned her annoyance at his choice. "How can you still feel for her after what she's done to you and the boys?"

"What my wife has or hasn't done is none of your concern. And as for my grown sons, they have a mother when they want and need her. She's always been there for them and always will."

"How can you say that? What about Marco?"

"Marco is a grown man," Arturo repeated coolly.

Realizing her angst over losing everything, she calmed herself. "Arturo, I'm sorry. I didn't mean for things to get out of hand. I'm just concerned, as any mother would naturally be."

"I repeat, Marco is not your concern, nor are you his mother."

"But I am his mother-in-law," she said indignantly. "I have every right to be concerned."

Arturo began walking toward to the courtyard gate. "Isabella." She felt his cold, patronizing tone like a slap in the face. "I have already been briefed and am well aware of the situation regarding my son. Now, I suggest if you have further concerns you may feel free to take them directly to Marco."

"I have, but to no avail. I was hoping you'd have some measure of control over our son's questionable behavior before it becomes scandalous. As you are well aware, scandals of this sort can reflect unfavorably on the entire Santos family." She was certain that he understood her meaning. The last major scandal surrounding the Santos family involved another outsider: Ava.

"Of which you are not a member." His words were blunt and wrought with meaning. He guided her through the gate and closed it soundly. "One last thing, Isabella. Marco is not *our* son. He's my son. Mine and Ava's."

"Of course, I was only . . ."

Arturo smiled politely and nodded. "Buenas dias, Isabella. Have a safe trip back."

Isabella slammed the door of the waiting cab. She ordered the driver to return her to the ferry dock. Reviewing the conversation in her mind, she searched for any words she could use to her advantage when she confronted the next person on her list. She smiled behind the dark sunglasses; there was still one person left to confront. And that, she assured herself, would be a pleasure. After all she was her mother's daughter.

Chapter 18

Marco frowned critically. He knew there wasn't much he could do about it, but the openly lecherous stares from the men as they passed were getting on his last nerve.

He had to admit, she looked incredible. The bright yellow shorts and bikini top bra with matching loose-netted pullover caught everyone's eye. With her cap turned backwards, Angela strolled along letting her two school-girl braids bounce lightly atop her shoulders. Remarkably, she was completely unconcerned about anything except the desert wasteland spread out before her.

"I can't believe how different the southern part of Puerto Rico is from the north. Just the other day we were in the middle of a wet tropical rainforest; then we swam with luminous fish and now look at this." She motioned around the vast area. "We're in a virtual desert."

Marco smiled, seeing her change from sultry, sexy siren to wide-eyed innocent schoolgirl again. He realized that he loved witnessing the transformation. Most of all, he loved being the cause of her pleasure.

His thoughts instantly went to their swim in Eden, the underwater cave. He could still feel the heated force of their bodies as they made love behind nature's drape. The water had poured down as their two bodies connected over and over again until the pleasure poured from his body and they screamed in ecstasy. The scene played in his mind like an exotic rerun.

Sleep had eluded him the nights since. Her exotic eyes and throaty voice beckoned him through the veil of nightly fantasies. She had gotten to him. He spent numerous hours remembering the feel of her body beneath and above his. His heart pounded each time he remembered that moment. The moment they'd reached ecstasy was beyond anything he could have imagined. All he'd thought about was her body, the feel of it, the touch of it, the smell of it and the taste of it.

He craved more.

And each time he saw her he wanted her more desperately. During the day he fantasized about her, at night he dreamt of her. Other nights he lay awake while fantasies of her invaded his thoughts. The sleepless nights had begun to affect his performance at the club. He could see his focus slipping.

He tried to reach her the next morning after Vieques, even going as far as to knock on her hotel room door. But, she had already gone out. He phoned all day and into the evening but to no avail. Her sudden disappearance consumed him. Her unexplained absence had sent him into a tailspin of worried anguish. He even went as far as to check and make sure Roberto was still out of town. That was two days ago.

He called her room early this morning to have her finally answer as if nothing was wrong. He knew he had no right to an explanation of her absence, so he didn't even bother asking. But one thing was certain. He was not going to have her out of his sight again.

His persuasive argument finally convinced her to allow him to drive her to Ponce instead of renting a car or taking a guided tour.

He could not spend another moment without her.

The seaside city of Ponce and its surrounding provinces was magical. The quaint 19th-century buildings of neoclassical and art deco styling captured the ambience of a moment untouched by the hands of a clock. Gas lamps and horse-drawn carriages added to the whimsical promise of days long-devoured by the ravages of time and civilization.

Restored to perfection, Angela marveled at the care devoted to the charming wrought iron balconies that surrounded the upper floors of the buildings that lined the tiny cobblestone streets. This was an architect's dream. Everywhere she looked she saw exceptional examples of Puerto Rico's quaint antique mastery. All were proudly displayed in restored perfection. The authentic splendor of old Ponce mingled readily with the complexities of its modern forms.

They'd spent the day seeing one wondrous sight after another. Angela had the time of her life and Marco enjoyed her reaction to the many attractions.

The journey back to San Juan was just as fascinating. Brightly hued homes stood out against the sprawling backdrop of the Cordillera Central Mountains. Contrasting mountain peaks and deep valleys leapt sporadically across the landscape, adding the perception of volume and texture to the scenery.

Marco delighted in watching Angela's reactions as she viewed the marvels of his homeland. Ponce, with its hidden treasures, was the perfect outing. The scenery was always unbelievably breathtaking, the smells delightful and the sounds enchanting. Marco glanced at Angela seated in the passenger's seat of his jeep. She seemed to be in a dreamlike state of euphoria.

Their long, exhausting day together had been perfect. So, when Marco suggested dinner, she readily accepted although she couldn't imagine anything more perfect than her last two outings with him.

Excitedly she dressed, anticipating a wonderful evening ahead. She wanted this night to be special. She'd purchased a beautiful dress in Old San Juan and decided that this would be the perfect time to wear it.

She'd just completed the finishing touches on her elaborate hairstyle when she was startled by a knock at the door. She looked at her watch. "He's early." She stepped into her heels then hurried, half walking, half hopping, to the door.

She flung it open expecting to see Marco, but was pleasantly surprised. "Roberto," she sighed then hugged him in welcome.

He beamed happily and looked her over completely. "Angela, you look fabulous," he offered after a short wolf whistle and a brotherly peck on each cheek.

"How was your trip?" she asked as Roberto strolled in, admiring the colorful sarong wrapped dress that seemed to dance over her smooth curves.

"Great," he said, smiling as he watched her walk away.

"Good," she called out from the bathroom mirror with one earring dangling and the other prepared to.

"I stopped by to invite you to lunch tomorrow. There are a few architectural sights on the west coast that might interest you."

"Really." She peered out of the bathroom; her interest was definitely piqued. "That sounds great. I'd love to go."

"Great, I'll swing by around noon."

"Okay, that'll be perfect."

"How have you been enjoying our fair country while I've been away?"

"It's absolutely beautiful. I went to the rainforest and Mosquito Bay two nights ago and Ponce and the southern coast this morning and afternoon. Everything was just incredibly breathtaking. I wish I could stay longer."

"Why don't you?"

She smiled wishfully. "Can't, I check out in three more days."

"So check out of here and come stay with me for a few decades." Angela giggled and shook her head after he eyed her jokingly. "My intentions are strictly honorable, I assure you," Roberto promised with the Boy Scouts' three-finger pledge. "I'll be a perfect gentlemen, for the most part."

She pouted her lower lip. "That doesn't sound like much fun. And for future reference, I believe Boy Scouts hold up two fingers, not three."

"Why, Ms. Lord, if I didn't know any better, I'd say you were flirting with me." He stepped closer and gently rubbed her soft smooth cheek with the back of his fingers. "It's a good thing I know otherwise." Angela intertwined her arm through Roberto's and sisterly kissed his cheek.

"And what do you think you know, Roberto?"

"I know, dear Angela, that you and my brother are a perfect match—that is, as soon as he stops acting like a complete ass."

"A perfect match?" she pondered. "What makes you say that?"

"I'm psychic."

She laughed as she walked back into the bathroom. "I have to finish getting dressed, although I'm sure that as a psychic, you already knew that. Tell me, Great Roberto, what do you see in my future?" she called out as she chose a perfume bottle.

Roberto walked over to the terrace doors and looked out at the star-littered twilight sky. "I know you have a dinner date this evening," he said, raising his voice slightly to be heard.

She walked out of the bathroom and crossed the room to the nightstand. "Very good, I'm impressed. I do have a dinner engagement this evening." She picked up her purse and checked its contains then picked up and deposited her room key.

"With . . ." he began, then turned to see a man standing in the open door, ". . . Marco."

"Wow, you are psychic," she said softly as she caught his eye then turned around to see what he was staring at behind her.

"Not really," Roberto said as his brother stood glaring at him in the slightly open door.

The sudden tension in the room was unmistakable. Angela instantly remembered the first night she'd met the two brothers and the argument that ensued. She tossed her purse down on the bed and planted her hands on her hips. "If this is going to be a repeat of the club scene my first night, you can both leave here right now."

Marco smiled tightly as he stared at Roberto and entered the room. "I have no intention of repeating that performance. "Buenas tardes, Roberto."

"Good evening, Marco," Roberto said with a hint of humor in his roguish eyes.

Still staring at his brother, Marco continued the civil dialogue. "I did not know you were back on the island."

"I got back a few hours ago." Roberto nodded his approval of his brother's new appearance. "I like your new look. It's good to see the old Marco back."

Marco nodded, accepting the compliment. "I gather the trip was productive."

"Extremely. But that's business and this isn't the time nor place to discuss such matters."

"I agree. We will discuss your trip later," Marco said as he stepped into the room further. For the first time since entering he looked to Angela. He raked his eyes over her sheer florid attire. His breath caught in his throat. She looked like an angel with gossamer wings.

Roberto watched his brother's reaction upon seeing Angela. He chuckled to himself then continued. "I'm on my way to the café. But I thought I'd stop by to persuade Angela to join me for dinner."

"As you can see, brother, Angela already has plans for the evening. She will be dining with me," he said with his eyes still glued to Angela.

"So it seems," Roberto said with pleasure.

Angela spoke up for the first time since her stern warning. She picked up her discarded purse. "Why don't you join us for dinner, Roberto?"

At this Marco shifted his eyes to Roberto, daring him to accept. Roberto chuckled at Marco's stalled expression. Roberto knew he would decline, but letting Marco sweat for his answer was well worth the trip home.

"Maybe some other time."

"Shall we go?" Marco said, moving to hold the door open. He watched the delicate wispy material composing Angela's dress drift out of the door and down the empty hall.

As Roberto passed he leaned near his brother's ear. "Don't blow it this time," he warned as Marco scowled and closed the door.

Heads turned with eyes focused to watch the handsome couple walk across the lobby of the elegant hotel. Marco and Angela, on the other hand, paid little attention to the many admiring glances.

Roberto smiled as he watched the elegant couple exit the elevators in front of him and continue walking across the lobby. He paused, proud of his most recent accomplishment. Marco deserved happiness and he was sure that Angela would bring it to him in abundance. She was his perfect match in every way. At that moment Angela turned and winked her good-bye. Roberto smiled fondly and blew her a kiss.

As they approached the exit, Enrique suddenly appeared out of nowhere. "Señor Santos," he called out several times before finally gaining Marco's attention. "Good evening, señorita," he gushed happily. He turned to look up at Marco. Marco's coal eyes still blazed with heated anger at seeing Roberto in Angela's room. Enrique panicked, his words immediately stammered and he began in his usual nervous stutter. "I . . . I . . . I . . . I . . ."

"Buenas tardes, señor," Angela said sweetly then glared at Marco. She politely held her hand out for Enrique to shake. Instead, he took her hand, turned the palm downward and lowered his plump face to kiss her hand. Afterwards he smiled and sighed happily.

"Is there something you wanted, Enrique?" Marco firmly asked.

"No, no, no, no, I, I, I just wanted to see if there is anything you needed and, and, of course to welcome you back to your hotel." As soon as the words left his mouth, Enrique wanted to cut off his tongue for his stupidity. He'd just welcomed the man to his own hotel again.

"Thank you. As you can see, we are on our way out. I shall come by soon and we will talk at leisure. Buenas tardes." He grasped Angela's hand and the couple began to walk away.

"Si, si, si, of course at your leisure, Señor Santos." He bowed then rose up in time to watch them exit the lobby doors. He hurried to the exit and waved several times. "Buenas tardes to you, Señor Santos. Uh, uh, uh, and to you also, señorita." The couple got into his car and pulled away from the curb.

Quietly berating himself as he turned back to the automatically opened doors, Enrique snapped at the grinning doorman. "What are you smiling at? Straighten your tie, tuck your shirt in and stand up straight. This is the Paradise Island Hotel, not a barnyard." The doorman grinned wider as he adjusted his already perfect tie and shirt. He chuckled openly as he watched his uncle disappear back into the lobby, still mumbling to himself.

Isabella stared in disbelief. How could this be? It just wasn't possible. Her eyes must have deceived her. She'd known there was a close resemblance, but she wasn't prepared to see this vision. It was as if Angelina had stepped out from her grave just to mock her. An icy chill sent a cold shiver through her slight frame. Her body physically shook.

"Astounding, isn't it?" The deep familiar voice jarred her from her troubled wayward thoughts.

Isabella spun around, her eyes were still wide and wild with alarm. She looked as if she'd seen a ghost. Her skin had gone from ashen to pale white, her facial expression was that of sheer horror. She nervously patted her bleached-blond hair already cemented in place with a heavy coat of gooey hair spray. Her hands trembled uncontrollably as she tried desperately to compose herself. Roberto grinned openly at her reaction. It was apparent that she was visibly shaken by seeing Angela and Marco together.

"What are you doing here?" she quietly spat in anger.

He shrugged his shoulders easily then glanced down at his highly polished manicured nails. "I could say that since I own the joint I came to check out the profits but I guess that would be bragging. What do you think?" he stated as cocky as possible.

"Don't flaunt your wealth," she snapped, then as an after-thought added, "it's gauche."

"Oh thank you, mother," he mocked. "I do enjoy our little daily lessons on morality."

"I find your impertinence offensive. I shall speak to Arturo about teaching you proper manners when addressing a lady."

"Lady?" he asked while looking around the nearly emp-tied lobby.

She sucked her teeth, rolled her eyes and began walking away. Roberto followed. "I noticed that seeing Angela really knocked you for a loop."

"Your colloquialisms are so trite. I do not get 'knocked for loops.' "

"But mother . . ." he began. She stopped cold, turned and stared at him with daggers in her eyes. He smiled with boy-ish innocence and roguish spite.

"Don't you ever call me mother again."

Roberto looked genuinely hurt. "Does this mean that you no longer wish to be my mommy?"

"You are so much like Ava," she hissed through squinted slit eyes.

"Why, thank you. How kind of you to notice," Roberto gleefully acknowledged, choosing to accept the insulting words as an endearing compliment.

"I hate you," she spat.

"I'm touched that you care." He placed his hand over his heart.

"Diablo! You are the devil himself. I will not stand here a second longer and listen to your devious lies and malicious tongue."

"Bye," he quipped tartly.

Isabella, completely speechless with anger, rolled her angry eyes then marched through the doors. She bumped right into the still mumbling Enrique who bowed and babbled his sincere apologies.

Roberto followed with humor in his eyes. He watched as Isabella angrily pushed Enrique to the side, marched to her car and slammed the door. His laughter never eased.

"Enrique, my man," Roberto began as he draped his long arm around the husky man's thick shoulder. "Tell me, how's business?"

By the time the two walked to Roberto's car, Enrique had only managed to stutter out his pleasure on seeing Roberto again. The doorman shook his head trying desperately not to laugh at his uncle's comical antics.

Chapter 19

Angela stood waiting on the candlelit patio. The light, gentle breeze had picked up and dark clouds threatened the stilled peacefulness of the evening. She watched as the wind wrestled through the surrounding trees. The increasing breeze toyed with the chiffon material of her delicate dress. A storm was coming. Shivering, she marveled at the odd change in events. "Are you chilly?" Marco asked as he returned to her side.

"No, I'm fine," she said as she looked at the curio's crackling fire glowing warmly in the corner of the patio. The sweet rustic scent of charred wood wafted through the air. It had been the perfect evening.

"Rare books, antiques, restaurants, nightclubs, this incredible house. You must be extremely rich."

"I am. Does all this impress you?"

"No. Not really. It must be nice though."

"I don't think about it."

"How can you not?"

"Because I've always had it." The innocence of his remark touched her.

"You're very sweet sometimes."

"And other times?" he asked, tempting fate, knowing her response.

Angela smiled and looked away. "Other times, I could strangle you," she joked.

Marco laughed openly, rich and joyous.

He poured more wine into her glass then set the bottle down on the side table. "I believe you actually mean that."

"Just sometimes." An easy silence opened between them, giving them pause for reflection. Their turbulent relationship had certainly endured its share of peaks and valleys. She looked out into the dark night. He looked at her. "It's so beautiful here. Does your home have a name?"

"Si, Colina del Sauce."

"Sounds like something you'd pour over mashed potatoes."

Marco laughed loud and long as he pulled Angela into his arms. He would never grow weary of her unconventional American humor. He embraced her then kissed her forehead lovingly.

"Colina del Sauce," she repeated. "What does it mean?"

"Hill of the Willow, or Willow Hill."

Angela looked around the garden surrounded by dozens of age-old willow trees. "Are the trees indigenous to Puerto Rico?"

"My ancestor visited what is now your Savannah, Georgia. His betrothed immediately fell in love with the weeping trees. She cried and cried, begging that he give her one. He brought back one for every tear she shed. It is said that she never cried again."

"This place has such great stories. I love it here. Sometimes I forget this is just a short vacation from reality."

He reached over and turned her chin with his finger to face him. "Stay." Gently, he stroked the side of her face then traced her smiling lips with his finger.

"I wish I could," she uttered honestly. "But I can't. I have to leave in a few days."

"You can do whatever pleases you. Stay here with me."

A warm blush crossed her lips. "It's not that simple; I have responsibilities. I can't just do whatever. I have a life in D.C. I can't just walk away from that."

"And what about what you want?"

"Could you just give up your life here, your friends, your family, your responsibilities and just walk away from everything you know and love?"

"I will never leave Puerto Rico. Never."

"You should never say never."

"I will never leave Puerto Rico," he reiterated firmly.

"That sounds pretty definite."

"It is definite."

"But there are so many other places to live in this world. "

"I've never found any place else I've wanted to live except here in Puerto Rico."

"You need to get out more."

"I get out enough."

She smiled. "I would have guessed that you were a man who'd traveled the globe, seen and done it all."

"I lived in New York for a time when I was a child. But since nine years of age I have resided on this island. And this is where I intend to stay. Does that surprise you?"

"I'm not surprised by much."

"I'll have to remember that." He smiled broadly, his dark eyes sparkling with mischief in the candlelight.

Angela had to avert her eyes to refrain from literally jumping on the man's body. How could any one man look so good, smell so good and feel so good? He was just too perfect to be true. She turned away, back to the dark night. "Dinner was wonderful, but I thought we were having dinner at the club."

"Were you disappointed?"

As a distraction she turned to him. "No, not at all." She glanced away to the open patio doors that led back to the large living room. "Your home is incredible."

"Thank you."

She looked around the expanded patio and then out across the lush green lawn. "The foundation looks old, the late 17th century I'd guess?" she questioned.

"Somewhere around in there." He sipped from his glass.

"Every stone was brought here over a century ago from Spain.

"Tell me about it?" she asked, her eyes sparkling with interest.

"About what?"

"Your house, its history. It must have one of those tragic love stories linked to it."

Marco smiled and dramatically looked up at the wrought iron lined balconies and stone facade of the second floors. He lowered his voice to almost a whisper. "The original structure was built by a nobleman of Spanish aristocracy. His name was Aleandro Migel Santos."

"An ancestor?" He nodded, confirming her question.

"It was completed in 1789. He built it for his new bride, a French noblewoman. Their fathers had arranged their marriage at birth. It was a commonplace occurrence that went along with the exchange of money, land and dowries. Aleandro's bride was to arrive from France with her courtier and handmaidens. Somewhere along the way she fell in love with the chaperone and when they arrived here she refused to marry Aleandro so he killed her."

Angela stood there with her mouth agape. She couldn't believe her ears. "He killed her? Just like that, end of story? He didn't try to woo her or challenge the lover or anything? He just killed her?"

"Yes, he killed her."

"What kind of love story is that?"

"It's what you asked for, a tragic love story. I merely gave you what you requested."

"So none of that was true."

"Yes, some parts were true."

"Which parts?"

"I have an ancestor who was a conquistador. He became rich by clearing this land after aiding in the massacre of its original inhabitants. His grandson was the father of Aleandro Santos who married Genevieve LaFore, a French maiden who stayed after her mistress jilted Aleandro and left him for an-

other. The once bride-to-be, the French noblewoman, sailed
back to Paris with her new beau. Unfortunately she wasn't
aware that there was a revolution going on at the time. Upon
their return, the two were immediately arrested, tried for
treason then promptly introduced to Madame Guillotine."

"So Aleandro and Genevieve lived happily ever after,"
she sighed, pleased with the revised ending.

"Actually, there was a huge scandal. You see, all members
of the nobility were required to marry of their same stature.
Genevieve was not of the aristocracy. The blue bloods were
appalled. Some had already arranged for their daughters to
be introduced to him. Aleandro didn't care. He was in love.
So, his family and his world disowned him. The only thing he
had left was this home, the land it stood on and Genevieve.
As far as he was concerned he had it all."

"Don't tell me. He couldn't hack it without the cash so he
got rid of Genevieve and married a blue-blood to please his
father and the rest of the aristocracy."

"No, actually Aleandro's father and family finally realized that they were destined and relented. The family was reunited. Aleandro and Genevieve lived to well into their eighties.
They had twelve children and fifty-three grandchildren. And
somewhere down the line they had me."

Marco moved closer and removed the wineglass from her
hand. "He died of a broken heart just two weeks after she
passed. They are buried side-by-side out there." He pointed
into the darkness. After setting the glass down he turned
back to her. "Come." He held out his hand and walked her
back toward the living room. She followed wordlessly as a
tiny raindrop fell from the sky.

"Angela," he whispered, "I'm delighted you decided to dine
with me this evening." She smiled, afraid her voice would
betray her if she spoke. He admiringly gazed down the length
of her. "You look exquisite. Puerto Rico truly agrees with
you." He barely heard the whispered thank you before he
took her hand and led her through the living room doors.

Dimmed lights and soft jazz guitar music surrounded them,

welcomed them to the soft ambience of lit candles and gentle breezes.

"What kind of music is this?"

"I like to call it Caribbean jazz. Do you like it?"

"Yes, it's wonderful. Kind of sultry and soulful all at the same time. I've never heard anything so beautiful. Who's performing?"

"A local group."

"Do they record?"

"No."

"They should, they're wonderful."

"I'll make sure to let them know the next time I see them. Come, dance with me," he requested, pulling Angela into his arms. He wrapped his arms around her, caressing the swayed curve of her form, molding her against his body.

"I never would have figured you for a jazz man."

"Why not?"

"Well, the music at Club Santos is hardly Motown, R&B or jazz. I assumed you were more of an island-calypso style."

"I enjoy most types of music." Without thinking he began stroking the length of her back. The soft chiffon material of her dress felt like heaven.

He closed his eyes and floated on the fantasy. She fit so indescribably perfect, he wanted to make love to her right there in the living room. Suddenly, he stopped and took her hand.

"Where are we going?" she asked as Marco led her through the wide hall to the front foyer. He picked up her purse and his keys.

"I can take you back to the hotel tonight, but I would prefer otherwise. The choice is yours."

She took her purse and walked to the door. He followed, disappointed. She turned the brass knob and opened the door. The rain began. She stood watching the water stream from the darkened sky. She sensed the moment he walked up behind her. "I'm flattered, Marco, but we both know that this would never end well. You have your world and I have mine.

We've shared some wonderful moments together. Moments that I will never forget."

"I fantasize about you, about us, about our bodies together." His words were a whisper of longing. He rubbed his hands slowly down her bare arms, stroking the tender points that made her stomach tremble with need. He knew her body too well, and he knew where to touch her and how to touch her. "I want to feel you beneath me again, and above me again. I want to hear my name on your lips when we reach our moment of pleasure. I want see the passion burn in your eyes and feel the heat of my touch. I want to touch you, Angela, like we touched in Eden." His words seeped through her and pierced her heart. The need of his desire matched the ache inside her.

Words could never express the feelings she had for him, so without uttering a sound, she answered him. The fullness of her feelings and the passion of the desire in her eyes said it all. Her heart thundered in her chest as she knew that this was what she wanted. She reached out to him and he was there to catch her.

In an instant she was swept up into his arms, embraced by his love, and being carried up the stairs to their destiny. The boldness of his actions drew a slight gasp of delight at the feel of his arms wrapped around her body. She grasped him tighter, reveling in the gentle strength of his caress.

As the world slipped slowly away and only the feel of their bodies together surged forward, she relaxed back in his arms. She touched his face gently, feeling the heat that penetrated his smooth skin. This was what she wanted. He was what she wanted. Gently, she ringed his soft full lips with her finger, enticing what she knew would come next. Then, she felt him gently pull her closer, lovingly and wholeheartedly obliging her desire.

With kisses as gentle and tender as the love they shared, he filled her fully with promises of more to come. Their lips mated as she wrapped her arms around his neck and pulled him closer. How could she ever have enough of this man?

The slow steady movement of his body as he carried her felt like heaven. When he had reached the second floor he went to the nearest bedroom.

When his tender lips left her mouth and found the sweetness of her neck, she leaned her head back giving him all he demanded. He buried his face in the arch of her neck and found his treasure. She moaned. He surged forward as the swell of her breath bade him to her chest.

Her body quivered in his arms.

Clothes were disbursed along the length of the room. When they reached his bed she fell across its length. Panting, groping, pulling, grasping, tugging at the remainder of the obstacles to their goal until they lay together, all hindrances gone.

The crazed hands ceased, replaced by sure fingers of steadfast diligence. They had reached the base of the mountain. Patience was needed to reach the apex of their desire. Slowly, gently he caressed her, cherishing every inch of her adored body.

Marco pulled a plastic package from the dresser drawer and handed it to her. She immediately tore it open and fit the condom snugly over his swollen passion. He gasped, the feel of her sure fingers sent a blaze scorching through him.

Then he ascended and they climbed in unison. The swell of desire engulfed them. Higher and higher, harder and harder their bodies forged, reaching peaks of pleasure previously unknown. They made love—slow, sensuous, mind-blowing, passion-forging, and torturous love.

The end was a climax of unimaginable force. Driven by the power of passion they soared on the crest all the way to top then spiraled downward in gasps of breathless wonder and spasms of sated joy. Rocked by love he poured his essence into her, filling a void of long-overdue love.

Hours later, Angela awoke to the sound of clashing thunder. The storm had returned. She sat up and looked around the darkened room, confused by the unfamiliar surroundings. Smiling, she eased back down, remembering where she was. She reached out to feel Marco's warm body beside her. She was alone. She sat up. Marco was nowhere in sight as the silent lightning flashed into the room.

Angela climbed from the bed and grabbed the black silk robe lying on the thick-carpeted floor. She felt at the sides for the sash and found it tucked in each side pocket along with several unopened condoms. She smiled and placed them back in the pocket then pulled the robe together and secured it.

She opened the door and peered out into the hall. It was shrouded in darkness. The whole house was in complete darkness. The storm had knocked out the electricity. As she cautiously stepped into the hall, she noticed a glow coming from an open door at the end of the hall. She slowly made her way down through the darkness toward the glow of light a few yards away.

She pushed the door completely open and peeked inside. The room was filled with the glow of candles. On the night stand, on the mantel in the fireplace, on the floor, everywhere candles flickered beneath clear glass hurricane covers. The soft glow illuminated her surroundings. She looked around; it was the most beautiful room she'd ever seen. This was straight out of a dream. She instantly knew that this was Marco's bedroom.

An ornate four-poster bed sat adrift on a sea of plush, deep blue carpet. Thin, silky, gossamer sheer netting was loosely draped above the tall posts then cascaded down into generous puddles at the head and foot of the large bed. The same sheer material blew uncontrollably into the room from the opposite wall. They seemed to beckon her through the twin doors and out onto the terrace. Gingerly she walked through the room, moving slowly toward the open doors.

The cool terra cotta floor tiles chilled her bare feet as she stepped onto the terrace. Squinting against the darkness she made out the figure of a man by the rail. Marco. He had his back to the terrace door, his head was down and his hands held the wrought iron railing tightly. His bare back glistened in the shadow of the candles inside the bedroom. He wore only black silk pajama bottoms; his feet were bare.

Angela walked up behind him and reached for him, but drew back, afraid that if she touched him there would be no turning back. She reached again, this time for the back of his head and felt the soft curls just above his neck. He did not move. She slowly ran her nails down his neck and onto his back. There she rested her face and gently kissed his smooth surface. She heard the sounds of the distant storm mingling with his low moan of pleasure.

"Angela," he said, his voice slow, deep and husky. She continued to drag her fingernails down his back, then around his waist and up to his chest. Slowly, gently she encircled his nipples as a gasp escaped his lips and a smile of power graced hers. She could feel the strength and control wailing inside of him. His breathing was sporadic and desperate.

"Angela . . ." he rasped again. She slid her hands down to the satiny-corded drawstring of his pajamas. Pulling, the cord gave way to a puddle of satin at his feet. She smiled, delighted with her find. Tiny silken curls brushed against her fingers as she grasped him in her hands, feeling his instant response.

The pleasure she had felt with him gave her boldness to stroke him now. Reaching, feeling, stroking, she felt the tremors of need rage through him. His heart pounded like the thunder above. Not yet satisfied, she decided that she wanted more. She kissed his back then raked her teeth, sending love bites to his heart. Then she kissed him again, slowly letting her tongue taste the pleasure of his skin. She slipped her hand away and reached into the pocket, pulling out a condom packet. She tore it open then began fitting it over him. He tensed. A giddy delight of power surged through her as he gasped then moaned his arousal. He grabbed her wrists before she could continue her torturous strokes.

He turned his face to his shoulder. "In your hands is the power to destroy me. Decide now, me or Roberto, stay or leave," he said. She opened the satin robe and pulled herself closer, molding her naked body against his. She bit him again, then let her tongue soothe the sting of his pleasure.

"Marco," she said, her voice huskier than she'd ever heard it, "I want to be with you. Only you, for as long as I can." In an instant Marco turned around, his eyes flooded with passion and desire. The storm had arrived. Thunder rumbled overhead as Marco grabbed her and held her tight. She couldn't move, even if she wanted to. The vice grip of his hands sent a shiver of passion through her.

The rain began to come all at once, fierce and hard. There was a flash of lightning and Angela found herself, in an instant, breathless and panting, on the cushioned chaise longue beneath Marco. His movement was so quick and strong she was dazed by the sudden turn of events.

He lifted her leg to his shoulder and embraced the sensitive feel of her skin. She writhed as his head dipped to her breast and suckled the begging nipple to pebble to its fullness. He moved lower, sending a quiver of lust as his lips kissed the flat of her stomach and eased to her hip.

She gasped as his hand found her treasure and his tongue tasted the richness of her body. A sudden flash of blinding light surrounded her as she arched back and anticipated the inevitable. She screamed with pleasure as he reached down to feel the moisture of her readiness for him.

Then, in one smooth surge, he entered her. She gasped loudly at the expected. He filled her completely, sending a bolt of pleasure straight to her heart.

His lovemaking was just as strong and fierce as the raging storm around them. He was wild and relentless in his power and passion. Untamed lust was matched only by the thunderous storm above them as passion exploded within time after time after time.

Angela had never before felt such complete ecstasy. The rhythm of his body rose and fell to the beat of their pounding hearts. Her nails dug deep into his skin as she pulled and held him tighter. There was no stopping, no turning back. Their soaring climax came as a burst of lightning lit up the sky. The poetic balance and rhythm of nature sent her soaring higher. She saw the strain of rapture on his face. Never before had anyone made her feel so desired, so filled, so completely loved. Marco collapsed. He lay still, spent and breathless.

"Angela," he whispered as he rolled over, taking her with him..

"Shhh . . . don't," she said, her eyes closed tightly, still bathed in the warmth of his passion.

"Angela, I love you," he said.

"Don't," she repeated.

Marco rose up and brought her with him. He took her into the bedroom and laid her on his bed, gently, softly, careful as not to disturb the muted candles still aglow. The soft new lighting inside made their passion swell again. This time slow and patient, they loved. He teased her body with his tongue, sampling every inch of her. She sighed and half moaned each time he caressed the inside of her thighs. By hour's end, he knew all there was to know about her body and used his new-found knowledge to bring her to heights of ecstasy she had never before experienced.

Several times he held her, restraining her attempts to end her torturer's passion. Angela begged for Marco to come inside of her. Each time he ignored her, instead delighting in the rapture of her wanton pleasure. Then finally he lay back and rolled her on to him. He reached over and grabbed a condom from the nightstand. She took it and smiled. She was in control now.

She wrapped him safely then impaled herself as Marco smiled up at her, delighted by her urgency. She began to move, slowly at first, back and forth, then faster and faster. Answering her body, he sat up with his hands coupling her breasts as his mouth consumed her. She raised and lowered her body quicker and quicker. Marco held her waist and slowed the rhythm down, prolonging the moment of pleasure. Again their passion climaxed with their cries drowned out only by the passing thunderclouds above. She fell against him and he held her, lying back down until the next time they would delight in each other's desire.

They made love again before the night was through. Each time was more passionate than the last. By morning's break the storm had passed and the lovers awoke in each other's arms, still reeling from the night of lovemaking. The candles had long since extinguished themselves, leaving hardened puddles of spent wax as the only evidence of the night before. The sky was clear and seemingly untouched by the power of the heavens that had raged just hours earlier. The world felt new and fresh. All was well.

Marco was the first to move; gently he kissed Angela's eyes to awaken her. She moved slightly as he pulled her body closer to his side. "Good morning." He kissed her forehead, nuzzling her wayward hair.

She smiled and groaned enticingly. "Buenas dias."

"Thank you . . . for staying."

"You're welcome." She reached out to him and caressed his chest, feeling the power of his strength.

"How long will it take you to pack and move in?"

She stopped. "What?" she asked, as the dizzying haze of sleep and lust vanished. He repeated the question while stroking her arm resting across his chest. "I'd rather stay at the hotel until my vacation's over," Angela replied.

Marco laughed and kissed her hand. "I was referring to your permanent move to the island. How long will it take? A few weeks? A month?"

She sat up. "My permanent move?"

"Of course permanently." He sat up and kissed her bare shoulder. "You'll never regret this, Angela; I'll give you any and everything your heart desires."

"Marco." She turned to him. "I can't move here permanently. I have a life in the States. I just can't up and leave like that."

"So last night meant nothing to you?"

"Of course it did. Last night was unbelievable. It was beyond anything I could have ever fantasized. You were wonderful. I'll always cherish our time together. You are very special to me."

He looked into her eyes. "As a footnote to your vacation."

"It's not like that. You know how I feel about you."

He turned to her. "No, I don't. Tell me, Angela, how do you feel about me?"

"Why are you being like this? You knew I had to leave sometime. We talked about this. I have responsibilities."

"You made a choice last night, remember? Roberto or me, stay or leave. You chose stay."

"Wait a minute. You're saying that because I stayed with you last night I can't be friends with Roberto and I have to move here?"

"Precisely."

"That's ridiculous."

"I don't understand your confusion. You have me, you have no further need of Roberto."

"I consider him a friend; what about friendship?"

"Is that what you call it?"

"Are you implying otherwise?" she warned.

Locked in a heated debate, they were stalemated as they stared at each other. The discussion had reached a critical point. A single statement from either could shatter the delicate thread they walked.

"You chose to stay," he reiterated.

"For the night, yes. Not for a lifetime." Those few words seemed to mortally wound him. She could see it in his eyes and feel it in her heart.

He stood and paused just long enough for Angela to see into his dark, smoldering eyes. She knew that look. He was angry and hurt. It was the same look that had stared back at her many times in her own reflection.

He spoke so softly she could barely hear. "Get dressed. I will see that you get back to your hotel safely." He turned and left the room.

By the time Angela showered and dressed Marco was no-where in sight. Carlos was waiting outside with instructions to take her back to the hotel. As he drove away, she took one last look at the huge white stucco home. She vowed to remember every square inch. She wanted the image of last night branded on her mind eternally. This was where she'd lost the man of her dreams.

Marco looked out from the side window as the car turned to drive away. His heart broke as he watched her turn one last time to him. He knew she couldn't see him, but still his heart opened up to her. She was everything he had ever desired and still she left him. For Roberto, for home, it didn't matter. The only thing that mattered now was that she was gone and he was alone in his pain again.

He willed the car to stop, just as he willed the plane to stop when his mother left. But it continued, just as the plane did several decades ago.

Chapter 20

Later that afternoon Marco angrily drove to the dock to catch a ferry to Vieques Island for the second time in four days. The overcast sky and troubled currents matched his restless mood. Over and over again he replayed that night in his mind. Angela had chosen to leave him just as his mother had.

Arturo met him at the dock; a proud smile and warm hug was his greeting. They didn't speak right away, only stood looking at each other. Arturo could see his son's pain and guessed at the cause. His son had been headstrong and blinded for years. It was time to bring it to an end. They walked to his father's car and drove in silence to his home; there they would talk.

"I've been expecting you," Arturo began, as he turned off the engine and got out of the car.

Marco, knowing never to underestimate his father's intuition, smiled. This man had traveled the world, was a member of the political reform, had his finger on the pulse of everything going on, not only in Puerto Rico, but the States and the world. And yet he still knew to expect him.

"Tell me about Angela Lord."

"There's nothing to tell."

They walked in silence. Arturo waited patiently for Marco to tell him about Angela. Marco looked over at his father. No one was more patient than Arturo Santos. Marco deliberated for a moment then asked, "What do you want to know?"

"Anything you wish to tell me."

"She's stubborn, argumentative, flippant, selfish, head-strong." He shook his head. "Beautiful, intelligent, vivacious, and confident." Marco looked at his father's grinning expression. "What?"

"You're smiling," Arturo said, studying his son's face. Marco tilted his head, lacking understanding. "I'm delighted to see that now you so relish all of these unique qualities in your woman."

Marco studied his father's words carefully. Arturo was correct, as usual. Never had Marco been attracted to a woman such as Angela. The women with whom he associated were all quiet, demure and subservient. Angela was different, very different. She was bold, poised and impossible to forget. The very memory of her had put a smile on his face.

They walked into the living room; Marco looked around. A delicate perfumed scent captured his senses. "You have company, Poppy?" he asked.

"Company? No, not really." Arturo smiled. "It is her home as well as mine."

"Who?" Marco frowned, then widened his eyes in understanding. "Mother? She's here?"

"Si. Of course, who else? What other woman would ever be so wholly welcome in this house?" Arturo continued across the living room through to the open patio doors. Marco followed.

"I knew Roberto saw her from time to time, but I had no idea that you . . . When did all of this happen?" he questioned, staring at his father in disbelief.

Arturo smiled. "She is my wife. Why wouldn't I see her? We have always been together." He watched a pack of wild horses gallop freely across the sandy beach.

"But you're divorced."

"No. You have always assumed we were divorced because

we did not live together as conventional man and wife. I assure you we are very married."

"You never told me."

"You never asked."

"But you never spoke of her. Ever."

"That was your choice, not mine. She is my wife. The
mother of my children and the woman I shall always love and
cherish."

Marco looked around anxiously. "Where is she?"

Arturo smiled and looked out across the sandy beach. A
slight figure covered by a large straw hat strolled barefoot along
the waterline. Arturo waved; she returned his gesture then
continued across the dunes away from the house. "Would
you like to meet her again?"

Marco turned his back and walked back into the living
room without answering.

Arturo stood and watched Ava disappear into the distance.
Then he walked back into the living room and found Marco
sitting at the dining room table with a drink his hand. "A tad
early for libations isn't it?"

"You never said a word."

"You are still so angry. Why? Your mother did not desert
you."

"No, she deserted you. She deserted us."

"No, Marco, it was I who deserted her." Marco looked at
his father oddly. "Let me tell you a story. A young man saw
a woman, a tourist on holiday, sitting in a café sipping morning coffee. This woman was the most beautiful vision he'd
ever seen." Arturo smiled at the fond memory. "He instantly
fell in love. Unfortunately, she didn't feel the same way.

"As a matter of fact she regarded him as arrogant, proud
and bigheaded, I believe she said." He smiled and chuckled.
"So, undaunted, this young man set out to woo her heart and
her affection. He threw his money and connections and everything he had at her feet, but she turned him away. He tried
everything to capture her heart. But to no avail. She would
still have no part of him."

Marco looked at his father with more interest. "What happened then?"

"Well, then he decided to come down off of his lofty money and his position and his family name and just be a man in love. She opened her arms and heart to him." Arturo looked outside and smiled. "He never regretted a single day since."

"You forgot the ending." Arturo looked at his son questioningly. "You forgot that still she left you. After all of that and still she left us."

"No, my son, your mother did not leave us. We deserted her."

"What?"

"Things were very different then than they are now. I was very different. I could not see my way into a new life. I could not live in her world and those in my world refused to accept her. So we parted. But never in our hearts. There, she is always, just as the first moment I saw her in the café."

The phone rang several times as Marco tried to comprehend Arturo's words. "Pridefully, I refused to live anywhere other than here. It was I who left her."

"Señor Santos." Arturo turned to his housekeeper. "El telephone," she said, offering him the cordless phone.

Knowing that it had to be important or a message would have been taken, Arturo took the phone and listened as Roberto spoke. A few seconds later he handed Marco the phone.

"Yes?" Marco questioned.

"Where is she, Marco?" Roberto demanded.

"What are you talking about, Roberto?"

"You know damn well what I'm talking about. Angela, where is she? We were supposed to meet. Her bags are still in the room but no one has seen her since last night. You were the last one with her."

"I no longer concern myself with Señorita Lord's whereabouts." He hung up.

"May I join you?" Both men turned. Ava walked into the dining room and removed the large brim hat from her head.

Arturo immediately stood and took his wife's hand. He kissed each hand in turn then both of her cheeks.

"Welcome, my dear." He wrapped his arm around her slim waist and pulled her tightly. Marco stood slowly. His black eyes glistened with threatened moisture. Then, just as quickly, he turned his back.

Ava smiled sadly, feeling the hurt that still consumed her son. The heavy clouds surrounding his heart would remain for now. She longed to open her arms to him, welcoming him back into her heart. He would come, of that she was certain. He would one day embrace the woman he'd spent a lifetime trying to forget.

Arturo tensed then moved to confront Marco. Ava placed her delicate hand on his arm. Arturo halted immediately. With great pain he stood to the side watching the love of his life and their eldest son. He lowered his eyes in regret. Had he not left, this would have never come to pass.

Arturo kissed her hand and she walked through the living room then up the stairs. Marco looked up and watched her go. He took a single step then stopped. Arturo nodded and smiled. *Soon.*

As soon as Carlos dropped her at the front entrance of the hotel, Angela went directly to her room. Angrily she stomped through the hotel room, grabbing, throwing and snatching up everything in her sight. She was furious. It seemed she'd been furious most of the trip. Ever since she'd first laid eyes on Marco, she spent most of her days and nights dreaming of him in one way or another. She grabbed her beach bag and stormed to the door not noticing the phone's blinking light.

Flinging the door open, she gasped in surprise. On the other side a woman stood with her fist raised high in preparation to knock. At Angela's sudden appearance, she also gasped. The woman slowly lowered her hand and just stood there staring at Angela.

"May I help you?" Angela asked as she remained with her hand on the doorknob and her beach bag slung over her shoulder. The woman smiled haughtily and, without invitation, sauntered into the room.

As she passed, Angela sized her up. The confidence she exhumed by simply strolling into a room gave her the air of money. She smelled of expensive perfume—crisp, light and delicately floral. Angela recognized the scent as one she'd worn on rare occasions. It was expensive, as were her slick designer suit and strappy Prada sandals with matching purse. The woman stood in the center of the room and nosily scanned the area. "May I help you?" Angela repeated louder.

The woman made a humorous *humph* sound then turned her back to look out of the terrace door. Angela recognized the approach before, having spent many years with foster parents who had performed the same floor show. The woman wanted to make a statement. She wanted to show power and control. She was out to intimidate her.

"I'll be out for a few hours. That should give you enough time to thoroughly clean the room. And don't forget to wash behind the commode," Angela said smartly.

The woman immediately turned to Angela and glared angrily. "I beg your pardon?" she huffed indignantly as her overabundance of gaudy expensive jewelry clinked and chimed in added response. Her awkwardly stretched skin remained an angry grimace.

Angela looked more closely at the woman's face. The thick layer of makeup did little to conceal the age lines deeply embedded there and the tight stress pulls of a recent lift. Once, she might have been attractive, Angela assessed. Yet years of sun-seared skin had left her looking taut and leathery.

"You *are* with housekeeping, right?" Angela asked innocently.

"I most certainly am not," the woman snapped, completely insulted by her reference to the humble position. She reached up and smoothed the bleached-blond, lacquered French twist she managed to coif atop her head. "I am Señora Rivera and you are Angela Lord." Isabella moved toward Angela and looked at her closer, eyeing her critically.

Angela raised a brow. "Have we met?"

The older woman smiled. "Not officially, not that you'd remember." Her eyes bored into Angela. Every inch of her face had been scrutinized and dissected.

"You must be Isabella." Angela smirked, realizing this was Angelina's mother. The woman who had literally driven her daughter to suicide. "Well, Isabella, as I'm sure you realized, I was on my way out when you arrived. So, if you don't mind getting to the point."

"I'll thank you to refer to me as Señora Rivera. And to answer your question, there is no point, as you say, Señorita Lord. I just wanted to see you up close and meet you face to face, woman to woman," she drawled out.

Angela understood immediately. The other woman was there to size her up. "Why?"

"Marco Santos is a very, very cherished friend of mine. He is my son-in-law and I love him dearly."

"And this means what to me?" Angela said impatiently.

"I understand the two of you have been spending time together recently. I wanted to see what was so distracting," Isabella said, raising her nose in disgust. She looked Angela up and down. "I don't see what all the fuss is about."

Angela walked to the door and held it open, indicating the end of their brief meeting. "In that case you wouldn't mind leaving."

"You do realize that he is well out of your league."

"Excuse me?"

"Marco is a Santos; he is descended from royalty, monarchs, kings. He is a leader of men. His lineage dates back centuries, even to the beginning of this land. Yet he stoops to wallow on your level. What is your lineage?"

Angela refused to let this woman hurt her with her bigotry and prejudice. "Marco is a man—that's it, that's all. He's not a king, nor a demigod or anything else you seem to make him out to be. He is a man, a grown man with his own mind.

He can decide for himself what and who he wants." Of that she could firmly attest having just spent the evening and night in his bed and in his arms; he was definitely a man.

"You are correct in that, Señorita Lord. Marco is a man, and as a man, he has needs, physical needs. That's where you come in. Do you actually think that you're the only woman to come to this island and garner his momentary attention?" Isabella laughed. "You're not. You are merely a passing amusement. He has no feelings for you other than lust." Her nose rose higher, detesting the thought of Angela and Marco together.

Angela smiled. Her knowing expression sent a chill through Isabella. "What Marco and I have or don't have is none of your business."

Isabella slowly walked to the door. She puckered the bright red lips and swiped at her golden locks again. When she came face-to-face with Angela in the doorway she smiled triumphantly. "You are so much like your mother."

Angela frowned in surprise. "What did you say?"

Isabella smiled broader and continued down the hall.

Angela hurried after her and stood in front of her. "What did you just say?"

"You heard me."

"What do you know about my mother?"

Isabella threw her head back in a cackling laugh and continued walking toward the elevator.

Angela just stood and watched her go this time. The woman obviously had no idea what she was talking about. How could she possibly know her mother? She didn't even know who she was. Angela hurried back to her room and grabbed her key and closed the door still thinking about what Isabella had said.

As soon as she closed the door she heard the phone ring. She considered answering for a few seconds then decided she'd had enough strangeness for one day. First Marco and then Isabella. All she wanted to do was forget about the whole morning.

* * *

Rita frowned and placed the phone back on the receiver. Excitedly, she'd been calling Angela since late last night. She had news, and was sure Angela would be interested.

Too excited to concentrate on her usual duties, Rita stood and walked out of her small office. She stood at the threshold, leaned against the heavy iron gates and watched as life continued outside. It was a beautiful day. Much too nice to be inside a musty old building digging through old files.

She watched happily as older children played ball in the small park across the street and busy workers rushed aimlessly from place to place. A bevy of giddy tourists snapped hundreds of photos for keepsake memories that they'd look at once and forever put away in dusty old albums.

A flood of memories overwhelmed her seeing a crying child being dragged along by a distracted parent. A feeling of sadness darkened her calm features. The world could be cruel, especially to children.

She walked back to her desk and looked down at the folder Angela had given her. She picked it up and leafed through it for the hundredth time since she found the clue last night. This was too obvious, she tried to assure herself. But each time she thought about it she came up with the same conclusion. And that could only mean one thing.

She picked up the newspaper spread across her messy desk. It was dated 1970. She opened it to the society page. There, smiling back at her in black and white, might be the answer to Angela's questions.

Rita smiled as she turned back to the cover page. The entire newspaper was dedicated to the island's carnival celebration, the marriage of Arturo and Ava Santos. Rita reread the lead articles. The more she read the more excited she got. This was definitely of interest. She had to find Angela. She picked up her purse, locked her office and the outside gate then climbed into her car, heading to Angela's hotel.

* * *

Luquillo Beach was packed, but Angela didn't care. She needed to relax and a swim in the sea was the perfect distraction. After dropping her towel she dove into the warm Caribbean waters. She swam far out into the serene blue. The solitude was a blessing.

Isabella stood hidden just beyond the grouping of tall, fanlike palm trees. She'd followed Angela to the beach and now stood watching as she dashed into the water and began swimming. Hate filled her cruel eyes. Hate for a woman she'd met only once before. Hate for a plan failing miserably and hate for a youth she no longer possessed.

Without a second thought, she waved her bright red scarf in the air then let it fall. It was out of her hands now. She would leave Angela's life up to fate a second time. She crossed herself faithfully, replaced her dark sunglasses and headed back to the car.

Prone and in position, the two young men lay on their sailboards discussing their good fortune. "Look," the one said to his partner. Both looked toward the sandy beach less than a quarter of a mile away. A blood red scarf gently waved in the breeze just beyond the trees.

Moments later they maneuvered their rigs into the wind to catch the slight breeze. Their brightly colored sails skimmed the surface of the calm blue water with relative ease. Their speed and agility increased as their taut, slim bodies leaned into the flow of the prevailing breeze. Windsurfing: the best of both worlds, sailing and surfing. It required technique and skill for beginners. Most who advanced in the sport chose the funboard, finding windsurfing less tame in medium and high winds.

Today's wind was perfect. The two maneuvered their sailboards through the throng of the seafaring tourists. Nearing their target they heard the faint sound of a blowing whistle, warning them of their trespassing status. Ignoring the slight annoyance they continued. Swimmers hurriedly dove away from the speeding boards, some yelled obscenities, others swam desperately for the safety of the shore.

Out on the water Angela drifted; afloat on the calmness she began feeling better. She closed her eyes against the bright afternoon sun. When she opened them moments later a mirage appeared and was come directly for her. She dove below the surface a split second later. Torpedoed. The brightly colored gossamer sails were the last things she saw before going under.

A loud piercing whistle blew repeatedly as the lifeguards ran across the packed beach and dashed into the water. A crowd gathered on the wet sand and watched as the windsurfers who'd seemingly lost control of their rigs continued to sail off.

Moments later the lifeguards pumped her chest with force as the sound of the approaching ambulance whirled in the distance. The young lifeguard stopped, listened at her mouth, then continued the lifesaving technique. The two other lifeguards worked feverishly as concern etched their young faces. The gash on her forehead continued to bleed through the makeshift padded gauze dressing.

Fifteen minutes later the ambulance's whirling siren silenced as it barreled through the gates of St. Nicholas Memorial Community Hospital. The staff awaited anxiously for its arrival.

"Damn!" Roberto cussed, causing Enrique to jump a few inches more.

"Señor, I am certain Señorita Lord is just out on tours. There are several leaving for Ponce every morning. I'm sure we will find that she was on one of them."

Roberto looked at him with impatience. "No one has seen her since she left the hotel last night with your brother," Enrique said. "She's not the kind of woman one easily overlooks."

Roberto stood and walked to the office door. "Call me as soon as she returns."

"No, señor; I mean, si, señor, of course, as soon as Señorita

Lord returns, I shall phone you immediately." Enrique winced as the door slammed. Slowly he collapsed into his office chair and whipped his sweating forehead with the damp handkerchief.

Roberto headed for Angela's room once more. Maybe Enrique was right; maybe Angela had simply gone to Ponce or to one of the many tourist locations on the island. But in his heart he knew better. There was no way Angela would forget or dismiss their afternoon adventure without calling him. As he walked down the hall, he noticed that Angela's door was open. Relief washed over him as he hastened his steps.

"Angela," he called out. "Angela."

A member of the housekeeping staff appeared at the bathroom entrance. "Señor?" Roberto, visibly disappointed, shook his head never mind and backed out of the room. As he did he bumped into someone, completely knocking them down.

Rita, thoroughly surprised by the wall of masculinity standing above her, shook her head to clear her vision. This had to be a hallucination, she fathomed. Then, from the deep fog still shrouding her thoughts, thick masculine arms came out of nowhere and gently picked her up.

"Are you all right?"

She heard echoes through the thick haze of shock and disbelief. She was speechless. All she could do was stare at him as he carried her to the bed and lay her down.

"Get water," Roberto ordered to the startled, staring housekeeper standing behind them.

"Si, señor," she said and hurried to the bathroom for a glass. She returned with the water then quickly disappeared to her next room, closing the door firmly behind her.

"Are you all right?" Roberto repeated.

Rita nodded gingerly and eagerly accepted the offered water. After a few minutes her head began to clear. Her breathing slowed and steadied but, her heart rate increased after one look at the man leaning over her. She knew him instantly, Roberto Santos.

They'd been in some of the same classes together in school. He, of course never noticed her. He was popular, athletic and head of most of the Senior class committees. She, on the other hand was quiet, brainy and studious. Hence, they'd never actually met even though they attended the same schools for almost twelve years.

Roberto stared at her curiously. "Don't I know you from somewhere?"

Uncertain of her trembling body, Rita mutely shook her head and tried to get up from the bed. Roberto laid his hand on her shoulder to calm and ease her back on the pillow. "Slow down," he assured her with a devilish smile. "I won't hurt you."

He stared as she gulped the rest of the water. When she finished it he took the glass from her chilled hands. Embarrassed by his touch she quickly grabbed her shoulder purse to her side and scrambled from the opposite side of the bed. "Pardon me," she began, "I was looking for a friend of mine. I must have the wrong room." She quickly rushed to the closed door. Then, realizing that Angela's folder had slipped from her open purse, she turned to look for it.

Roberto was already scanning the contents. He looked up at her as she slowly approached. "Where is she?" he asked with a tone of voice so menacing, it would have halted Hannibal's mighty forces.

Rita stopped. Her heart rate increased and her hands began to tremble and sweat even as her mouth went dry. Roberto stood and moved toward her. "Where's Angela?"

The timid knock on the door took his attention away from the computer on his desk. "Yes, yes, come in," he called out. Helena opened the door and stepped in. Enrique looked up. "What is it now, Helena? I'm busy." He frowned until he saw the lines of concern etched in her face.

"You wanted information about a guest, Angela Lord?"

"Si, si. What is it? Did you find something out?"

"I'm not sure. But there was an accident yesterday morning at Luquillo Beach. A tourist was badly hurt." Enrique stood slowly.

"What tourist?"

"I called the hospital, they still don't know who she is. She had no identification. But her description matches that of Angela Lord."

Enrique sat slowly. He was ash white. How was he going to tell both Marco and Roberto if this woman was truly Angela Lord?

"Get the hospital on the line," he ordered instantly.

"I already did; they're on line one." Enrique looked down at the red blinking light on his desk phone. He picked up the receiver and spoke to the woman on the other end. He nodded a few times then hung up.

He looked up, seeing Helena still standing in the doorway. She smiled and shifted her purse on her shoulder. "I'm on my way home for the evening, but I thought that you might like company going to the hospital."

Enrique smiled; sometimes his niece's caring, gentle ways were so much like his sister it brought a knot to his throat. "Yes," he said, "that would be very nice." He grabbed his jacket and together they hurried to her car.

Chapter 21

Roberto sat behind the Marco's desk. Something was going on; he was sure of it. He was disturbed by Angela's sudden disappearance and equally questioning of the timid figure in her hotel room. She'd said that she was a friend, yet Angela had mentioned that she knew no one on the island. He frowned with frustration. Her face was familiar. If he could place where he'd seen her, then maybe he could figure out what was happening.

Her elusive answers about having the folder with Angela's name on it were evasive and vague. Yet he was sure that if he had pressed further, she would have surely collapsed and fainted. But, he was by no means through.

Without a knock, the office door opened. Roberto looked up and glared at the woman calmly strolling into the room. "What are you smiling about?" he asked.

"Why wouldn't I?" She smiled even broader. "It's going to be a beautiful day outside," Isabella said, unable to contain the glee she felt after checking on the apparent fatal condition of the Jane Doe earlier. She looked around the office. "Where's your brother?"

Roberto looked at her suspiciously. "Why?"

"We have business to discuss. Personal business, nothing that concerns you."

"I doubt that, since we're business partners; whatever concerns Marco, concerns me."

"Not this time, junior." She puckered her shiny gloss-covered lips sparkled with ruby-red luscious radiance. "Oh, and I'd get used to being left in the dark if I were you," she said smugly as she ran her finger across the surface of the desk.

Interested, Roberto leaned back in the leather seat and chuckled, causing Isabella to frown. "So, you think you know something, huh?"

"I know that Marco has finally come to his senses. He wants me."

"For what?"

"What else?" she said slyly as she perched her bony hip on the desk and leaned her newly acquired breasts into his face. "You see, my darling Roberto"—she ran a long painted nail down his tensed jaw and across his full mouth—"your brother phoned me earlier and asked for me to meet him here today. He said that it was very important that I see him. He needs to ask me a question. A question he should have asked me years ago." She smiled at the thought. "I think he's finally come to his senses. He realizes that I'm what he's been searching for all along. Only I can satisfy him." She swung her long bare legs around and seductively laid them on the desk. "If you're a good little boy, maybe I'll offer you a few crumbs."

"My God, I knew it," he exclaimed in a whisper. "I knew it was bound to happen one day." She sat up seductively, smugly anticipating his conformation to her new status. "I just didn't expect it so soon." He paused. "You've lost your mind. You've gone stark raving mad." He began laughing then quickly roared until remnants of moisture appeared in his eyes. Isabella instantly hopped down from the desk.

"Laugh as you like while you can, Roberto; soon you will answer to me," she said confidently. "Angelina could never handle a man like Marco. He was too much for her poor delicate sensibilities."

"I don't believe you. You're actually serious aren't you? You actually believe that Marco wants you?"

"And why wouldn't he?" she stated indignantly.

"Aside from the fact that you're old enough to be our grandmother"—she gasped quietly at the insult as he continued—"the two of you have nothing remotely in common."

"We are the upper class," she stated proudly. "He is Santos; I am Rivera; that, in itself, is enough. Age is unimportant. Families such as ours are born to merge. But if you want more"—she smiled enticingly—"I am a very sensuous woman. Few can handle your brother properly."

Roberto's grin broadened. "And I suppose you feel that *you* can?"

"Imbecile. Of course I can. He is Santos. His body burns hot with Spanish blood, our blood. Every core of his being pulsates with our conquistador ancestors. We are of royal lineage, descended from cultures beyond your meager understanding. He is Santos." She raised her head higher, haughtier, prouder. "I am Rivera. We are one."

"Okay, that was way over the top, even for you."

"I despise you," she snipped.

"Be that as it may, I have a small problem with your otherwise wonderful rendition of hail to the Spanish conqueror. I too am of Santos blood as well, half Santos blood. If you'll remember, our . . . mother . . . is . . . not . . . Spanish." He spoke very slowly as if speaking with a child. "And I think that you should seriously consider having your physician adjust your prescriptions. You're way too medicated."

"Fool. Angelina informed me of their few moments together. It seems your brother has an insatiable appetite. And as it happens, I too am somewhat ravenous at times. In that we are extremely well suited. Everything else will progress in time, of that I assure you."

"There's that medication problem again."

"You are beyond reproach," she spat through gritted teeth.

Roberto smiled and nodded. "Yeah, I get a lot of that."

"You'll see," Isabella warned.

Roberto's laughter was uncontrollable. Each time he looked at Isabella he began laughing all over again. She stood stoic, anger surging as she stared at him until he finally calmed himself. She turned her back to him.

"All of this is a moot point, although I do thank you for the comedy relief. I can always use a good laugh. But, in case you haven't heard, Marco has been seeing someone."

"Cretin. Did you honestly think some cheap New York knock-off could handle a man like Marco? Do you honestly think I would allow her to come down here and destroy everything with her lies? She is nothing, comes from nothing, and will always be nothing."

"By that snappy remark, I presume you're referring to Angela. You might remember her. She looks a lot like a child you once had."

Isabella turned and gasped unexpectedly loud, surprised by his innocently insightful statement. Her eyes were wide with stunned surprise.

Roberto tilted his head in added interest. "What? Why so surprised, Isabella? All I did was mention Angelina." He smiled then removed it just as quickly. "No I didn't, did I? I didn't say Angelina by name, did I? I said *a child.* Now, why should that upset you?" He leaned back in the chair.

"*You* upset me boy. Your very being upsets me," she hissed. "I hate you."

"No." He arched his palms together and tapped his fingers lightly together. "That's not it. You were scared."

"I hate you."

"Now you're repeating yourself."

"I hate you!" she screamed.

"What am I missing here, Isabella? What do you know that I should? What has you running so scared?"

"I am not afraid of you. You are nothing to me."

"Disappointing." He smiled seductively. "What about my crumbs?" He inched closer to her and opened his arms to her.

"How dare you, you impudent pig?" she hissed.

Roberto smiled triumphantly seeing she picked up her purse and moved to the door. "Now when is that anyway to speak to your future brother-in-law and lover?"

"You will most certainly burn in hell," she spat out.

"For tormenting you, probably."

"You disgust me!" she screamed across the room.

"I have that effect on a number of people. Don't take it personally; it's just my Santos conquistador charm."

"If you think that I'm going to just sit by again and let some no-name bastard's child take what is due me, then you don't know me as well as you think you do."

Roberto eyed her suspiciously. "Meaning?"

"There is more than one way to skin a cat."

Roberto eyed her more seriously. He didn't like the way she uttered her warning. He had sparred with Isabella enough times over the years to know when she was bluffing and when she wasn't. This was no bluff. His playful tone turned serious as he stood. "Whatever you're up to, Isabella, or think you want to do, I suggest you forget it, or the very least of your problems will be dealing with Marco."

She smiled, understanding his meaning all too well. But her assurance was Marco; he would never betray their bond, ever. Not even for Roberto. "Inform Marco that I was here. I shall be at my suite the remainder of the day, awaiting his arrival." She turned and stormed from the office.

Roberto sat back down thinking about Isabella's obscure ramblings. Why should the mention of Angelina get such a rise from her? he wondered. Surely she wasn't still mourning. No, there was something else. There was fear in her eyes. Something had definitely spooked her.

Absently, he turned back to the computer and continued typing in his monthly orders. After a few minutes he stopped in midair. What was it his mother said? Something about there being a reason why the two resemble each other. Why was Isabella so afraid at the mention of her child?

He leaned back in the chair and smiled to himself. His imagination was getting the best of him. As soon as he found Angela, they'd have dinner and laugh about his wild imagination. Nothing could go wrong, he assured himself as he picked up the ringing phone. "Hola," he greeted the caller happily.

"Señor Roberto Santos, por favor."

"Si, this is Roberto Santos. Who is this?"

"Señor, this is Enrique; I have been looking for you since this morning. I am at the St. Nicholas Hospital. I have found Señorita Lord. You might want to come—"

Roberto never heard the rest of Enrique's message or hung up the phone. By the time Enrique realized that he was no longer on the other end, Roberto was charging out of the club and running to his car.

She looked so frail lying in the tiny hospital bed. Her head was still wrapped and she remained unconscious since the accident. Roberto sat by her bed the rest of the day. He felt completely helpless. How could this happen? It was senseless.

He'd spoken to the attending doctor earlier. He informed Roberto that Angela had a bad concussion, a hairline fracture and numerous abrasions and bruises. He predicted the black-and-blue swelling would subside with time; he assured Roberto that they weren't as ominous as they looked. She should expect headaches, stiffness and general body aches, but he'd supply pain relievers. As soon as she awoke they would know more. The question was, when and if she'd awaken.

"Hello."

Roberto turned. "You."

Rita stood in the doorway, her eyes filled with tears and glued to the figure lying still in the bed. Machines beeped and blinked while a continuous stream of life-affirming liquid seeped through a tube attached to an IV bag near the bed. Roberto stood and opened his arms to Rita. She tucked herself into his embrace as if she'd done just that time and time again.

"What are you doing here?"

She chose to ignore the question. "How is she?" she finally muttered.

"Pretty banged up. But the doctors say that she should be okay in time." Rita nodded her understanding. "How did you know to come here?"

"I didn't. There was an article in the paper this morning about a Jane Doe accident at Luquillo Beach yesterday. Angela once mentioned that she loved to swim in the water at Luquillo. Since she missed our appointment yesterday and I still hadn't heard from her today, I took a chance and came down after work."

"That was very smart of you. But then again you were always the smart one, weren't you?" Rita looked surprised. "Yes, I remember you from school, Rita Mendez. It took a few moments, but I pride myself on never forgetting a beautiful face." Rita lowered her eyes. Roberto tipped her chin upwards. "I must admit, sometimes I wondered about you. You were always so quiet. I wondered what you were like—really like."

Rita blushed as she shyly moved her hands behind her back. Roberto reached back and took her hands to kiss the tops. "We've never been formally introduced. Me llamo Roberto Santos, encanto. Command me, I am your obedient servant."

Rita blushed bright red and looked away. "What do the doctors say about Angela's condition?"

"Bruises, swelling aches and pain but nothing permanent." He intertwined her hand in his arm and walked to the bedside. "Their only concern is her emotional state. She had earplugs in so she never heard the warnings from the lifeguards. Apparently the windsurfers plowed right into her and never looked back." Roberto pulled a second chair to Angela's bedside. Rita sat next to him.

"That's very strange. When you hit something in the water you usually feel it, particularly if you're on a windsurf board. I wonder why they didn't stop?"

"My thought exactly."

Rita turned to look into Roberto's eyes. "You don't think this was an accident do you?"

Roberto shook his head then turned back to Angela lying in bed still unconscious. "I don't know. But who would want to harm Angela and why?" He turned to Rita. "Do you know?"

"No."

"Tell me, Rita, how do you know Angela? She told me once that she didn't know anyone here; yet you said the two of you were supposed to get together. What were you meeting to do?"

"I'm helping her with a project."

"You're an architect?"

"No. It's a personal project."

"In other words, mind my own business."

"When she's ready to tell you, Roberto, I'm sure she will. Until then there's nothing more I can tell you without violating her trust."

Day turned into evening, and evening into the night. They'd talked the entire time. Late that night Rita fell asleep, her head on Roberto's shoulder as they sat side by side at Angela's bed. The room, a muted flow of deep shadows, belied the time of night. "Señor Santos." Rita awoke; Roberto turned around. The nurse knocked on the door frame again then stepped into the room. "Señor Santos, we need more information on Señorita Lord. Her chart must be completed so we may take tests."

"What do you need?"

"Driver's license, credit card, medical card, anything will be helpful."

He nodded. "I'll get what I can from her hotel room. Her bill will be paid by me personally, is that understood?"

"Si, señor." The nurse nodded and left the room.

Roberto picked up Rita's hand. "Come, I'll take you home."

He smiled. "You need to get some rest. I'll call you if anything changes in Angela's condition."

"I'd rather stay."

"You need your rest. Come, we'll talk later."

"Okay," she agreed, then turning to him noticed his broad smile. "Why are you smiling?"

"It's not often that I sleep with a woman and actually sleep." Rita blushed bright red. Roberto decided that he liked seeing the spread of color on her cheeks. Together they smiled and left the room.

Juan replaced the receiver as Marco walked into the bathroom to finish changing his clothes for the evening. "So what were Roberto and Isabella arguing about earlier?"

"You, of course."

"Me?"

"They got pretty loud at one point. It sounded like she was about to strangle him."

Marco chuckled to himself. "Roberto has that effect on a lot of people. Did they say where they were going?"

"They didn't leave together. Isabella left first then Roberto came barreling out. He almost knocked me through the wall as he flew down the steps."

Marco grimaced at this news. Very few things would get Roberto upset. "Do me a favor, Juan," he called from the bathroom, "get my father on the phone."

Arturo picked up the phone on the second ring. The conversation was brief. He hadn't heard from Roberto all day. The next call was to the café. When the manager picked up, Marco asked her about Roberto's whereabouts. She'd spoken to him earlier. He wouldn't be in for a few days. Marco was troubled. Something was definitely wrong. Roberto would never disappear like this. He may be a lot of things, but irresponsible wasn't one of them, particularly when it came to Café Santos.

Marco picked up the receiver again. His fingers dialed the

hotel but he hung up before the connection was complete. Dressed for the evening, he walked out of the office, spotting Juan in the front lobby. "I'm going out for a while. I'll be back later. I'll call you if I'm detained."

"Something wrong?" Juan asked, seeing Marco's concerned look.

"I don't know yet, but I intend to find out."

Roberto hung up the phone just as Marco let himself into the room using the third duplicate key. The two men glared at each other for a few minutes until Roberto dropped Angela's purse into her oversized straw bag.

"Where's Angela?" Marco asked.

Roberto glanced at Marco, shook his head, and went back to gathering Angela's belongings.

"I asked you a question, Roberto: where is Angela?"

Roberto shook his head. "She's no longer your concern, remember, brother?" Roberto mimicked. "I believe those were your exact words." He looked around the room for anything else that might be of some help to the hospital staff.

Marco circled around the suite and stopped at the patio door. He glanced out at the darkened night sky then turned back to the Roberto. "So she made her decision, she went to you—how typical."

"Given your attitude lately, I'd say she didn't have much choice."

"You have no idea what you're talking about, Roberto."

"You're right, I don't. And I may never find out."

"What's that supposed to mean?" He circled back to the dresser.

Roberto tossed Angela's cellular phone into her bag. "I don't have time for this."

"Why not, is she waiting for you?"

"Yeah, in a manner of speaking, yes. Angela is indeed lying in a bed waiting for me. But not at my villa." Roberto looked fiercely at Marco's unyielding expression. The silence between then filled the room as each man's rage grew.

The telephone rang, drawing their attention. Roberto, closer, immediately picked it up. He spoke briefly, jotted down some information on the nearby notepad, then hung up. "I have to go."

Marco stood. "Who's Rita?" He'd obviously overheard part of the conversation.

"A friend."

"What about Angela?"

"What about her?"

"You're just going to play Angela now that you have Rita."

"I never had Angela, Marco, you did, and if you had any sense, you still would." Marco turned to leave. "It's not what you think, Marco. Rita is a friend of Angela's." Marco kept walking to the door. "There's been an accident; Angela's been in the hospital for the past two days." Marco's legs froze solid, cemented in place. His hearing hollowed as his mind whirled down a deep dark tunnel. Slowly he willed himself to turn around.

"What?" Marco whispered in total disbelief. "How? Where? When? We were together just . . ."

"I don't know a lot of the particulars yet. I do know that it was in some kind of windsurfing accident."

Marco's thoughts instantly raced to the incident a month earlier when a tourist was fatally injured in the same type of accident. "How is she?" Roberto looked away, remembering his first sight of Angela's bruised and gauzed face. "How is she?" he reiterated louder and more firmly.

"She's banged up pretty badly, although the doctors assured me that she'll be fine once she regains consciousness."

"She's unconscious still, after two days?"

Roberto nodded. "Yes, even though she avoided most of the brunt of the board by diving under the water, she still got hit pretty hard."

"Who did this?"

"The police are still investigating. There were dozens of witnesses to the accident, but nothing definitive. I'm on my way back to the hospital now. I just came here to get some of her things for registration."

Marco ran from the room. "Let's go!" Roberto barely heard his fearful command as he ran down the hall.

"So this is Angela," Ava said, as she grasped the young woman's hand. "It's true, even with the bandages, she has the face of an angel. She's beautiful. No wonder my boys are so smitten with her."

Arturo placed his arm around his wife and held her close. He felt a sense of loss and sadness at seeing Angela lying motionless in the bed. Although he'd never met her, he felt a closeness toward the woman who had touched his sons so completely. Silently, the doctors slipped into the room. Several other men accompanied him. The physician introduced them as members of the hospital board.

Each man shook Arturo's hand and nodded politely to Ava. The doctor gave his assurance that the facility was doing everything it could to aid Angela's recovery. But at the moment there was little to be done until she woke up. The room fell silent as all eyes turned to Angela, lying so still in the bed.

A loud bang turned everyone's attention. Marco had arrived, slamming the door so wide it hit against the back wall. He went straight for the bedside. He knelt down by Angela's side and took her hand, kissing it lovingly. The doctor and board members quietly slipped out, leaving the Santos family together.

Roberto stepped into the room after stopping at the admittance with Angela's information. He stood next to Ava and she took his hand. Arturo turned to Roberto. "I need to speak to someone about the financial obligations."

"I've already taken care of it, Poppy," Roberto whispered. "The bursar will bill me directly."

"No, change it," Marco demanded, still focused on Angela's face. "Angela Lord is my responsibility."

"It's already done, Marco."

"Then undo it."

Roberto opened his mouth to protest, but felt the gentle squeeze of his mother's fingers. "Sure." He looked at Arturo. "I'll show you to the bursar's office." The two men left the room leaving Marco alone with Ava and Angela.

Ava stepped closer to Marco and laid her hand on his. Marco immediately grasped her hand and rubbed his cheek against it. "There's nothing we can do at the moment. Angela will awaken in time. The doctors gave her something for the pain and a sedative to help her sleep," she said. Marco nodded his head, his eyes still on Angela.

Ava looked down at Angela. "Roberto tells me she's a very strong woman. She's had difficulties before and came through. She will come through this as well."

"I can't lose her, not now, not this way." Marco spoke his first words to Ava in over twenty years. "She's so still."

"She's resting peacefully. She needs to reserve her strength. She'll need it when she recovers."

"I can't lose her."

"You won't. She'll pull through." Marco looked at his mother as if seeing her for the first time. She looked at her son, her hand still in his.

"Come, we should allow her to rest."

"You go ahead, I'm going to stay for a while." Ava nodded, gently squeezed his hand then turned to leave. "Mother." Ava paused, her heart soaring at the sound of her maternal name from Marco's lips. "Thank you; I love you."

Unable to turn around without completely breaking down, she nodded as tears streamed down her soft brown cheeks. "I love you too."

Late that same night Angela stirred. Marco immediately hurried to her side. Watching her face closely, he saw that she'd crinkled her nose and batted her eyelids several times.

He ran to the door. "She's waking up!" he hollered to no one in particular.

Within seconds the room was crowded with a bustle of hospital employees and Santos family members. Marco was right in the midst of the commotion. Like the calming center of a raging storm he stood placid, controlled. He knew she would need his strength.

Juan replaced the receiver in its cradle then dropped down exhausted in the seat near his wife. Rosa frowned, troubled by her husband's deep thoughts. "Juan, what is it?"

Juan shook his head sadly. "There's been an accident."

Rosa gasped then quickly retrieved the beaded rosary ever constant on the mantel. Slowly she slid down into the seat beside her husband. She took his hand. "Tell me, what has happened. Is it my sister?"

Juan turned to his wife. "No, Rosa. Your sister is just fine. It is a friend of the Santos family. You remember the young woman you saw on the plane, Angela Lord?" She nodded, slowly afraid of what she was sure she'd hear. "There was another windsurfing accident; she's in the hospital. She's just regained conscious so the doctors will just now be able to assess the full extent of her injuries."

"Accident. She had a windsurfing accident. Oh no," she cried over and over again as tears fell from her eyes. "Please no. What have I done?" Juan looked at his wife's deep concern for the woman she barely knew. He took her in his arms to calm her.

"Shh, Rosa, I'm sure she will be better in no time."

Through fits of hysterical crying Rose spoke incoherently. "No," she sobbed uncontrollably. "You don't understand; it's all my fault," she wailed. "I never should have helped her. I never should have helped her," she wailed louder.

It took the better part of thirty minutes to calm Rosa down. Still she continued blaming herself for Angela's accident.

She insisted the accident was her fault, and that she would be punished.

"Why, Rosa? Why would you be punished for an accident you had nothing to do with?"

"Because of me she will die just like the other one." She began crying again.

"Listen to me, Rosa, Angela Lord had an accident, nothing more. These things happen. You remember, just a month ago another tourist was struck by a speeding windsurfer. That too was an accident. Boys drinking, playing, not paying attention; I'm sure it was the same thing in this instance."

Rosa shook her head no. She was emphatic.

"Rosa, your seeing Angela on the plane had nothing to do with any of it. Us speaking with her at her hotel had nothing to do with it. It was an accident; that's all. Just like before, two careless youths out joy riding on windsurfers. They ran into Angela while she was swimming. Apparently, they didn't even see her. You had nothing to do with it. Do you understand me?"

Rosa calmed herself. She sat still staring down at her hands. "It was no accident, Juan. They saw her in the water. The boys knew what they were doing because"—she paused to look up at her husband—"I told her; it was I who gave her the idea."

Juan took Rosa's hands in his. A kernel of hesitancy in the pit of his stomach began to ache. "You gave who what idea, Rosa?"

"Señora Rivera, Isabella, when she came pleading for my assistance to save Marco from the tourist woman."

Juan sighed heavily then gritted his teeth, looking away from his wife. "Isabella was here? When?" He stood and walked to the window. His mind whirled as he watched his small grandchildren playing in the front yard. They tossed a large round ball into the air to see it soar. Then they'd all scatter when it came crashing down to the ground. Laughing wildly, the children began again.

This is not good, he thought to himself. Anything dealing with Isabella always meant trouble. Ever since they were children together she'd had an agenda that detailed her life. And when something didn't go as she planned or to suit her, she either forcibly changed it or, like his marriage, turned her back and walked away.

Rosa came up behind him with her arms wrapped around her body. "Days ago. She came needing my help to prevent Angela Lord from infesting Marco with her lies. And from tarnishing Angelina's good name. She asked for my assistance. How could I turn her down? She is familia."

Juan continued to watch the ball soar into the sky. "Exactly what did you tell Isabella?"

"I told her about the tourist last month. The one who died from injuries. I told her what I'd read in the papers about the windsurfing accident and that the ones responsible were never found." Tears streamed from Rosa's face, following the same path as the many others before. "I said that Angela should have been here a month earlier." She hunched over and began to cry openly. "I didn't mean to hurt her; I didn't mean for her to die."

Juan took her in his arms. "Shh," he soothed calmly. "You had nothing to do with the accident, Rosa, and Angela will not die." He turned to watch the ball fall from the sky one last time. This time it eclipsed the setting sun as it fell to the giggling children. "Now go, dry your eyes, I will take care of everything; I will speak with Isabella."

Marco paced the waiting room like a caged animal. The doctors were still in the room with Angela. After she awoke everyone was immediately ushered out to give the doctors room to assess the extent of her injuries.

"Sit, Marco," Ava instructed calmly. "You'll exhaust yourself and be no good to anyone, least of all Angela."

Marco stopped then plopped down in the nearest chair. The chair was across from Roberto. Roberto lowered the outdated magazine he'd been scanning and looked over to Marco. He smiled as Marco turned from him. "I see you've shaved your goatee and trimmed your hair even more." Marco didn't speak. "It's about time."

Both Ava and Arturo scolded Roberto silently. They knew he was leading to trouble. They knew that it was only a matter of time before all hell would erupt. Ava smiled to herself. This was a picture right out of her memory. It was one of the last times her family was complete.

Roberto, the youngest, most playful, would always taunt his older, more serious brother, Marco. And Marco would allow him to up to a point. Roberto would pick at, taunt and noodle Marco like the constant swell of waves on sand. Then eventually Marco, with the force of a tsunami, would retaliate. At that point there was nothing more to do than soothe bruised egos and bandage scrapes and scuffs.

"Excuse me, Señor Santos?" Three men stood and turned to the nurse when she walked in. The woman looked down at the chart she held in her hand. "Señor Roberto Santos?" Roberto stepped forward and walked to the nurse's side. "Señor, I need your signature here, here, and here."

Marco followed. He frowned as Roberto took the chart and began to sign. "What is he signing?" he asked the nurse.

"These are for the señorita's recovery. She must have a local address listed for our files."

Marco saw Roberto's address listed as Angela's recovery location. He snatched the chart before Roberto finished signing. He quickly scanned the wording then pulled identification from his wallet. "Redo these," he ordered. "Use this address." He gave the chart back to the nurse. She looked around, confused.

Roberto grabbed the chart from the nurse and finished writing his signature. He pulled Marco's card from the clip and handed the chart back to the nurse. "You have my signature, go." The bewildered nurse took the chart, then, just as quickly, Marco ripped it from her hands. As expected, the room erupted into total chaos.

Ava sat quietly as Arturo tried to regain calm and order between his two sons. Although he'd managed to rescue the nurse by using his address for her forms, it did little to placate the brothers. They were at each other's throats over where Angela would stay after she was discharged.

"You didn't want anything to do with her," Roberto accused.

"She doesn't belong with Roberto," Marco countered.

"You don't want her; you said as much."

"Forget what I said; she needs to be with me."

"What she needs," Arturo began calmly, "is a quiet place to recover and recuperate. A place without hassles and aggravation. A place where she can relax and forget about what happened."

"That would be with me," both Marco and Roberto said in unison, then turned and glared at each other.

"Yeah, right, if I know you, you'll badger her until she gives you a detail description of each and every person on the beach that day," Roberto accused Marco.

"Like you wouldn't."

"No, I wouldn't. I'll let the police handle the investigation. I bet you already have Juan checking into this, don't you?"

"Juan has nothing to do with this. Angela is staying with me at Willow Hill and that's final," Marco insisted loudly.

"She's staying with me in Ponce, as far away from you as possible!" Roberto shouted emphatically as he pushed Marco aside.

Marco grabbed Roberto's arm and shoved him away. Both men glared at each other and they prepared to do battle.

At this point Ava stepped up. The argument was about to get physical and although they were already in a hospital, the last thing she wanted to hear and see were broken bones and fresh stitches. "Boys, boys." She stepped between them. "This is neither the time nor place for this nonsense. When the time comes for Angela's discharge, all will be decided then."

They were immediately silenced.

Arturo stood behind Ava, placing his hand lovingly on her shoulder. He was so proud of her. She was the only person who could ever soothe their sons to complete silence.

"Gentlemen, gentlemen, please, this is a hospital," one of the doctors spoke as he came from Angela's room. All eyes turned to him. "I have received Señorita Lord's test results. If you'll have a seat we can discuss them calmly."

Unlike the rest of the Santos family, Marco wasn't completely satisfied with the doctor's report. The open questions bothered him and he made his feeling known. Ava, who sat by his side, helped sway his mind and calm his fears.

The only good news from the report was that now that Angela had regained consciousness, she would be free to leave the hospital in a few days.

When the doctors excused themselves to see other patients, Marco stepped out of the room. He called Enrique at the hotel and instructed him to have Helena personally pack all of Angela's belongings and have them delivered to his home by the end of the day.

Chapter 22

"Nice place you got here."

Rita jumped, startled by the now familiar voice. "Where did you come from?"

Roberto tilted his head to the side. "Do we really need to get into that now? But if you insist, I'll be happy to give you a demonstration on the facts of life this evening." Rita blushed, embarrassed by Roberto's roguish suggestion.

"How's Angela?"

"She's awake." He walked further into the room and eyed her messy desk. "Marco is with her; she's in good hands. Meanwhile, you and I have some unfinished business." He walked behind her desk and looked over her shoulder at the notes she'd been so consumed with when he first entered. "What are we working on?" She covered her notes with a folder and her hands.

"*We* aren't working on anything. I am working on an assignment."

"Angela's personal project?"

Rita hesitated. "Yes."

"You might as well tell me what it is; she will anyway."

"Fine, then let her tell you."

"We don't want to put her through all that right now, do

we? She's just regaining her strength. Why don't we discuss it? I'm a big help with personal projects such as these. By the way, what type of project will we be working on?"

"You and I won't be working on any project as far as I know."

"Dinner then." He smiled the smile of a man who knew something, a man determined, a man about to succeed.

Rita looked at her watch; it was much later than she realized. With very high windows along the ceiling of her office, she had no idea the early morning hours had passed quickly into late afternoon. "I'll order something in later."

He pulled a chair from the sidewall, sat down and grabbed a yellow legal pad from off her desk. "You're right; it's much too early for dinner; we'll order out later. We had better get back to work." He pulled a gold pen from his pocket, cleared a space on her desk and prepared to write. He looked up at her expectantly. "Shall we begin?" he asked encouragingly.

Rita laughed. "You are too much."

"Actually I've been told that I'm just enough," he countered seductively, leaning closer with a glint of mischief in his eye. A leery, flustered Rita stood abruptly, nearly knocking her chair over. Roberto stood as well. "Where're you going?"

Rita took a deep breath and nervously held her hand to her chest. Her intense movements visibly shook as he circled the desk coming toward her. Rita took a step back. "I . . . I . . . I have work to do. You have to leave now." Her eyes dashed around the room wildly. She was on the verge of panic.

Roberto's expression changed. He instantly backed away. "Rita." She didn't answer or look at him. "Rita," he repeated, softer, gentler. "Look at me, Rita." She didn't. "Please." She turned and looked at him. "I'm sorry, I didn't mean to frighten you. I was only joking." He held out his hand to her, palm side up. She stared at it, not sure what to do. Slowly she reached out her hand to him. He took it and slowly raised it to his cheek.

At first the coldness of her hand chilled his face. She pulled to withdraw but he held tight until she relaxed. He slowly took her other hand and held it also to his cheek. He kissed the palms. "I would never harm you, Rita, and I would never allow anyone else to." She was silent, her head bowed, her eyes closed. "Do you believe me?"

Time passed before she finally spoke. "Yes," she said, surprising herself because she did trust him. Without really even knowing him, she felt protected and safe. Something she seldom felt, even as a child.

His larger hands covered hers, warming them with the heat of his face. "Do you want to tell me what just happened?" She shook her head no. "Are you all right?" She shook her head yes. "Are *we* all right?" She shook her head yes again. "Are you going to tell me what you and Angela are doing?" A slow, comforted smiled graced her face as she slowly shook her head no. "Then let's go eat. I'm starved."

Just moments later Rita sat opposite Roberto in a small outdoor café off the boulevard. Their chairs were turned to face the setting sun. She smiled happily and shook her head in amazement. This was like a dream come true. Roberto Santos was one of the island's most popular personalities as well as its most notorious bachelor. His scandalous reputation clung to him like a newborn to its mother.

She knew Roberto was only there with her for one thing, to pry information from her about Angela's case. But she didn't care. For that moment in time she would pretend that he was there for her. He reached over and took her chilled hand. She let him. He entwined his fingers with hers as casually as taking a breath. Rita's heart pounded hard against her chest as she wondered to herself, *How do you say no to a man like Roberto?*

The next morning Roberto charmingly persuaded the nursing staff into letting him visit Angela hours before the regularly posted visiting times. He promised them each a complimentary admittance pass to Club Santos. They gladly accepted.

"Good morning, beautiful." He peeked his head through the door as Angela continued to turn her nose up at the early morning offering from the meal cart.

"Hardly," she slurred, smiled, then winced, in that order. A shadow of pain from a bruise on her cheek pulled at her lips. "Buenas dias; come on in."

Roberto stepped all the way into the room carrying a large bouquet of mixed flowers. He tilted his head in sympathy. "How do you feel?"

"Like I've been run over by a Mack truck, twice."

"No truck, just two careless windsurfers."

Angela sighed heavily as she struggled to take a deep breath. "The flowers are lovely, thank you," she said.

Roberto glanced around the room and noted an enormous bouquet already in a huge vase of water on the side dresser. "Looks like I'm too late. The room already looks like a flower stand.

"It hurts to laugh, so no corny jokes," she warned.

"I wouldn't think of it." He smiled innocently. He placed the large arrangement next to the other already on the side table. He bent down to smell the sweet aroma. "Nice buds."

Angela held her hand to her chest and took a deep, ragged breath. "Yes, they are beautiful. They're from an Arturo and Ava Santos, your mother and father, I'm told." Roberto nodded. "I was under the impression that your mother didn't live on the island."

"She doesn't. She lives in New York. She's visiting my father for a few days."

Angela smiled. "They must have had a great divorce if they're still so close."

"They're not divorced."

"He lives here on the island and she lives in the States?" Roberto nodded. "And they're still married? Why . . . ? Oh, never mind. I bet this is one of those conversations that's going to make my head hurt again." Roberto immediately rushed to her side.

"Your head hurts? You're in pain? What can I do? I'll summon the doctor." He reached for the call button.

"No, no, I'm fine, I was only joking. You're so serious this morning. If I didn't know any better I'd say you and your brother exchanged bodies some time over the past few hours."

Roberto smiled, relieved. "Scary isn't it?" He leaned in closer. "As quiet as I try to keep it"—he looked around suspiciously for listening ears then continued—"I have an incurable illness called *concern*. I've had for years. No matter how hard I try to get rid of it, it always returns. I've even had several operations to have it surgically removed, yet it still comes back."

Angela smiled and tried to laugh but reached to hold her ribs. "Don't make me laugh."

Roberto took her other hand. "I wouldn't think of it."

An instant later he crossed his eyes and made a silly face. She laughed then winced.

"Sorry, bruised ribs," Roberto said as he took a decidedly serious stance.

"The doctor says I'll be fine after a few days of rest."

"When are you being discharged?"

"I don't know yet. Soon I hope."

In typical Roberto style, he picked up her chart and began studying the notations.

"Do you know what you're reading?"

"Have no idea."

She shook her head at the purely Roberto answer. "I heard about the argument in the waiting room. Actually I think everyone in the hospital has heard about it by now."

"Good news travels fast," he quipped, still scanning the chart. He flipped a few pages, turned the chart upside down then right side up.

Angela smiled and held her chest tighter. "I'm going back to my hotel room when I leave here."

Roberto looked up seriously. He opened his mouth to object but Angela shook her head no. "There's nothing you can do about it. I've made up my mind and that's final."

"I can cancel your reservation, have your bags packed and taken to Ponce." He smiled smugly with his veiled threat.

"Then I'll take the first flight back to Washington, doctor's orders or not."

"Okay, okay, you've made your point. Stay in the suite. Although I think my brother might have something to say about that."

"I doubt it." Her heart sank as she remembered the last time she and Marco were together and his reaction to her not instantly moving in with him. "Marco isn't exactly my biggest fan at the moment."

Roberto chuckled, showing deep dimples and the clear bright sparks in his dark eyes. "That's where you're wrong, my dear. The poor man is head over heels, crazy-in-love with you. He nearly ripped my head off when I suggested you come to Ponce with me. That is what the argument in the waiting room was about. The man is truly smitten."

Angela turned away as emotion threatened to spill forward. The thought of her feelings for Marco was still too raw. She loved him, of that she had no doubt. She was also certain of Marco's feelings for her. He loved her. But she couldn't spend the rest of her life not knowing her past.

"I hear I should thank you for bringing some of my things from my room."

"The administration needed information that I didn't know and Rita suggested that I pick up a few other things."

Angela stilled. "Rita?"

"Rita Mendez from the Hall of Records."

"You know Rita?"

"Oh yeah, we go way back. She and I practically went through school together."

"I see."

Roberto smiled. "She's a wonderful woman. Only thing, she has this annoying little habit about a thing called trust and loyalty. She absolutely refused to tell me what the two of you were working on. And believe me, I used every trick in the book, and then some." Angela brightened.

"She didn't tell you about my search?"

"No," he said as he sat on the bed beside her, "she didn't. Angela, if you're looking for someone on the island, why didn't you just tell me? I can be a big help. I have resources that even the Hall of Records doesn't have."

"It's not that simple, Roberto."

"It is that simple, Angela." She shook her head. "No," he continued. "Look at yourself; you can't continue this search from a hospital bed and when you get out of here there's no way you're going to be able to do it. Rita can't continue on her own; she has other work to do." He took her hand. "Let me help you, Angela. Trust me, it's an option you *can* afford this time," he said, reminding her of a talk they once had.

Every fiber in her being shouted *yes, do it.* So she did. She told him everything she'd told Rita. Her entire life lay before him, from the abandonment bin to there in the hospital room. Maybe it was the painkillers or maybe she was just tired of carrying it around all these years holding it inside.

Roberto, as expected, took it all in stride. He nodded when necessary and stroked her fingers with his thumb when she tensed up. When she'd finished her tale, he stood. "We will find the truth; this, I promise you." He bent down to kiss her teary eyes.

"I see you already have company," Marco said as he entered Angela's room with an arm loaded with calla lilies. He walked over to the table and laid the flowers down.

Roberto leaned in and kissed Angela on the forehead. "I've got to get going. Seems I have a lot of work ahead of me. Rita says that she needs to talk to you. I'll have her call later." He stood to leave; the impish smile was unmistakable. "Marco."

"Roberto," Marco said, his eyes still riveted to Angela lying in the bed.

The door closed, leaving Marco and Angela alone together. The room fell silent as Marco slowly eased toward the side then moved to the window. He absently fingered the small white blinds then pulled the cord to bathe the darkened room in early morning sunlight. Moments passed with the room still.

Angela watched Marco finger the blinds and took the opportunity to observe his newest appearance. His hair was now trimmed even shorter than the last time she'd seen him. There was a full thickness of short wavy curls tasseled atop his head that diminished as they reached through to his sparse sideburns. He looked younger, more like Roberto than before. The goatee he once donned had been completely removed, replaced by a clean-shaven jaw tightened with strain.

"What was Roberto doing here?" he asked accusingly.

Angela shook her head and smiled weakly. "Great opening line, Marco. How long did it take you to come up with that one?" Silence hung heavily as the two stared at each other for a time that seemed like an eternity.

"I sorry, you're right," he whispered.

She looked away. It hurt too much to see him. A slow, silent tear rolled down her cheek as she shook her head to regain control over her runaway emotions. This was impossible. Angela looked to the streaks of sunlight as they broke the shadows on the wall and floor. "What are you doing here, Marco?" she asked without looking up.

Marco turned to her. "I never should have left you like I did. I was wrong."

Angela shook her head no. "It doesn't matter anymore who was right and who was wrong. We never should have started this. We knew it wouldn't end well. She was right: we are worlds apart."

"Who was right?" Marco turned with interest.

"It doesn't matter."

"Angela." She turned away from him. "It doesn't have to end at all."

"We should just leave it alone, Marco."

"I love you and you love me. I can't just walk away from you, Angela, not now, not ever."

"You don't have a choice."

"Yes. We do have a choice."

"Marco. We had a few laughs. We enjoyed the moment, but that's all it was, a moment."

"I can't accept that. What we started here was more than a few laughs and you know it. Angela, I can't just let us go."

"You have to. I have to. We have no choice."

"Nothing is ever over."

"This is."

"No."

"What do you what from me, Marco?"

"I want you, Angela. I want us to be together." He took her hand. "Angela, when a man finally finds his perfect mate, he'd be a fool to walk away. There's nothing he can do. He's like a raging waterfall. You don't stop it. It can't be stopped." He caressed her face in his hands. "I'm no fool, Angela. We belong together. In your heart you know I'm right."

"I can't talk about this now."

"Okay." He moved closer; concern shadowed his dark features. "How do you feel this morning?"

"Better. Although I'm sure I look like crap." She reached up to smooth her hair with her bandaged arm.

Marco smiled pleasantly; his eyes gleamed with love. "Muy bonita. You are more beautiful than you have ever been, my sweet Angela. You are the sunshine that lights the darkness of my world."

"You, señor, are an awful poet and lousy liar."

His smile faded almost as soon as it appeared. "Have the police been in to speak with you?"

"Yes, late last night."

"Good. Have you told them everything and given them complete descriptions?"

"Yes, I told them everything I remember."

"Excellent." He turned his back, calculating how soon it would take to solve the crime. "I guess you've heard that something like this happened just last month. Unfortunately that tourist wasn't as fortunate. The authorities still haven't captured the culprits. I intend to go to Luquillo this afternoon. I'm sure I can find several more witnesses for the police to question." When he turned around Angela was frowning. "Are you in pain?"

"No, I'm not in any pain."

Marco backed off, remembering what Roberto said about Angela needing peace. His brow-beating her about her conversation with the authorities surely wasn't what the doctor ordered. "Maybe we should talk about something else."

"Good idea."

"You'll be getting out soon and the doctors want you to stay on the island for a few extra days. You'll be staying with me at Willow Hill."

"That won't be necessary; I'll go back to the hotel."

"Willow Hill will be more comfortable."

"The hotel would be just fine, thank you."

"I've already had your bags packed and moved to my home." Marco moved to her side and took her hand.

"Presumptuous."

"Persistent, remember?"

"No. Move my things back." Angela shook her head and sighed heavily just as Marco opened his mouth to rebut. "Marco, this will never work. There's an old saying, 'A bird can't swim and a fish can't fly.' There is no middle ground for us. We both know that. I don't fit into your world and you can't live in mine."

Suddenly, he thought of what his father had told him about his own marriage. There was no way he was going to repeat their choices and decisions.

"True," he said with finality. Angela lowered her head at the absolute word he'd chosen to agree with her. A part of her had always nurtured a small seed of hope and wishful thinking. Marco tipped her chin up to examine her bruises closer. He tilted her chin from side to side until he was satisfied there'd be no permanent damage. "Since," he began, "our worlds will never mix, we'll have to do like as Aleandro and Genevieve. We'll create our own world."

The words were sweet; the kiss was even sweeter. She didn't even feel the slight twinge of pain as she wrapped her arms around him, drawing him closer to her bruised ribs.

"I'll let you rest now. I'll be back later this afternoon." She nodded. "Angela, I will always love you."

He touched her lips gently then turned and walked out. She watched the door quietly close as a well of tears poured from her eyes. "I love you too, Marco."

As soon as Marco left the room he looked up, seeing his mother sitting in the waiting room across the hall. She smiled as he walked over to her, meeting her halfway. He leaned down and kissed her cheek. Ava's heart lurched with joy.

"How is Angela today?"

"She's still in some pain."

"And you, my son? How are you?"

"I've been better."

The conversation was awkward at first but Ava allowed him to talk and state his feelings. And for the first time in years they communicated as mother and son.

"The doctors have informed me that Angela will be discharged very soon. Has she accepted your offer to recuperate at Willow Hill?"

"No."

Ava smiled knowingly. "Maybe I can persuade her to reconsider."

Marco looked to Ava. He instantly recognized the determined expression of persistence he'd seen in his own face and in Roberto's stubbornness. Marco smiled and nodded. He left the hospital assured, knowing that leaving this up to his mother was the perfect idea. She would take care of everything.

The timid knock drew Angela's attention away from the bouquet of flowers that Marco had just brought. She looked up and smiled, immediately recognizing the woman as the matriarch of the Santos family. Both Marco and Roberto had her full lips and sparkling, open smile.

"Angela," Ava said as she opened the door further, "my name is Ava Santos, may I enter?"

"Yes of course," Angela said openly and attempted to sit straight up in the bed. "Come in, please. Thank you for the flowers; they're beautiful."

After social pleasantries had been exchanged, and Angela's current health detailed, Ava got right to the point. She gave Angela numerous reasons to recuperate at Willow Hill.

"And lastly, my dear," she added, "my son loves you like I've never seen before. Go to him, stay with him. Know the man that I know. Yes, he's stubborn and determined, but he's also determined and stubborn." She smiled with motherly love then tilted her head in acknowledgment. "And he loves you as strongly and completely as I suspect you love him."

Angela was instantly drawn to Ava's sweet kindness, gentle humor, and motherly concern. That was the beginning of a newfound friendship. Ava was funny, charming and it was quite obvious that she loved the Santos men beyond reason. She still had no idea how Ava so easily talked her into recuperating at Willow Hill.

"This is an unexpected visit," Isabella said as she sauntered back to her living room followed by Juan. "It's been a long time, Juan. Shall I pour you a coffee?"

"Save it, Isabella. This isn't a social call."

She smiled to herself. "Somehow I didn't think it was. Please sit down." Juan remained standing. "As you wish."

"Tell me about your little visit to my home a few days ago."

Isabella tensed as she picked up her cup and placed the brim to her ruby red lips. She hadn't expected Rosa to confess quite so quickly. "I stopped by to visit, is that so wrong?"

"You have no family at my house."

"Not true, you were once my family, my friend, my brother." She raised her brow for emphasis. "Whatever happened to brotherly love?"

"Get out of the past, Isabella. What have you done?"

She turned, her mouth open and aghast. "What are you implying, Juan?"

"I think you know. But if you'd like me to spell it out I will. You had something to do with an accident on the beach, didn't you?"

"Juan, how could you even suggest something so vile? I am not the monster you seem to think I am. I could never hurt anyone."

"Yes you could, both intentionally and unintentionally. You forget who you're talking to."

"You may show yourself out." She stood and began walking to her bedroom door.

Juan grabbed her arm. "Not so fast. You still haven't answered my questions. What have you done?"

"I have done nothing," she spat out.

Juan glared at her. "You've implicated my wife in one of your deceitful schemes," he warned.

"Your innocent little wife implicated herself." She snatched her arm away. "I wasn't here when the first tourist was attacked, she was. I wonder what the police would say if I told them that Mrs. Juan Martinez was involved in the recent attacks on tourists? She already has a record from an attack on a tourist, doesn't she?" Isabella walked back to the sofa and picked up her cup. "Oh yes, we had quite the little chat, girl talk, really. She's a very interesting woman with an even more interesting past. One would say she has a problem with tourists, wouldn't one?"

"I'm warning you, Isabella, whatever you're doing or plan on doing, stop it now before someone really gets hurt."

"You, warning *me*—how comical," she said spitefully. "If I remember correctly, I warned you about this marriage. You married so far beneath our level it's an embarrassment to everyone."

"My marriage is none of your business. You decided that a long time ago. You chose to stay out of our lives."

"You left me no choice. Rosa Delores, of all people—my God, Juan, what were you thinking? You could have done so much better. You should have done so much better." Juan turned and walked away from her in anger. She came up behind him. "You and I used to have such good times together, didn't we?"

He turned to her, smiling. She wasn't sure what to make of his expression. "Very good, Isabella, you played that quite well. But you have underestimated one thing." She stood with her hands planted on her hips, poised and ready to hear his next words. He turned to walk out.

"What?" she screamed as he opened the door to leave. "What?" The door closed behind him. "What?" she screamed to the closed door and the echo of silence.

"Is he gone?" Chevis de Long whispered, peering out of the bedroom as soon as he heard the door close.

Isabella turned to the hiding man, peeking out from her bedroom. "Get dressed and get out," she ordered angrily.

Chevis ducked his head back into the bedroom, put on one of Isabella's pink ruffled robes and came out into the living room.

Isabella sat on the sofa stewing, her mind flying a million different directions. Mentally she traced every line of logic that could possibly connect her to Angela Lord's unfortunate accident. Each time she came up clear. She was certain she'd planned it so that if ever suspected or questioned, she could honestly say that it was Rosa Martinez who talked of harming Angela. And who should the police believe, her or some ill-mannered, no-titled housewife?

Isabella didn't notice Chevis enter until he touched her neck. "He's gone. Let's get back to bed."

"Didn't I just tell you to get out?" she said without looking at him.

"But I just got here," Chevis complained. "I thought we'd spend the rest of the afternoon together." He reached down and crudely placed his hand over her breast. He massaged it roughly, knowing she would like it. The rougher the better, she always requested.

Chevis found that Isabella had acquired strange and unique

appetites lately. She insisted he do things he'd never even imagined possible. But Isabella had always been savage in her way. She was an animal once she entered her boudoir and he enjoyed every moment they spent together. Unfortunately, whatever time they spent together was of her choosing. He wouldn't dare come to her suite late one evening expecting a quick roll in the hay. Yet, she had no qualms paging him for a quickie, even on the night of his twentieth wedding anniversary party.

Chevis continued his awkward massage. And since Isabella didn't stop him, he boldly grasped the other breast with his other hand. Harder and harder he massaged until she threw her head back, inviting him to savor her neck. He did.

The coffee carafe and several porcelain cups tumbled to the carpeted floor when he clumsily thrust his body over the back of the sofa to be by her side. He grabbed a condom from the pocket of the robe and quickly dressed himself. He quickly entered her and within seconds moaned in his pleasure.

"You oaf," she raged. Angry and unfulfilled, Isabella kicked him away. "Get out!" she screamed. "You're useless."

Chevis, barely recovering from his intense pleasure, tumbled to the floor crushing the two coffee cups and denting the carafe beneath his weight. "What?" he questioned. "What did I do wrong?"

"Get out!" she screamed louder.

Chevis scrambled up, gathering the pink flouncy robe together. Isabella looked at the ridiculous sight. She sucked her teeth and turned her head in disgust. This is what her life had come to, an idiot with a hair-trigger hard-on. She looked up in time to see Chevis disappear into her bedroom, the robe hiked up and twisted, showing his bare bottom. Isabella moaned distressfully. She'd seriously consider suicide if she didn't owe her plastic surgeon half of Fort Knox.

Chapter 23

"Girlie, where have you been? I been calling your cell phone for days and I've called your room so many times, I'm starting to have a relationship with the front desk clerk. But we'll get back to him later. So where have you been? Your butt was supposed to be back here last night. I waited for three hours at the airport and no you. And don't even get me started about the twin idiots. Your ex-bosses are about to burst a serious blood vessel. They've gone berserk."

Angela collapsed back into the chair beside her hospital bed and closed her eyes, allowing the medication to take effect. She'd just shooed Marco and Roberto away after pleading for a moment to herself. "Believe it or not I've been in the hospital for the past three days."

"What?"

"I had a little accident a few days ago."

"Say what? Are you all right? Just give me a few hours. I'll be right down there."

"No. Elliot, really. It's not necessary. Believe me, I have enough mother hens chirping over me already. I'm fine, really. It was just a stupid swimming accident."

"That laid you up in the hospital for three days? I don't

think so. Either you tell me what's going on right now or I'll grab the next flight out of here with Mother Mitchell in tow."

"And I'll never speak to you again."

"I'll risk it."

"Elliot," she said.

"Yes?"

Angela rolled her eyes to the ceiling. She hated it when Elliot refused to budge on an issue, which was most of the time. "I told you; it was a stupid accident, that's all. I was floating in the water and got hit by a couple of windsurfers. It was an accident. Apparently they didn't see me because they never even stopped."

"What do you mean, they never stopped? You mean to tell me, you were run over by someone floating in the middle of the Caribbean Sea and you don't even see them? That's ridiculous."

"That's what happened."

"What are the police doing?"

"They're asking questions, getting witnesses, you know, the whole nine yards." She paused.

"And . . ." Elliot prompted.

"And?"

"Yes, and what's going on with the investigation now? You know, what leads do they have as to the identities?"

"None—as I said, the windsurfers kept going. Apparently all the witnesses were on the beach and too far away to get a viable description."

"And how are you doing now?"

Angela was relieved that he'd finally decided to change the subject. She still wasn't comfortable discussing the accident, even with Elliot. "I'm fine now, just a few scrapes and bruises."

"Exactly what kind of scrapes and bruises?"

"A few bruised ribs, a sprained wrist and a hairline fracture." His gasp said it all. "If you come down here you'll only make it worse. Elliot? Elliot, answer me!"

"A hairline fracture. What the hell kind of windsurfers

were they? How can you not see someone in the water? Didn't the lifeguard blow his horn or whistle or something?"

"Apparently he did but I had my earplugs in. I didn't hear him."

"Tell me, Angel, for real, how are you? Do you need me there?"

"For real." She paused. "I'm tired, the side of my face is swollen, it hurts to take a deep breath and I have to go to the bathroom."

"Do you need me there?" he repeated.

"No, I'm getting out of here today and I'll be back home in a few days. I'm just going to hang around for a little bit, doctor's orders."

"Going back to the hotel?"

"No, the room's already gone. There's some kind of carnival, holiday going on. So the island is pretty much booked. The hotel already packed my bags. I'm staying with Marco Santos at Willow Hill."

"Is this a good thing?"

"Yes, it's a very good thing."

"This sounds serious."

"I think it is."

"For both of you?"

"Yes, for both of us."

"Are you sure?"

"Absolutely."

"All right, but if you need me, I'm there. Call me tomorrow, okay? You know how I worry."

"I know. So tell me, what's going on up there?"

"Nothing much, oh, except that my best friend won best of show in the Washington, D.C., Design Show."

Taken off guard by the jubilant news, Angela screamed with joy then held her ribs in delayed pain. Marco and Roberto came charging through the hospital door then stopped, each bumping into the other nearly knocking the flowers onto the floor. Startled, Angela jumped and held her ribs at their unplanned comedic routine. Their concerned, confused expression was almost as good as winning the design show. While listening to Elliot continue to pour out the particulars of her unanimous win, Angela pointed to the door and demanded they leave.

Completely baffled, the brothers looked at each other, then back to Angela who was still emphatically pointing to the door. "You have offers from several serious design firms," Elliot continued, unaware of the confusion.

Angela hung up ten minutes later. Her satisfied smile said it all. Finally she was being appreciated for her talent and skills. But she meant it when she told Elliot that it was too late. She had no intention of going back to Carter Architectural and Design firm again.

Ava popped her head into the room. She smiled warmly. "Are you ready to go?" Angela nodded slowly. "Okay, let's go." She opened the door wider, allowing Marco and Roberto to enter. They immediately grabbed for her overnight bag then raised up and glared at each other before Roberto started laughing playfully and backed off with his hands raised in surrender. Ava just shook her head and looked away. Her boys would never change.

The rest of the journey was less eventful because Roberto said his good-byes at the hospital entrance when Marco left to get the car. He promised to stop by Willow Hill after catching up with Rita who had left several messages on his cell phone.

Roberto was feeling extremely good as he took the marble steps of the Hall of Records two at a time. Apparently, things were getting back on track as far as Angela and Marco were concerned. That alone had him smiling and humming a current hip-hop Latin favorite.

"How is Angela doing?" Rita asked, hearing Roberto coming a mile away.

"She's fine. Still sore, but fine." Roberto walked further into the building, watching Rita admiringly as she led the way back to her office. "I just left the hospital. My mother and Marco are talking her to Willow Hill."

"That's good to hear. I'm sorry to disturb you, but you did ask to be informed if I ever found anything interesting," Rita said as she and Roberto entered her office. "I'm sure you have more important things to do besides hang out in a dusty old building searching through microfilm and old newspapers." She stood safely behind her desk and offered a seat to him. "Angela must be very special to you," she said, hoping she didn't sound as curious about his relationship with Angela as she really was.

Roberto smiled at her veiled attempt to gain personal information. "Angela *is* a very special lady."

Rita smiled half-heartedly as she sat down and pulled out Angela's file. "I must admit, I don't know her very well but she seems like a very nice person. I hope you two are very happy together." Roberto smiled but chose to remain uncharacteristically silent. "If you don't mind my asking," she began, "how long have the two of you been together?"

"I've only known Angela a short time."

"Really, you seem so close."

Roberto stood and came around the desk. He cleared a space and sat on her desk and leaned back so as not to alarm her. "Rita," he began, "Angela and I aren't a couple. She's a friend, that's all. But if all goes well, I'm hoping she'll be a sister-in-law as well." Rita looked at him questioningly. "Angela and Marco, my brother." Finally she nodded her head in understanding as she smiled and blushed.

"I didn't mean to pry," she said softly.

"Yes, you did," Roberto offered with his usual charming self. Rita blushed bright red and looked to her messy desk.

"Look at this," she said, examining a copy of an old newspaper.

Roberto inched closer to Rita. Unlike the previous time, she didn't jump away from him. Roberto quickly read the article that Rita pointed out. "So? Pedro Martinez was having an affair with another woman."

"Isn't Pedro Martinez Angelina Rivera's grandfather?"

"Yeah, so, Angelina's grandfather had an affair years ago,

nothing unusual about that. A lot of men have affairs, no big deal."

Rita scoffed at his cavalier attitude. "No, look at the photo here." She pointed to a grainy black and white print of a couple sitting in an outdoor café with the young girl between them. "Look at the woman and young girl's face, particularly around the eyes. Don't they look a little like Angela?"

Roberto leaned in closer and squinted at the small photo. "Yeah, now that you mention it, they do. But, no, look at the date. That was way before Angela was born. It couldn't be her."

"No, not Angela but maybe her mother."

Roberto looked at Rita and smiled. He instantly knew where her thoughts were leading. And if she was even half close to the truth, then maybe Angela would have her answers sooner than she thought.

"Pedro Martinez was unquestionably Angelina's grandfather. And that is definitely not his wife nor Isabella in the photo. So, who are they? And more importantly, where are they now?" Rita wondered aloud.

"Good questions."

"How do we find the answers?" Rita looked up to Roberto. "This social register has been out of publication for at least twenty years. I doubt anybody knows now."

"Actually there's one person that might know."

"Who?" Rita questioned.

"Isabella Rivera."

"No way," Rita warned before he could go any further. "There's no way I'm gonna walk up to Mrs. Rivera and ask who her father was sleeping with."

Roberto smiled mischievously. "You won't have to. I will." He stood up instantly.

"You can't."

"It would be my pleasure, I guarantee you. Nothing would make me happier than to confront Isabella with this photo," he assured her, too anxious for his own good.

"No, you don't understand, if she does know who the

women in the photo are, she'll never tell. It's the code. Ignorance is bliss. Yes, men have their affairs and mistresses; the wives and children know about it, but no one ever openly acknowledges it."

"Well, they will today." He picked up his sunglasses to leave.

"No, Roberto, please." Rita grabbed his arm and held tightly. "Don't do this. There has to be another way."

Roberto paused and looked down to the petite fingers wrapped around his muscular arm. He smiled. The delicate flower had more strength than he'd expected. Itching to kiss her but not wanting to frighten her away, he relaxed his posture and turned back to face her. "Okay, we'll do it your way. But there's still one more person who knows as much about this as Isabella."

Rita smiled until she realized that she was about to be kissed senseless.

"Ava is a remarkable woman."

Marco walked across the room and sat down on the side of the bed. He smiled at Angela and stroked the side of her face lovingly. "Yes she is."

"Is she going back to New York soon?"

"No, she's going to Vieques. She and my father have a home there. She told me that she'll be back to visit you in a few days."

"I see where you get your persistence from. I still can't believe how easily she talked me into staying here."

"I'm glad she did. It's good to have you home again." She opened her mouth to correct him but closed it again as he continued, "I know, I know. This isn't home yet. But I'm working on it."

Angela had to laugh. His persistence was dangerous. And as far as she was concerned, not going back to Washington was a real possibility.

"How do you feel?"

"Better."

"Can I get you anything?"

"I'm fine, sleepy. I think that the medication is beginning to work."

"Good, why don't you rest? I'll be here when you wake up."

"Don't you have a club to run?"

"I've taken the night off."

"No. Go to Santos, I'll be fine. The nurse you hired is here and I'm just going to sleep anyway. You might as well get some work done."

"Are you sure?"

"Positive," she said as she settled beneath the lightweight coverlet. She yawned sleepily. "I'll see you when you get back."

He leaned in and kissed her lips gently. By the time he stood and walked to the bedroom door he heard the soft slow breathing of her drifting off to sleep.

This was how it should be, he decided. He could see himself in a few years kissing her good night with their babies in her arms and their sons already asleep beside her. The fantasy was as clear and perfect as he'd ever imagined. This was how it was going to be. Angela would be his wife and bear his children.

Chapter 24

Marco looked up to see Isabella burst in through the office door.

"I am appalled," she declared without hesitation.

"Not now, Isabella; I'm busy."

She marched across the office and stood right before Marco's desk. "How could you?" she accused.

"How could I what?" Marco asked, his voice low and noticeably drained of emotion.

"How could you do this to me, to us? After everything we've been through. You've stabbed your family in the back for a cheap lay with a tramp," she demanded, fanning her long red nails out across his desk.

He gave her a warning look. "What are you talking about, Isabella?"

"I just came from your hacienda," she spat out in disgust. "I was told that woman is there, at Willow Hill. What is she doing there? I demand an explanation." The elevated octave of Isabella's tone was dramatically piercing.

"Angela is a guest in my home."

"Since when? She has no right."

Marco leaned back on the chair and slowly looked up as he angled his fingers beneath his chin. He bit at his lower lip patiently before answering. "Willow Hill is still my home, Isabella. She is my guest for as long as she likes."

"How blind can you be? Don't you see what this woman has already done to you? Look how she's come between us already. She's taken you from the ones who truly love you, your family. She will only succeed in hurting you, Marco. As soon as your back is turned she will stab you. I know this."

"Isabella."

"Don't." She held her hand up to stop him. "She is using you, Marco. She will twist her lies around you until she has choked the life from you. She and Roberto are together in this."

"Roberto?"

"Yes, Roberto has always despised me, you know that. He has brought this woman here to torture me with her face and tempt you with her body. She will destroy you and leave you penniless. She and Roberto will have it all. Even now they plan on your ruin."

"What are you saying?"

"I was just at your home, Marco; Roberto's car was there. They're there together."

"You lie. Roberto would never."

Isabella smiled a conquering smirk. "Go, see for yourself. I'm sure he's still there with her."

Anger prompted Marco to hurry from the office.

Twenty minutes later Marco pulled his SUV behind the familiar red Mercedes sports car. "Roberto," he growled through gritting teeth. Within seconds he entered his home. The rooms were empty. He hurried to the steps but paused when he heard the gentle pull of guitar music being played from the living room.

He stepped down slowly, walked trancelike toward the open door. His heart raced with anticipation. He parted the door slowly and easy into the room. The terrace doors were open and music flowed through the opening like a gentle breeze.

Marco crossed the room and stepped out onto the terrace. He saw Roberto perched half on the cement planter surrounded by a halo of bright red blossoms. His eyes were closed and his fingers moved skillfully against the thin wired strings just as Marco had showed him years ago. He played a tune they'd learned as young boys at their father's knee. A gentle melody composed of soft harmony and flowing rhythms.

Marco looked around for his audience. Angela was nowhere in sight. Marco continued to watch as Roberto played. The song neared the end, but Roberto stopped suddenly when he opened his eyes and spotted his brother standing in the doorway. "Marco."

"Roberto."

Roberto lowered the guitar and spun it around several times, then stopped and smiled mischievously. He returned the guitar to its original position and began strumming the cords harshly for added drama. His fingers moved with added speed as he smiled broadly at his annoyed brother. Building faster and steeper toward the unknown ending, with frenzied proficiency he played with passion and assurance. Then, just as suddenly as he'd begun, he stopped.

The air hung heavy with turbulence. Roberto put the guitar aside. "Angela's asleep."

Marco took a deep breath and moved to stand by his brother. "What are you doing here?" His question was biting and direct.

"Yo, slow your roll; I'm just visiting a friend."

Exasperated, Marco ran his hand through his newly cropped hair. "Again we play these childish games."

Roberto laughed. Marco spun around and glared at him. "Brother, you have got to be the most obtuse man alive. You obviously still don't get it. I'm not a threat to you. I never was."

"No, brother, it's you who doesn't get it. Leave Angela alone."

"I can't."

"You will." Marco's tone was unmistakable in it's ultimatum.

"I'm helping Angela with something."

"She doesn't need your help. Angelina didn't need your help. So back off."

"Sorry, Marco, not this time. I can't. I gave my word to Angela that I would see this through."

"See what through?"

"She'll tell you when she's ready."

"More secrets, more lies. Enough!" Marco slammed his palm against the cement planter. "This sibling rivalry between us has gone on long enough. I will not do this again. Angelina, Angela. Who's next, Roberto? You claimed to help Angelina too, remember?"

Roberto laid the guitar on the table and walked toward the open living room doors. "This has nothing to do with you, Marco."

Marco followed. "It has everything to do with me. I love Angela and I will not allow you to destroy that. Isabella said you were here sneaking around with Angela behind my back just as you tried to do with Angelina."

Roberto stopped and spun around. "Okay, if you really want to do this now, fine, let's do it. It's been a long time coming. You want to know what happened that night, the night of Angelina's accident?" Marco walked back across the room to the patio door. "You always thought I wanted Angelina back. Your pride would never allow you to see the truth. I didn't want Angelina and she didn't want me. We were friends, that's all. She needed protection. I gave it, since you wouldn't or couldn't."

"Protection from what?"

Roberto shook his head. "You're so stubborn and pig-headed; you still don't get it, do you?"

"Enlighten me."

"You were supposed to protect Angelina from Isabella. But instead you were so blinded by disdain for our mother that you believed everything Isabella told you. You left Angelina long before she walked out on you that night."

"Why would Angelina need protection from her own mother?"

"Angelina wanted to escape, to get away from Isabella anyway she could. Marrying would do the trick, and marrying a Santos would secure her future."

"Are you trying to say Angelina married me for my money? She met you first, why didn't she go after you for the money? You're equally wealthy."

Roberto smiled. "That's the humorous part. She wanted to, but than Isabella found out about you, the oldest son. By rights everything would go to the oldest son not the youngest."

"That's ridiculous, nobody thinks like that anymore."

"No one except Isabella."

Marco thought long and hard. Isabella was a slave to the old ways. She lived for tradition. She still, even now, adhered to the prejudice of class structure. She equated her Rivera name with that of Santos. Names that meant something long ago in a different place at a different time.

Roberto continued. "Isabella Rivera had the name but not the money. That's when you came in. Angelina came down the first time for me, that much is true, until Isabella met you. She persuaded Angelina to switch brothers, so to speak."

Marco looked away. "You and Isabella have always had your differences."

"True, I never trusted her and never made any bones about it."

"So you're saying that it all comes down to Isabella."

"No. Angelina had her part. She lied." Marco turned to look at his brother questioningly. "Everything, from the very beginning." Marco looked as if he'd been punched in the stomach.

"She lied about the baby, didn't she?" Marco asked.

"Yes, I'm sorry, man. There was no baby, there never was."

Marco sat down heavily on the side of the bed. "I suspected as much."

"Is that why you had the marriage annulled?" Roberto questioned.

"The marriage was a mistake, it was over long before the

annulment papers were signed, and long before the night she died."

"Angelina never told Isabella about the annulment."

"What?"

"Isabella still doesn't know that the marriage was annulled."

"How do you know that?"

"Angelina told me that last night, the night of the car accident."

"She was with you that night? I thought as much."

"Yes, she came to me after she left you. She told me that she'd begged you to reconsider the annulment and that you refused. She said that you told her that the papers had been filed weeks earlier and the annulment had been final for over a month."

"It was over."

"That's when she told me that Isabella didn't know."

"Did Isabella know that there was no baby?"

"Probably. I don't know for sure."

"So Angelina lied to her too."

"She was desperate. She told me that you were going to personally escort her to the doctor because at six months she still wasn't showing any signs of pregnancy."

Marco nodded and lowered his head. Those were the last words he'd spoken to her. After that she slammed out of the door. He never saw her again.

"She came to me terrified," Roberto continued.

"Of me?"

"No, terrified that Isabella would find out about the annulment. She confessed what she'd done to trap you into the marriage. She said she hoped to get pregnant soon after you were married but it didn't happen. I told her that she had to tell Isabella the truth and that if she didn't I would." Roberto fell silent, lost in his memories.

"And?" Marco prompted.

"She refused. She was too afraid to go back to Isabella."

"She didn't have to go to Isabella, she could have lived

comfortably anywhere in the world she chose. I would have seen to that."

"She didn't trust that you wouldn't listen to Isabella and not her. Remember, you believed everything Isabella said. As far as you were concerned, she was the perfect mother."

Roberto lowered his head in his hands. "That night, when she left me, she ran out and jumped into her car. By then the storm was just threatening. I swore I'd never allow her to go out in that storm. The next thing I heard her car was being pulled up from the canyon. I'm sorry man. None of this was supposed to happen."

Marco looked at his brother. "It's not your fault. We all made our choices. Now we have to live by them every day of our lives."

"No, you can use the past to change your future."

Marco looked at Roberto and cocked his head in wonder. "When did you start being so smart?"

Roberto smiled. "It's been coming on for a long time now."

"Tell me about Angela. What does she need your help with?"

"She's going to have to tell you, Marco, in her own time. She's suffered what no one should ever have to live with. You say you love her; show her. Give her time; give her room. Be patient."

Marco didn't respond. He knew that he couldn't promise to just step aside and do nothing if indeed Angela was in need. His heart would not allow him to be patient any more than his heart would allow her to leave him.

After he walked Roberto to the front door, Marco turned and looked to the top of the staircase, then slowly ascended; his thoughts were still on Roberto's comments. The hired nurse sat in the hall. She looked up from her book when he approached. She greeted him in their native tongue and gave him a brief report as to Angela's current condition and well-being.

He opened the door and walked over to the bed. Angela

lay still asleep, perfectly peaceful. Marco reached down and brushed a stray hair from the side of her face. Undisturbed, she rolled her head to the side and snuggled deeper beneath the silk coverlet.

Marco's eyes narrowed in speculation. Roberto's words continued to play in his mind. If Angela was in trouble, he would help her. But he couldn't help if he didn't know what the problem was. He looked over to the side table. Angela's cellular phone lay on the table. He picked it up and walked out of the room.

He was confused, and for the first time, not about Angelina but about Angela. The past two weeks with her was like magic. He'd never been so alive. She enjoyed hanging out with him at the club, shopping for knickknacks or just sitting by the pool or on the beach doing nothing. She was interested in his thoughts and concerned for his feelings. She was everything he'd ever wanted in a woman.

The confusion was so unlike him. All of his life things had been black or white, never gray. That's why Angelina had fooled him so easily. Now there was Angela, by all accounts her physical twin. He knew without a doubt that he wanted Angela in his life.

Marco was pensive the entire evening. He remained in his office alone, brooding the rest of the night. He barely spoke when Juan came into the office with the night's numbers. His demeanor was unnerving, even Juan was taken back by his placid mood.

Marco took Angela's cell phone from his pocket and placed it on the desk. After spinning it around several times, he picked it up and opened it.

The last number dialed was to a D.C. exchange. He pushed redial and waited. The call was answered by a man's deep voice in a veiled Cuban accent. "You got some 'splaining to do, Lucy," Elliot began, doing his best Ricky Ricardo impersonation. "You were supposed to call me this morning. Where are you, Angel?"

Marco cleared his throat. "This is Marco Santos in Puerto Rico."

"Where's Angela?" The seriousness of his tone was obvious.

"Angela is fine. She's recuperating at my home, Willow Hill. We need to talk, Elliot."

The conversation lasted forty-five minutes. When Marco hung up, he had a clear understanding of Angela's reason for coming to the island.

Angela and Angelina, Angelina and Angela. The similarities were too close to be mere coincidence. There had to be a connection between the two women. And only one person would know what that connection was.

Chapter 25

Isabella opened the door wide, barely dressed in a frilly robe draped over her shoulders, revealing the thin straps of a body-hugging negligee beneath. She had been expecting Chevis, and was astounded but pleased to see Marco standing at her hotel door.

"Come in, come in," she cooed warmly. "I was just getting ready to lay down for the evening. Join me."

Marco anxiously marched inside almost as soon as the door opened. He barely noticed Isabella's scant clothing. "I'm sorry to come so late, but I had to see you tonight. This can't wait any longer." He stopped in the center of the room then walked over to the mantel.

Isabella sauntered behind Marco, draping the robe's material lower to expose her perky bosom and smooth neckline. She stole a quick glance at her reflection before laying her hand on Marco's shoulder and dropping it down his back. "Of course, Marco. You must come to me as often as you like, whenever you like. I will always be here for you. What would you like?" she asked temptingly.

"I need answers."

"I presume you went to Willow Hill as I suggested."

"Yes, I did."

"And Roberto was there with her."

"Yes."

A slow, pleased smile curled her painted lips. She had him just where she wanted him. Roberto and Angela had been found out and Marco had come to her for solace. *That* she would surely give him, plus more.

Marco turned and looked at Isabella for the first time. The glare in his eye was fierce. "Did you know about the baby?"

The sudden halted screech of her libido was almost audible. "What? What baby? What are you talking about, baby?"

"There was no baby, Isabella. Angelina was never pregnant. She lied to me. Did you know?"

"Lies, lies, all lies," she screamed. "That woman has poisoned your mind with her lies about my Angelina and your son."

"Stop it, Isabella. There was no child."

"There *was* a child, Marco, I swear. Angelina carried your child until the day she died. She carried your child to her watery grave."

"What do you know about Angela?"

"I know her New York tricks won't work down here."

"New York? Angela's from Washington, D.C. How did you know that she's originally from New York?"

"Roberto must have told me."

"I doubt that." Marco rubbed his hand across his jaw, considering her remarks. He looked back to Isabella questioningly.

"You know more than you're saying, don't you?"

Isabella eyes widened as she looked around the room, completely off-balanced by the question. "How could you ask such a question? How would I know anything of this woman?"

She backed away from Marco and eased closer to the bedroom door.

"You knew she was originally from New York."

"She has an accent. If you'd ever leave this island you'd know that a New York accent is unmistakable."

"She has no accent to speak of."

"I would not lie. How else would I know this?"

"That's what I intend to find out." Marco turned to the door to leave.

"Marco, please, wait, listen to me. You don't need this distraction. Come with me back to Miami. Let me take you away from her destructive lies." She took his arm and pulled him toward her bedroom door.

"No." He yanked away, throwing her off guard. "I will find the truth." He marched to the door, opened it and slammed it behind him.

Isabella grabbed the nearest breakable item and flung it across the room. The crash sent a thrill tingling through her. She chose another item and also sent it sailing to meet its destiny against the far wall. Five minutes later her excitement level had raised so much that she barely heard the sound of the timid knock on the door.

She smiled anxiously. Marco had returned to her. She removed her robe and ran to the door. Panting heavily, she opened the door wide, showing all of her newly purchased glory. Chevis stood leering at her nearly exposed body. He hardened instantly, thinking that she had anticipated his arrival.

He grabbed at the lace covered straps of her high-French-cut teddy and pulled hard. Her breasts popped out, sending a wave of excitement through each of them. Without hesitation he delved in head first.

There, in the hotel's empty hall, on the tenth floor, at three in the morning, against the door frame of her suite, condom-covered, they made love like ravenous heathens. Pulling, panting, greedy, and gluttonous, they tore at each other's bodies with unabashed hunger.

Then, finally, spent and sated, Isabella pushed Chevis back and looked at the ridiculous offering. His pants were down, tangled at his ankles. His white socks were high, just below the knee, and his shirt, tie, and jacket were still neatly in place. She sucked her teeth in disgust at the sight of him and slammed the door in his face.

Chapter 26

Early the next morning Isabella was on a mission, and Willow Hill was her first stop. She'd had enough of tip-toeing around this. It was time for this Angela woman to know the truth. It was time for her to leave Puerto Rico and go back where she belonged.

Angela opened the door. Isabella marched in without a word of greeting. Angela noted the familiar behavior from their first meeting in her hotel room. "If you're looking for Marco, he's not at home," Angela said as she held the door open for Isabella to find her way out just as easily.

"I am not here for Marco; I'm here for you."

Angela closed the door and walked into the living room. She sat patiently waiting to Isabella to speak.

Isabella angrily followed Angela through the foyer and into the living room. She hissed at Angela's audacity and presumptuous attitude. It made her blood boil to know that she might one day be mistress of the Santos home.

She looked around the once welcoming room. There was nothing remaining that reminded her of her child. Once a frequent visitor, she'd grown accustomed to having her every desire attended. Every employee yielded to her needs no matter how obscure. She was the power behind her child. A child whose memories had been washed away and forgotten. Lost in the midst of sadness she allowed tears to fall from her eyes. Tears, not for her child, but for herself.

"You are just like your mother," Isabella spit out. "You ruin everything you touch."

"You knew my mother?"

Isabella laughed heartily then smirked at Angela. "Yes, I knew her, briefly."

"Who, where is she?" The excitement in her voice was evident. For the first time in her life, Angela felt a connection. This is what she waited all of her life to hear.

Isabella walked over and opened the veranda doors. A gentle breeze rushed in as she walked outside and stood at the rail. She looked off into the distance.

"Upon his death, my father's lawyers had informed my mother that the sum of the money she'd been entitled to had been divided in half between her and his late mistress's children. My mother was appalled. Of course he'd had a mistress; they all did. But no one ever left money to their bastard children.

"Later, years after my mother died, I went to New York to finally confront this person. I wanted to meet the child of the woman who had stolen first my father, then his money. I found her in labor, with you. She was rushed to the hospital. I registered her under an assumed name for fear of repercussions."

"Where is my mother now?"

Isabella shrugged matter-of-factly. "The woman died in childbirth, and it was presumed that I, being the one who brought her in, would care for the child. They assumed wrong. I left and returned to my home. Two weeks later I realized that I too was two months pregnant.

"You left me there?"

Isabella looked at Angela with all the contempt she'd felt all of her life. The smile of relieved joy sparked her to continue. "Yes."

"Why?"

"You were nothing to me; you *are* nothing to me."

"You just left me there?" Angela repeated, still stunned by her admission. "You were my mother's sister and you just walked off and left me there?"

"I was *not* your mother's sister!" Isabella screamed. "She was nothing to me. Your grandmother was the whore that my father slept with. You are nothing to me; you never were and never will be."

Angela's head spun as her mind whirled in dizzying directions. "How can you say that? My mother was your half-sister. She was your family. Your father was her father."

"You have no idea the hell I endured alongside my mother because of that trash my father loved." Angela looked stunned. Isabella's brow raised as she smirked at Angela's shocked expression. "Yes, loved. My father married my mother because of who she was. She was his equal. But he was in love with someone else. Pearl, your grandmother."

"My grandmother?" Angela's shallow breathing barely formed the words. She had a grandmother out there somewhere.

Isabella's voice became haughty as she raised her inflection. "The affair itself was tolerable, it was with whom, she objected. Pearl Richards, born in squalor, died in squalor."

"She's dead?"

Isabella took pleasure in enlightening Angela with her grandmother's demise. Her vindictive laugh brought tears to Angela's eyes. "When my father found out about Pearl's death months later, he vowed to give your mother and her brother everything. He offered it all, his heart, his time and his love. The only thing your mother never accepted was his money." She sneered and looked directly at her. "But I did—what was left of it anyway. After my mother was through with him, he had very little to give. Eventually he began spending all of his time in New York. He left us to care for your mother and her brother. And my mother eventually turned her back on him because he never openly admitted his love for Pearl."

"None of this has anything to do with me. It was his decision to leave. If your mother didn't want him why didn't she just divorce him?"

Heat still raised in Isabella's face when she recalled that the entire time her parents had been married, her father was having an affair. "Never. Filing for divorce was socially unacceptable, so my mother did what anyone in her position would do: she spent him into the poorhouse. Even then, he would not return to us. Hence, his untimely death couldn't have come at a more opportune moment."

Angela looked into the coldness of Isabella's eyes. Lacking feeling and devoid of emotion, she stared straight ahead, her head tilted upwards in arrogance and conceit.

Isabella glared at Angela. Her spiteful look was murderous. "So you see, you have no past here. You have no future here. You have no right to be here. I will not allow you to steal from me again."

"I don't even know you, and you don't know me."

"I know your kind. Do you think Marco will still want you after I tell him who and what you are? I told you before: he is a Santos and you are nothing, merely a distraction. He will soon be through with this amusement, then he will go to someone of his own echelon."

"You obviously don't know Marco very well."

"I know him better than you think. I assure you." Isabella walked over to the sofa and picked up her purse. "Tell me, what will he do when I tell him that you lied to him all along? That you and Roberto conspired together? That you used him? That I have proof that you came to this island for revenge and to destroy his family and mine?"

"You lie."

Isabella smiled as she pulled a folded paper from her purse. She slowly opened it and handed it out to Angela. It was her original birth certificate. "Maybe," Isabella continued, "but who do you think he'll believe? You or me?"

Angela's mind whirled in confusion. The knowledge of her grandmother's affair with a married man, her mother's pride in disowning her father and Isabella's lies turned the pain she once had into a pounding, blinding headache. Angela gripped her head and turned away.

"Leave here now and I will spare Marco of the embarrassment, pity, and contempt of his friends and family. What do you think they'll say about him? How long do you think Santos Enterprises will last once this comes out? Go, get out; leave this place now!"

Angela dropped that paper and ran.

Marco arrived at Juan's home unannounced. To his surprise Roberto's red sports car was already parked outside. Rosa ushered him through the courtyard and into the house. Juan immediately stood and greeted his friend at the front door. "Marco, come in, come in; Roberto has already arrived."

Roberto stood as Marco approached. The brothers looked at each other guardedly, not knowing what the other's reaction would be after their last meeting. Roberto held his hand out. After several nervous heartbeats by everyone in the room, Marco grasped the offered hand and pulled his brother toward him. They hugged warmly for the first time in years.

Juan and Rosa smiled and looked to each other before she disappeared into the kitchen. Juan opened his arms up to the brothers. "Come, sit." He beckoned them back to the seating area. "Rosa has gone to prepare coffee." He looked at the brothers' faces. Their intense expressions bespoke a need for answers. Juan sighed heavily. He knew it was time. If what he had suspected since first laying eyes on Angela was true, it would mean that the past had finally caught up to the present and that there was no need to continue with the secrets. "I presume you've both come for the same reason."

"If you're talking about Angela's past, yes," Marco said. Roberto looked at him, surprised by his newly acquired knowledge.

"Angela told you?" he asked.

"I spoke with Elliot."

Roberto nodded, remembering his conversation with Elliot when he visited D.C. earlier. The closeness of their friendship was more like brother and sister. Angela had trusted Elliot all of her life. And if Elliot had felt assured enough to disclose Angela's most guarded secret to Marco, then he must have also felt that Marco was the man for her.

"How is Angela related to Angelina?" Marco asked.

"We will get to that in time."

Rosa returned with a tray of morning drinks and refreshments. She poured coffee into three cups and set out several dishes of pastries, breads, cheeses and fruit. Roberto immediately grabbed a plate and began filling it. When he'd finished his first plate, he went for seconds. Juan settled down with a coffee across from the brothers and began telling the story of his family; his mother and father, Mariah and Pedro Martinez, and his younger sister, Isabella Martinez Rivera.

Isabella walked over to the mantel and picked up the beautifully adored vase. The light gentle sway of its line bespoke that it was extremely expensive. She held the vase up against the light, seeing through the thin porcelain material. She turned the vase upside down. The artisan mark was evident. It was an original, and it was priceless. She smiled and replaced it. It would soon be hers, along with houses, land clubs, restaurants and Marco.

"What are you doing here? Where is Angela?"

Isabella spun around. "Marco, I am so glad to see you." She ran to him and threw her arms around his neck. She hugged him closely, breathless with anticipation. "We must talk."

Marco removed Isabella's arms and held her away.

"Talk; I'm listening."

"She summoned me here."

"Who?"

"That woman, Angela Lord. I came because I assumed that you needed me. But, when I arrived, she told me that she never wanted to see you again." The piercing darkness of Marco's eyes was too intense for her, so she turned away and continued. She walked to the veranda doors and closed them soundly. "I didn't know what to make of her announcement until I realized that she was only after you to get what she could."

"Is that right?" Marco asked, his voice threaded with anger and contempt.

Isabella whipped around. "Yes, I don't blame you for being angry; she had us all fooled." A short nervous laugh bubbled. "I was actually beginning to accept her as a part of our family."

"Were you?"

"Yes, I was. But, of course, after her lies and deceit, what can I say? I'm just happy that you found out the truth before it was too late."

"I think you've said quite enough."

Applause rang out and got closer as Roberto entered the room and approached. His cynical laughter echoed throughout the first floor. "I sincerely commend you, Isabella. That was truly an Oscar-worthy performance."

"It was him," Isabella instantly accused and pointed her finger across the room at Roberto as he came to stand beside Marco. "It was him all along. He put that trash up to deceiving you. They were in it together."

Roberto began shaking his head and sucking his teeth in pity for her outrageous attempt to still lie about the truth. "Now, dear," he began patiently, "is that anyway to talk about your favorite son?"

"Marco, listen to me," she pleaded. "You know that I would never do anything to jeopardize our love or your trust. It was him. You know me."

"Apparently, not well enough." Marco crossed his arms over his chest and glared at Isabella with contempt. He looked to Roberto as Isabella continued to panic. "Handle this, brother." The startled shriek of Isabella's gasp sent another wave of chuckles through Roberto. "I'm going to see about

Angela." Marco exited the room and took the stairs two at a time.

The joyful smile on Roberto's face was beyond exhilaration. Never had he been given a gift as perfect as this. Marco had given him the astute pleasure of removing Isabella Martinez Rivera from their lives permanently. How sweet was that?

Arturo sat beside Ava on the wide sofa and listened patiently. When Roberto had finished the tale he stood and walked over to the window. He looked out at the seagulls in flight. "That was very enlightening, Roberto," he said.

"Yeah, it took us all by surprise," Roberto answered.

"Where is Marco now?" Arturo asked.

"On his way to Angela."

Ava stood. "Marco left the island?"

"He sure did."

Ava smiled as Arturo returned to her side. "It seems we have come to the end of this journey."

"Not quite," Roberto interjected. "Angela left here after talking to Isabella. We don't know what Isabella told her to drive her away. Yes, she loves Marco, but whatever Isabella told her had to question her faith in his love for her."

Ava reached up and stroked the bleached-blond streaks from Roberto's brow. She smiled and tilted her head in wonder. "When did you become so astute at feminine emotion?"

"A librarian told me."

"Should we meet this librarian?" Arturo asked.

Roberto smiled boyishly. "Nah, we're just friends."

Chapter 27

Angela arrived at the airport in time to purchase a ticket, get seated and leave the beautiful island she'd grown to cherish. So many emotions washed over her as regrets of a lost love ate at her heart. She was confused and ashamed, but she could never allow Isabella to destroy Marco.

She knew that her leaving would hurt him badly. But in the end Isabella was right. It would be best for everyone if she just went back where she came from. After all this was probably just another island romance to him. But she knew better in her heart even before the words formed in her mind. She knew Marco loved her.

Eastway Island Air, true to the motto, left the island paradise on time and swiftly. There was no turning back. She sat by the window staring out as the tiny island slowly disappeared into a mist of memories. Angela flew out of Marco's life as quickly and easily as she came.

By the time she had safely arrived back to her home she was exhausted. Elliot was there waiting for her. He told her of his conversation with Marco and she told him about the dramatic ending to her search.

"You know what you need to do."

"Don't start with me, Elliot."

True to form, a romantic at heart, he pleaded with her to contact Marco. "I know you're not gonna let Miss Thing just get away with this."

"Not now, Elliot, I just want to sleep for the next few days."

"Girlie, you are not gonna let Marco go, just like that, not without a fight. What happened to you down there? Where's the tough girl who beat me up the first day we met?"

"She still might if you don't drop it."

"Angela Lord, martyr to love. I don't buy it."

"I'm being realistic here. Marco is over, I have to reconcile myself to that. He's hundreds of miles away with no intention of ever setting foot in North America. End of story." She turned and walked upstairs.

"Whatever happened to *and they lived happily ever after?*" Elliot called out from the landing.

She stopped and turned. "That's only in fairy tales." Afterwards, she went directly to her room and closed the door. The familiar silence welcomed her like an old friend.

She sat down on the bed. As soon as her head hit the pillow, she regretted her decision. She could never return to Puerto Rico. The memories of lost love were too strong. Marco would never accept her back, not now, not after she left the island without one word to him. She closed her eyes and tears dampened the pillowcase. She decided to call Roberto later and explain as much as she could about her feelings for Marco and why she chose to leave. That made her feel much better; at least one Santos wouldn't hate her.

Moments later, she had just begun to drift in a warm mist of Eden's memories when she heard the commotion downstairs. She sat straight up in bed and listened to the voices. It was Elliot and he was talking with someone else. A man. Her heart leapt. Could it be?

She hurried down the steps and into the living room. As soon as she entered, her ex-boss, Lewis Carter, turned. Elliot glared at Lewis then spoke to Angela. "You have company."

Lewis immediately began. "It's about time you got back.

I've been covering for you for days. Your vacation is days overdue. I'm afraid we'll have to dock you the extra time." Angela looked at him like he'd gone mad. "But, now that you're back, you may start work first thing in the morning. I've already taken the liberty of setting up appointments with some of our new clients."

Angela looked at Elliot who had gathered his jacket and was standing at the door shaking his head. "Handle your business. I'm going out." He nodded to her then left.

Angela walked over to Lewis. "What are you doing here, Lewis? You obviously don't remember that you fired me weeks ago."

"Don't be ridiculous. You took your time off; you had your vacation. Now, it's time to get back to work. We've had numerous calls about the work at the design show and several clients are anxious to speak with you."

"I have no intention of going back to Carter Design."

"All right. All right. You can have your five percent raise." She began walking toward the door; he followed. "Fine, ten percent. We'll also throw in another assistant and forget about the time lost."

"No thank you."

"Okay, okay, fifteen percent."

"It's too late for that."

"Come back and we'll make you a partner in six months."

Angela looked at him oddly. She had no job and no idea what she was going to do with the rest of her life. But one thing was certain; she wasn't going back.

"What do you want, Angela, anything; tell me, it's yours."

"I want you to leave." She grasped the doorknob and turned. "Good-bye Lewis." She yanked the door open just as Marco raised his hand to ring the doorbell. Angela let out a small gasp of surprise. Lewis stepped closer to see who was there. Angela's mouth fell open as the two men looked at each other.

"Who the hell is this?" Lewis asked indignantly.

"Marco?" Angela said, completely ignoring Lewis's remark.

"Marco? Who the hell's Marco?" Lewis said, ignoring Angela and watching Marco intently.

"What are you doing here?"

"I came to live in the States, to be near you, to be with you."

"Someone from another design firm, no doubt," Lewis interjected. He eyed Marco suspiciously as he looked him up and down to size up his intent.

"Shut up, Lewis," Angela said automatically.

"My mother is searching for a home for us even as we speak."

"Ava?"

"Yes."

"Hey, you can forget it, Marco Polo; Angela is already taken."

For the first time Marco directed his attention to Lewis. "My name is Santos, Marco Santos, and you are?" Marco asked.

"Who am I?! Who am I?!" Lewis repeated impatiently.

"But you said that you would never leave Puerto Rico."

Marco smiled. The hypnotic sparkle of his dark eyes captured her instantly. "I've recently learned never to say never."

"I'll tell you who I am," Lewis began on a new tirade.

"Shut up, Lewis."

"Angela's with me," Lewis continued to Marco. "And I intend to keep it that way." He stepped past Angela and loomed over Marco as he remained a step lower.

"Get out, Lewis," Angela said.

"And there's nothing you can do about it," Lewis added to Marco.

"That would be unfortunate," Marco said to Lewis.

"Why's that?" Lewis asked skeptically.

Marco stepped up a step then moved forward. The impressiveness of his body dwarfed Lewis by comparison. "Because Angela is with me now." He looked at Angela with eyes that promised forever.

"Good-bye, Lewis." Angela held the door and pointed

Lewis outside. Lewis tripped down the first step but caught his balance on the rail as he continued further down. "You be to work first thing tomorrow morning, Angela, or you can forget about your job or getting a reference from me. Did you hear me?" The door closed soundly before he finished his veiled treat.

Angela turned. Marco was right there. "I can't believe you're here," she said, still too stunned to see him there, standing in her foyer.

"Where else would I be?"

"You came all the way here for me?"

"Angela. I love you. I would travel to the ends of the earth for you."

"Marco." She swallowed hard. "There's something about my past, my family that you need to know."

"I've already spoke to Juan."

She looked puzzled. "Juan?"

"Yes. Juan and Isabella are brother and sister."

"He knew all along?"

"No, he only suspected when he saw the resemblance. He knows the whole truth now."

"Then you know everything."

"Yes."

"I can't go back there."

"Yes you can."

"What about what Isabella said? She could ruin your family, and your business."

Marco began laughing. "Isabella doesn't matter. She can do nothing. And as soon as we can prove that she hired the two windsurfers, I'm sure she'll be much too busy with the police to cause any more trouble."

"She hired them to . . ." Angela's body began shaking. "I was never a threat to her. Why would she want to hurt me?"

Marco stepped closer and drew Angela into his arms to still her anxiousness. "Isabella is a troubled woman. She will get the help she needs."

She stepped back and turned away. "Marco, I've been piecing together my past for as long as I can remember. What Isabella said about my mother and grandmother was true."

"Let it go, Angela. The past is just that, past. What happened or didn't happen makes no difference to me. I love you now and forever; that's all that matters."

An avalanche of emotion swept over her as he took her hand. "Give us a chance," he whispered, pulling her into his arms and kissing her softly and passionately. "I love you; I will always love you."

With tears in her eyes, she answered softly, "I love you too, Marco. But . . ."

"Shhhh. Don't speak, my love. Angelina is gone; she's been out of my life for a long time now. What was between us is in the past. It has taken me a long time to reconcile my feelings about that. Now I see things so very clearly, thanks to you. I needed to let go of my past even as you searched to find yours. Together we have found our future."

"But where do we go from here? Where do we live?"

Marco smiled warmly. "I know what I want; I know who I want; I want you, Angela, so just love me; we'll work everything out in time. We have the rest of our lives." He kissed her again, this time forever.

Epilogue

Angela stood on the edge of the hill, beneath the willow trees, and looked out at the calmness of the turquoise sea. The gentle waves lapped leisurely against the white sand as the crystal-blue sky opened its wide arms to a panorama of perfection. This was truly paradise.

Marco came up behind her and wrapped her in his welcoming arms. She instantly felt the solid wall of his chest and the sweet hunger of his desire. She snuggled closer, letting her head lay back against his shoulder. He dipped his head to nibble her neck. A thrill of excitement shot through like an electric shock and she swayed to the music they both felt.

"We have to stop meeting like this, Señor Santos."

He smiled as he tucked his new bride close into his arms. "Never, Señora Santos, not in a million years."

They stood like that until the sun gently climbed further into the sky and the early morning mist that swirled around them was driven away by the warm breeze. "Happy?" he finally asked.

"Deliriously happy," she said, as she snuggled deeper into his embrace.

"Are you sure that this is what you want?"

She turned to face him, looking questioningly.

He continued. "To live here on the island instead of the States while you design Santos North?"

Angela began laughing. "Let me think, my mother-in-law is busy scouting property for a second home in Miami, while in the meantime, I get to live here with the man I love in this beautiful home in the middle of paradise. Are you kidding?"

"Sarcasm again."

"Get used to it," she said as she returned to her place in his arms.

Marco reached down to caress the flat of her stomach. Angela immediately knew what he was thinking. "So, how many children do you want, two, three, four?" she asked.

"Hundreds." Angela instantly stepped away again, turned and looked up into his humored eyes. "But I'll settle for one at a time, right now." He smiled proudly. "Sarcasm?"

Angela chuckled and shook her head. "Close enough." He reached out to pull her back into his arms. She laughed and stepped back. He reached out to her again; she swiped her hands away. Then finally she took his hand and pulled him into her arms. She looked up into his dark eyes. She saw there the overwhelming love reflected in her own eyes. This is where she belonged. This is what she'd been looking for all her life, a reflection of love.

"Hundreds, huh?" she asked. He nodded with a contented smile. "Well, I guess we'd better get started."

Marco laughed and within an instant swept Angela up into his arms and walked back toward the house. Like an ending to a great movie, they walked into the sunrise of a new day and a new life.

Roberto got out of the rental car and looked up at the sign above the door. This was his place. His solo venture and his joy. *Club Phoenix.* He smiled at the appropriate name. As was the ancient Greek mythological bird, it was indeed a life born from the ashes and raised up anew.

He opened the door, breezed through the club's inner sanctum then continued to the manager's office. He smiled as soon as he saw her face.

There she sat at the window in the private dining area, overlooking the lush green of the surrounding outside landscape. Roberto sat down and picked up the drink that had been waiting for him. He took a long sip and smiled, leaning back in the chair, relaxing for the first time in a long time.

"How was the wedding?"

"Small, charming, perfect."

"Good. Wish I could have been there."

"That would have caused quite a stir."

"Are they happy?"

"Beyond delirium."

She smiled and pushed a package across the table. Roberto sat his drink down and opened and pulled several old books from the package. "What are these?"

"A wedding gift from me."

Roberto opened the first book and flipped through pages and pages of old photographs and journals. He stopped on a particular page. The black-and-white photo, now crystal clear, was familiar. He touched the stilled, smiling faces of the loving couple and teen looking back at him. "Is this . . . ?"

"Yes."

"Where did you get . . . ?"

"I found them. They were hidden in the bottom of a trunk that was sent to me years ago. I didn't know what to do with them until now."

"This is incredible," Roberto said in wonder, as he continued to flip through the last two photo albums. "Everything is here." Suddenly, he stopped and looked up. "You knew about Angela all along, didn't you? Why didn't you just tell me? I would have helped."

"You did."

"No, I mean from the beginning. We could have done this together."

"No, no one would have believed us. Mother had to be

found out and Marco had to see this for himself. And Angela, she suffered for so long in her search; she needed Marco in her life and he needed her."

"You're such a romantic," Roberto quipped easily.

"So you approve?" she asked. Roberto nodded and smiled as he closed the last journal. "Do you think she'll like them?"

Roberto looked up into the face he'd adored and protected for years and sighed. "She's gonna love them."

"Good. I'm glad."

"Okay, señorita," Roberto began. "How's my club doing?"

Angelina Carita Rivera smiled warmly. She had never been happier and her world had never been more at ease. Being washed up on shore and contacting Roberto only after she'd already been presumed dead was the best thing she could have done. Her rebirth away from Isabella had been her miracle. Here, in Club Phoenix, she had been reborn to a happiness she now knew was possible.

Dear Reader,

I hope you really enjoyed reading the story of Angela Lord and Marco Santos in *Reflections of You*. The idea of a sexy hot romance set on the island paradise of Puerto Rico was just too tempting not to pursue, especially since I wrote it in the middle of winter.

What do you think: does Roberto Santos need his own story? Write me and let me know. If you want it, I'll write it. Watch for more hotter-than-hot romances set in other Caribbean islands in the coming months. But for right now, the Mamma Lou series continues with JT Evans in *Irresistible You*, coming August 2004.

As always, I thank you for your continued support. Please feel free to contact me at conorfleet@aol.com or Celeste O. Norfleet, P.O. Box 7346, Woodbridge, VA 22195-7346. Watch my Web site for contests and special surprises, http://www. celesteonorfleet.com.

Best wishes,
Celeste O. Norfleet

ABOUT THE AUTHOR

Born and raised in Philadelphia, Pennsylvania, critically acclaimed author Celeste O. Norfleet currently has more than six novels to her credit. An avid reader and writer, she lives in Northern Virginia with her husband and two children.